A desperate woman in a deadly trap

"Hell, here they come!" shouted the slender woman on horseback as she whipped her rifle from it's saddle boot.

Younger's bend was so close, and yet so far. A band of twenty-two men led by Colonel Coffee was hot on Belle's trail as she and her Cherokee cohorts herded the stolen cattle away from the storm-swollen river.

But now they were being backed up against the river and cornered, with twelve of Coffee's men spreading out to close in from the east, and another dozen coming head-on in a single inpenetrable unit.

"Blue Duck," Belle said to the Indian beside her, "we've got no choice but to move the herd across the river. You and the boys get going—I'll hold them off as long as I can."

As Blue Duck and the others started the cows down the slope behind her, Belle peered out through the hanging willow branches at the oncoming riders. She could forget about the group circling from the east—she'd outsmarted them by sending her men west to ford the raging river.

Alone, and determined to stand her ground, Belle Starr turned to face her twelve angry assailants. Her finger tightened on the trigger of her carbine as they dismounted. They approached her cautiously, guns at the ready, behind a wall of moving horseflesh . . .

The
WOMEN WHO WON THE WEST
Series

TEMPEST OF TOMBSTONE

DODGE CITY DARLING

DUCHESS OF DENVER

LOST LADY OF LARAMIE

FLAME OF VIRGINIA CITY

ANGEL OF HANGTOWN

BELLE OF FORT SMITH

WOMEN WHO WON THE WEST

Belle of
Fort Smith

Lee Davis Willoughby

A DELL/BRYANS BOOK

Published by
Dell Publishing Co., Inc.
1 Dag Hammarskjold Plaza
New York, New York 10017

Dell ® TM 681510, Dell Publishing Co., Inc.

ISBN: 0-440-0575-2

Printed in the United States of America

First printing—August 1982

1

THE CHEROKEE STRIP of the Indian nation, September, 1876 . . . It was perfect weather for herding stolen livestock. The wind was out of the south and it had been raining fire and salt all week. So Belle and her gang were soaked to the skin, chilled to the bone, and feeling mighty pleased with the way things were going as they drove the stolen herd into the cottonwood thickets of Catfish Draw on the flooded bottomlands of the brawling brown Arkansas.

Despite the rain and the fetlock deep floodwaters all around, the wet furry hides of the hard-driven cows were steaming and their tongues were hanging out. So Belle raised a gloved hand and called out, "Mill the leaders and hold 'em here for a spell, boys! We could all do with a trail break and it ought to be half safe, now."

She saw Blue Duck circling the herd on the far side, but the Osage kid on the calico gelding was moving too slow. Belle spurred her big mare to full gallop and passed him, riding gracefully sidesaddle, despite her own weariness, as she snapped, "Get the lead out, boy! If you wasn't ready to ride, you should have stayed home with your mamma!"

Belle loped old Venus even with the herd leaders, turned

them with curses and waves of her soaked plumed hat, and
reined in with a satisfied sigh as she saw the critters were
safely bunched and starting to steady.

Belle brushed a strand of wet black hair from her rain-
soaked face, and put her soggy hat back on before she
clucked her mount into a slow walk and started circling the
milling cows, softly singing *Rock Of Ages*. Cows seemed to
find more comfort in old hymns than Belle did, for some
fool reason. She hated hymn singing. But it was important
to soothe and steady the stolen critters in unfamiliar surroundings with no graze worth mention to occupy their
bovine minds. She saw some of the critters were nibbling
experimentally on cottonwood twigs. If they were that hungry, they weren't likely to bolt in the near future, so Belle
relaxed a mite. The raid had gone well and they were halfway home free. But halfway wasn't all the way, so as she
spied Blue Duck riding to meet her, she called out,
"Who've you got on lookout to the north, honey?"

Blue Duck, who could have been taken for a white cowhand until one rode close enough to see the Indian features
under his dripping black hat brim, looked blank and said,
"Hell, Belle, what do we need with a lookout? The creeks
have riz and we left no trail worth mention. I thought that
was the reason for driving through all the flooded draws in
the first damn place."

Belle swore under her breath, shook her head wearily at
her lover and second-in-command, and said, "Damn it,
Blue Duck, it's no wonder you poor heathens wound up
losing so much land to my kind. These cows used to be the
property of Colonel Coffee and they won't be our'n for
certain 'til we sell 'em across the Arkansas. As anyone but
a fool Injun can see, we ain't about to ford the Arkansas in
high flood and I reckon Colonel Coffee can figure that
out, too!"

She turned in her sidesaddle and called out, "You there,
Sparrow Hawk, lope your pony atop that rise to the north
and keep your eye peeled for that infernal posse!"

The Indian youth called back, "What posse, Miss Belle?"
and Belle yelled, "The one following us, you lame-brained

Osage! There's always a posse following raiders. Didn't your mother tell you anything whilst you was growing up?"

Sparrow Hawk shrugged and spurred his pony into a lope, splashing water stirrup deep as he rode back to cover the trail break. Belle shook her head wearily as she turned back to Blue Duck and said, "We'll hold 'em here until they look like they can make it to that willow-wooded high ground to the east. There's fair grazing over there amid the trees, and they'll stay bedded for the night."

Blue Duck stared past her to the north and said in a worried tone, "I ain't worried about these cows as much as I am about your words about Colonel Coffee's riders, Belle. What makes you think they might have followed us over the line into the strip? White men ain't supposed to, you know."

Belle swore softly and said, "For God's sake, Blue Duck, Colonel Coffee's been knowed to gun a man for smiling at his woman, and we just run off with half his beef! You think him and his riders give an infernal damn about imaginary lines on the map?"

Blue Duck frowned and answered, "They ain't supposed to follow us into the Indian Nation. White man's law don't count on this side of the line, imaginary or not. They can't arrest us even if they did manage to cut our trail, now!"

Belle rolled her eyes heavenward and marveled aloud, "I just can't understand it, Lord. Anyone can see the man's full growed, and he ain't all that bad in bed, but you surely failed to create this pretty Injun with a lick of sense!" Then she stared soberly at Blue Duck and added, "Colonel Coffee and his posse riders ain't figuring on arresting nobody, Blue Duck. The law works both ways in the Cherokee Strip."

"What law, Belle? There ain't no law worth mention in the Indian Nation. Ain't that why we've been using it as our home base between raids?"

"It is. No white man but a federal officer can arrest anybody here in the Indian Nation, but Colonel Coffee ain't figuring on any such formal proceedings, and his riders outnumber me and mine two to one. So if he catches up with us on this side of the river, well, it's been nice knowing you, Blue Duck."

It wasn't raining in Missouri, but Jesse James looked broody as a wet hen when his older brother Frank joined him in the back room of a house of ill repute on the outskirts of Liberty. A man had a right to feel broody when it wasn't safe to show his face in public, even in his own home county. Frank James sat down across the table from Jesse and spread the newspaper out between them as he said, "Well, it looks like they ain't fixing to hang old Cole and the others after all. It seems the state of Minnesota don't hold with capital punishment. Ain't that a bitch?"

Jesse growled, "Don't never mention Minnesota to me again, Frank. We was crazy to raid so far apart from kith and kin in the first place. In the second place, the law took three of our gang prisoner, and by now at least one must have talked!"

Frank shrugged and said, "I ain't so sure, Jesse. We left poor old Clell Miller and Billy Chadwell dead in front of the damned bank. Charlie Pitts was kilt by the posse. So all the law took alive was our kin, the Younger boys. We know Cole would never peach on us, and I don't reckon Jim or Bob Younger would, either."

Jesse James grimaced and said, "It's one thing to reckon and another thing entire to know for certain. So we dasn't go back to Mamma's spread, and the Youngers know every other place we might hide out in Clay County, too!"

Frank James soothed his brother. "Well, they don't know about this place, Jesse. For, 'til Bob Ford told me just the other day that Madame Olive was a sort of understanding woman, none of us ever holed up here. None of her regular customers ever come back here, and nobody comes in at all until the Madame looks him over personal. So simmer down. This is as safe a hide-out as we're likely to find for now, even in our home county."

Jesse James took out a smoke, thumbed a light, and muttered, "I don't feel safe. There's something about this whorehouse as spooks me. Do you trust Bob Ford, Frank?"

Frank James pursed his lips and said, "I reckon. Don't you?"

"Mebbe. He's kin, at least. But him and his brother ain't wanted by the law for anything serious, and that's a mighty handsome reward they just put out on us."

"Yeah, since the Northfield Raid we seem to be sort of famous. But hell, Jesse, no kith or kin from Clay County would turn us in for no reward. How in thunder would they ever live to spend it? Old Bob ain't much, but he's got enough sense to see that. Nobody as knows us will ever turn us in. We got too many blood relations as wouldn't like it all that much."

Jesse James blew a thoughtful smoke ring and said, "Madame Olive ain't kin. She's an old whore who sells her all to the highest bidder, and the Pinkertons are bidding mighty high. I don't like this setup, Frank. I felt the hairs on the back of my neck tingling like this that day we rode into Northfield. I knowed something was going to go wrong with that infernal raid, and my hair tingles was right! We got to get us outten here, Frank. We got to get us clean outten Clay County. Too many knows our faces hereabouts, and it only takes one false friend at a time like this!"

Frank James nodded as he stared down at the newspaper. He considered some other hide-outs and discarded them. Then he brightened and said, "Younger's Bend!"

Jesse looked blank. Frank smiled and said, "See? You never heard of it, neither! It's a shantytown in the Indian Nation. Cole Younger told me about it, one time. The law would never look for us there."

Jesse frowned and asked, "How come Cole never told *me* about this town named after him, and how come it is?"

Frank smiled and said, "You was to home with your woman and childer, I reckon. Anyhow, you remember that time old Cole helt up the bank, here in Liberty?"

"I do. It was about the dumbest thing Cole ever did."

"Well, we was all new at the game in them days, Jesse. Anyhow, after Cole helt up the Liberty Bank, he naturally had to do some serious running. So he run off to Texas and took up with a gal called Belle Shirley. Texas was all right, for ordinary outlaws, but Cole was hotter than a whore's pillow on payday. So even Texas wasn't safe."

Jesse snorted in disgust and said, "It surely sounds like a dumb time to saddle one's self with an infernal she-male. But Cole always has been a lady's man."

Frank said, "It turned out to be a good move. This gal, Belle, was the proper daughter of a Texas judge, so she knowed the law better than Cole did. Cole said she was one of the slickest gals at thinking crooked he ever met. Anyhow, Belle run away from home with Cole and led him to an old cabin she knowed about in the Cherokee Strip. They shacked up there for quite a spell, and even gathered together a modest gang of 'breed and Injun crooks. It was Belle's notion to name the settlement Younger's Bend. She told ever'body she was Cole's wedded wife, even though Cole never was the marrying kind."

Jesse James motioned impatiently with his hand and growled, "What's all this ancient history got to do with here and now, Frank? Cole's in State Prison, where he figures to stay for life."

"Yeah, but his gal Belle ain't. You know how Cole likes to travel. But the gal said she'd keep a candle burning in her window for him just the same. The night Cole told me the tale, he said the last he'd heard she was still there, stealing livestock for a living, and that as far as he knowed, she was still fond of him."

Jesse James blew another smoke ring and mused, "Shirley is her maiden name, you say? I know some Shirleys over near Carthage."

"That's her kin, Jesse. Belle was birthed a good old Missouri gal. Her brother rode for the South in the war, like us. So she's our kind of folks. You want to ride down and see if she has room for us at Younger's Bend?"

Jesse James got to his feet. When Jesse was on the prod he tended to move sudden. Frank got up from the table and headed for the door. But Jesse said, "No. Let's not go out the front way, Frank."

"Our horses are in the livery across the street, Jesse."

"I don't care. My hairs is tingling. So we'd best go out the back."

It was twilight outside when Jesse James opened the back door, stared soberly at the trees in the woodlot behind the whorehouse, and drew his six-gun. Frank didn't see anything, but he drew his gun, too. He didn't view the universe with his younger brother's sometimes unreasonable suspicion, but he'd learned to follow Jesse's lead after the suspicions had panned out true more than once in the past.

And so, as the quartet of lawmen staked out behind the house opened fire, the James boys were set to fire back, and did, crabbing sideways along the clapboard wall of Madame Olive's as bullets slivered the planks where slower moving owlhoots might have still been!

They were outnumbered two to one, which was sort of ridiculous odds when one considered them. The rest of the posse was covering the other three sides of the house, so the four men covering the back were in big trouble as Frank and Jesse James took bearings on their gunsmoke and charged, firing less and aiming better! The deputies were part-time gun slingers, and Frank and Jesse James were masters of their deadly craft, so while one lawman's bullet ticked the brim of Frank's hat, and another round made a hole in Jesse's coat-tail, three deputies were laid low, and the other had the sense to bury his face in the dirt and stay there until both brothers had run through them into the woods, and helped themselves to two of their tethered horses. Neither Frank nor Jesse had said a word during the gunfight, and they saw no need to speak until they'd ridden a couple of miles. Then Jesse reined in, looked back to see how wide a lead they had, and said, "Well, Frank. We'd best ride down to Younger's Bend and see if old Belle has room for us."

Belle wasn't as far from Younger's Bend as the James brothers, but she was still a long way from home, and Colonel Coffee had a Black Seminole tracking for him and his riders. It was still raining, and starting to get dark, but nobody tracked like a Black Seminole, so when the scout reined in on a rise ahead, the colonel rode forward to join him, asking, "What's up, Chief? Have you cut sign?"

The Black Seminole said, "No. The thieves have been driving the herd where the flood waters cover their tracks. They think they are so smart. I told you they were stupid Cherokee."

Colonel Coffee shifted his weight in the saddle. He was soaked to the bone and feeling his forty-odd years more than he had when starting out on this long chase. He knew he had a temper, so he deliberately kept his voice laconic as he said, "I'm missing something, Chief. You say you can't cut their sign, yet you say they're dumb?"

The Black Seminole pointed with his chin at a distant rise covered with crack willow as he answered, "I track like human being, not like a dog. If a man thinks ahead, he doesn't have to sniff at hoof prints. Hear me. The Arkansas is just beyond that timbered rise. The river is in flood. No cow could cross it tonight, so the thieves have to bed them down and wait out the flood."

"I can see that, Chief. But why that particular rise?"

"I said Cherokee were stupid. I didn't say they were crazy. They have to bed the herd for the night on high ground. They would look for high ground they can hide in. That rise is timbered. The ones up and down the river for miles are not. Can you see it now?"

Colonel Coffee frowned and said, "Makes sense. I don't know anywheres better to look."

He turned in his saddle and waved his other riders in. As his *segundo* rode within earshot, the colonel said, "Somerville, take half the boys off to the east and hit that wooded rise, spread out and gun in hand. I'll lead the rest head-on. What are you waiting for, a goodbye kiss?"

The *segundo* nodded and started riding, trailed by a dozen others. The colonel wondered if he had time for a smoke as he waited for them to get into position. He decided to forget the notion. The boys were riding tolerable, and he'd never light a match in this infernal rain, anyway. He drew his saddle gun, levered a .44-40 round in the chamber, and said, "Ready when you are, Chief."

Naturally, the picket Belle had posted saw the two-pronged attack coming at them across open ground and yelled a warning. Belle leaped into her sidesaddle and rode to join him. As Blue Duck fell in beside her, Belle swore and said, "That tears it! Blue Duck, you and the boys had best start the herd across the river, sudden!"

Blue Duck gasped and said, "Belle, that's mighty wild, even coming from you! It's almost dark and the river's over her banks! We'll drown our fool selves as well as the cows if we try to ford!"

"Would you rather drown, or dangle from a cottonwood? Get cracking, damn it! Like your folks say, I have spoken!"

Blue Duck called out, "Jerry, Sparrow Hawk, get the leaders started across and keep the others close bunched. Let's go!" Then he turned to Belle and added, "We'll try. You'd best go first, Belle."

But Belle shook her head as she drew her carbine from its saddle boot and said, "Get going, now! I'll cover for you!"

"Honey, talk sensible for a change! There's two dozen pissed-off riders headed this way, and you're just a gal!"

Belle swore and snapped, "I said to move the herd and I meant it! I know who I am and I know who's coming, and if they hit you boys afore you make her across with the cows you won't have a chance! Move it out, God damn your eyes!"

So Blue Duck did. He knew Belle was in one of her stubborn moods and, in truth, Blue Duck wasn't half as brave as Belle. Few men were.

As Blue Duck and the others started the cows down the slope behind her, Belle peered out through the hanging willow branches at the oncoming riders. She saw that half of them were circling to the east, so she could forget about them. It was a slick enough move, she allowed, but she was even slicker.

She'd seen right off that a run in that direction was expected, and hence foolish. Belle took a deep breath as she cocked her carbine. She felt sort of lonesome right now, but what the hell, they couldn't see her, and she had every one of the rascals out in the open. Her own boys needed time. So she raised her gun, sighted on the heavy-set gent who seemed to be the leader, and fired.

Her mare spooked under her. Belle didn't try to stop her, for she knew better than to stay in one place after firing from cover. Belle rode along the inside of the tree line as a volley of bullets whipped through the cloud of gunsmoke she'd left behind. When she reined in again for another look-see, sure enough, she had the man she'd fired at on the ground. The others were dismounting to take cover behind their mounts as they walked them toward her in a moving barricade of horseflesh.

Belle liked horses. She liked them better than some folks she'd met, but this was no time for sentiment. She took aim, gut-shot a pony so it would bust free and run back to die, then fired twice more and rode back the way she'd just come. When she reached her first firing position, the smoke was still hanging in the air amid the shot-up willow branches, but everyone on the other side was dusting up the place she'd just been. Belle grinned like a kid stealing watermelons and shot another man. She only hit him in the leg, but it put him out of action, so now they were all moving back to reconsider their options.

Belle saw that they were carrying the first man she'd blown out of his saddle. She laughed. That meant he was a big shot, and if there was one thing Belle hated, it was big shots. She saw she'd stopped the first rush, but she'd lost sight of that other bunch riding east and had to consider them. It was well for her she did so. As she spurred Venus east behind the tree line, Somerville and his dozen riders were moving in dismounted. The *segundo* had made it into the willows on foot as Belle encountered him, riding her big thoroughbred at a considerable lope. The last thing poor Somerville had expected to meet up with in the willows was a she-male riding sidesaddle in full skirts, so he made the mistake of dropping his jaw instead of the hammer on his Winchester, and the next thing he knew Belle had dropped him with a bullet in his shoulder. As the *segundo* lay groaning in the wet grass, Belle rode off, laughing, with her long black hair streaming in the wind and rain.

Her earlier marksmanship had considerably dampened the enthusiam of her enemies, and since it was getting mighty dark by now, Belle followed her gang and the stolen herd across the brawling Arkansas unmolested. She was unmolested by bullets, anyway. The river damned near drowned her and Venus before Belle swam her to the far side.

The riders who had forced her to cross the river in such unseemly haste built a thoughtful fire in the willows and gathered in their wounded. Nobody had been killed outright by Belle's fire, but Colonel Coffee and the other wounded were feeling mighty poorly. The posse improvised lean-to shelters for the wounded to dry out under as they nursed them. As they were bandaging the *segundo*, Somerville, he attracted not a little interest from Colonel Coffee and the others as he told them his tale. He said, "I know you boys think I'm outten my head, but I swear to God it was a woman as gunned me. She looked like a damned spook as she rode outten the willows at me, sidesaddle, screaming like a banshee and shooting like Wild Bill Hickok!"

Someone asked, "Are you sure it wasn't a Cherokee boy with long hair?" and Somerville snapped, "God damn it, I reckon I know a she-male from a he-male by now! Besides, she was white. A man would have to be blind to mix a white woman riding sidesaddle with an infernal Injun buck!"

Colonel Coffee sat up on one elbow, favoring his wounded side, as he asked, "What did this she-male cow thief look like, Somerville?"

The *segundo* said, "Crazy. I didn't get much time to study her features afore she layed me low, but I'd say she was mebbe thirty, give or take a year or so either way. She had a right trim figure and long dark hair. Her face was glaring too ornery to tell if she was pretty or just tolerable. Like I said, we didn't spend much time together."

The Black Seminole lit his inverted corncob pipe carefully before he said quietly, "I have heard there is a white woman dwelling among the Cherokee, over near Fort Smith. My people and the Cherokee are not on friendly terms, but we hear things. They say she lives with a bad Creek or Cherokee. I do not know his name. She has had two children, a boy and a girl. The boy is dead. I am not surprised. She does not sound like a very good mother."

Colonel Coffee grimaced and said, "She's a damned good shot, though. Do you know her name, Chief?"

"Not her white name. They call her the bell. Cherokee say their Indian names in American. I don't know what a bell would be in Cherokee. It's a stupid language."

A cowhand came in from the trees and hunkered down, wet, to say, "Well, Colonel, they got the cows across the river. Don't ask me how. I would have said it was impossible. But the rascals done it."

Another man asked if they were going on after them, come morning. The wounded Coffee shot him a withering look and said, "Not hardly. I need a doctor more than I need them cows. That gang was tougher than I figured, and I'm sorry as hell about that, boys, but we'd best leave them to the federal lawmen for now. They say they got a new hanging judge over to Fort Smith who means to clean up the Cherokee Strip."

Another hand said, "It's about time!" and the colonel nodded and said, "Yeah, cleaning up the strip is long overdue. But if you boys can get me home alive, I mean to leave it to the full-time law. Male or she-male, that leader of their'n is a mite rich for my blood."

The next morning they carried Colonel Coffee and their other wounded back to Kansas. When they told the tale of their wild adventure with Belle and her wild bunch, it occasioned considerable excitement in the local newspapers. So the legend of the "Bandit Queen of the Cherokee Strip" was born.

A lot of what they wrote about Belle was exaggerated. Much of it wasn't at all true, but the West had never had a bandit queen before, and so, while she lasted, they meant to make the most of the only one they'd had.

* * *

The Redbird's cabin lay well back from the brawling brown Arkansas, but it still stood on the wooded bottom-lands and the river was over her banks. A sheet of mustard-colored water covered the dooryard, and Pearl couldn't go out to play.

Granny Redbird had said it was all right to set on the front veranda, so Pearl was rocking herself and the corn-husk dolly her Uncle Blue Duck had made for her when she spied the riders coming.

There were eight of them. They were white men, and they were soaked liked drowned cats, despite the wool hats and yaller slickers they wore. The trail from Fort Smith lay stirrup deep in places, and the afternoon rain was coming down in sheets that whipped back and forth in the wind. The men spotted the girl-child on the veranda as she rose. Pearl knew it wouldn't look Christian to duck inside and lock the door. On the other hand, Granny Redbird had warned her not to talk to strangers, and Granny Redbird knew everything. Granny Redbird was so old she remem-bered the Trail Of Tears, and she was a spey woman be-sides. Mamma had said she'd never have birthed Pearl alone without the help of the old Cherokee spey woman, and that when she and Uncle Blue Duck were away on business, Pearl should do what Granny Redbird told her to do, even if it didn't seem sensible.

But the little girl was alone as the riders splashed across the dooryard. There was nobody to tell her what was need-ful. Pearl smiled up at the white men as they reined in to face her in a long mounted line. Not one of them smiled back.

Pearl licked her lips and said, "I bid y'all welcome and offer shelter from the storm, sirs, but I dasn't offer coffee and grub without asking my elders. Granny Redbird's out herbing in the woods, but she ought to be back directly."

The leader of the posse, a likeable enough man under other circumstances who had kids of his own, stared down at the child on the veranda. He didn't like what he saw. This young white girl was living among the 'breed and full-

blood trash in the Strip and was only maybe eight or ten
and sort of pretty. Her straw-colored hair was neatly
braided and ribbon-bowed, but she stood barefoot on the
rough pine planking, clutching that fool Injun doll, and the
shift of cotton sacking she wore barely covered her skinny
legs to the knee. She seemed well-spoken, considering, but
it didn't seem likely she was still a virgin, young as she
might be. The scum is these parts weren't safe to leave
alone with livestock, let alone a white girl old enough to
walk.

The head deputy asked, "What's your name, sis?"

The child answered, "If you please, sir, I'd be Pearl Shirley."

Another rider snorted in disgust and said, "Rafe asked
your full name, girl. Don't you know your daddy's name?"
He chuckled and added, half to himself, "I reckon you
wouldn't, at that."

The head deputy silenced him with a look and said,
"We've come to the right spread, boys. Shirley is her last
name." He smiled down wolfishly at Pearl and added,
"Ain't that right, sis? Ain't your mamma Belle Shirley,
from Scyene, Texas?"

Pearl nodded and replied, "Yes, sir. Mamma is away on
business and I'm to stay with Granny Redbird, here, 'til she
comes home again."

"Do tell? What sort of business did your mamma say she
was riding off to with that buck of her'n, this time?"

"I don't know, sir. Mamma says I'm too young to study
on her comings and goings. She says to always remember
she loves me and to mind Granny Redbird when she ain't
here to tend to me."

"That sounds reasonable, sis. So where in thunder is the
old witch this afternoon? The law has got some questions to
ask and, no offense, you ain't likely to have the answers
we're seeking."

Pearl didn't know where Granny Redbird was. The old
Cherokee spey woman had been fixing vittles on the stove
inside when she came out here, but Pearl didn't even have

to turn about to know the one-room cabin behind her now stood empty.

Pearl couldn't have told anyone how she knew. The other white children figured she was spey from living so much with Injuns. Pearl didn't feel like she was spey. She just knew things. What she didn't know, however, was that growing up among a folk who lived close to nature had honed her senses keener than they might have been had she been reared more to Queen Victoria and other white ladies' liking. So, when her sharp ears detected a slight change in the pattern of the falling rain, Pearl brightened and said, "I hear someone coming now, from the woods out back." Sure enough, Granny Redbird came around the corner of the cabin, soaked to the skin in her calico Mother Hubbard and sunbonnet.

She was not alone. A wet and sullen looking older Cherokee man stood beside her with the rain running off the muzzle of the shotgun he held, lowered polite-like.

The old woman said, "Pearl, go inside and shet the door."

As Pearl turned she saw two other Indians down at the other corner of the cabin. They were younger than the tribal elder with Granny Redbird. One of them nodded at her, then turned to gaze at the white riders with scornful distaste.

Pearl stepped inside the damp, moldy darkness of the little cabin and shut the door as she was told. She ran over to the window made of bottle-glass so she could listen. Granny Redbird was the first to say anything.

"You folks are on Indian land, as well as mine. I hope you have a reason."

Pearl could only make out distorted forms through the thick bottle bottoms set in pitch, but she recognised the leader's voice as he answered in a warily polite tone. "We have, Granny Redbird. You folks over here in the Strip likely heard what happened last month up to Northfield. That's up Minnesota way. Your friends, the James-Younger clan, tried to hold up the Northfield First National in broad daylight."

Granny Redbird said, "The James and Youngers are not friends of ours. I have never met Frank or Jesse James. I swear this."

"Yeah, but they named this stretch along the river "Younger's Bend" after Cole Younger, though. We know the whole tale, Granny. Younger holed up here a spell back, hiding out after sticking up the Liberty Bank. That little gal you just sent inside was the result of his stay here with Belle Shirley, right?"

"If she was, it was many summers ago, many. You have no right to bother us about Cole Younger. I read the papers from Fort Smith. The Northfield raid went badly for the Younger boys. You will not find Cole Younger in the Cherokee Strip. He is in the prison hospital in Minnesota, with eleven bullets in him. He is not expected to live, but anything is possible. Ride to Minnesota if you want to talk to Cole Younger. He has not been seen in these parts for a very long time."

The older male Cherokee, who Pearl knew as the Elder Swan, interrupted by shouting in a high sing-song voice, "Hear me. We are not bad people. We robbed no bank in Minnesota. Even if we had, white lawmen hold no writ in the Indian Nation. I think you should ride back across the line to Fort Smith. Why are you bothering my daughter of the Redbird clan? You white people have Cole Younger and the others in jail!"

The rider called Rafe shook his head and said, "Not all of 'em. The gang split up outside Northfield when their raid went sour. The posse caught up with the Younger boys and Charlie Pitts. Frank and Jesse James rode clear, and are still at large."

The Elder Swan asked, "What of it? They say the James brothers are Welshmen. Do we look like Welshmen? Go away. You are starting to make me very cross."

Rafe said soberly, "Lots of folk are cross, Chief. We're riding with a federal warrant as carries more weight than your tribal council here in the Strip. Before you cloud up and start something the U.S. Calvalry can finish if we

can't, I'll tell you true we're not looking for any Indian in connection with the James boys."

"Then why are you here? Frank and Jesse James have no kith or kin in the Indian Nation."

"Well, now, mebbe they do and mebbe they don't. We never come across the Arkansas line to trifle with Granny Redbird or any other Cherokee. But that child inside is said to be Cole Younger's daughter, and her mother, Belle Shirley, is said to be his common-law woman."

The Elder Swan hesitated. Then he said, "Go away. Our little white sister Belle is the woman of Blue Duck now. If she ever was the woman of Cole Younger, it was long ago. She would tell you this herself, but she and Blue Duck are not here. I don't know when they will come back."

Rafe shifted in his soggy saddle and said, "We heard about the business trips Belle takes with her stock-stealing buck, Chief. A man could get wet, waiting about for their return, but I did want to jaw with old Belle some. So I'll tell you what we'll do. We'll just carry that young girl of her'n back to Fort Smith with us, and whenever Belle comes back from wherever, she can come by and tell us what she knows about, oh, hideouts and such."

Pearl gasped and moved back from the mottled glass. She didn't want to ride off with the surly looking white men, but what was she to do if they tried to make her? Maybe if she ran out the back door and hid in the tanglewood until Mamma and Uncle Blue Duck came home. . .

Then the Elder Swan's voice snapped like a whip as he told the posse, "Hear me! You will not take any child left in our care as I draw breath! You are talking silly, even for white men! You have no right to arrest little Pearl! She is only nine years old and has done nothing. Nothing! Your hanging judge, Isaac Parker, will laugh at you if you bring in a little girl for bank robbery. But you will not do it, even as a joke. I, the Elder Swan of the Cherokee Council, have spoken!"

"Look, Chief, nobody said anything about arresting Cole Younger's bastard child. We just aim to use her to sort of twist her missing mother's arm a mite. We'll treat the kid decent."

The Elder Swan said, "I told you I had spoken. You will ride out now, alone, unless you mean to fight these boys and me. You may kill us here and now. We are outnumbered, but the sound of gunfire will bring others. They will not be white men. You are far from the Arkansas Line for a running gunfight all the way back. Do you feel like dying today?"

"Not hardly," Rafe admitted. "You win this hand, Chief, but when Belle and her buck ride in, you tell her if she don't come in to Fort Smith on her own, we'll come back again in greater numbers, hear?"

Pearl heard the sounds of splashing hoofbeats fading off in the rain as Granny Redbird entered the cabin with the three male Cherokee.

"Lord of mercy, we'll all die of the ague, as wet as we are. You gents set whilst I get coffee and grub, something warm, into us all. Pearl, child, be a darling and fetch me that tin of Arbuckle down off yon shelf whilst I fire up the range."

Pearl climbed on a bentwood chair to get the coffee, but before she could reach it, one of the Indian boys had stretched his longer arm and handed her the tin.

"I am called Sequanna. I speak your tongue, but I have not taken a white man's name," he said.

Pearl thanked him and hopped down with the tin, wondering why he looked at her with such a queer expression. Sequanna was a nice-looking boy of seventeen or so, but his sloe eyes glittered bright, like he was held busy thinking behind the otherwise impassive features of his dark, hawkish face.

Pearl took the coffee over to the range and handed it to Granny Redbird as she asked, "Granny, what's a bastard?"

The old spey woman closed the stove lid on the burning alderwood as she answered impassively. "A bastard is what the white folks call a child whose mother and father weren't married lawful in their eyes."

"Oh, you mean like when my daddy, Mister Younger, made me with Mamma that time?"

"Something like that, child. Now put the cups on the table like a good girl."

Pearl wondered why Granny Redbird looked so flustered whenever anyone asked about her father.

The Elder Swan, sitting at the head of the bare table, smiled at Pearl and said, "Hear me. There was no shame in the way you came forth from the Great Creator, Little Pearl. Your mother and father could not marry under white law at the time."

Granny Redbird muttered something in Cherokee. Pearl knew just enough of the language to know she was telling the old man to drop it, but the Elder Swan persisted.

"No. Everyone has a right to know where they walk under the stars. Pearl asked a question. The way a child learns is to have her questions answered." He smiled at Pearl before continuing. "Cole Younger could not marry your mother under the laws of the white men while the two of them hid out here in the Strip. The white law was looking for Cole Younger at the time. Your mother was hiding out, too. She had run away from home and was under age. If your grandfather, Judge Shirley, had known where she was, the two of them would have been in even more trouble. You are not to feel any shame because you are what the white people call a bastard. We Cherokee don't say bad things about people unless they did something bad themselves. You had nothing to say about the way your parents had you. Do you understand me, little Pearl?"

"I think so. Are my Mamma and Daddy wicked folks, Elder Swan?"

Granny Redbird brought the coffee over, softly scolding the talkative tribal elder in their own tongue. As she poured, the Elder Swan ignored her and said to Pearl, "Your parents are what the Ruling Spirits made them. Your father might have been another sort of man had he not ridden for the losing side in the big war over the black people. Your mother was from a good family, as the white people count good families. She was not able to live as they wanted her to live, so in the eyes of the white people she is what they call an outcast. The daughter of a Texas judge is not supposed to run away with handsome young outlaws. Since then, of course, other things have happened."

Pearl took a seat next to the old man as Granny Redbird put their tin plates of rabbit stew in front of them. Pearl waited until the old woman took her own seat and said grace in Cherokee, for although she was a spey woman—a witch and a soothsayer—as well as a full-blood, Granny Redbird was also a Christian. As soon as it was seemly to speak again, Pearl asked more questions.

"If my mother and father loved each other, how come he rode off afore I was birthed?"

The Elder Swan said, "I don't know. Maybe the law was breathing down his neck. Maybe Changing Woman led his heart away from your mother. Maybe, in truth, your mother tired of him. These things happen. Only Changing Woman knows why, and the spirits seldom tell us anything. Anyway, your mother rode off in good time with another white man named Jim Reed."

"I remember Uncle Jim. He was good to us and bought Mamma that nice mare, Venus. He and Mamma had me that baby brother as died. How come the law shot Uncle Jim when I was little, Elder Swan? I was here with Granny Redbird when Uncle Jim was gunned in Texas, and Mamma never told me why."

Even the Elder Swan could see he'd started something more than he'd intended. He looked down at his stew and answered, "These things happen when a woman takes a fancy to following men who live by the gun. Eat your rabbit before it gets cold, Pearl."

Pearl tasted her stew. It was all right, but she wasn't hungry. Whenever she asked Granny Redbird about her elders, the old spey woman got all flustered and told her to chop wood or something. With the natural curiosity of her years, Pearl pressed the old Indian for more of her shadowy history.

"I was mean-mouthed by some white kids over to Fort Smith one day when Mamma and Uncle Blue Duck took me shopping. This prissy boy snickered at us and said I looked mighty light for a 'breed. What did he mean, Elder Swan?"

The old man took a swallow of coffee and put down the cup. "You were right. He was mean-mouthing. Some white people think it's wrong for a white woman like your mother to live with an Indian like Blue Duck. You are not a 'breed. There is nothing wrong with being part Indian, but, if it's important, you come from good white stock on both sides."

Pearl sipped her own bitter brew, put down the cup, and frowned at the old Indian. "What's so awful about Mamma and Uncle Blue Duck being friends? I like Uncle Blue Duck. How come the white folk in Fort Smith think he's bad?"

The Elder Swan shrugged and said, "They judge a man by the color of his face. Maybe, to be fair, they don't understand how Indians feel about the ownership of stock."

Down the table, Sequanna said, "I stole a fine horse the other day. A foolish white man left it in his pasture, untended. No Indian would leave such a good horse out where anyone with eyes could see it wanted to be ridden."

Pearl frowned and said, "I didn't know Uncle Blue Duck was a stock thief. The Good Book says it's wrong to steal."

"Not livestock." Sequanna insisted. "Ripping clothes off the line or taking money from someone's house is stealing. Taking horses or cattle is the way of our people. It always has been; always will be. Blue Duck is not a bad person. He's just acting Cherokee."

Pearl didn't answer. She knew the folks she spent so much time with while Mamma was away had different customs from her own, but stealing was stealing, and it sure seemed odd how Mamma always seemed to wind up with men friends who took things they didn't own.

By the time they'd finished their skimpy meal, the rain seemed to be letting up. The Elder Swan cocked his head to listen, then said he and the youths should make a break for it before it settled in for the night. Sequanna said he'd best stay at least until dark lest those riders return. The other Indian boy laughed and said something in Cherokee that sounded slightly wicked. Pearl wondered why the old man looked thoughtfully at her, then shook his head and said something in a sterner tone. Pearl followed just enough of his drift to understand that someone around here was too young to do something. They likely meant her, as she was the youngest person hereabouts, but when she asked what they were talking about the Elder Swan said it was "man talk" and that they were fixing to leave.

So they did, and when Pearl and Granny Redbird saw them to the door they could see that the yard water had lowered some. The raindrops spangled the muddy overflow from the river, yet there were mud banks beginning to show as the sun tried to break through, hanging low in the west.

As the three Indian men faded away in the rain, Granny Redbird sat wearily in her rocker to dip some snuff and ponder something she seemed to see in the flooded dooryard. Pearl sat on the steps, knowing better than to ask for a dip of snuff. She'd tried it once and it had tasted awful. Old Granny Redbird liked her coffee bitter, too.

The setting sun broke through a hole in the blanket of clouds. Granny Redbird spat like a grasshopper and nodded with approval. Open sky at sunset generally meant a dry night, and her old bones ached in the damp. She didn't say anything. She knew Pearl could read signs well for a white child, and it was not the custom of Real People to twitter, like mockingbirds and white women, when there was nothing to be told. Pearl watched a little island in the subsiding waters of the dooryard until, sure enough, it started moving.

"That bitty turckle's headed back for the river, Granny. Do you want me to catch her?"

"No, it's too small to be worth shelling out for the pot, child. It is not the way of Real People to catch anything just for sport."

Pearl sighed, rested her chin on her small fists, and said, "I know. I was just asking. Gol' damn, I hate white folks!"

"You mustn't swear, child. You mustn't hate your own kind, either."

"Well, I do, Granny. White folks is mean as hell. What do you reckon makes white folks so mean?"

The old woman spat and said, "I don't know. It must just be their nature. The bluebird sings pretty and the crow bird raids the cornfield. All of us creatures act as the Great Creator fashioned us from the dust of time. I have never understood white folks. I have tried. My people have been trying since before any of us now alive were born. Back in the eastern hills where I was born, the Five Civilized Tribes took up the white man's way of life to try and get along with them, but the first white men I can remember were white soldiers. They came to my father's homestead along the Tennessee to tell us that we must move out here. It was very bothersome. I was too big for my mother to carry and too little to walk the Trail of Tears. I don't know how I did it, but I must have, because I am here. Many children of our people died along the trail. Old people, too. The Trail of Tears was very hard on anyone who was not strong, and the soldiers were very hard on the strong who resisted."

She spat again and added, "You never walked the Trail of Tears, child. Why should you hate white people? You are white. Your father and mother were white. Even the polecat must be fond of its own kind."

"Well, I ain't feeling fondly toward white folks, for they've surely been mean as hell to me and mine! Look how they mean-mouth Mamma, and why in thunder did they have to go and put eleven bullets in my dad?"

The old woman shrugged. "Fair is fair, child. When a man holds up banks for a living, he has to expect folks to act surly toward him."

"Well, it seems mean to shoot anybody eleven times. Do you reckon my dad will die, Granny Redbird?"

"I don't know. It depends on where they shot him. I never got to know Cole Younger well. He was well-spoken and polite, for a white man. He was a big man, hard and tough from riding and fighting so much. I can see why it took eleven bullets to bring him down."

"What was my father like, Granny Redbird? I've always wondered, but when I ask Mamma, she gets all dewy-eyed and flustered, and tells me not to ask fool questions."

The old woman frowned and said, "I told you what Cole Younger was like. He was a hard, tough man who always looked like he was fixing to move, even when he was set- ting still. You mustn't vex your mother with fool questions about what's past and done with, Pearl. You never saw your father and it don't seem likely you ever will."

"Well, he's got out of jails afore. Mayhaps when he busts out again, he'll ride back to me and Mamma. Wouldn't that be grand, Granny Redbird?"

"Not for Blue Duck. Mayhaps not for your mother, ei- ther. You're a mite young to understand such things, Pearl, but a woman deserted by a man whose child she carries ain't always filled with fond memories toward him. You'd do best to consider your father dead, no matter what the law does to him."

"I want my father to come home to us. I want all my folks together. Uncle Blue Duck's nice, but it ain't like having my real father about! Do you reckon if I wrote to him in prison, so's he'd know how much I loves him, he'd bust out and head this way, Granny Redbird?"

"You're talking foolish, child. I know your mother's taught letters to you, and Cole Younger might know how to read, but after that it gets complicated."

Before Pearl could ask any more questions, her keen young ears picked up the sound of muddy hoof beats. She sprang to her feet, crying out, "That's old Venus I hear coming from the west! It's Mamma! Mamma's coming home!"

She splashed out to the ankle-deep mud in the dooryard in her bare feet, calling out, "Mamma! Mamma!" as a pe- tite figure rode into view, waving.

Belle Shirley sat on her big chestnut mare sidesaddle. She wore a mud-spattered black velveteen riding habit. Her

waistline measured no more than eighteen inches, partly
because of the corset she wore, but mostly because she was
a very slender woman to begin with. A big black hat, be-
decked with a soaked and sagging black ostrich plume,
perched atop her pinned up mop of luxurious dark hair.
From middle distance she looked like a well-born gentlewoman who'd somehow decided to ride to the hounds with
a brace of six-guns strapped around her hips. The illusion
faded as she came closer.

By no stretch of the imagination had Belle Shirley ever
been really beautiful, and the hard living of her twenty-
eight years was starting to show on her rawboned features.
The face that went with her petite feminine figure seemed
more suited to a handsome young man. Her eyes were
friendly, but inclined to glare wildly at a world she'd found
hard to get along with. Her teeth were white and even, but
her lips were thin for a woman's, and her jawline betrayed
the stubborn nature of her North Saxon and Celtic blood-
lines.

But to Pearl, she was beautiful, and as Belle dismounted
to take her in her arms and kiss her, she sobbed, "Oh,
Mamma, I misses you sore. Where have you been so long
this time?"

Belle laughed and replied, "Me and your Uncle Blue
Duck was out gathering stock, like I said we'd be. Let me
tether Venus, girl. We'll ride off on her together, directly,
but first I got to put some coffee down my gullet, for I'm
chilled through to the bone."

Pearl released her, and as Belle tied the mare's reins to
the veranda rail she nodded at Granny Redbird and said,
"Blue Duck and the others are driving the herd to the
Carson's spread for safekeeping. Has Pearl been a burden
to you while we were away, Granny?"

The old woman shook her head and said, "Pearl is always tolerable to have about, Belle. I'm not sure you
should leave that stock with the Carsons, though. Some
lawmen come by just a short spell back, and they was on
the prod, looking for you specific."

"Shoot, the Carson spread's a two days' ride from here, Granny. What did the lawmen say they wanted of me and mine?"

Granny Redbird waited until they'd all gone inside for coffee and grub before she filled Belle in on the posse's visit. Pearl sat by her mother adoringly, as Belle sipped her coffee daintily. Pearl thought it sure was odd how Mamma's eyes glittered when mention was made of Cole Younger's arrest up North.

She hoped her Mamma wouldn't cry when she learned her father was in jail with eleven bullets in him. She didn't, but she stared hard into space for a spell when Granny had finished. Then she said, "They had no call to pester y'all about old Cole. He ain't been here in the Strip since afore the child here was birthed."

"That's what I told them, Belle, but they said that if you didn't ride into Fort Smith to tell them what you know of the gang, they're fixing to come back again. What do you aim to do now?"

Belle shrugged. "I reckon I'd best ride in, then. I'll go come sunrise. I've rid all I aim to this evening, and it'll be pure heaven to spend the night in my own sweet bed at our cabin."

"Hear me, do think that's wise, Belle? What if they arrest you? They say Judge Parker in Fort Smith is very strict."

"Shoot, Granny, I know how to talk to judges. My own papa was a judge. I growed up hearing law talk. They have no call to arrest me for what the infernal James boys done. I'll just tell them I've never been anywhere near Northfield, and that's the honest truth."

"Yes, but what if they ask where you have been, Belle?"

"It's none of their business. I told you I know the law."

She laughed and added, "Besides, by now Blue Duck and the boys have them ponies halfway to the Carson's in the tanglewood. What can they arrest me for, for being so pretty?"

Granny Redbird shrugged and said, "Being sassy is more like it. Most folks in these parts are *afeared* of the law! I expected you to run off when you heard they was looking for you, Belle."

Belle nodded. "That's 'cause you Injun folk don't savvy the law as good as me. Running off when they don't have a charge they can make stick is just foolhardy. That's likely what they want me to do, but I'm not afeared of Hanging Parker and it's time he figured it out. Like I said, I'll ride in tomorrow and have it out with the old buzzard, and that'll be the end of it, for now."

"For now, maybe. What about the next time, Belle? What will become of Pearl if you and Blue Duck get caught with a herd you don't have a bill of sale for?"

Belle laughed and replied, "We always have a bill of sale, Granny. I spent eight years at the Carthage Female Academy, and I writes with a fine Spenserian hand. I told you my papa was a county judge. I reckon I write as good a bill of sale as any you ever laid eyes on. I'd show you the one on the stock we just found sort of grazing untended, but Blue Duck has it with him at the moment, just in case."

Belle lowered her empty tin cup with a sigh of satisfaction. "That surely pleasured my insides, but my outside is still wet and clammy, so whilst I'd like to set a spell and jaw with you, Granny, I'd best carry me and Pearl over to my place and put me and mine to bed."

"Can I ride pillion on Venus with you, Mamma?" Pearl asked excitedly.

Her mother smiled at her. "Of course you can, little darling. Do you think I'd let you walk barefoot in all that mud out there? Kiss your Granny Redbird goodnight, and let's get home and dry."

The child did as she was told and followed her mother outside. "Oh, I'm so glad you're home again, Mamma. I love Granny Redbird, but it feels so grand to have my real mother about."

The cabin that Belle shared with her daughter and her Indian lover lay a country mile from Granny Redbird's. Younger's Bend was a tolerable place for fishing when the river was low and a little shantytown of squatters had sprung up along its banks. Belle's shack had been there since the time an outlaw on the dodge, and she, as a run-away schoolgirl, had found and repaired an abandoned trap-per's cabin.

The interior was neat and well-furnished, for despite what scandalized whites might think of her, Belle Shirley was personally fastidious. However, her liberal views on pri-vate property accounted for the somewhat luxurious fur-nishings.

The oil lamp on the rosewood table shed a warm friendly glow on the whitewashed log walls as Pearl poured boiling water into her mother's tub. Pearl was just as glad Uncle Blue Duck was away on business, for when he was home, Mamma never bathed in front of her. Pearl liked to watch her mother at her toilette. There was so much work to being grown-up and pretty. The big wooden tub smelled like violets from the bath salts her mother used, and she looked so queenly when she relaxed in the big tub.

"Your tub is ready, Mamma," Pearl said.

Belle came over, naked, and patted Pearl's head as she tested the water with one small foot.

"Bless you, darling. It's just right," she said.

Pearl drew up a three-legged stool and sat by to watch gravely, as Belle ran the bath sponge sensuously over·her skin. It was odd how white her Mamma's skin was where the sun couldn't get at it. Her face was tanned and, with her high cheek-bones, she didn't look much different from the 'breeds and full-bloods living up and down Younger's Bend.

"Gee, Mamma, you surely have pretty tits," Pearl said.

Belle gave her a thoughtful look before replying. "I thank you kindly, Pearl, but it ain't seemly to talk about things like that. Tits is a country word. The polite thing to call them is breasts, if you have to speak on them at all. A girl your age ain't supposed to notice such things."

"Well, I sure wish my durned old, ah, breasts would grow some. How old do I have to get afore I can have 'em too, Mamma?"

Belle laughed and said, "Don't worry. You'll find out soon enough. To tell the truth, they're more a bother than a blessing. Save for the time I nursed you at 'em, they've mostly just got in my way."

She sank down in the water as she added, "Sometimes I sure wish I'd been birthed a boy. Men folk get along just fine without the complications that goes with a she-male form."

"I think I'd rather have been a boy, too, Mamma. Do you reckon my father would like me better had I been birthed a boy?"

Belle frowned and said, "You're talking foolish, child. Cole Younger doesn't know I had you, boy or girl, so it wouldn't have made one bit of difference about his feelings. The rascal has no feeling worth mention about either of us."

"How come, Mamma? Weren't the two of you in love when you went to all that trouble to have me?"

Belle laughed bitterly. She said, "To tell the truth, having you was the furthest thing from our minds at the time, but, yeah, I reckon we must have felt something for one another. I know I did. Your father never was a man to let his real feelings show."

Pearl said, "Granny Redbird says he had to leave 'cause the law was after him. Do you reckon he'd have stayed here in Younger's Bend with you and me had not the law been after him?"

Belle shrugged, and stared into space again with her haunted deep-set eyes. "Might-haves, and might-haves only unsettle a body's mind, Pearl. Your father and me might never have met, had not he been on the run after holding up the Liberty Bank that time, for Cole come from Clay County, in Missouri, and I was going to school in Texas when he sort of caught me on the fly as he was passing through," she said.

She soaped herself as she added wistfully, "He might not have seen fit to take up with me even if we had met in the county of Clay, had he not been on the dodge. He was a

with old squaws. I'll tell you all about such doings when the time comes for you to know."

An appalling thought flashed unbidden into Belle's mind, and she asked. "You ain't been fooling about like that with any of the boys hereabouts, have you, Pearl?"

"Of course not, Mamma. My tits ain't even growed yet. That big boy, Sequanna, acts like he admires me some, but he ain't asked me to make babies with him, yet."

Belle's eyes blazed dangerously as she turned in the tub. "God damn it, he's an Indian! I'll kill that Sequanna if he trifles with you! You're to tell me at once if any of these infernal Cherokee bucks lays a hand on you, hear?" she said.

"Why are you looking at me so wild, Mamma? I told you I ain't been doing anything country with any boy, and I thought you liked Injuns," Pearl replied.

"It's not the same thing, damn it. I'm me and you're you. I want you to always remember you're the granddaughter of Judge Shirley of Scylene, Texas, and pure white on both sides. Do you understand me, girl?"

"Not hardly, Mamma. Why is it so awful for me to take an Injun when the time comes, if it's good and proper for you to live with Uncle Blue Duck?"

Belle grimaced and said, "A woman has needs. It ain't that good and proper, even for me, but when a woman can't have the man of her choice she takes the man she can get. I got other plans for you, Pearl. You was birthed with your father's looks, and though that hair figures to darken some as you get older, you're still fixing to grow up a head-turning gal. I never went to all this trouble rearing you to have you waste yourself on some damned buck, or even worse, a white man who can't draw fast enough to back his boastful nature."

Belle rose from the tub and Pearl handed her the towel.

"I felt bad when Uncle Jim Reed got gunned down Texas way, too, Mamma. Is that why we live with Uncle Blue Duck, now? I reckon Uncle Blue Duck could have beat that rascal who gunned Uncle Jim to the draw, don't you?" Pearl asked.

"I don't know. Jim was about as fast with a gun as a natural man comes. The advantage Blue Duck has is that he don't start up with strangers in saloons just for practice. If there's one thing I've larnt about men, child, it's to stay clear of the ones who strut about telling the whole world how dangerous they are. I should have knowed Jim Reed was due for a short life on this earth when I heard the way his spurs rang when we danced. Let me slip into my robe and I'll help you empty that tub," Belle said.

"Can I take a bath in it first, Mamma?"

"Are you sure you want to? I just washed off a heap of trail dust in that same water, honey."

"I don't care. It smells so pretty. I want to smell pretty, too."

Belle shrugged and said, "All right. But make it a fast one, for it's fair late and we got some riding to do, come sunrise."

Belle sat down to comb out her dark hair as Pearl slipped her shift over her head and stepped into the tub. Belle didn't comment, but she noticed the way her child was starting to fill out. At nine, Pearl's chest and hairless pubic mound were still childlike, but anyone could see she figured to start blossoming in a year or so. Belle remembered how she'd been shamed by her folk for maturing earlier than most of her classmates. The resentment she'd felt at being blamed for things she had no control over had likely led her down the primrose path a lot sooner than she'd have found it on her own. Belle had never read a book on raising children, and would never see one, but she knew all too well that she'd never have started masturbating at such a tender age had not her puritan mother and maiden aunts dwelt so on an awkward young girl's private parts. It had been Aunt May, insisting on her showing them the peach fuzz on her tender groin that Sunday afternoon, that had gotten her so interested in the infernal thing in the first place. Once she'd come with her hand, or a candle, and just about every other thing in the house that would fit, she been in no shape to resist the first fool man who'd offered to pleasure her right!

She surely hoped her daughter hadn't inherited her warm nature. Even a girl as pretty as Pearl had enough on her plate without having an insatiable craving for anything in pants.

Belle sighed as she ran the comb through her long hair, wishing Blue Duck was waiting for her in yon bedstead across the room. They'd have to think about building a lean-to for Pearl to sleep in this coming winter. A mother had to set a proper example for a daughter, but whenever she was in that strong buck's arms, it was hard to remember the infernal kid was above them in the loft, and Pearl had sharp ears.

Belle didn't remember hearing her own folks doing anything like that in the big old house in Texas. It was hard to picture her severe father and her prim little sparrow of a mother actually kissing, let alone rutting hot and heavy. But they must have, or she wouldn't be here to fret about it.

"Sneaky," she muttered. "The whole world's at it sneaky every night. By day everyone walks about looking like butter wouldn't melt in their mouth, but at night, behind closed doors, the whole world goes crazy, and it's cocks and cunts from the preacher's rectory to the bawdy houses down along the dead-line."

"Did you say something, Mamma?" Pearl asked from her bath.

"Yes. I said it was time for you to be in bed. Get out of that infernal tepid water afore you catch an ague, and make sure you wear your flannel nightgown under the quilts. It's a raw, wet night, even with the rain stopped."

"Are you taking me with you into Fort Smith in the morning, Mamma?"

Belle said, "Sure I am. Don't you want to go? I fancy them white kids as teased you the last time will leave you alone from now on. I had a talk with their folks, and you'd be surprised how polite folks can act to keep their barn from burning down some night, sort of mysterious."

* * *

Pearl was awakened at midnight by the soggy sound of hoof beats on the flooded riverside trail. She sat up on one elbow in her bed under the eaves of the loft, as her keen hearing detected that two riders had slowed their trotting ponies. As they approached, she knew they were strangers, for she knew the hoof beats of the neighbor's mounts. Sure enough, the mysterious riders reined in just outside. One of them spoke in a voice too low for most white folks to hear from this far. Pearl wondered what tribe he hailed from as he said, "Dyma'r fan, Jesse. Belle fawr sy fod fan hyn."

Another louder voice growled, "Talk English, damn it. You know I hardly remember the old Valley Talk. I know this must be the place. The question's who might or might not be here yet!"

Downstairs, Belle called out, "Get off them horses with your hands held polite, unless you aim to ride on. Either way, I got the drop on you from in here with a Patterson .36!"

"Is that you, Belle? Put away your shooting iron. It's Frank and Jesse."

"Frank and Jesse who, damn it?"

"We'd best discuss that inside, Belle. For public consuming we're using the last name 'Howard,' these days, if you follow my drift."

Pearl climbed out of bed and crawled over to the edge of the loft as below, her mother opened the door. Belle waited until the two men were inside before she struck a light and, as she lit the oil lamp, Pearl saw that the strange riders wore slickers and rain-wilted wool hats. Her mother grumbled, "Well, I'll coffee and grub you, but then you'd best ride on. The law's already been by looking for you, and you boys have no call on my hospitality in the first damned place. Who in thunder told you to come here, damn it?"

The taller of the two men peeled off his slicker, exposing a brace of six-guns worn low around his hips, and he folded it over the back of a chair, "Old Cole mentioned this cabin fondly on many an occasion, Miss Belle. Mentioned you fondly, too. Now that we've met up with you, I can see why."

"Bullshit. You men are all alike when it comes to seeking any old port in a storm. There's Arbuckle on the stove but it'll take a spell to heat."

The older man took off his hat and said, "Cold will do just fine, Miss Belle. We're sorry to trouble you like this, but we had nobody else to turn to in these parts."

"Yeah, I read the posters the Pinkertons has put out on both your fool heads. Which one of you is Frank and which one's Jesse?"

The older brother replied, "I'm Frank, and he's Jesse, Miss Belle. We don't ask even old friends to help us unless we make it worth their while. I fear we can't give you as much for hiding us as the Pinks would give you for turning us in, but it's cleaner money."

"I know where your money comes from. Cole bragged a lot when he was down here trifling with my affections. We'll talk about that later. I don't see as how I'd be able to let you boys hole up here, Frank. I got a date to ride into Fort Smith in the morning to discuss your possible whereabouts with Hanging Judge Parker, and other lawmen too numerous to mention. I'd feel foolish as anything if you two were to be caught under my roof whilst I was swearing on a stack of bibles I had no notion where you might be."

As they sat down, Belle brought the cold coffee and cake tin over to them and added, "Besides, my man might not understand if he was to ride in whilst I was in town, to find you rascals sitting here."

"We heard Jim Reed was gunned in Texas back in '74, Miss Belle."

"Well, that was two years ago, and I ain't too ugly to get another man in two infernal years, no matter what Cole told you! My current man's called Blue Duck. Before you ask, he's a full blood Cherokee. Want to make something out of it?"

There was a moment of silence. Then the one called Jesse shrugged and said, "Well, everyone to her own taste. I got nothing agin Indians, as long as they know their place."

Belle said, *"This* place happens to be Blue Duck's. You're

the ones as rode in uninvited. He ain't all that fond of your breed, and he packs a Walker .45 he knows how to use. So, to save all sorts of accidents, you'd best light out when I do. You can bunk here for the night, but you can't stay here alone, and if I don't ride in to Fort Smith, the law figures to come looking for us all."

She sat down and started slicing the cake.

"I'll tell you true, Miss Belle, me and Jesse here are in one hell of a mess. The wet trails has likely throwed the posse off our tracks for the time being, but the last time we swapped shots they was crowding us a mite. We dasn't ride by daylight until we gets deeper into the Indian Nation. Can't you fix it it up with some of your neighbors to tell your man we ain't here wrongful, if he rides in afore you can get back from Fort Smith?" Frank James asked.

Belle snorted in disgust. "Jesus H. Christ, you boys sure have trusting natures, considering the business you're in. Have either of you the least notion how much that reward would mean to a hardscrabble squatter along these bottom lands? It's a pure wonder someone hasn't collected on the two of you long before this!"

"We never lower our guard about folks we don't think we can trust, Miss Belle. Cole said you was a good old gal, and it's sort of knowed in certain circles that we're all in the same line of work. How come your Injun neighbors don't turn you in if they're so fond of the white man's law these days?" Jesse asked.

Belle shrugged and said, "You've been mighty polite about mentioning it, but I'm living in the Indian Nation as a squaw. My man's a Cherokee, and the only law in these parts is the Cherokee Police, which puts a different complexion entire on what I may or may not be doing in my spare time. You boys don't qualify worth a damn as members of any of the Five Civilized Tribes. The Indian Police likely won't bother with you one way or the other, as long as you behaves in The Nation, but getting any Indian to help you is another matter entire."

Then she called out, "Pearl? Are you awake, child?"

"Yes, Mamma," answered Pearl.

"Get down here, then. There's some gents here I want you to meet."

Pearl slipped down the ladder in her bare feet and flannel nightgown. Frank James rose from the table, looking surprised, but politely, down at her. Jesse just looked surprised. Pearl noticed he had granulated eyelids and blinked a lot. Pearl curtsied, and Frank James bowed gravely to her as Belle said, "If you must know, she's a byblow of your friend Cole Younger's last ride through these parts. Notice how she favors him?"

Jesse grinned and said, "I'll be damned. Cole never mentioned any such misdeeds in his past. Does he know about this kid, Belle?"

"Why should he?" she answered. "It ain't like he ever sent me as much as one letter after. What's the latest on him from that prison hospital up North?"

The brothers exchanged glances. Then Frank answered, "We don't know any more than the newspapers tell us, Miss Belle. Things went poorly up in Northfield. We never saw Cole after those of us still able got away, with half of Minnesota throwing lead and cuss words after us."

Pearl joined them for coffee and cake. She chose to sit near Uncle Frank, since he seemed the nicest. Uncle Jesse was nice-looking, but his eyes scared her. It wasn't just that they were infected some way, he had spooky little haunts living inside those cold sick eyes.

As Belle cut Pearl a slice of cake, she explained how she wanted her to stay here as look-out and go-between in the morning while she rode into Fort Smith to talk to Judge Parker.

Pearl said she understood, but asked, "Won't it get you in trouble to fib to Judge Parker, Mamma? You told me more than once it's a sin to lie."

Jesse James muttered ominously, but the older and steadier brother, Frank, took the child's free hand and said, "It is a sin to tell a lie, honey. Leastways, it is to tell black lies. But you look old and smart enough to know there's white lies as well as black lies, right?"

"Yes, sir. A white lie is when you tell a lady with a

dumb hat how much you admire it, whilst a black lie is one as hurts somebody."

"There you go, honey. What your mamma has to tell the law in Fort Smith is white lies, for they'd hurt Uncle Jesse and me severe if your mamma told them true. You see, the law has lied a heap to folks like us in the past. So it's only natural to pay them back with harmless fibs of our own. Do you understand me, honey?"

"I think so. What sort of lies do law folk tell, Uncle Frank?"

"All sorts of lies. They got them a thing they calls the Constitution. It's packed full of lies put there to make the little folks think the big folks ain't out to rob them blind. Do you love your mamma, Miss Pearl?"

"Of course I does. Don't you love your'n?"

"We sure do, honey, and whilst your Uncle Jesse and me was off fighting in the war, the law lied to our mamma to steal her land for the railroad. They spread all sorts of lies about us being bandits instead of Confederate soldiers, too. They lied us up, down, and crossways, and they're still saying mean things about us in the papers. They have us robbing banks and trains in places we've never been in our born lives! You can surely see the disadvantages of telling folk like that the truth, can't you?"

Pearl answered, "Well, I reckon it's all right to lie to liars. Are you a friend of my Pappa's, Uncle Frank?"

Across the table, Jesse snorted, "If he's your father."

Frank silenced him with a look and said, "We rode in the war together, honey. The Younger boys growed up with us over to Clay County, and are cousins besides. Save for my kid brother, here, I don't know any man I admire more than your father, Cole Younger."

Pearl nodded gravely and said, "I 'spect that makes me your friend, too, then. For I purely love my Dad, even if he don't know about me. Do you reckon he'd like to get a letter from me in that prison, Uncle Frank?"

"Well, it might surprise him, some. But I see no harm in it," Frank replied.

Jesse laughed. "He'd admire it even more if you could manage a saw in the envelope."

"Don't fun the child, Jesse. She ain't old enough to savvy your sense of humor." Frank turned back to Pearl and said, "I want to be your friend, too, Pearl Younger. Is that all right with you?"

Pearl squeezed his big horny hand and said, "Oh, yes. You're a nice man. Are you two some sort of Injuns?"

"Not hardly, honey. What makes you ask?"

"Before, when you was outside, I heard you talking in some furrin lingo. It wasn't Cherokee or Creek, but it purely wasn't American. I took you for maybe Comanche or Sioux or something."

Both brothers laughed, but Frank's face was respectful as he nodded at her and said, "You have good ears. Sometimes on the trail we talk in Welsh to throw off anyone listening in on us. Welsh is a valley over in the old country, where our clan come from long ago. I disremember most of what I larnt at our old granther's knee, and Jesse here, barely savvies it at all. But it comes in handy at times, to come from a solitary race, for you never know who's listening. We didn't know, when we rode up, how friendly you two ladies might be, but now I can see it's safe to talk American here."

Pearl laughed and said, "I'm glad we're all going to be friends, Uncle Frank."

Frank James looked at Belle with an inquiring smile.

Belle said, "Oh, eat your damned cake, and we'll see about finding some place for you two to bunk. I can see my fool kid's taken a shine to you, and you had the good grace to call her Pearl Younger. So that's good enough for me. I'm still mad as hell at that infernal Cole, but I can see his friends, at least, have good breeding. But if you boys get me hanged, I swear I'll never speak to either of you again!"

The next day broke clear. The trail was starting to dry as Belle rode off, leaving her daughter in the care of Frank and Jesse James, or, perhaps it was the other way around.

Nobody ever came to anyone's cabin uninvited along Younger's Bend, but that fact didn't seem to reassure Uncle Jesse as he paced the cabin like a caged tiger, peering out each curtained window he passed with his blinking eyes. Uncle Frank seemed more relaxed as they waited for Mamma or Uncle Blue Duck to ride in. Pearl showed him her coloring books, and he said he admired how she stayed inside the lines so neatly with her crayons. Uncle Jesse stopped pacing long enough to look at the coloring books, too. He said he had two childer of his own, living with their mother, wherever she might be. He even touched Pearl softly on the head as he muttered, half to himself, "Folks in our line shouldn't sire no kids, damn it. And damn it, where the hell is everyone?"

Frank, seated with Pearl at the table, soothed, "Take it easy, Jesse. No one coming is better than the wrong one's coming every time."

Jesse turned away from one window and headed for another. He growled, "Who's to know what anyone coming up on a man might have in mind, even if you know 'em? I still say we were betrayed in Northfield, Frank. Someone told them townies we were riding in to make a withdrawal from First National."

"Jesse, we've been over it time and time again. The only ones who knowed what we was up to was riding with us. So how in thunder could anyone have betrayed us? You reckon it was Bill Chadwell or the Miller boy, Clell? If they was in cahoots with the law, the law sure paid them back funny by shooting them both dead in the streets of Northfield. The posse kilt Charlie Pitts as we rode out, so I doubt it was him. Nobody else was there with us but Cole, Bob, and Jim Younger, and you don't pump police informers full of lead and throw them in jail. So that leaves me and you. Are you suspicioning me of being a lawman in disguise, Baby Brother?"

"Of course not. But things should have gone smoother. We planned that job good. How come every damn thing went wrong that could have?" Jesse answered.

Frank shrugged. "If I knew how to hold up banks without folks on the other side objecting some, I'd likely die rich as a Vanderbilt, but the only way I know is the hard way. Forget old Northfield, Jesse. It's over and done with. The two of us are still alive. That's more'n some of the boys who rode with us that day can say, right now."

"We ought to go back and get that sheriff. What was his name, Crispen?"

"Glispen, Jesse, but let's forget him, too. Once the heat dies down, there's this place I told you about over in Tennessee, near Nashville. We got enough to buy the land I mentioned and settle down a spell."

He glanced down at Pearl and added, "Maybe settle down for good. You're right about this being a lousy life for folks with kids. Your young'uns would like it on that farm in Tennessee, Jesse. It's time to start thinking ahead. The war's been over almost a dozen years, now, and I'm finding it sort of tedious to go on fighting on the side as lost in the first place."

Jesse moved to the other window again as he said, "You know they'll never let us live peaceable, Frank. No matter where we go, they'll search us out. Meanwhile, they may as well pay our traveling expenses. I see two riders coming. Looks like Belle and some Injun."

Pearl and Frank rose as Jesse went to the door. As they joined him there, Belle and a friendly Cherokee, who Pearl knew only as Uncle Sam, reined in to dismount.

Belle and the Indian came inside. "Boys," she said, "this here is Sam Starr. He may look young to you, but he's mean as hell. I run into him in town and as we rode back I explained your problem to him."

Sam stated simply, "You two can't stay here. Belle just lied her way past Judge Parker again, but there's a limit to anyone's luck, and they know you two are in the territory. I'm headed for the Texas line on a trail no white man knows. I have to deliver a few head of cattle to a place their old brands ain't knowed well enough to spot. I could use a couple of extra hands. I have spoken."

"He means he don't give shucks either way. That's the way Indians tell you it's up to you if you're in or out."

The two brothers hesitated. Jesse asked, "How can we be sure this pal of yours can be trusted, Belle?"

Sam Starr looked disgusted and started to turn away, but Frank quickly said, "We're in, Chief. Don't mind my baby brother's manners. He's just feeling broadly about another business deal that fell through. None of the folks who might or might not have double-crossed us were Injuns, and if Belle says you're all right, that's all we need to know. Ain't that right, Jesse?"

Jesse James shrugged and said, "We have no choice. But you'd better not be playing us false, Injun. For if you are, you know what will happen to your red ass."

Sam Starr's face went from Cherokee to Cigar Store Indian, and if anyone ever said that only blue or grey eyes could look cold, they'd never gazed into the black gunflints of a thoroughly annoyed Indian.

"What's going to happen to my red ass, Mister, ah, Howard?" Sam Starr asked.

Belle tried to calm him down. "Now, Sam, is that any way to talk in front of womenfolk?"

But Sam Starr merely spoke in a quieter tone. "Stay out of it, Miss Belle. The man just made his brag. It ain't my fault it was under your roof. What's it going to be, White Boy? It's your move."

Jesse James gasped like a man who'd been about to put on a boot and just noticed a scorpion in it. "You're talking mighty dangerous, Starr. Don't you know who I am?"

"I know who you are. You don't know who I am, or you'd act more polite. I'd tell you of the wonders I'd done, but I'm not a bragging man. So if you want to shoot it out, just say so," Starr said.

Frank James led Pearl into a corner and stood between her and whatever was about to happen as Belle jumped between the two men.

"Both you boys just stop it, hear? What's got into you, Sam Starr? I've never seen you fly off the handle like this afore," Belle demanded.

Starr said, "He started it. I'd be obliged if you'd stand

aside, Miss Belle. I come here to do a favor for your friends as you asked me to. I come in peace and good will. What happens now ain't up to me."

Frank spoke calmly from the corner. "Jesse ain't fixing to draw on you, Sam Starr. And if you draw on him it'll be two agin one, for he's my brother, even if he do get testy at times."

Starr shrugged and said, "I said it was up to him. The two of you can do as you like. I'll not back down."

Frank continued, "Nobody's asking anyone to back down, Sam. Anyone can see both you boys have sand in your craws, so let's talk about brains in your heads. Jesse, the man says he don't want to fight you unless you make him. I'd say you ought to tell him it's a Mexican standoff, and that you'll allow you was in the wrong as much as anyone. How about it, Baby Brother?"

Jesse James blinked his granulated eyelids rapidly, and his gun hand hovered menacingly out to one side as he said, "Nobody backs me down and lives to brag on it, Frank."

"Hell, Jesse, the man just told you he don't brag worth mention. I don't see this as a backing-down matter. I see it as two good old boys who locked horns sort of accidental, and now it's time to make up and ride off to Texas together, lest all three of us aim to stay here and do our drawing at the next federal deputy who comes down this way," Frank said.

Belle agreed. "Frank's right, Jesse. I ain't sure they believed every word I said in Fort Smith this morning, and this misunderstanding is likely more my fault than anyone's. I should have told you boys that Sam, here, has a rep of his own to defend. But he ain't here to add to it. Ain't that right, Sam Starr?"

"My cards are all on the table, Miss Belle. I'll fight the both of them or carry them to Texas. It's up to them to decide. I can chaw it either ways," Starr answered.

Frank James said. "There you go, Jesse. The gent said he didn't want a war with us, and we sure as hell ought to be thinking about Texas. Let's all shake on her and ride, hear?"

Pearl came out of her corner. She said, "Please don't fight each other, Uncle Sam and Uncle Jesse, for I likes you both and it would vex me awful if either of you was to get hurt."

Jesse James' face softened. "Oh, hell, I was only funning, Sam Starr. You know I'd never slap leather agin a friend of Belle and Cole Younger's daughter. Let's get the horses, Frank."

The three of them left, joshing back and forth like schoolboys. After an even fight they didn't aim to start again, and Belle sat down weakly to marvel. "Woosh! Who'd have ever thought that of Sam Starr? There's more to that young buck than meets the eye."

"Do you think the law will catch them on their way to Texas, Mamma?" Pearl asked.

"Not if the law knows what's good for it! The next time you're told to stay in a corner I want you to do it, Pearl. You're too little to understand what just happened, but your poor old mamma just had a year's growth scared out of her. Fetch me the jug from under the dry-sink like a good child, will you? They may be gone, but it's going to take me a spell to settle my nerves. Who'd have ever thought old Sam had the sand to face both the James boys at one time? I'd hardly ever noticed that young buck afore today, but ain't he something else?"

Blue Duck came home late that evening, drunk and sullen. The Carsons, trash whites and receivers of stolen goods who dwelt deeper in the Nation, had taken advantage of Blue Duck, or at least Blue Duck thought they had. Blue Duck wasn't a deep thinker, drunk or sober, and he had deep-rooted feelings of inferiority to whites. Like everyone out here under middle age, Blue Duck had been born at this end of the Trail of Tears. Like other Cherokee children, he'd been reared on bitter tales of past injuries to a proud, bewildered people.

The brutal and unjust removal acts, engineered by Andrew Jackson and land-grabbing slave state politicos, had in truth been more horrendous that even white friends of the Five Civilized Tribes could know. The formation of the so-called Five Civilized Tribes, composed of the Cherokee, Chickasaw, Choctaw, Creek and Seminole, had been an oversimplification as well a gross injustice.

In theory, the Five Civilized Tribes were Eastern Woodland Indians who'd bowed to the inevitable, and had tried to assimilate to the culture of their white frontier neighbors. The Cherokee, in particular, had progressed, if that was the word, to where they'd published their own newspapers in the alphabet devised by the great self-taught sage and educator, Sequoyah. Most, however, were by then speaking English as well as their own Iroquoian dialect. They had needed to. The Cherokee had taken to "living white" with a vengeance and enthusiasm, after fighting on both sides in the American Revolution. They'd dressed like rural whites, lived in cabins like rural whites, and farmed the bottomlands along the Tennessee with perhaps more skill than their envious poor-white neighbors. By the time of the removal acts, the Cherokee were enjoying a standard of living better than many small-holding white farmers, north or south. They'd used the same implements, including slaves, and had grown the same crops as the white farmers they competed with. So, naturally, they had to go. It wasn't fitting in the eyes of the Lord or Andrew Jackson that such an odd, unclassifiable breed prosper on lands that common sense could see was prime farmland, meant to be settled right by decent folk. The Cherokee and other civilized tribes seemed spooky to the white Southerner. They didn't fit right in God's scheme. Everyone knew that white folks lived in houses, drove wagons to market with bumper crops and generally behaved civilized. Black folk had been put on this earth to chore for the white folk. Indians were supposed to wear feathers and paint and traipse around in the woodlands 'til some red-blooded white frontiersman saw fit to clear them along with the trees. Then they were sup-

posed to move further west or fight. It made no never-
mind to folks blessed with the Good Book, long rifle, and,
in a pinch, the U.S. Army.

The Cherokee were not only prosperous, they were good
looking, or perhaps one should say that since Iroquoian fa-
cial features were closer to the white European's standard
of beauty than some other tribes, white people found them
a good looking kind of Indian. So, from first contact,
there'd been lots of inter-marriage.

Blue Duck was a pure blood, or pure-blooded enough to
look like an Indian was supposed to look. He was a handsome man for any race to boast, and was inclined to be
soft-spoken and friendly when sober. Like many men of a
proud but defeated kith, he made a very ugly drunk, so
Belle sent Pearl up to the loft when she saw the way he
was walking toward the shack.

"You ought to rub that pony down and put him in his
stall agin the night air, honey, for you both look hard rid.
How did it go over to the Carson's spread?"

Blue Duck growled, "Fuck the pony and fuck the Carsons. I've rid high and I've rid low and I feel like I've
been drug through the keyhole backwards. Is my supper
waiting on the table, Old Woman? For if it ain't, I mean to
beat the shit out of you!"

"Now, Blue Duck, you don't mean that. You just come
inside and set down to your steak and beans. I'll tend your
pony."

He missed the step up to the veranda, and would have
fallen had not the small but wiry Belle grabbed his arm to
steady him. Blue Duck wrenched free and stood there,
swaying, as he stared at her owlishly with bloodshot eyes.
Then he shook his head as if to clear it and said, "Howdy,
Old Woman. If you're here, I must be home, but I dise-
member how in hell I got here. Who was we just fussing
at? Has someone been rawhiding you about being my
squaw again? Just point the son of a bitch out to me and
I'll stomp his ass!"

Belle took a deep breath and answered, "Come inside

and set before you fall like a fool in the dooryard, Blue Duck. Your supper's ready, and a body can see you need something warm inside to sop up what you've been drinking."

As she led him in he protested, "I only had a couple, damn it. Are you saying I'm drunk?"

"No, dear, I said you looked trail weary. Come set yourself down like a good boy."

Blue Duck reeled to the table and almost missed the chair as he took a seat, protesting, "I ain't no boy, God damn your eyes! I'm a full growed man, and I rode in the war as a cavalry corporal. Where's my old butternut uniform, Belle? I want to put her on. It's Saturday night, and my Injun blood is up and I sure looked fine in that uniform."

Belle went to the range to take his tin plate from the oven. She said, wearily, "You don't have your Confederate kit no more, Blue Duck. You told me you had to get rid of it when Lee gave up the fight years ago. Besides, you'd only get in trouble wearing it. The Reconstruction's about over, but the B.I.A. is run by Yankees just the same."

Blue Duck ignored the food she placed before him to roar, "Fuck the Yankees. Fuck their mothers, too! Fuck Robert E. Lee for giving up so easy! He never should have done that, Belle. Didn't we have us enough on our plates here in the Nation without Lee surrendering our last rights to the Yanks?"

A tear ran down his saddle-leather cheek as he sobbed. "God knows we tried, Belle. How the hell was we supposed to know the South would lose when us Cherokee rode for her? What the hell's the matter with our tribal council? They should have knowed enough to pick the winning side!"

Belle poured coffee, strong and black, for him. "We all thought the confederacy would win, Blue Duck. Even though my daddy moved from Carthage to Texas to avoid the border fighting, it sure looked like our side would win."

"Well, they didn't, damn it, and now them damned Yankee sissies has stripped us of the few rights we had and put white men in the Bureau of Indian Affairs over us, just like we was infernal Sioux."

"Now, honey, you know they still let the tribal council run things more or less. You got your own Indian Police and such."

"It ain't the same. They told us when we come out here that the Five Tribes would have total self-government. Now they say we four-flushed our rights in the war some way. How come they done that, Belle? You've got more book larning than me. You're a white gal besides. So tell me how we four-flushed our rights away in the war."

"Likely by choosing the wrong side. The reconstruction was hard on Texas, too. Eat your supper, Blue Duck. I'll see to putting your pony way," Belle said.

She went outside. Blue Duck took a sip of coffee, groaned, and laced it with four spoonfuls of sugar before experimenting again. He nodded and said, "That's more like it." Then he called out, "Pearl? Where are you at, Pearl?"

Pearl came to the edge of the loft. "I'm up here, sir. Mamma said I was to play with the doll you made me up here and not to pester a tired man," she said.

"She did, huh? Well, come down here and keep me company, damn it. What in tarnation do I look like, some kind of ogre?"

Pearl came down the ladder in her bare feet and sacking shift and stood near the table. "No, sir. I admire the way you look, Uncle Blue Duck. Did you have a nice time over to the Carson's spread?"

"I never have a nice time with white folks. Not white men, anyway. I gits along better with white women."

He stared at her oddly, and Pearl felt uneasy. He laughed. "I know what you're thinking, girl. I could likely get horse-whipped for what I'm thinking, too."

"Sir?"

"Why don't you hoist that skirt up so's I can see if what I'm thinking about is worth it, Pearl? Go on, give old Uncle Blue Duck a friendly peek at your pussy. Has it got hair on it yet? Let me see."

Pearl blushed and said, "Uncle Blue Duck, you hadn't ought to talk that way to me. I'm only a girl-child."

He laughed and joshed, "Hell, when they're big enough they're old enough, and you're, what, twelve or so?"

"If you please, sir, I'm only nine."

"Shoot, your mother lies about your age because it vexes a woman to have daughters old enough for men to pleasure, Pearl. She's twenty-eight, and she run off with Cole Younger when she was sixteen. I may be an Indian, but I can add. Say she was seventeen when she had you, you'd have to be at least twelve by now, and you sure are filling out nice. Let me see your pussy."

"I 'spect I'd best not, Uncle Blue Duck. Mamma says things like that ain't seemly. Besides, I'm still only nine. Mamma and my pappa spent some time together afore they had me. I reckon they didn't get about trying 'til they knowed one another a spell."

Blue Duck laughed. "Hell, Old Belle likely screwed him the first night she saw him, knowing her warm nature. I'll tell you how old you are once I see your pussy, girl. I'm a fine judge of she-male privates. Hoist that shimmy shirt and let me see. I ain't asking you, girl. I'm telling you. You want me to take a switch to you for being a willfull child?"

Pearl felt a lump in her throat and she feared she was going to start crying. Fortunately, Belle came back in at just that moment, saying. "Well, your pony will likely live, but you sure are hell on a horse, Blue Duck. Howdy, Pearl. What's the matter with you, honey? You looks upset about something."

Pearl didn't look at Blue Duck as she whispered, "I come down to ask if I could go outside a spell, Mamma. I know the leaves is turning, but it's a warm evening and I thought I'd search for crawdads along the riverside."

"All right, but mind you come in afore sundown," Belle said.

Pearl promised, and turned away to run out the door, feeling oddly like she was being chased by something spooky. As she closed the door behind her, she heard her mother saying, "Watch them hands, you fool Indian. It's broad day out. Can't you wait for a seemly hour?"

Pearl didn't stop until she'd run down to the river bank, and then she had to. She was out of breath and feeling queer. She sat down on a cottonwood log and gazed out across the rolling river. She didn't feel like searching for crawdads. She didn't know what on earth she'd do with an ugly old crawdad, even if she got her hands on one. She was sorry that the winds had shifted to the west again, with the smell of snows warning her not to swim in the cold Arkansas if she didn't want to come down with an ague again. She didn't know why she wanted to go swimming, but she did. The river now ran low and the water was clear, and Pearl felt soiled. She didn't know why, for she'd bathed just the night before in Mamma's sweet salted tub. She'd gotten out of the tub so clean her skin had squeaked. What made her trembling flesh feel so dirty all of a sudden?

A haunting soft sound drifted through the trees along the riverside, like a lovestick dove crying on some willow limb. But no bird made a sound like that. Pearl followed her ears with her eyes until she saw the Cherokee boy, Sequanna, up the bank blowing on a turkey bone flute and pretending he didn't see her.

"Menfolks!" Pearl sighed, looking away from him again. She was too young to grasp what all the fuss was about, but she'd been reared among Indians, so she knew their courting customs. What in tarnation was getting into the menfolk hereabouts? Uncle Blue Duck had been too drunk to know what he was saying, but couldn't Sequanna see she was too young to haunt with his courting flute?

She knew he wasn't going to come any closer. It wasn't the custom to blow a courting flute close to a gal until you'd done it for some time and been offered some encouraging smiles, but it still made her uneasy to sit here with a fool Indian twittering at her like an infernal bird. She debated with herself about marching right over to Sequanna, stamping her foot, and telling him to stop pestering her, but she knew Cherokee gals did that when they wanted a boy to know they were interested in them. The way a Cherokee gal got rid of a boy she didn't fancy was to just ignore him until he got discouraged and went to blow his infernal flute at someone else. It could take some time, if a gal was pretty, but it was the only way to handle an Indian boy who'd taken a shine to you. She just wished it didn't make her feel so uneasy. She wondered why she felt so spooked by Sequanna's dumb old tune. Despite her youth, Pearl knew what rape was, and that Indians who followed the old ways never did such unseemly things to anyone but the women of their enemies. So she didn't have to worry about that, because she and her mother were on tolerable terms with everyone on Younger's Bend.

She wondered what it felt like to get raped. The confusing part was that older women seemed to feel so excited about whether a man took them willing or by force. She'd seen plenty of critters doing it, and though the critters seemed excited by it, too, the whole thing struck Pearl as plumb disgusting, and mighty silly besides. She crinkled her nose at the thought of the time those two dumb hound dogs got hung up in the road, and how the folks had laughed when Charlie Bluefeather came out and splashed a bucket of water over the two of them. She wondered if human folk got hung up like that and how they got unstuck. It hardly seemed likely that grownups went to bed with a bucket of cold water handy. She'd never seen exactly what Mamma and Blue Duck were up to down there in the dark, although, from the odd noises, they were up to something mighty wild. She was suddenly aware of her body in a way she couldn't remember before.

She felt like that silly Sequanna could see right through her shift as he stood up there in the alders, blowing at her on his dumb flute. She got to her feet with a flounce of her head, and turned her back on him to march grandly back to the cabin. Uncle Blue Duck never teased her when Mamma was about, and Sequanna was acting too silly to bear another minute.

She stepped up on the veranda in her bare feet and opened the door softly, so as not to disturb Uncle Blue Duck if he was sleeping off that red-eye, so neither Pearl's mother nor her Indian lover noticed as she stood there, thunderstruck, for the brief moment it took her to gather her wits, back out, and close the door behind her. Then she ran as hard as she was able, all the way to Granny Redbird's cabin.

The old Indian woman was rocking on her veranda as Pearl ran to her. "I seen them! It was awful! Mamma and Blue Duck was acting dirty as all get out, and I'll never be able to look either in the eye again!"

The spey woman gathered the bewildered child in her arms and soothed her. "Now, just you hush that crying, child. Young'uns have always walked in on their elders unexpected, and they likely always will. You only seed what comes natural to older folk, Pearl."

Pearl buried her face in the old woman's motherly bosom and sobbed, "I reckon I know what comes natural or not, Granny. Mamma was atop old Blue Duck, naked as a jay, and she was puffing on his dirty old thing like it was a peace pipe whilst he licked at her privates like a yaller dog!"

The spey woman repressed a chuckle as she said, "They calls that French loving, Pearl. I reckon others has took up the custom, too. Sometimes when a man's likkered up he ain't good for much else. Did they see you spying on them, Pearl?"

"No. I wasn't meaning to spy. I ducked out as soon as I seed how dirty they was acting. Why in thunder would anyone want to act so dirty, Granny Redbird? You wouldn't do a thing like that, would you?"

"Not lately," the old woman said, sighing. She patted the frightened girl to calm her as she added, "The ways of a man with a woman have always been nicer to do than to look at, honey. You mustn't trouble yourself with things you ain't old enough to understand. What other folks do with their own bodies is their own business. Your Romeo and Juliet must have looked silly as all get-out whilst they was playing slap and tickle, but it was important enough for them to die over. Someday when you're a woman growed and married up, you'll understand. Until then it's not for you to worry about, understand?"

"No, I'll never understand why Mamma has to act so crazy and dirty," Pearl said.

Granny Redbird didn't answer. It was not her place to teach a virgin child anything a future husband wouldn't likely be more convincing about in times to come. They just rocked a spell in the gloaming light, and when she'd sobbed herself calm, Pearl said, "I don't know how I'll ever be able to go home, and I promised I'd come in before sundown."

Granny Redbird said, "Surely you know how to go home, child. You just take the same trail back that you followed here. You'll make it well before the sun ball surrenders to the owl birds, if you hurry."

"I knows the way home, Granny. I just don't know how I'll ever face the two of them again! What can I say to them when I come in the door?"

The spey woman patted her again and said, "You could say 'Howdy', for openers. They don't know you saw them going French. Now that you've larnt the advantages of knocking on doors before you opens them, it won't likely happen again. But what if it does? Your mother is foolish about some things, but she is not a bad person. What you saw her doing was not as rare a thing as you might think, silly as it must have looked to a child. Farther along, you'll know about such matters. Now, all you have to know is that your mother loves you, in her own odd way. I want you to go home and say nothing about it. Do you understand me?"

"Lord of Mercy, of course I dasn't tell Mamma I saw her puffing on a man that way. But why do grown folks do such things, Granny? What does it feel like to go dirty with a man?" Pearl asked.

The spey woman shrugged and said, "There's no way to tell you. Do you know that blind child who lives down around the bend from you?"

"Yes, Creek Alice. I ain't allowed to play with Creek Alice. Uncle Blue Duck says Creeks are part nigger, albeit

Creek Alice looks Indian enough to me. I find the part about her being a nigger a mite confusing."

Granny Redbird nodded soberly and said, "Being blind from birth, little Alice Ferndancer must find it confusing enough to be an Indian. But getting back to more important mysteries, how would you tell that blind child what a sunset looks like, Pearl?"

Pearl thought for a moment before answering. "Lord, I don't see how I could, since she's never seen color once, and don't know the difference betwixt light and darkness."

The spey woman nodded and said, "That is why nobody can tell a virgin maid what sex feels like. It would be easier to explain the sunset to a blind person. You are luckier than Alice Ferndancer. You already know what a sunset looks like. Someday maybe both of you will understand the other beauties of this world. But whilst we admire yon sunset, the hour's getting late. Go home, Pearl. I have spoken."

So Pearl did as she was told, and Granny Redbird got up wearily to go inside. She lit a candle on a shelf under a tinted print of the Virgin and spoke in Cherokee as she murmured, "Hear me, Mary, Changing Woman, or whatever your name is. You spirits had better do something about that white child I brought forth from a troubled womb. I did not go to all that trouble to see her ruined. I want you spirits to think of some way to get her out of this life before it's too late. I will be very cross with you if that child I worked so hard to save turns out another white trash whore. I have spoken."

2

His Honor, Judge Isaac Parker of the Federal District Court of Fort Smith, Arkansas, didn't look like a hanging judge and, in fact, had not hanged nearly as many criminals as he had felt were worthy of the distinction.

Parker was a handsome, courtly man in his youthful middle age. His people hailed from Chestershire, in the old country, and in an earlier time he'd have made a perfect country squire of the Old School.

Judge Parker had also had the obvious good sense to pick the winning side in the recent war, and had first come to public notice as an official of the Reconstruction. Those ex-confederates unfortunate enough to be hailed before his bench had found that Isaac Parker made little distinction between a man who'd actually fought in the southern forces or simply cheered them on. Parker considered the Rules of Evidence to be Holy Writ engraved on granite, so he had earned the reputation in criminal circles of being a fair judge if you were innocent, but if you were guilty, watch out!

Judge Parker held, rightly or wrongly, that attempts to reform an habitual criminal were a tedious waste of the taxpayer's money while, on the other hand, once you'd hanged a rapist or murderer, he'd surely never rape or murder again. But while he could sentence a guilty man to death in front of his weeping wife and mother, Isaac Parker prided himself on¹ clean law. More than one surprised and doubtless guilty defendant had been released by Parker for lack of evidence when he found the arresting officers hadn't done their homework.

As he sat in his chambers that morning with the Fort Smith marshal and two deputies, Judge Parker was at ease with his conscience and the world as he found it. His robes were hanging in the closet, and he sat in his swivel chair in a fresh-pressed suit of snuff-brown serge, regarding his visitors with polite distaste.

The marshal said, "You gotta give us a search warrant on Belle Shirley, Your Honor. Like I told you, the James boys has been seen in these parts, and everybody knows old Belle and Cole Younger are lovers."

Judge Parker corrected him. "Were, Marshal. Past tense. At the moment, Cole Younger faces life-at-hard in Minnesota State Prison, so I very much doubt you'll find him in that woman's cabin."

"Yes, sir, but Cole Younger is kin to the Jameses, and they was seed crossing into the Indian Nation mebbe a day or so ago."

Judge Parker smiled. "I follow your drift, boys, but I can't issue a federal warrant on such flimsy grounds. The Constitution says we have to show cause before we go busting in on folk. The fact that a woman shacked up with someone the James boys know, ten years or so ago, is slicing the Constitution mighty thin. Besides, you wouldn't find Frank and Jesse in Belle's cabin at this late date, even if I gave you leave to search for them there."

One of the deputies frowned and said, "No offense, Judge, but you don't look like you got telescopes for eyes. How can anyone say for certain what we'd find or not find in that trashy bawd's cabin?"

"I talked to the woman the other day. And by the by, you deputies had no call to send her to me on mere suspicion.

She told me her father was a judge in Texas. I believed her, for she could talk the horns off a billy goat when it comes to knowing her law. If such a monstrous freak wasn't against nature, she'd have made a tolerable she-male lawyer herself, had she not gone so wrong. The reason I know she's not hiding the James boys is because she's too slick by half to do such a fool thing."

"Well, can't we just sort of poke around over there in any case, Your Honor? The woman's a known receiver of stolen goods. There's no telling what could turn up on or about her spread."

Parker shook his head. He said, "You come to me with exactly what stolen object you have in mind, and show me probable cause for it to be in her possession, and I'll be proud to issue you a search warrant. I know I'm new here, so I'd best explain my views on 'rough' justice. I don't hold with it. Two wrongs don't make a right, so don't ask me again to issue fishing licenses in the guise of proper papers. I don't work that way."

One of the deputies said, "Judge, you don't understand what we're up agin, trying to keep order in these parts. That woman Belle is smart like you say. Everybody knows if it wasn't for her brains, the gang of thieves she sends out every which ways from the Strip would have been caught long ago. She's a regular bandit queen!"

"That's hearsay evidence, son. Hearsay don't cut much ice in my court. I've heard the tales about the woman. They may be true, She was a shifty-eyed slick talker when I met her the other day, but I can't order folk arrested on idle gossip. You boys have to get some proof on her and that buck she lives with."

The youngest deputy in the room scowled and said, "Hell, Judge, she's shacked up with an Injun. Don't that prove she ain't no good?"

Parker smiled crookedly as he replied. "It proves she's not particular who she bestows such favors on."

The marshal said, "I don't see how a white woman can dwell over in the Strip in the first place, Your Honor. Ain't the Indian Nation supposed to be just for Injuns?"

Parker said, "Yes, but that's a matter for the B.I.A., not the Justice Department. The B.I.A. is Department of the Interior. You may have noticed they don't co-operate with us worth mention. I had a talk with them about the whites squatting in the strip. They said their condition with the old tribal councils in delicate, so that they generally let the Indians decide such matters. That kind of co-habitation is against the law here in Arkansas, but that's a delicate matter the B.I.A. is working on. Indians don't see the mixing of blood as the same sin we do. Chief Quanna of the Comanche Nation has a white mother he's right fond of. He could get mighty surly if we were to insist he was an unlawful bastard and that his mother was a criminal, so the B.I.A. hasn't seen fit to pester him about it, seeing as his mother's living willingly with the tribe, and the Comanche are at peace with us at last, praise the Lord."

"Hell, Judge, Belle Shirley ain't married up with no chief. She's living in sin with a no-account Cherokee thief calt Blue Duck!" said the marshal.

"I chided her about that the other day, Marshal. She tells me they're married lawful in Indian eyes and mayhaps they are, since I'm not up on the subject. She said she'd have to leave the Strip if she didn't have a Cherokee man. Our hands are sort of tied. It's up to the B.I.A. and their wards what Belle Shirley does or doesn't do over yonder in the Strip."

"Damn, that Strip sure vexes me!" the marshal complained. "I surely wish Washington would make up its mind about that infernal Indian Nation. It ain't run right by neither us or the Injuns. Nobody seems to know what the law in the Nation is these days, so there's no law at all worth mention. The James boys ain't the first to use it as a no man's land to hide out in!"

Judge Parker nodded and said, "I'm not supposed to take sides in the pending election this November, but if Rutherford Hayes wins, you may see some changes for the better. Hayes is running on a reform ticket, and I agree the Cherokee Strip is overdue for some reforming. Meanwhile, we have to just keep cool and bide our time until they sort the mess out. As you know, the original Indian government was disbanded because of the Cherokee in particular siding with the Confederacy."

"The Creeks and Seminoles was on our side, Judge, likely 'cause so many of 'em was really runaway slaves passing as redskins."

Judge Parker raised a hand and said, "No matter, the experiment in self-determination didn't work as it was supposed to, so now the Indian Nation is under reservation status like the other B.I.A. reserves. The point is that Washington dissolved the old government without making sensible plans on providing a new one. The handful of white agents spread across enough land to make a couple of eastern states have to use the Indian leaders to get anything done at all."

"Hell, that's not saying much, Judge Parker," said the marshal.

"I know. The B.I.A. ain't happy about it, either. The council elders go all cigar-store-sullen if they're prodded too hard, so the agents have to concentrate on keeping them content enough to keep what little order there is. The Indian Police seem willing enough to arrest someone caught red-handed over a raped and mutilated squaw, and they tend to frown on anyone stealing directly from an Indian, but that's about the size of it. It's a waste of time trying to get them to think as delicate as we do about critters like that infernal Shirley woman and her thieving buck. But, like I said, let's just wait until the election's over. If the new administration doesn't see fit to put up the money it would take to run things right over there, they might at least give me a freer hand to deal with it."

The marshal nodded and said, "I purely hope you're right, Your Honor. If you ever turns me and the boys loose, I got a list of renegades as long as my arm for you to study on hanging high, and I'd sure like to see what a white woman looks like swinging on a rope," he added as he rose to leave.

"You reckon you have enough to hang Belle Shirley on?" Parker asked.

"I'm working on it. Lord knows, she has it coming," replied the marshal.

Pearl sat at the table frowning down at a sheet of yellow foolscap and wishing her mamma was to home. Pearl's spoken vocabulary exceeded her spelling, but her mamma could even spell Constantinople because she had been to the Carthage Female Academy to almost the eighth grade, and was smart as anything. But she and Uncle Blue Duck were out on errands that afternoon, so Pearl had to compose her important letter as best she could.

She was writing in blue crayon. There wasn't any ink, but it hardly seemed proper to write a letter in pencil. Her block letters were neat and legible, only she wished she knew how to write in longhand like a fine lady. She was desperately trying to make a good impression, as she sensed a certain delicacy in the way her parents might feel toward her. She wanted no more misunderstandings.

This was the third time she'd started. The first two letters had ended as angry crumpled balls of paper. It was sinful to waste, so this time Pearl was more careful, and got all the way to the end without making a single mistake. She signed it and sat back to read it over.

DEER FATHER:
　　HOW DEW YEW DEW? I AM YEWR DOTTER PEARL YOUNGER AND I AM SORE VEXED TO HEER YEWR IN THAT OLD JAIL. I SURELY HOPES YEW GITS OUT. WHEN YEW DEW Y DONT YEW COME BACK HEER AND LIVE WITH MAMMA AND ME AGIN? WE MISS YEW SORE. MAMMA DONT LET ON. BUT I GNOW SHE STILL LUVS YEW AND I LUV YEW TEW. HARDLY NO LAW EVER COMES HEER AND YEW MUST BE MITEY TIRED OF TRAIPSING ABOUT NOW THAT YEW GOT ALL THEM BULLITS IN YEW. YEW COOD REST UP HEER UNTIL YEWR ALL BETTER AND THEN WE COOD ALL RIDE OUT TO CALIFORNEE AND

LIVE. MAMMA WAS OUT TO CALIFORNEE WITH UNCLE JIM WEN I WAS LITTLE AND SHE ALLOWS ITS RIGHT NISE OUT THERE. NOBODY IS LOOKING FOR YEW IN CALIFOR- NEE IS THEY? MAMMA SAYS IT DONT SEEM LIKELY THE CALIFORNEE LAW IS LOOKING FOR HER THERE CAUSE UNCLE JIM GOT SHOT DOWN TEXAS WAY AND NOBODY SEEN HER FACE WEN THEY GOT ALL THAT GOLD OFF A MEAN OLD RICH MAN AS MADE IT OFFEN THE SWEAT OF OTHERS. SO Y DONT YEW JUST COME HOME TO US AND BE MY DADDY RITE?

YEWR LOVING DOTTER PEARL YOUNGER

The child nodded in satisfaction and neatly folded the letter. When her mamma came back she'd ask her for an envelope and a stamp. She knew where Belle kept such things, but she'd only gotten permission to use the note pad and might need help addressing and all. Her father was in Minnesota State Prison, but she didn't know where it was at.

The door opened and Blue Duck came in, cussing under his breath. Uncle Blue Duck did that when he'd been drinking, and he'd been doing that a lot of late.

Pearl smiled at him uneasily and asked if he wanted her to fetch him some Arbuckle as he sat down across from her. He stared at her and said, "Don't want no coffee. Want whiskey. You got any whiskey on you, girl?"

"I fear I don't, sir. You drank all we had in the brown jug."

"Hell, what good are you if you don't have nothing decent to serve a man? What are you doing with that writing pad, girl? That's your mother's writing pad. Don't you know it's a sin to steal from your kin?"

"If you please, sir. I asked Mamma's permit. She said it was all right with her if I used a sheet."

The Cherokee nodded grudgingly. Then a crafty look came into his bloodshot eyes. He pointed with his chin at the balls of foolscap on the table between them as he said, "You used more than one sheet, missy. Your mother only said you could use one, so you disobeyed her. What have you to say for yourself on that score, eh?"

"I'm sorry, Uncle Blue Duck."

"You are, are you? Well, sorry ain't good enough, I fear I'm going to have to punish you for stealing."

Pearl stared at him aghast. Uncle Blue Duck joshed a lot, but this time he looked like he meant it. The thought of being switched made Pearl feel slightly ill. Her Mamma had threatened her with a switching more than once, but had never done it. She was an obedient child. Even her Mamma said so.

The Indian rose, frowning down at the terrified child. He looked around as if for something to switch her with. Then he came around the table, took her by one arm, and pulled her to her bare feet, saying, "You'd best come with me so we can punish you right."

The thought of resisting an elder never occurred to Pearl. She started to cry as Blue Duck led her out and around to the back of the cabin as she pleaded, "Please don't switch me, Uncle Blue Duck! I'll never do it again. I swear I'll be good from now on. I'll do anything you say if only you won't switch me!"

Her words seemed to be having a good effect on Blue Duck, because he was smiling as he led her past the outhouse to the back stable. The small log outbuilding was empty as they entered. On a warm fall day such as this the ponies were grazing in the back lot. The dark interior smelled of hay, horse and spider webbings. Pearl could smell Blue Duck, too. He smelled of sweat and red-eye and something else. A musty chestnutty odor rose from his worn overalls. The odd scent made her uneasy. Blue Duck looked around. Then he moved over to the loose hay piled in a corner and sat down, pulling Pearl after him into his lap.

The child sat quietly, wondering if he was just funning her after all. She didn't see how he'd switch anybody sitting in his lap, and the other times she'd sat in Uncle Blue Duck's lap he'd been telling her a story. Uncle Blue Duck was a sweet-natured man, when he hadn't been at the likker.

A sudden awkwardness seemed to have come over the grown man as well. He sort of snuggled her closer to him, like he'd forgotten about switching her after all, and Pearl wondered what that was she was sitting on in his lap. There was a funny bulge in the front of Blue Duck's overalls, pressed up between the cheeks of her trembling rump, and the bulge was sort of trembling, too, like it was a mouse or something. Blue Duck held her firmly with one hand but the other hand was strangely gentle as he slowly moved it up her slender young thigh, under the skirt of her thin cotton shift.

He said, "I got to punish you, girl. But there's punishments and punishments. Would you rather be punished in a way that don't hurt?"

Pearl nodded eagerly and answered, "I sure don't want you to hurt me, Uncle Blue Duck."

"Well, maybe I won't. Give your old uncle a kiss, little darling."

So Pearl twisted around to kiss him like he asked. It felt nice to kiss, but the way he stuck his tongue in her mouth was frightening and distasteful. He held her closer, breathing husky, and she was afraid she'd gag if he stuck his tongue any further in betwixt her lips, but he seemed to like it and anything was better than getting switched.

She'd never been kissed like that before and it distracted her enough so that Blue Duck's big brown hand was between her thighs and cupping her naked privates under her shift before she realized what was going on. She flinched as he parted her small opening with sneaky fingers. As one finger entered her she tried to pull away, pleading, "Please don't trifle with my privates, sir. I don't like it!"

He rolled her off his lap and on her back in the hay, still molesting her with his hand but moving his lips from hers to say in a funny sneaky voice, "Hesh, honey. You know you likes it. All she-critters does. Besides, you said you'd do anything I asked, and this is what I'm asking. You're a willful child and you must be punished, but I may as well enjoy my duty. Open your legs, girl. I'll switch your bare behind if you don't stop trying to cross your legs like that, hear?"

Pearl started to sob uncontrollably as she allowed him to spread her slim thighs and cock a denim-clad knee over between them. Some remaining spark of humanity in the drunken Blue Duck made him say soothingly. "Hesh your tears, honey. I ain't going to hurt you. I'm fixing to break you in gentle as anything."

"What are you going to do to me, Uncle Blue Duck?"

"Nothing hurtful, honey. I'm just out to make a woman outten you. There, you see? I got two fingers in you, now, and it don't hurt a bit, does it?"

Pearl sobbed, "Please take them fingers outten me, sir! You're shaming me awful, hurtful or no!"

Blue Duck chuckled and moved his hand skillfully as he jeered, "You gals is all alike. I can feel you just gushing for what you are about to receive, but how in thunder am I to get my old organ grinder in whilst wearing these fool bibs? I should have studied on this more afore I started. Reach up and unhook the straps like a good little gal, Pearl."

She didn't want him taking off his durned old overalls. It was broad day and she didn't want to see his old thing again, but she was afraid to disobey him. He was staring down at her wolfish and wild. She sensed he'd do something mean to her if she didn't do exactly as he said, so she reached up and started fumbling with the snaps as Blue Duck drove his fingers deeper into her cringing flesh and gasped, "Oh, Lord, hurry! You're going to be tight as a drum but I see I was right about you being big enough!"

She closed her eyes and swallowed a scream. She was innocent, but no rural child was too innocent about barnyard matters to fail to grasp what he intended, and she knew he'd do something awful if she screamed. She knew she was going to get raped, and now she knew why womenfolk thought it was so awful. She pleaded, "Please, sir. If it's all the same to you, I'd rather be switched!"

He growled, "Not hardly. I've better things to do with your sweet little bare ass than switching the same! Hurry up with them straps. I'll hit you sure as hell if I wastes this wad by coming in my pants. I've been saving it up to come in you for quite a spell!"

Pearl unsnapped him, and Blue Duck reached one hand up to pull down the only barrier between her exposed naked groin and his raging erection. She was resigned to what she knew was coming, and despite her terror some detached part of her wondered if his old thing would feel any worse than those infernal knobby fingers. Blue Duck was experienced as well as depraved, by Indian as well as white standards, and the way he was fooling with her down there was starting to feel sort of interesting. She knew Mamma liked it, but what on earth was Mamma going to say about all this?

What Belle had to say sounded more like the roar of an enraged tigress, for as she came in the doorway looking for them, and finding such a sight, Belle screamed mindlessly, snatched a pitchfork from the wall, and drove the tines into Blue Duck's denim rump with all her strength, which was considerable.

Blue Duck howled, as much in surprise as pain. He rolled off Pearl and tried to grovel out of reach as Belle stabbed down again, missing the small of his back by inches and driving the tines deep in the earth floor. This gave the Cherokee time to spring up, holding his perforated bleeding rear, and roar, "Have you gone crazy, woman!"

Belle yanked the tines out of the dirt, hissing, "No, you have, you filthy red-skinned son of a bitch!"

She went for him again, aiming for his eyes. He reeled out of the doorway and did the only thing anyone could have under the circumstances. He ran like hell, with Belle in hot pursuit, and cleared the fence like a deer to vanish into the woods while Belle yelled, "Come back and face me like a man, you baby-raping bastard!"

She started to climb over the fence, but she knew she'd never catch him, and there were more important things to worry about closer to home.

Belle ran back to the stable, tossed aside her weapon,

and sank to her knees by Pearl, gathering the weeping child in her arms.

"Oh, if only I hadn't hung my guns in the house. Tell me what he done to you, child. Granny Redbird can likely save you if I come too late!"

Pearl clung trembling to her mother and answered, "Oh, Mamma, Mamma, I'm so glad you're here! I think he was aiming to rape me. That's what you calls it, ain't it?"

Belle gasped with relief and said, "Oh, thank God! Are you sure he didn't come in you? You do know what I'm talking about, don't you?"

"Yessum. He never got his old thing in me if that's what you mean. He was fixing to. He said he was, But you saved me, Mamma. Did you hurt poor Uncle Blue Duck sore?"

"Not as sore as I aimed to, from the way he was running. Oh, Jesus, I've never wanted to kill anything so bad in my life, and my son-of-a-bitch guns was out of reach!"

"I'm glad you didn't kill him, Mamma. He was acting crazy, but he was likely just drunk."

"Nobody gets that drunk around my child and lives if I have anything to say on it! We'd best get back to the cabin, Pearl. If that fool buck comes back I mean to kill him dead as a turd in a milk bucket, and it's tedious trying to do it with a pitch fork!"

They went back to the cabin, holding one another and crying all the way. When they got inside, Belle sat Pearl down, barred the door, and took her brace of six guns off the wall to strap around her own trim hips before she went to the stove and poked the coals alive.

"Please, Lord, make that crazy Indian come back. It ain't fair to let him off so easy. A mother has rights, you know," she said.

Pearl was glad Mamma had recovered her poise, although, in truth, Belle's face was so filled with cold hate that she hardly looked pretty, even to a loving daughter. Belle put fresh firewood in the stove and moved the coffee-pot over on the cast-iron top where it would heat best.

"Well, we'll coffee in a minute. But I'd best sit down, for my legs are still shaking," she said.

She came to the table and sat across from Pearl. Belle knew she scared folk when she was in one of her serious moods, so she attempted a smile and said, "I'm glad you've stopped crying, honey. What's all this paper doing here?"

"That's what Uncle Blue said he was punishing me for, Mamma. I fear I used more than one sheet of paper from your pad. I didn't know I was being willful. But you can switch me all you like, 'cause you're my mamma."

Belle's grim visage softened and she said, "Pearl, honey, you can use the whole pad if you like. There's plenty more over to the trading post. What was you doing when that dirty old Cherokee started up with you, drawing more pictures?"

"No, Mamma. I wrote a letter to my pappa in prison. Would you like to see it?"

"I reckon I would. This surely comes as a surprise. What on earth made you do a thing like that, Pearl?"

Pearl handed her the folded foolscap as she said, "I wanted to tell him how much I loved him. You don't think it's too mushy, do you?"

Belle unfolded the letter and read it. She put it back on the table quietly, and then for some reason Pearl couldn't fathom, she started to cry again.

Pearl got up, came around to her, and put her arms around her mother's shaking shoulders. She asked, "What's the matter, Mamma? I didn't think it was a sad letter. I tried to make it cheerful. Did I say something wrong to my daddy?"

Belle sobbed, "Oh, God help me. What am I to do with such a sweet fool girl in the Cherokee Strip?"

"Did I spell all the words right, Mamma? You wasn't here when I needed you."

"I know," said Belle. "I feel awful about that, too. It's a fine letter, Pearl, but I ain't sure you ought to send it. You see, Cole Younger don't know you all that well."

"I'm his daughter, ain't I?"

"You are, God help you, but he don't know that. Besides, it ain't a good notion to put things about your Uncle Jim and me pulling off that gold dust job in any letter sent to a state prison. Honey, you see, they reads the letters prisoners get. What your Mamma done in California that time is a family secret," said Belle.

"Oh, dear, I'd best write another one and leave that out, then. Will you help me with the spelling and show me how to post it, Mamma?" Pearl replied.

Belle started to shake her head. Then she said, "Sure I will, honey. Later, after we settle some."

She didn't tell the child the letter would never be sent. That infernal Cole would likely laugh fit to bust if he was still alive by the time such a crazy letter reached him. Belle had thought more than once of writing a letter very much like the one Pearl had in mind, but she had one advantage over her love-child. She knew the sardonic son of a bitch who'd sired Pearl. She knew he hadn't meant a thing he'd whispered in her teenaged ears as he used her for his love toy all that time. Damn, men folk were rascals when it came to getting around a woman that way. She'd thought he loved her. She'd loved him so bad she could still taste it after all these years, But when he'd heard they'd lost interest in that old bank job, he'd just up and rode off, without so much as a farewell kiss.

They supped light, for neither felt hungry. As the evening crept up on them, things seemed to be normal again. Belle busied herself with some overdue house chores, and Pearl helped by sweeping out the cabin. As it got dark, Belle left the lamp unlit. She'd thrown Blue Duck's possessions out on the veranda, and if he had any sense he wouldn't come for them personally.

Pearl went up to bed in the loft, but she couldn't sleep. An owl was hooting lonesome in the dark outside, and she didn't know what she'd say if Uncle Blue Duck came back. Mamma might take him in again, and then what would she do? She'd never be able to look that man in the eye after the way he'd trifled with her. She rolled over to catch some shut-eye. However that durned old owl was still hooting and, down below, Pearl heard her mother crying. Belle was crying with her face buried in her pillow, but Pearl heard things others often missed.

She rolled out of bed and climbed down from the loft. "What's wrong, Momma? Why are you crying?" she asked.

Belle stifled a sob and curtly answered, "Go back to bed. I'm crying 'cause I feel like crying. That's why I'm crying, damn it!"

Pearl climbed into bed with her mother. It was all right, tonight, because they were alone. She snuggled up and soothed, "Don't cry, Mamma. It's awfully late and I don't reckon Uncle Blue Duck's coming back no more."

Belle gathered the child in her arms and sobbed, "I know. I hate myself for missing him, too!"

"Hush, Mamma. You don't have to miss him on my account. I 'spect he knows enough to leave me alone, now that you've showed him you don't like it."

Belle laughed wildly. "If I ever lay eyes on that no-good Injun again, one of us figures to die. You don't understand, Pearl."

"I sure don't, Mamma. First you say you miss him, and then you say you want to gun him. I don't understand you growed folks at all."

Belle sighed. "Sometimes I don't, neither. You see, honey, I got to kill Blue Duck if ever I get the chance. He knows I got to, so he won't likely give me any such chance."

"But you said you miss him, Mamma."

"Not him. Only one part of him. You see, honey, your mamma is a warm-natured woman, and that fool Injun was about as hot and hung as they come. A woman has needs. I don't miss Blue Duck, but I sure miss having a man in bed with me at night."

"I'll sleep with you, if you like."

"It ain't the same, honey. Sleeping with she-males only pleasures lizzy women, and I ain't a lizzy woman. Besides, even if I was, you ain't, and you're my own flesh and blood. We got to draw the line somewheres, no matter how hard-up we gets. Shoot, I'd try it with a dog or ram afore I'd turn into a lizzy woman."

"Can't I sleep down here with you, just tonight, Mamma?"

"Well, just for tonight, but we'd best not make a habit of it. I told you I'm warm-natured, and I've heard that's how lizzy women get started. It ain't natural for folks to sleep together past a certain age unless they sleep together serious, but it's comforting to have you here just the same, honey."

Pearl lay quietly in her mother's arms, and she thought Belle was starting to drift off. But then Belle suddenly sobbed aloud and said, "Oh, Sweet Jesus, what's to become of me without no man! You're so lucky to be pretty, Pearl. I'm glad you turned out pretty. I always wanted so to be pretty, and it's a comfort you got your father's looks, even if he was a trifling son of a bitch."

"I think you're pretty, Mamma. But I wish you wouldn't call my daddy names. Ain't we both supposed to love him?"

Belle laughed bitterly. "I used to. Lord, how I loved that outlaw rascal! You should have seen him when we first met up, child. He rode so proud in the saddle and scared hell out of every man he wanted to, but he had soft gentle eyes for womankind, the horny old thing. He could shuck a gal out of her corset and all from twenty paces with them mocking eyes of his. He was tough, too. You didn't mess with Cole Younger if you knew what was good for you. No, sir. How many men do you know who it takes eleven bullets to bring down? And the last I heard, he's still alive after soaking up all that lead! Ain't you proud to have a father that tough?"

"I reckon so, Mamma, though I'd likely love him just as much if he wasn't. Do you mind if I ask you about that, Mamma?" said Pearl.

"About what?" Belle asked. "Me and Cole Younger? I never denied I let him make a fool of me"

Pearl said, "That's the part I don't understand, Mamma. About you and tough men, I mean. I reckon I wouldn't be here if you hadn't run off with that one outlaw, but how come you keep doing it? First there was my father, riding with the James boys and all, and then there was Uncle Jim Reed and he was nice to me when I was little, but he was an outlaw, too. Then, after he got killed in that shoot-out, you took up with other uncles who stole for a living, like old Uncle Blue Duck and them other thieves. I mean, wouldn't it make more sense for you to make friends with easier-going gents, Mamma? You said your own self a man is a man. So why don't you get a boyfriend who ain't as likely to wind up dead or in prison?"

Belle didn't answer for a time. Then she said, "I follow your drift, honey. You got uncommon good sense for a gal so young. I've studied on the men in my life, and you're right that it'd make more sense to tie up with a gent who didn't live such an active life. But, I dunno, I've never been attracted to weak men. I can't abide 'em, as a matter of fact."

"Shoot, Mamma, I'm only nine and I know men with honest jobs who're strong. I seen that Saunders boy over to the trading post unload a wagon one day. He picked up a heavy hogshead of nails like it was nothing. I'll bet the Saunders boy is twice as strong as most men, and there's no papers out on him, neither."

Belle answered, "Well, he's a little young for me, and too old for you, so we'll say no more about him. I wasn't talking about that kind of strength in a man, Pearl. You see, lots of things in pants *look* strong, until push comes to shove. I reckon your grandfather, Judge Shirley, looked strong to most folks. He was a big man, and most feared him, for he stood for the law and sent many a man away to prison or worse. Jesus, how I hated him."

"I didn't know you wasn't fond of my grandfather, Mamma. What did he do to make you revile him so? You just said you admired strong, feared men."

Belle's voice dripped venom as she said, "He was weak. Hardly anyone ever knew that, but he was a spineless jellyfish under all that bluster."

"Mamma, no offense, but you ain't making much sense about Grandfather. You just told me he was feared by everyone," said Pearl.

"Oh, sure, in his courtroom, wrapped in the majesty of

the law, he acted like he could do wonders and eat cucumbers, but I found out what he was when I was not much older than you are now, Pearl."

Pearl waited for her mother to continue. "We was walking back from church one Sunday. Him, me, and your grandmother. I told you how we moved to Texas to get out of the war zone. Texas men have a mighty cruel sense of humor. They think it's funny to mock womenfolk with barnyard talk. Anyways, as we-all were walking home, we passed these two young cowhands spitting and whittling on a doorstep. They'd said awful thing to me before, but this time I knew they wouldn't rawhide me. Hell, I was walking with my folks, and my father was Judge Shirley, right?"

"What happened, Mamma?"

"I'll tell you what happened. As we approached, this one old boy looked me right in the eye and said, 'Howdy, miss, you sure are flat-chested!' I expected the sky to open up and a thunderbolt to strike him dead on the spot, for he said this in front of my father, Judge Shirley, in the flesh!"

"That cowboy sure was mean, Mamma. What did Grandfather do?"

"Nothing. He pretended not to hear, but he must have. I know he heard what the other one said, for we was directly abreast of them and the cowhand said it loud and clear. He said, 'Hell, her ass ain't bad. A man could always throw a flag over her chest and fuck her for glory!' "

Pearl gasped and said, "Oh, Mamma, that was ugly of him! What did your father say to them?"

Belle's voice was dry and bitter as she answered, "Nothing. Not a single solitary thing. He just kept walking like he didn't hear them 'til we'd left their jeers behind. My face was red, and my mother's face was red, too, but I was the one crying. When we got home my father stared at me like I was the one in the wrong, and then he roared at me and slapped my face for shaming him in public by carrying on so. I told him he was the one who had shamed us all by not standing up for me, so he hit me again and sent me to bed without no supper."

"Heavenly days! Didn't Grandmamma say any defending words for you?"

"She couldn't. She was afraid of the mighty Judge Shirley, too. He was mighty free with his hands around womenfolk. He was brave as anything about sending men to the chain gang, too, when he had his robes on and armed bailiffs standing by. But I never forgave him for showing such a yaller streak in front of his own women on the streets of Scyene."

Pearl gently patted her mother's shoulder and said, "Oh, poor Mamma. You must have felt just awful."

"I did. Then Cole Younger rode into town. I met him at a church social. He was on the dodge, but he knew it was safe enough 'cause he had friends in the crowd. They started to dance and, like always, I was over at the side with the rest of the wallflowers, for nobody hardly ever asked me to dance. I didn't know who he was then, but I'd never seen such a handsome brute. I watched as he danced with a pretty gal in an organdy gown. I knew her slightly as a mean-mouthed little bitch, and she must have said something spiteful about us wallflowers as they danced past us. I reckon it struck your father wrong. He told me later that he'd never liked folks who picked on others when they had the edge on 'em. The first thing I knowed he came over to me, eyes sort of twinkling like he figured to play a trick on somebody, and the next thing I knowed I was in heaven, sweeping about the dance floor with the best looking man in Texas!"

Pearl sat up in bed and clapped her hands. "Oh, that must have made you feel grand, Mamma!"

Belle said, "It did. Looking back, I can see he was just mocking that spiteful gal, but then he found out I'd been birthed in Missouri like him, and when I told him how we'd camped here in the Strip on the way down to Texas, he said he liked jawing with me and asked if he could walk me home after the dance. Well, I can tell you true he didn't have to twist my arm much. And that's when I fell head over heels in love with the rascal."

"Oh, did he kiss you the first night, Mamma?"

"He did something better than kissing. Remember those two cowhands who'd shamed me in front of my folks? Well, as we was walking along we run into them. They sort of brightened up when they saw me again, but then they saw how big Cole was, so all they did was grin silly. Cole stopped, swung about, and asked them what they were grinning about. You should have seen it, Pearl. He crawfished 'em! They said they wasn't grinning at us at all. So we walked on, and then it got even better. I'd been so afraid those mean boys would start up with me again that I was trembling like a leaf. Cole noticed and asked why. As we walked on a ways, I told him. We was in front of the lumber yard by then, and naturally there was nobody about at that hour. Cole picked me up like a doll and set me on a lumber pile like it was a high-chair. Then he said to wait right there, and he turned away to go back after those fresh cowhands. I called after him that there was no need and that it was two to one besides, but Cole paid me no heed. He just walked off, tall and sort of cat-like. I was trying to figure how to get down off that lumber without tearing my party dress, and I thought I'd wet my pants when Cole came back directly with them two cowhands. They looked scared as hell. I reckon the Walker .45 he was holding in his hand, sort of casual, had a lot to do with it."

Belle stopped, chuckled to herself, and said, "You know what your father did then, Pearl? He made both them rednecks apologize to me formal, and promise never even to look at me again. Then he made them both get down on their very knees and kiss my feet! I swear to God that's what he done! My legs was hanging down off the lumber pile so my high-button shoes was maybe waist high off the ground. They was both red-faced, and one of 'em was crying. Cole made each one kiss both my feet before he told them to go off and not to show their faces in town no more 'til he rode out. He rode out about a week later, and I rode with him. We come to this very cabin. It stood alone in the bend, then. So now you know why I admire tough men. Tough men are the only kind worth having. That's a mean old world out there, honey. A woman needs a man who can shield her some from it. And, damn it all, where am I to get me another, now?" ❧

3

RUTHERFORD B. HAYES, Republican, won the election that November. He stood for sound money, administrative reform, a conciliatory policy toward the South, ending the last annoying Reconstruction regulations, and a total reorganization of the badly run Bureau of Indian Affairs. Nobody in Younger's Bend had voted for him. The Indians couldn't, and Belle, other whites, and 'breeds in the Strip weren't all that interested. But they should have been. President Hayes was one of those rare political figures who thought promises one makes to get elected are binding. Therefore, when Agent Stover of the B.I.A. rode into Younger's Bend one afternoon, he was thinking of his own job as well as the sloppy conditions along the frayed edges of the Indian Nation.

Stover thought the whites and 'breeds squatting on federal lands were scum, and as scum tends to rise to a surface, the shady squatters and the type of 'breed or full-blood who associated with their kind had formed a sort of crust along the border, facing Arkansas and white man's law. Save for licensed traders and other whites with sensible reasons to live around there, the squatters were becoming a bother to law-abiding Cherokee and whites alike. Stover's mission, as he saw it, was simple. There was plenty of open land suited for settling on legally under the Homestead Act in other parts of the West. The Cherokee Strip was Indian land. No others need apply to live there.

Belle had sent Pearl to the trading post on an errand. She sat alone on her veranda when Agent Stover rode up, dismounted, and introduced himself. Belle invited him in for coffee and cake. Stover shook his head and said, "I thank you, ma'am, but I can't stay long. What I dropped by to tell you is that the U.S. Government is giving you ninety days to clear out."

"Clear out?" Belle gasped. "By God and little fishes, you're talking about my home, mister! I've lived here in this very cabin nigh a dozen years or more! I've lived here longer than anyone in Younger's Bend. There was nobody for miles when I moved in!"

Stover smiled thinly and replied, "So I understand. I know your story, ma'am. It's the talk of Sebastian County, just across the line. I'm not here to judge you or your way of life. I'm an Indian Agent, not a lawman. The point is that there's no such place as Younger's Bend on any U.S. Survey map, and no white person has ever filed a homestead claim in the Strip in any case. You folks are squatting on government property. These lands have been set aside for Indians and their dependents."

"Oh, it's all right, then. Everyone over to Sebastian County will tell you I'm living as a squaw with a Cherokee," Belle said.

"Forgive me, ma'am, you used to be. They told me about you running Blue Duck off a while back. It wouldn't help you if you hadn't, but since you haven't seen him in some time, I'd better tell you about the federal warrant out on Blue Duck. It seems he sold some cattle and at least one horse he says sort of followed him home from Arkansas. The Indian Police are looking for him, too. He, ah, trifled with a young Creek girl shortly after you ran him off for whatever reason, so both red and white men have agreed to testify against him before Judge Parker in Fort Smith as soon as someone or other catches him. I doubt the Creeks mean to take him alive."

Belle shrugged, "I'll kill him if he ever shows his face in these parts, now that I see how he treats little gals. But you've still got no call to run me off my own spread, Stover. I'm here with the approval of the Cherokee Tribal Council. Ask the Elder Swan if you don't believe me."

Stover sniffed. "It's not a matter for the Indians to decide, ma'am. Under the new regulations they can only decide on Cherokee matters, and you're hardly a Cherokee, or even the dependent of one. The Tribal Council has no right to assign tribal lands to outsiders. If President Hayes gets his full Indian policy passed, all Indians living on federal land are to be wards of the state from now on. They won't be allowed to sign contracts or have any business dealings with whites without the approval of the B.I.A. and, no offense, the B.I.A. doesn't approve of you at all. So, like I said, you have ninety days. Don't ask for more. I couldn't give them if I wanted to. The matter is out of my hands."

As he started to remount, Belle rose and shouted, "Hold on a minute, damn it! You can't just evict folk on the fly like that! I ain't had my own say yet!"

"Miss Shirley, what is there to say? I'm only a messenger. I didn't ride in to hold a hearing on the matter. It's been decided at headquarters. Unlicensed whites are to remove themselves from Indian lands, period. You can take it to the Supreme Court if you like, but the answer will be the same. Grant's Indian Ring has been too busy exploiting the poor Indians the last few years to bother all that much about keeping house, but the new administration means to do things right. Washington set this land aside for Indians to live on, and that's who we mean to see living here!"

"Just a second, damn it. You said Indians and their dependents, before. Does that mean if I get me another buck I can stay here?" Belle asked.

Stover's lip curled as he said, "You must have mighty good reasons for wanting to stay, but everyone to his or her own taste. It's true that since there were so many 'breeds among the Five Civilized Tribes we have to allow for, well, a certain type of white, or almost-white, if they can show some claim to tribal membership. But I fail to see how you can, Miss Shirley. Casual living doesn't qualify you for anything but more gossip over in Fort Smith. You don't get to be an Indian just by, well, being friendly with one or more."

"What if I was to marry up lawful with a Cherokee?" asked Belle.

"You'd have to do so within ninety days. You understand, of course, that no white justice of the peace would perform such a ceremony," Stover replied.

"I ain't all that worried about white man's law. What if I married an Indian under his tribal law?"

"I don't see how I could stop you. It's illegal in Arkansas, but we try not to interfere in tribal matters. I take it you're engaged, Miss Shirley?"

"Yeah, you might say that. Don't look at me like that, damn it. I know how you B.I.A. men carry on with the prettier squaws every chance you get."

She'd either hit a nerve or disgusted him too much to answer. Stover got back in the saddle and rode off, looking like he was sucking on a bitter lemon.

Belle sat on the steps, her mind in a whirl. She didn't know nearly as much law as she thought she did, but she could see they had her over the barrel. Where in thunder were she and Pearl to go if they got run out of the Strip?

She hadn't come up with an idea by the time Pearl came home with the sack of sugar, but no refill for the jug.

"Mamma, the trader told me to tell you he ain't allowed to sell likker here no more. He says there's a new president, and even though he ain't took office yet, word's been passed that traders selling likker to Injuns won't get their licenses renewed, whatever that means."

Belle frowned and said, "Thunderation! I heard about the new First Lady, Lemonade Lucy, not holding much with strong drink for anyone. I reckon from now on I'll just have to get my medicinals over in Arkansas and, hmm, a body could show a modest profit if they was to carry home a few extra jugs in the buckboard for the poor deprived

Cherokee. Damn! Just as things get so's you can show a profit, they go and tell you you has to move! Set the sugar down, honey. I got some news for you."

Pearl did as she was told and said, "I got news for you, too, Mamma. You remember Uncle Frank and Uncle Jesse? Well, Sam Starr says they got away. I just met him over to the trading post. He's rid back from Texas and he said they had no trouble at all."

"Do tell? I'd like you to do me another errand, honey. I know you just come from the trading post, but would you be a lamb and run back there to tell Sam Starr he's invited to supper?"

When Agent Stover rode back on a cold winter's day to see how they were coming with their moving, he found Belle Shirley had changed her name to Belle Starr, and there wasn't much he could do about it. Belle and the quiet Cherokee had married lawfully, as the Nation saw it and, unlike Blue Duck, Sam Starr had no reward posters out on him. As a full-blood, he had tribal rights to the land the Elder Swan and other council members had assigned him with a certain sardonic amusement.

Pearl liked Uncle Sam much better than she had Blue Duck. Sam was better looking and, while he didn't want her sitting on his knee drunk or sober, he treated her with grave courtesy, as if she was a woman grown. Sam drank as much or more than most, especially since Belle had started running contraband corn back from Fort Smith in the buckboard as a sideline to her horse trading, but all that happened to the gentle Starr when he drank was that it made him sleepy.

When Pearl thought of Sam Starr as gentle, of course, she meant toward her, her Mamma, and other folks he liked. He was known as "Bad Injun" to the folk in Fort Smith. Few white men cared to make slurring remarks about his white squaw where Sam might hear of it. Indians didn't mess with Sam, either.

One night at the table, Pearl heard the soft sound of a

turkey bone flute and murmured, "Oh, dear, that fool Sequanna is at it again, and it's fixing to snow, too."

Sam, seated at the head of the table in his clean but sun-faded denims, stared thoughtfully at his stepdaughter. "You seem troubled, Pearl. What is the matter?" he asked.

Pearl told him about the shine Sequanna had taken to her. Belle, seated down at the far end of the table, snorted and said, "He must be moon-struck. You're far too young a gal for any man to pester, Pearl. I'd best have a talk with that young rascal."

Sam Starr got to his feet, "You won't have to, Belle. I'm the head of this household, now," he said.

He went to the door and stepped out into the cold night wearing only his shirt-sleeves as Belle stared thoughtfully after him. In a short time, Pearl heard Sequanna's flute stop in mid-trill, as if it had been stepped on. A few minutes later, Sam came back in, resumed his seat, and said, "It's over. Would you please pass the butter, Pearl?"

Belle gazed admiringly at her new husband and asked, "What did you tell him, honey? Did you threaten him good?"

"I don't threaten, Belle. I told the boy my stepdaughter didn't want him pestering her anymore. He knows who I am, so we didn't have to go into it much."

Sam buttered his roll, then turned to Pearl. "Hear me, Pearl. If anyone else bothers you, you tell me. Your mother is my woman. That makes you my child. Do you understand what I am saying, Pearl?"

"Not surely, Uncle Sam. Ain't Cole Younger to be my father no more?" Pearl asked.

Belle shot her daughter a warning look that Pearl failed to see.

"That is up to you to say, Pearl. Nobody can tell a child to deny a father. Let's say for now you have a white father and a red father. Your white father is in prison for life. Your red father is here. Your mother is my wife. We Indians don't look at things as your people do, but even the white people would say that you are my stepdaughter. If

you don't want to call me your father, call me your stepfather. Don't call me Uncle Sam. I'm not your uncle, and
even if I was, Uncle Sam sounds silly," said Sam.

"Can I call you just plain Sam, then?" asked Pearl.

"Why not? It's my name. What's for dessert, Belle?" answered Sam.

And so this illiterate, inarticulate, and rather dreadful
person was to become the nearest thing to a father figure
Pearl would ever know. Sam Starr was known even to his
more decorous Cherokee tribesman as a killer and a thief
who drank more than he should, but although it would
take a while to sink in, he was a vast improvement over the
various "uncles" Belle had taken up with in the past. As a
parent, Sam was an improvement on Belle, too. He simply
had better instincts about the rearing of children.

Belle Starr was a good mother to the extent a bitch wolf
or she-bear is a good mother to her cubs. She'd fight anything that physically menaced her only child. She had
sense enough to keep Pearl warm and dry and made her
wear shoes in cold weather. If Pearl asked for anything
else, Belle would buy or steal it for her. She never switched
Pearl because Pearl was an obedient child who never
needed switching, which was probably very fortunate for
Pearl when one considered Belle's temper.

Sam had more delicate notions. He was a naturally fastidious man who donned a fresh shirt every day and took a
bath once a week whether he needed it or not. One of the
first things he did, on assuming his duties as Pearl's stepfather, was to load her in the buckboard and drive her over
to the trading post to get her dressed properly.

The nearest trading post was down the Arkansas a couple of miles, where the B.I.A. maps said a settlement belonged. Like other traders on Indian lands, the white pro-
prietor paid the B.I.A. for a license and was loosely
supervised, lest he exploit the poor savages. Washington
seemed oblivious to the fact that the Indians of the Five
Civilized Tribes had been as financially sophisticated as
any other American rural folk for at least a hundred years.

As they drove up to the general store with other log cabins clustered about it, a cruel children's game of blindman's bluff was going on in the dirt street out front. A band of local children were circling Creek Alice, taunting and poking at her with sticks, as the little blind girl struck out wildly, trying not to cry, at her unseen tormentors.

Alice Ferndancer's misfortune was heightened by two things. She was helpless and outnumbered, which tends to bring out the worst in most people, child or adult. The children taunted her also because of the fact that the blind girl's Cherokee father had married a Creek, or as they preferred to be called, Muskeegee.

It was all right for the Cherokee to marry whites. Most Cherokee admired the whites they'd been aping for so long, and in truth, many Cherokee were of partly white blood by this late date. Many Muskeegee, including Creek Alice, were part white, but back east in the olden times, the Muskeegee and their Seminole cousins hadn't understood the peculiar institution of chattel slavery. Therefore instead of keeping black slaves as the Cherokee and their white neighbors had done, the Muskeegee had sheltered runaway slaves and, it was whispered, were inbred with them.

The great Black Warrior of the Alabama Creeks had been an Ashanti spearman from West Africa, who, when captured and sold as a slave, hadn't played the game according to American standards. Creek Alice was paying for this unfortunate lack of decorum in her mother's people.

As one of the boys teasing her threw a horse apple from the road at the blind girl, Pearl cried out, "Oh, make them stop, Sam! Please make them stop before they hurts her!"

Sam Starr reined in, stood up in the buckboard, and called out in Cherokee. The game of blindman's bluff ended in a general dash for the surrounding cabins. The children knew who Sam Starr was, and even their elders feared him.

Pearl leaped down from the buckboard and ran over to the blind girl, who flinched and stared defiantly in her general direction.

"Are you hurted, Alice?" asked Pearl with concern.

The pretty dark girl shook her head. "No, but I think they got me with some horse turds. Is my dress dirty?"

"Uh, I fear it is, Alice, but it'll rub off once it's dry. I'll help you, if you like."

"Help me? Why should you help me? Who are you?" asked Alice.

"Oh, I'm Pearl Younger. I 'speck you didn't know 'cause you can't see. I know who you are 'cause we've passed more than one time, and I've nodded. Now that I study on it, I can see you might not have noticed. Since you can't see me, I'd best tell you I'm a gal about your age. I'm a white gal, by the way."

Creek Alice nodded soberly, and staring past Pearl, she said, "Well, I thank you for being so neighborly. Who was that man as yelled at them to stop? I want to thank him, too."

Sam Starr had dismounted to tether the carriage horse to the hitching rail in front of the store. Pearl took Creek Alice shyly by one hand and led her over to him, saying, "Sam, Creek Alice here would like a word with you."

The Cherokee stared impassively down at them as the blind girl thanked him for helping her. He shrugged and said, "I only done what was right, girl. It ain't seemly to pick on blind folk, so we'll say no more about it. Let's go in the post, Pearl."

"Can my friend come with us, Sam?"

"If you like, but let's not tarry about out here."

The two young girls followed Sam inside. Pearl liked the way it smelled in the trading post. She figured Creek Alice would, too. That was why she'd brought her along.

Like most general stores, the trading post sold everything from fertilizer to soap and candy, so every breath smelled different. As Pearl led the blind girl to the counter near her stepfather, Creek Alice sniffed and said, "What's that I smell so strong? It smells like anise seeds."

Pearl looked for the source, sniffing herself, and said, "Oh, them's licorice whips you're smelling, Alice. They're a sort of candy made to look like shoe strings. They taste nice, but they're right dear, and I'm sorry but I don't have no pennies."

Sam starr nodded to the white man behind the counter and said, "Well start with a couple of them licorice whips, Doc. How much do they go for?"

The trader was a father and the candy was cheap, so he smiled and said, "I'll let the young ladies have 'em on the house, Mister Starr."

Sam reached in his jeans with a shake of his head and said, "No. I'll pay. How much?"

"Two for a penny?"

"That sounds fair. Pick out the whips you fancy, Pearl."

"Can I give one to Alice, Sam?"

"I'm paying for two, ain't I?"

Pearl handed the blind girl a licorice whip, and, as they both stood sucking on them with the delight only a child not used to sweets can know, Sam Starr spoke to the trader.

"Pearl here is getting too growed to run about like a trash kid. I don't know much about women's unmentionables, but I want her fixed up with proper stockings, underdrawers, and such. She could use a couple of more seemly dresses and a sunbonnet, too."

The trader nodded and called his Indian wife out from the back. "Mary, this white lady here needs to be outfitted Sunday-Go-To-Meeting from the hide out. I reckon it would be more seemly if you was to see to it."

The motherly Cherokee woman smiled down at Pearl. "You just come along with me, honey. We'll go in the back and I'll show you what we has in the line of duds," she said.

Pearl said, "Come on, Alice." The trader's wife shot an odd glance at Sam. Sam shrugged and said, "My daughter's taken a shine to her. It's no never mind to me."

The trader's wife sniffed and said, "Well, if you say so. Follow me, girls."

As they were moving back through the piled bales of merchandise, Sam called after them, "While you're about it, give the Creek kid a Mother Hubbard. The one she's wearing's covered with dung."

After they were out of ear-shot, the trader nodded at Sam and said, "That was right generous of you, Sam. I feels sorry for that blind kid, too. But do you really want your daughter playing with an outcast?"

"It's up to Pearl. Some youngsters make pets out of frogs and crawdads. I reckon she can pet a Creek if she wants. I don't think anyone hereabouts will have much to say about it," replied Sam.

"That's for damn sure. Is there anything else I can do for you, Sam?"

"Yep. I'd best bring home some ribbons, bows, and a new plume for my old woman. And we're running low on salt. Is it true you won't be selling no more trade likker, Doc?"

The white man smiled wearily, for he'd had this discussion before, and it got tedious having Indians cussing at him.

"It ain't my notion, Sam. I've still got a few jugs left to sell discreet between now and the time that infernal Hayes takes office in the spring, but keep it to your own self, for I've heard him and Lemonade Lucy are keeping a list on traders selling the stuff, with a view to not letting them trade with your folks no more once they have the power to stop us. How many jugs do you kind of need against unfortunate encounters with snakes?"

Sam answered, "May as well take home some Maryland Rye as a surprise to Belle. She likes the good stuff. The reason I was asking, though, was I could still get you all the likker you could sell, over to Fort Smith. My woman's a white, and so she can buy all she likes across the Arkansas line."

The trader looked wistful and said, "I know. I could, too, but that ain't the problem, Sam. I can't sell it here at the trading post no more."

"Well, my people figures to buy it one damn place or another. We've been drinking the stuff about as long as anyone else, and you can't expect folks to change their ways just 'cause the new President's lady is a tea-total busy-body."

"We've tried to tell them that, Sam, but nobody in Washington listens to folks who deals with Indians regular. Them dudes has you all lumped together and wouldn't know a Cherokee from an Apache or a Pueblo from a Sioux. They study Indian folk in books instead of looking at 'em and, no offense, they think you all run about out here in feathers and paint."

Sam frowned soberly. "Hear me, Cherokee never wore feathers, even in the Shining Times. When the first white men met us we were wearing turbans on our heads and pants on our legs."

"Hell, Sam," the trader retorted, "don't tell me, tell Washington! I'm married Cherokee. Don't look so mean-eyed at me, old son. Ain't it true that white men who live among you folks has always took your side agin' Washington?"

Starr nodded gravely. "Yes. Sam Houston was a friend of my grandfather. He traded among us, like you, before he went to Texas. He was a good person."

"There you go, Sam. Your white enemies ain't us western folk who know you. It's them infernal squat-pissers in Washington as can't get it through their sissy skulls that you folks live just as sensible as anyone else."

The trader's wife came back with two young girls. Pearl looked like a totally new person in her new print dress, sunbonnet, and high button shoes. Creek Alice was running her hands in wonder over the new calico dress Sam had bought her, her blind eyes glistening with silent happy tears. Pearl smiled up at Sam and said, "Don't Alice look fine, Sam? Tell her how fine she looks."

Sam said, "You both look a lot better than when we come in. Stand aside whilst Doc and me finish up."

Pearl nodded and took the blind girl by the hand and led her outside. The braver of the children who'd been tormenting Creek Alice before had moved into sight again. The boy called out, "Well, I'll be stung by bees! What are you doing holding hands with a nigger gal, Pearl Younger?"

Alice flinched. Pearl held her hand tightly and called

back, "You listen to me, Arthur Bluefeather. I knows where you lives, and if you ever pester Alice here again I'll come looking for you, and I mean to have me a big stick in my hand, too! I'd like to see you throw horse turds *my* way, you big bully. I've eyes to see with, so I can dodge and hit."

The boys neither retreated nor advanced. They weren't really afraid of Pearl, even though she was said to be a fair scrapper, for a gal. But, while any two or more of them could likely whup Pearl, her crazy mother was something else, and her new stepfather had an awesome reputation.

Sam came out with his other purchases and told Pearl to say goodbye to the blind girl.

"If they pesters you more, come and tell me about it, hear?" she added to her farewell.

For some reason this made Creek Alice cry. Pearl hugged her and said, "I got to go now, Alice, but we'll likely see more of each other. Leastways, I'll see you, and you'll know who I am when I say howdy."

Sam made no comment on the incident, and Belle made such a grand fuss over Pearl's new outfit that they'd forgotten the small kindness by the time they'd supped and were sitting on the veranda to watch the sun go down. Belle was rocking in her chair. Sam and Pearl sat on the steps. Pearl sensed her new father didn't like to be talked to when he was smoking his pipe unless it was important.

As they sat there quietly, a raggedly dressed Cherokee came up the wagon trace on foot, carrying a burlap sack on his back. Sam rose.

"Evening, Ferndancer. What can I do for you?" he said.

The blind girl's father put the sack down and answered, "You've already done it, Sam Starr. My child told me. I thought you folks might have use for these turnips. I dug 'em fresh just now." He nodded to Belle, turned to Pearl, and added, "You must be the kindly child Alice told me of. This is for you."

He handed Pearl a worn rubber ball, saying, "The paint's sort of wore off, but it still bounces. I knows you rates better, but we ain't rich folk."

Pearl accepted the pathetic offering with polite thanks. She knew Indians were insulted when one refused a present, whether you thought you had one coming or not.

Bob Ferndancer turned back to Starr and said, "I hope you won't take this wrong, Sam Starr, but I want to know how much that dress you bought my girl cost you. I ain't got any money right now, but I can give you an I.O.U."

Starr shrugged, "I disremember how much it might have cost. It wasn't much. I'll settle for fifty cents, when you get around to it. I don't need no I.O.U. I know you'll pay up when you can."

Ferndancer shook his head and said, "I know you thinks I'm trash, being married to a Creek, Sam Starr. But I ain't ignorant. I know what new duds cost. God, how I knows! Alice ain't the only woman I has to try and dress. A dress like that would cost her mother at least two whole dollars, and Alice comes to her mother's shoulder now, so it couldn't have been much less."

"All right. You can owe me six bits, if you want to be so infernal proud about it, Ferndancer."

The defeated looking Indian sighed. "Pride's about all I has. You may think it's odd for a man married up with a Creek to feel proud, but I don't feel as low as folks hereabouts try to make me out."

He stood taller as he added, "Damn it, Sam Starr, my woman is good-looking, and it ain't true she's part nigger!"

Sam said, "I never said she was. Belle, do you reckon we could all go inside for some Arbuckle?"

Belle rose, smiling, for she didn't see why Indians were so picky in the first place. "I can do us better than coffee, husband. I baked a cake today, as you know, and we only et half of her at suppertime."

Bob Ferndancer shook his head and said, "I thanks you, ma'am, but y'all has already stuck your necks out for me and mine enough this day. Sam, here, is too nice a cuss to say it, but I ain't all that popular with your neighbors."

Sam Starr said, "My woman just invited you inside, Bob Ferndancer, so that's where you'll be going. I don't give two hoots and a damn what the neighbors say. They say enough about me and mine, ahind my back. I doubt they'll say anything about this to my face."

"I knows that, Sam, but you got certain advantages others don't. I ain't just poor. I've never been worth much as a fighting man."

"How are you at taking orders, Ferndancer?"

"Orders? What kind of orders, Sam?"

"We'll talk on it inside, where the sparrow birds can't carry our words to the law. I see some changes coming to the Cherokee Strip, Bob. I've been studying on how a tolerable bright cuss could mayhaps take advantage of 'em. I see a lot of work ahead, and I can't do it all my own self. I'll need some help, and you look fair strong, brave or no."

As he followed Sam Starr inside, Ferndancer said dubiously, "Lord knows I've been searching high and low for steady work, Sam, but I ain't up to any deed as takes steady nerves."

"You already told me that. You has the guts to load a buckboard and drive at night, don't you?"

"Well sure, anybody can do that, Sam."

"That's what I figured. We'll talk about it inside."   ✑

4

THE NEXT FEW years would be remembered by Pearl as the happiest time of her childhood. Quiet Sam Starr treated her and her Mamma nice, and her momma blossomed like a rose.

As Sam and many other worried Cherokee had foreseen, the greenup of '77 brought many changes to the Cherokee Strip, and the Starr family prospered from them in a way that President Hayes and the reorganised B.I.A. had never planned.

The first noticeable change around Younger's Bend was that most of the trash whites were forced to move out. Squatting on Indian lands by whites had ended, at least for now, and while the Indian Police or white B.I.A. agents seldom rode through, they did so often enough to evict anyone dwelling in a cabin they couldn't show title to and to show title, at least one member of the family had to be an Indian, approved as such by the local tribal elders. The tribal elders naturally approved very much of Sam Starr, since he was their main source of medicinal alcohol in these parts.

Their bootlegging was so uncomplicated that it was more like a steady job than criminal activity for Sam and Belle

Starr. As a white woman, Belle was legally entitled to pur-
chase all the cheap booze she wanted in the Arkansas town
of Fort Smith. The white merchants who sold it to her by
the barrel saw no reason to question the fact that an apparently very hard-drinking white gal had Indian hired hands
to load and drive her buckboard. The nearby border of the
Cherokee Strip was unguarded and unpatrolled by whites.
The Indian Police liked to drink as much as anyone else, so
as long as she didn't move the stuff past them in broad
daylight while beating on a drum, they couldn't have
cared less.

Be it recorded that the Indian Police were no more cor-
rupt than white lawmen. That is to say, some took their
duties seriously and some didn't. It was easy enough, however, for Sam to find out when the occasionally strict Indian lawmen were likely to be patroling. Most, while they
felt duty-bound to arrest anyone actually committing what
they regarded as a crime, resented being told by Washington that they were forbidden strong drink, as if they were
white children or other legal incompetents who had to be
protected from their own weaknesses by the Great White
Father. (As a future President named Wilson would discover to his chagrin in the coming century, it was one thing
to prohibit grown people from drinking. It was another to
make them stop).

Bootlegging was not considered a crime by either whites
or Indians in the rural South and, as more than one Indian
peace officer pointed out to chiding B.I.A. agents, what
could they have done to Belle, even if they caught her with
a wagonload? She might be married to an Indian; she
might be living on Indian land; but she was a member of
the superior race Washington seemed to feel could bathe in
the stuff, if they had a mind to. It was no business of theirs
if Belle Starr seemed to buy more booze at a time than a
platoon of white cavalry men could have consumed on pain
of death. Nobody'd ever seen her selling any of the stuff to
any Indian, had they?

This was true. Belle only bought the alcohol. Sam sold it.
It was sold at night in isolated places at a handsome profit,

save for some few jugs distributed, gratis, as a good will gesture, to those few Cherokee officials who could have caused them pain. The quiet Sam Starr could have died a rich man, unmolested by an uncaring world who was hardly aware of him.

Pearl, as she began to mature, was turning into a very attractive young miss, but she was hardly noticed by the outside world, either. Mamma was the problem.

Belle Starr enjoyed her new-found prosperity, and was proud of her notoriety. So proud in fact, that she tended to flaunt it. Her husband, who might have been able to control her since she was very fond of him in bed or anywhere else, seldom strayed into Fort Smith, and was too unsophisticated about whites to really see the picture Belle presented to whites who considered themselves "quality".

Belle rarely rode in the buckboard. She let Sam's Indians drive it as she led the way rather grandly, riding her chestnut mare, Venus, on a new, fancy side-saddle with silver mounted harness and martingale. Belle favored expensive velvet riding habits. She would have been noticed even without the habits, as she sat her mare well and had a very attractive figure. But she wanted attention. She sported a big Texas hat, pinned up on one side and decorated with plumes. She rode armed to the teeth, with a saddle gun with polished walnut stock and decorated with finishing nails in the shape of a bell and a star. In addition to her saddle gun, Belle favored a brace of ivory-handled, silvermounted six-guns in a buscadero gunbelt of tooled leather. And she was noisy!

Belle had taken to matching her Cherokee husband drink for drink in the cabin at night, or any other time. Sam had a good forty pounds on his petite Belle, and could absorb far more alcohol without getting drunk. Even when he did, he was a quiet drunk. Belle was just the opposite.

She'd learned in Texas that a cowboy full of red-eye was just naturally supposed to let the whole world know he was coming, so it could get out of his way, and Belle regarded herself as a sort of cowgirl. She didn't just let out a war whoop when she reined in from a full gallop in front of the liquor wholesalers. She was inclined to fire at least one shot at the sky to let them know she'd arrived. Then she'd swagger in like a tiny trail hand and announce her presence further with a banshee wail that pained people's ears in a confined space.

The dealer had to put up with her. She was, after all, one of his best customers, but things were surely more peaceful once she'd gone.

This public display naturally attracted a lot of attention in Fort Smith, and since very few of the local residents were in the bootlegging trade, there was a certain amount of talk, and numerous complaints to the town law.

Sam Starr had naturally made business contacts with the Fort Smith constabulary, so all they did was ask her discreetly to keep it down to a roar, and not to frighten the pure at heart.

They could have saved their breath. Belle enjoyed upsetting the pure at heart. She knew what they thought of her. She gloried in it, and in truth worked to make herself look ten times more like a female Wild Bill Hickok than the family business called for. Even Sam tried to explain to her after one of her noisier outbursts that she wasn't supposed to be the family gunslinger. He was the head of the household, and he would attend to such gunslinging as was needed.

She didn't listen to Sam, either. She'd do anything in bed with him that didn't hurt, but, by the High Almighty, she'd spent eight years at the Carthage Female Academy and didn't need advice from any ignorant Indian on how one conducted oneself about her own kind!

Belle wasn't just flamboyant, she was ambitious. Her husband's bootlegging, while flourishing and profitable, hardly justified itself to a woman who admired men like Cole Younger and the late Jim Reed. So one night at supper she proposed they branch out.

"We've gathered us a fair-sized gang of good old boys, honey, and it vexes me to have to share out the little we make with so many hands," she said.

Sam asked Pearl to pass him the salt before he answered.

"I have to share with the boys, Belle. Fair is fair, and they take more risk than you and me. Ferndancer and Osage Bill almost got picked up the other night. I've been meaning to talk to you on that, too. How come you stayed in Fort Smith and sent them pure-bloods home alone with all that red-eye?"

"Hell, honey, I wanted to scout that new bank in town, and anyone can drive an old buckboard. Pay attention to what I'm saying. I know we has to pay our bootleggers right, but there's more money out there to be had, and I mean to get me some."

"Please don't hold up the Fort Smith bank, Mamma! My true dad got eleven bullets in him messing with banks, and they still ain't let him out of prison!" Pearl pleaded.

Belle laughed. "I was just funning about the bank, child. I ain't that dumb. I know we depends on good will in Fort Smith, and there's no telling how many of our friends could have money in that bank."

She turned back to Sam and continued, "We has us contacts all over the Indian Nation, and on the white side of the line, too. I was thinking of the way I used to sort of transfer property rights when we first met up, Sam."

Sam shook his head. "Fencing stolen goods don't mix with bootlegging, Belle. That's why I told you to stop when we got hitched. Fencing is another line of work entire. Different folks has to be fixed. A lawman as will wink at a Cherokee buying something for snakebite can take an entire different view on stealing. Horse stealing in particular gets folks too excited to make it worth it. That's why I made you get rid of that pinto you had when I married you."

"I thought you had more sand in your craw, Sam. I never had to fix anybody toting a badge when I was fencing stock and such. Hell, the first day I met you, you was off to Texas with some other folk's stock!" she said.

Sam chewed the food in his mouth, swallowed, and said, "You was lucky, and I was a couple of years younger in them days, Belle. Things has changed since Hayes is president. There's more whites living along the edge of the

Strip, which makes it harder to ride cross country without being seen. I used to steel critters 'cause there wasn't a better way to make money. Now that Washington's gotten so strict about likker for my people, there's a better way. We're making money hand over fist, and I bought you the new curtains you wanted. What are you fussing at me about? If you needs something, just say so and I'll buy it for you, lawful. You have no call to deal in stolen goods no more."

Belle started to say it was more fun, but she knew her man didn't hold with fun much. She got up from the table with a flounce instead.

"Oh, hell, you'd be as easy to talk to if you was standing before a cigar store, holding wooden cigars," she said as she stormed out to sit on the veranda.

Sam looked at Pearl. "What's got into her, Pearl? Ain't I been good to you both?"

"You've been more than good to us, Sam. I'll see if I can find out what's troubling her. May I be excused from table?" Pearl replied.

Sam nodded, and Pearl followed her mother outside. She found Belle sitting on the steps, dipping snuff and scowling at the sunset.

Pearl sat at her mother's side and said, "My, don't that look pretty? Poor old Alice Ferndancer's never seen a sunset. I mind one time Granny Redbird told me something about sunsets and the way we gets to be women. Since Alice and me has been friends I know better what she meant. Can I ask you some woman lore, Mamma?"

"Shoot, what do you need to know about woman lore? You ain't but twelve yet. Has anybody been trifling with you again?" Belle asked.

"No, Mamma. I 'spect they're scared of Sam. I'm still pure, but, well, I suspicion I must be getting sick. I got this funny bleeding betwixt my legs this afternoon and I can't get it to stop. I didn't think it seemly to mention it in front of Sam. You know he don't allow me to get dressed in front of him of a morning."

Belle gasped, spat out her snuff, and took Pearl in her

arms as she said, "Oh, my poor little lamb! I should be switched for not watching you better! I have noted the way you've started to fill out this past year or more, but I clean forgot young gals don't know about the vile curse."

Pearl looked startled. She'd thought there must be something wrong with her, but 'vile curse' sounded like she was in a worse fix than the suspicion warranted.

She asked, "You reckon I've been hexed by a mean spey witch-woman, Mamma? I've been cramping the last few days like I'd et green apples, but I didn't know I was cursed."

Belle laughed. "It ain't a hex on you personal, honey. It's a dastardly trick nature played on all womankind. I've always resented it like hell."

Then, as Pearl listened, wide-eyed with wonder, Belle Starr told her the facts of life, albeit in words and with some notions that medical opinion might have objected to.

When she'd finished, in her own rough, barnyard way, Pearl grimaced and said, "Well, if it's the price one pays for being a growed woman I 'spect I'll have to just bear it, as hard a row as it may be to hoe. But now that I'm cursed, does that make me a growed woman like you, Mamma?"

"You'll always be my bitty baby, Pearl, but I fear you are a woman now. We'll fix you up with some rags so's not to soil your petticoats."

"It ain't bad yet, Mamma. I wanted to talk to you like a growed woman, now that you admit I am one."

Belle kissed her and said, "I thought I covered everything, Pearl, but if there's anything you still want to know, I'll do my best."

"Oh, I ain't worried about my privates, Mamma, now that I know it's natural to do that once a moon. I wanted to talk to you woman-to-woman about some other things."

"Well, go ahead then. I reckon you've earned the right, you poor thing."

Pearl searched for words before she finally said, "Well, Mamma. I am a Christian gal, ain't I?"

"Of course you're a Christian. What did you think you

was, a Mormon? I was brung up Baptist, and I think Cole was a Methodist, so you're a sort of Christian breed. What made you ask a fool thing like that, Pearl?"

"Well, Mamma, thanks to you I can read. The Ferndancers have a Good Book over to their cabin. Neither of her elders knows how to read, and of course Alice is blind. Bob Ferndancer said the Good Book is a family heirloom. Anyways, I've been reading from it aloud to Alice and her folk from time to time. It sure has a lot of interesting stuff in it."

Belle nodded. "Yeah, I admire that Samson slewing all them rascals with that jawbone, and wasn't that little David something with that slingshot?"

"There's other things in the Good Book than tales of blood and slaughter, Mamma. It tells how Moses went up on a mountain to jaw with the Lord and get the Lord's views on right and wrong. The Lord gave Moses his laws on these sort of gravestone things."

"I know about the Commandments, girl. Your grandfolks had 'em framed on the wall back home in Texas. I've always tried to live by 'em, within reason."

"Forgive me, Mamma, but if you live by the commands on your pappa's wall, he must have got them from another Good Book. The one over to the Ferndancer spread said it's wrong to steal and, no offence, Mamma, you've been stealing things since I've known you."

Belle shook her head and said, "That ain't true, Pearl. Have I ever stole from you?"

"Of course not. We're kin. But the Good Book says it's wrong to steal from anybody, and livestock is mentioned specific!"

Belle sighed, took another dip of snuff, and said, "Honey, you just don't understand how the war and all changed things. Moses and the Lord had that talk back before the war, didn't they?"

"I 'spect they must have, Mamma."

"Well, there you go. The Lord didn't know about the carpetbaggers and such when he handed down them laws to Moses. The Children of Israel likely had finer neighbors, so it wouldn't have been right to rob them. Though, now that I study on it, it was jake with The Lord for them to rob the men of Canaan. You see, Pearl, there's white stealing and black stealing, just as there's black and white lies. It's all right to steal off folks you ain't friendly with. You mind me telling you that tale about Robert E. Hood and the sheriff of Lincoln County?"

"Yes, Mamma. Where's Lincoln County at?"

"Over New Mexico way. Old Robert E. Hood's long gone, but the Greenwood Gang's led by a boy calt Billy the Kid these days, and they're still paying that mean sheriff back for wronging poor folk. Anyhow, Robert E. Hood comes from a book, too, just like Moses. It was writ plain that Robert E. Hood was in the right to steal from the rich and give to the poor. You mind the presents you've taken over to that blind child on her birthdays? Well, where in thunder do you reckon your stepdaddy and me could have gotten the wherewithal to buy such play pretties if we didn't rob the rich bastards?"

"Mamma, Sam ain't a thief. He's a bootlegger. That's not the same as stealing."

"Why not? They're both agin the law, ain't they? You got to understand, your momma ain't talking about cruel stealing, Pearl. You know I'd never rob a *poor* person, don't you?"

" 'Course not. Poor folks don't have nothing worth robbing!"

"There you go, Pearl, you're learning. It's a comfort to know you're growing up your father's daughter, even if he was a rascal."

Pearl Younger was fourteen when they shot Uncle Jesse. It was in the newspaper Sam Starr brought home from the trading post and placed on the table without comment. As he went back out to tend the horses, Pearl read about it, and it was just awful.

Uncle Jesse had been living up in Saint Joe with his wife and children when the Ford brothers rode down one Sunday morn to visit. They came invited, for they were distant kin to the James boys, and, worse yet, they sat down to table and broke bread with Uncle Jesse before they murdered him. The paper didn't call it murder, but what else could one call it when a rascal shoots his own kin in the head whilst he's up on a chair straightening a picture frame with his back to one and all?

Pearl cried, but not much, for in truth she hadn't really been all that fond of Uncle Jesse, and Uncle Frank was still at large, with the whole infernal country looking for him. The Ford boys had lit out, too, as well they might when one considered how many James, Youngers, and even Fords would be after them for being such rascals!

The death of Jesse James called for a rehash of his past in the papers. Pearl gasped in surprise when she saw the photograph of her real father, Cole Younger, on the third page.

She muttered, "So that's what he looks like. Whoever would have thought it?"

The stranger in the old photograph was a man with a beard, a puffy face, and starting to go bald. The picture had been taken when they had captured him after the Northfield job, so Pearl allowed one couldn't expect a man to look his best after a posse had pumped eleven bullets in him and likely roughed him some, but she'd still expected something else. To hear Mamma tell it, he'd been better-looking than anyone else in Texas. If he had, life surely had played hell with his youthful looks.

She wondered why he'd never answered the letters she'd sent to Minnesota State Prison. Mamma had said she'd mailed them, and it wasn't that far to Minnesota. She'd looked it up in the atlas.

Pearl had written a dozen or more letters before she'd given up. She finally realized that they either wouldn't let him read them in jail, or that if they had, her father wanted no truck with her. That was a painful thing to suspect, for she'd never done anything to make a father dislike her.

Pearl went to the sideboard, got a pair of shears, and carefully cut the photo from the paper to put with the other mementos of her father she'd saved. She even had a reward poster that said he was worth a thousand dollars to the Missouri Central.

A week later, Pearl Younger was to learn more of her birthright when she was visiting Fort Smith. Belle was on an innocent shopping mission, and she was on her best behavior, too. She enjoyed the way the la-di-da ladies of Fort Smith stood rooted and gasping when she loped by on Venus, but she didn't want her budding daughter exposed to ugly looks.

As the county seat, Fort Smith prided itself on being up-to-date, so a colored street singer on the corner near the depot had the newest version of a song set to an old country hymn. As Belle and Pearl drove by he was singing,

> "Oh, 'twas on a Wednesday night when the moon
>   was bright,
> They robbed the Glendale train,
> And in less than a day you could hear the people say,
> 'Twas Cole Younger, Frank and Jesse James!"

Pearl gasped. "Listen, Mamma! They're singing songs about my pappa."

Belle nodded cheerfully. "There you go, I told you he was famous, honey. I heard the song before. It's about your Uncle Jesse's death, but you can't tell the tale of Jesse James without including Cole Younger, for they all rode together all the way back to when they was kids in Colonel Quantrill's Fifth Confederate Calvary."

Even Pearl knew Quantrill's guerrilla cavalry was a myth, for it was a matter of public record that the Confederate Army had disowned William Quantrill as a surly lunatic who'd never held commission in any army on either side. Pearl and her Mamma had had that out before, so there was no use discussing it.

Pearl knew her pappa had indeed ridden with Quantrill, for a Cherokee that Sam Starr knew had told her they'd rode with Quantrill's Irregulars, too, and if she ever met up with her pappa, Pearl meant to ask him why he'd been so silly in his teens.

She wished colored folk wouldn't make up songs about her pappa and that Mamma would stop bragging about all them banks and trains. Pearl had heard that sometimes, after a man had been in jail a spell, the law sort of forgot what they'd put him in for and let him go free, but it hardly seemed likely the law would forget Cole Younger and his brothers unless folks kept quiet about him.

They stopped in front of the dry goods store near the center of town and Pearl hopped down to tether the horse. A tall, hawk-faced man walked over, touched the brim of his hat, and said, "Howdy, Belle Starr. I'm glad you come to town this day. Saves me a ride. You're wanted over to the courthouse."

Pearl's mouth went dry, but Belle just smiled and said, "I come to town to do me some shopping, Rafe. What do you want with me in the courthouse?"

"I don't want you worth mention, Belle. Judge Parker wants you. Leastways, he wants a word with you. You ain't under arrest, exactly, but if I was you I'd go on over peaceable."

"Well, it's best to get it over afore we have our shopping in the wagon bed. I hear tell there's thieves about Fort Smith," said Belle.

Deputy Rafe smiled thinly and said, "That's true, Belle."

Belle met his eye, laughed and said, "Come on, Pearl. Let's get this over with."

The terrified teenager followed as her mother marched rather grandly to the courthouse a city block away. Pearl wanted to beg her mother not to march them into the lion's den, but the deputy was right behind them. Surely her Mamma knew what they said about Hanging Judge Parker! Pearl wondered, if they threw her in jail, if there was some way she could get locked up near her daddy.

Judge Parker was in his chambers when the deputy herded them in. The judge rose from his desk, for he was a courtly man, and offered them both seats. Hanging Judge Parker looked at Pearl sort of oddly when her mother introduced them.

"I had no idea your daughter was such a refined looking

young lady, Belle. Rafe, see if you can rustle up some refreshments for the ladies. You do like lemonade, don't you,
Miss Pearl?" he asked.

Pearl managed a silent nod as she sat down, weak-kneed
and full of butterflies. She could see Hanging Judge Parker
wasn't as mean looking as she'd expected, but she could
also see that there was an iron fist in that velvet glove, so
she hoped her Mamma wouldn't sass him.

When the deputy left, Issac Parker said, "I'll come right
to the point, Belle. You know what happened up to Saint
Joe. Bob Ford's been spilling all he knows about the
James-Younger gang, and, being a junior member for some
time before he decided to file for that reward, Bob Ford
had a lot to spill."

Belle sniffed. "I figured he might. The statute of limita-
tions has run out on anything you have on me and mine,
though. The one I knew best is in prison. You won't find
Cole Younger hiding under my skirts, Judge."

Parker nodded. "We're not looking for the Younger
boys. We're looking for Frank James. Bob and Charlie
Ford told us where Frank had been the last time they
supped with him, but Jesse getting shot must have spooked
Frank, for he'd lit out by the time the law got to his last
known address."

Belle laughed and said, "I figured he might, Judge, but
don't ask me for his new address! I'll tell you true, I
wouldn't give it to you if I had it, but to save us all a
bother, I give you my word I don't. I ain't seen hide or hair
of any of the old bunch, recent."

Judge Parker smiled pleasantly. "I know how recent that
was, Belle, and you slickered us good. I feel sort of dumb
about that, too. The boys wanted a search warrant on your
spread when the James boys were hiding out with you a
few years back, and I refused it. I said I thought you were
too smart to be hiding them. I fear I misjudged you. Later
on, a Cherokee informant told us the whole tale. Your Sam
Starr led them to safety in Texas, along with a mess of
livestock I'd like to talk to Sam about if we could prove it."

Belle's eyes were mocking as she replied, "You can't

prove nothing on mere hearsay, Your Honor. I told you I knowed my law, and the law says you're just fishing. I'd like to set and jaw a spell, Judge Parker, but I got shopping to do, and we both know you ain't got doodly-boo on Sam and me."

Isaac Parker snapped, "Sit down!" as Belle started to rise. He added in a softer tone, "The young lady here hasn't had her lemonade. As for what I may or may not have on you and Sam Starr, the Interior Department doesn't go out of its way for us, so I see no call to do the B.I.A.'s work for it. The bootlegging over in the strip is between you and them, Belle. I've enough on my court calendar between murders and robberies hereabouts."

Rafe came back in with two glasses of lemonade. Belle refused hers with a disdainful look. Pearl accepted the offer gratefully. Her mouth felt like it was filled with spider webs and sawdust. The lemonade tasted fine, but it didn't help. She was too afraid Mamma would say something to make that hanging judge throw them both in jail forever.

"All right," Belle said, "let's get down to brass tacks, Judge. Just what in thunder do you want from me? I swear on my honor as a southern gentlewoman that I've no notion where Frank James might be these days. I 'spose, since you're a carpetbagger, that ain't good enough for you."

Parker smiled humorlessly and said, "I know the store your kind sets on its given word, Belle. I know Frank James isn't hiding out at your place, right now. Some, ah, Indian scouts just told me that. I hope you understand that I've got my eye on you, Belle Starr."

"You don't have to drop a brick wall on me, Judge. I can take a hint. The Ford boys just showed how some men will sell their souls for Judas silver, and they was both white. But since your spies told you how often we'uns use the outhouse, what are you pestering me about Frank James for? I know he ain't hiding out with Sam and me, and you know he ain't hiding out with Sam and me, so this is getting tedious. Finish that lemonade, Pearl. We got us some shopping to do."

Judge Parker shook his head. He said, "I haven't finished. The last we had on Frank James, he was heading this way. I sure admire the imagination of those boys. It's getting so you can set your clock by them. We'll probably get him before he makes it to the Strip this time, but if we don't, it's no mystery where he'll look for help over there. You do understand what I'm asking, don't you, Belle?"

Belle frowned and said, "I ain't as dumb as I look, but my maiden name was Shirley, not Ford. I swear I don't know where old Frank might or might not be headed, but if you think you could get us to set him up for you, you've been drinking more than lemonade! Do I look like a Judas to you, Judge?"

Isaac Parker was too polite a man to tell any lady what Belle Starr looked like to him. So he simply replied, "This time you have no say in the matter, Belle. I told you I have my eye on you and Sam. If you try to help James again, you'll all just wind up behind the same bars. On the other hand, there's a fair reward on the head of Frank James and, since we all know he's going to get caught one place or another, why should the Ford boys be the only ones to profit from the inevitable?"

Belle didn't answer. Parker mistook her silence for agreement and continued, "Here's what I want you to do. When Frank James comes to your spread, you're to go ahead and offer to hide him out. I'd bed him out back in that stable you have, since it might get noisy toward the end. Anyway, once you have him bedded down someplace, you're to send one of Sam's bootleggers to us, sudden. Once you've done us this small favor, I promise none of you will be involved any deeper in the case. I can fix it so's you get the reward without your names being mentioned in any papers. The Ford boys made themselves a lot of dumb trouble by running all over bragging about it when they turned Jesse in, but . . ."

"Damn it, Judge," Belle cut in. "They never turned Jesse in. They murdered him! They broke bread with him on the Sabbath and then they shot him from the back, in his very own front parlor, with him not armed!"

Parker grimaced. "I can't say I find their conduct worthy of my unqualified admiration, Belle, but I'm not asking you or Sam Starr to gun down Frank James. You won't be present when my men close in."

"Mayhaps not, but we'll purely hear the noise, and every shot would be a coffin nail in the soul I still got left! There's got to be a better way, Judge. I'd never Judas a jasper I didn't know, and it's a free country, ain't it?"

Isaac Parker shook his head and said, "Not for you and Sam, Belle. If we take him within ten country miles of your spread, and you haven't done your duty as law-abiding citizens, I'll have you so deep in a dungeon cell that you'll have forgotten the color of the sky by the time you ever see it again."

Belle shrugged. "Can we go now?"

"You can go on over to the dry goods store if you like, Belle. Your daughter, here, can catch up with you directly. I haven't had a chance to get to know Miss Pearl, and I'd like a chat with her alone before she leaves."

Belle started to object. Then she laughed and agreed. "You think you can get my child to Judas her mother? Well, that makes you the fool of the world, but go ahead."

She rose. "Don't be afraid of him, honey. If you ain't with me when I'm ready to head back I'll make some charges my own self."

Pearl couldn't believe her mother was abandoning her to these frightening strangers, but she couldn't cry out or say a word as Belle stamped out, cursing under her breath.

Judge Parker waited until Belle's footsteps faded away before he said, "We won't need you, Rafe."

The deputy looked as puzzled as Pearl, but orders were orders, so he left them alone.

Pearl's heart was beating like a triphammer as she faced the terrible old man. She didn't know what she'd do if he started acting like Blue Duck had that time. Could they do anything to a judge for raping a gal?

"I won't keep you long, miss. I won't bite you, either. Do you know what a ward of the state is?" Judge Parker asked.

Pearl licked her lips and said, "Yes, sir, the Indians are."

"Indians, incompetents, and minors. You're a minor, Miss Pearl. No offense."

"No offense took, Your Honor, but I've never been near a mine in my life."

Parker chuckled and said, "Let's put it this way, then. You're not an adult. The law takes the view that young folk without proper adult supervision, or abused children, must be defended and protected by the state."

"Oh, you mean like if I was an orphan child, sir?"

"Yes, but you don't have to be an orphan if you're not being treated right. I've heard conflicting stories about you, Miss Pearl. Now that I've met you, I see some of them can be dismissed. I can't figure out how it could be possible, but you seem to be a very well-behaved young lady."

Pearl smiled shyly and answered, "I thanks you, sir. I 'spect I owes my proper manners to my Mamma and Sam Starr."

Judge Parker frowned and said, "That's what I meant. I'm not sure I understand just how electricity works, either. The world sure is filled with wonders."

"What was you wondering about, Judge Parker?"

The old man didn't look nearly as old or mean now, as he smiled at Pearl and answered, "Well, you may find me nosey, but it's my duty to ask certain things, Miss Pearl. Some of the ladies here in town have complained about a young white girl living with, ah, a woman like your mother and a, well, Indian buck, in a one-room cabin."

Pearl shook her head and said, "It ain't a one-roomer no more, Judge. Shortly after Sam wedded Mamma, he built me my own lean-to. So I sleep in my own room and I got it fixed up right pretty."

"Hmm, I heard gossip about you being molested by one of your mother's Indian lovers. You know what molesting means, don't you?"

"Yes, sir. You must be talking about the time Uncle Blue Duck tried to trifle with me. But you don't have to worry about Uncle Blue Duck doing that again. Sam says he'll stomp him good if he ever shows his face in Younger's Bend again. Sam don't let nobody trifle with me. He says it ain't seemly to pester gals as young as me," Pearl answered.

Judge Parker made a check mark on a legal pad before him and muttered, "So much for the incest complaint. Tell me, Miss Younger, how do you feel about an Indian switching you when you've been sassy?"

Pearl looked blank and asked, "Why would he want to switch me, sir? I get along just fine with Sam. Neither him nor Mamma has ever hit me. I don't hold with being sassy."

Judge Parker made another mark of dismissal and said, "I see I'm barking up the wrong tree. I've heard Sam Starr's a decent cuss, for a Cherokee. Let's try it another way, Miss Pearl. You seem to be a decent, law-abiding young lady. How do you feel about the way your folks abuse the law the way they do?"

Pearl sighed and said, "I feel poorly about them having to live so much like Robert E. Hood from Lincoln County, sir. But they don't listen to me about such matters, so I don't see what I can do about it."

"You don't have to live with them, you know."

Pearl stared wildly at him and gasped, "Leave my Mamma! You must be joshing me, sir! Why on earth would I ever want to do that?"

"Listen to me, Pearl. I know you love your mother. I can see she's done a better job on you than I'd have thought possible. But what's to become of you out there, Pearl? You're almost a young woman, and a very pretty one to boot. I'd hate to see you turn out bad."

Pearl said, "I'd hate that too, Your Honor, but I don't mean to. You may think I'm too young to understand, but I know all too well what being bad can lead to. If there's one thing I've studied on, it's the fruits of going agin the law. I don't mean to be an outlaw when I grow up. Can I go, now, sir? Mamma will be worried about me."

Judge Parker sighed and nodded dismissal. Pearl got to her feet and almost ran out of his chambers, but she turned in the doorway, curtsied, and said, "I thank you for that fine lemonade, sir, and I don't think you're really as ornery as they say you are."

When she'd left, Rafe returned to the judge's chambers.

"How did it go, Your Honor?"

"Not the way it was supposed to. We'll never get that girl to press charges of abuse against Belle and that bootlegging rascal, Starr. I sure hate to have to leave her with them, though," Parker replied.

"Can't we just take her away from them trash, Your Honor?"

"On what grounds? Belle's the poor girl's natural mother."

"That's true, Judge Parker, but if you leave that pretty little thing to be raised over there in the Strip, we both know she'll wind up a whore or worse."

Judge Parker pursed his lips and said, "Maybe. Genetics are a funny thing, Rafe. Somewhere in her thorny family tree that child has quality in her. She is tidy and well dressed. They must let her pick out her own clothes. She tells me she has her own room and that the buck doesn't abuse her sexually or otherwise. You can see she's well fed and has no nits in her hair. Hell, she's living a damn site better than half the white kids in this county! Our hands are tied, Rafe. There's nothing we can do to get her out of there unless we get lucky when her Uncle Frank comes to visit."

"Lucky for us or lucky for her, Your Honor?"

"Maybe both her and us. The girl's honest. Her mother would lie when the truth was in her favor, but I don't think young Pearl knows how to lie. So, if Frank James should dare to show his fool face in the Cherokee Strip, it might turn out handy to have a friend of the court in Belle Starr's cabin, when you study on it some."

Rafe grinned and shouted, "Hot damn! Do you reckon you could get her to witness agin her trashy mother, Your Honor? Would she do it for us?"

"Not for us, Rafe, but I suspect if she was sworn to tell the truth in my court, she would. Tell the boys I want a sharp lookout along the trails leading to the strip, but tell 'em not to crowd too close. We'll give Frank James enough rope to hang the whole infernal crew. We'll let him bed down a spell at Belle's before we move in. You call that getting two birds with one stone, Rafe."

Rafe said, "I know how to round 'em up for you to sentence, sir. It'll be more like three birds than one, if the Starrs are dumb enough to shelter old Frank. Do you reckon anyone could be that dumb, Your Honor? You just told Belle we had our eyes on her."

Judge Parker sighed and said, "They'll be that dumb, God help them. If serving with the Reconstruction taught me anything about the sort of folks we're dealing with, it's that they carry clan loyalty past all common sense."

Judge Parker stared vacantly into space, seeing faces he'd like to forget, as he added, "It's such an infernal waste, Rafe. There's so much raw animal courage and, well, what you could almost call nobility, being wasted in a prison or the end of a rope. I don't mind the plain vicious ones ending that way, but there's so much good in some of them. I've always thought Frank James would have turned out better in another world, and Belle Starr can't be all that bad, to have such a daughter. But, God help us all, there's only one way they can all end up. You're probably right about the kid, too!"

5

THE REST OF April was quiet but tense in Younger's Bend. Belle Starr was deathly afraid that the last of the old bunch would come to them for help and hiding, and if Frank James did come, she wondered what she and Sam would do.

Sam soon learned of the white and Indian lawmen pestering his neighbors with questions about him and Belle. There were even some infernal Seminole deputies guiding the white federal men. Sam knew they were up against a dangerously slick checker player in Judge Parker. Sam knew it was Judge Parker.

Parker was the smartest white man for miles around. It hardly seemed fair. A judge was supposed to just sit tight and let marshals and sheriffs figure out how to catch folk, but Hanging Judge Parker had vowed to clean up the Cherokee Strip for Washington even though Hayes wasn't President any more.

The B.I.A. had slackened off some since old Chester Arthur had taken office after someone had gunned President Garfield. President Arthur wasn't much on speeches of reform like Hayes had been, but he'd confirmed Parker

117

as the local terror, and Hanging Judge Parker was getting mighty uppity about it.

Naturally, Sam pulled in his horns and told the boys not to run any more likker whilst the infernal Seminoles were scouting them. Sam had never studied on the Roman Empire, but he was Cherokee, hence, he was all too well aware what "divide and conquer" meant.

The Seminole were mighty odd Indians. They even made their Creek cousins nervous. They didn't think or fight like other sensible tribes, and it was likely because they'd mixed so much with blacks who'd escaped slavery by running off to the swamps. They hated the Cherokee, and the feeling was mutual. The white man had found the Seminole to be a deadly enemy and a handy ally after some of the bands moved west on the Trail Of Tears and took jobs as army scouts or Indian police. Seminoles made deadly night fighters and were almost as fearsome in broad day. A Seminole could find cover behind a stem of grass, and they ambushed silently. The whites said they were the best trackers of all their Indian scouts, too.

Sam made Belle get rid of a roan colt in the corral that she'd promised to sell for Charlie Bluefeather. Then, having neatened up, they could only sit tight and hope Frank James would search somewhere else for help. Sam, of course, had agreed that they'd have to help a man who had a claim of friendship on Belle, but figuring out how to flap their wings and lay eggs seemed easier than figuring out how they were going to be able to lift a finger for old Frank without going to jail with him.

Belle had been a mite hesitant in mentioning the reward when she told her man about the conversation she'd had in town with Judge Parker, but, to her considerable joy, he'd dismissed it as a notion about as attractive as cannibalism. He said he'd *eat* Frank James before he'd Judas him to the *law*! That night, when Pearl went to sleep in the lean-to, Sam Starr got some loving that wore him to a frazzle.

It was pushing May Day, and the alder leaves were the size of kitten's ears. Then the lightning struck. It was silent lightning, for a man on the run with the whole world after him moves mighty quiet.

Pearl was sitting on the steps of the Ferndancer cabin, reading the Good Book to blind Alice, when Frank James made it across the line into the Cherokee Strip. He got there crawling on his belly through the brush. He'd abandoned his spent pony before noon in the Arkansas hills, along with everything he owned in the world but a few dollar bills and his guns. He crawled with his holstered six-gun swung around to the small of his back, and the Winchester .44-40 cradled in his elbows, using them for forelegs as he bulled through the thickest brush he could find. His drawn and haggard face was unshaven and scratched up. His haunted eyes would have been frightening to look at, if he'd been anywhere where other folk could see them. He had no intention of letting anyone see his eyes or anything else before he reached the dubious safety of Belle Starr's spread. Unfortunately, one part of his wary mind warned him he was likely a fool for heading there. After all, what was Cole Younger's erstwhile mistress, when a man got down to it? Sure, Belle and that Indian she was said to be living with these days had helped him and Jesse in the past, but Bob and Charlie Ford had done more in their day, and were distant kin besides! If a man couldn't trust a gang member he'd invited for Sunday dinner, how in thunder could his brother trust a pair of bootleggers he barely knew?

But he kept crawling. He had nowhere else to go in these parts, and the law was pressing him close since that fancy gal in Little Rock had turned him away from her parlor house door and likely gone to the law by now. In the good old days, the Cherokee Strip had been easier to hide out in. You could just camp out alone in some draw or other and rest up a spell, but now they had patrols of Indian Police prowling all over in here, and unless a man could bed down under some friendly roof for the night he figured to be prodded awake with the unfriendly end of a rifle. A man alone couldn't post a night guard, and sooner or later everybody had to fall asleep.

Lord, how he needed sleep. He hadn't had any for the past two nights, except when he'd nodded off for a few minutes hiding in a cornfield. Frank James knew his weary mind was likely not working as well as usual. Was he making a terrible mistake in heading for Belle's cabin? Who was Belle? Oh, yeah, she was old Cole Younger's gal. Or maybe she had been at one time. It was hard keeping things like that straight. Cole had so many gals spread out across the country, but he'd said of all the gals he'd had, Belle was the most faithful. Belle would help him. She had to help him. If she wouldn't, he was a gone cuss!

Over at the Ferndancer cabin, blind Alice was saying, "Hold on, Pearl. Where did them other sons of Noah come in? I disremember them being on that boat with the others.

Pearl looked up with a frown "What others, Alice? There was just Noah, his old woman, their three sons and their wives, and of course the critters."

"Then who was Mustard and Bread? Noah surely gave his kids funny names if you ask me."

"Mustard and Bread? There's nothing in here about any mustard and bread, Alice. I don't think they had mustard and bread in them days. I never read you nothing about mustard and bread."

"You surely did, Pearl Younger. You read it. You said Noah sent Ham into the wilderness and his descendants, Mustard and Bread."

Pearl laughed. "You fool Indian, that's not how it goes. The Book says Ham went into the wilderness, and his descendants mustered and bred. That means they tallied up and had a mess of young'uns. Old Ham's family become the Hammites, whilst Shem's become the children of Israel, save for the branch of the family fathered on that slave gal when Father Abraham trifled with her one time. But that comes later in the book. How many times do I have to read this infernal Good Book to you, Alice? We've been over it more than once, now, and I don't think you understand it worth mention."

"Some of the words is hard to follow, but I likes it when you read to me, Pearl. Read me some more, will you?"

"I'd best call it a day now, Alice. The sun ball's going down and the light's getting poor for reading this small print."

Alice frowned. "I've always had trouble following that, too. How come you sighted folk lose the gift when that sun thing goes off somewheres?"

Pearl started to josh her blind friend about not knowing the difference betwixt night and day, but then she realized why she didn't, and it made her shudder inside. "We've been over it time and time again, Alice. Since you can't understand, you'll have to take my words in good faith. In the daytime we have the gift you was birthed without. At night, we're sort of like you, unless we light a lamp or something, and there's no lamp handy," she said gently.

"Oh, are you blind like me right now, Pearl?"

"Not hardly. I can still see to get about, but everything's gone sort of orange and purple. It's too dark to read small print by, but it's pretty. I like the way the world melts soft and gentle at this time of the day. I sure wish you could see a sunset at least once, Alice."

"I wish I could, too. Tell me about it again."

"Honey, you know I've tried, but words like orange and purple or light and dark don't mean a thing to you."

"I know, but I can tell by your tone they must be grand. Tell me what you see out there, Pearl."

Pearl sighed and said, "Well, the tree tops over to the west are standing agin the sunset sky like black lace. You know what lace is, and I reckon all the lace you've ever felt must look black to you."

"Lace feels pretty. Go on, Pearl."

"Well, the sky is sort of like a big peach skin with the colors running together, and some birds are flying north across it now in a line of winky black dots. I'd say they was whooper cranes, from here. Things seem smaller as they get farther way from sighted eyes, Alice."

Alice said, "Mamma told me that. She's tried to tell me what it's like to be able to see, too. She ain't as good with words as you are, Pearl. Sometimes when she's talking to me about my curse she gets all choked up, so I don't ask her much about it any more. Why do you reckon it upsets her so?"

"I don't know. Mammas are like that, I reckon. My mamma worries more about me than she has a call to. You have to understand how it vexes sighted folk to try and explain things to you, with you not being able to understand so many words the rest of us take for granted."

"Do you find it hateful to talk about it with me, Pearl?"

"Sometimes. But mayhap it's good for both of us, Alice. Since we've been pards I've noticed things about being blessed with sight that I might not have never noticed. If you'd been able to read this Good Book your own self, I'd have missed out on some things about the Lord my folks never got about to telling me. Sam and Mamma say they believe in the Lord, but that they take this book with a grain of salt. Sam says walking on water and stopping the sun ball in its tracks don't sound natural to him."

"They sound all right to me. If the Lord runs everything, He can likely do anything, right?" Alice asked.

"I reckon He can. He sure does a lot of odd things. I never understood that 'til the Book explained how 'the Lord moveth in mysterious ways his wonders to perform.' That means we have no call to question some of the funny things as happen, Alice," said Pearl.

"I know. My mamma says it was the Lord's will for me to be birthed blind, but that He might have had the good grace not to heap so much on anyone already birthed Indian. I've never understood just what an Indian is, Pearl. Would you settle that for me?"

Pearl gaped at her teen-aged friend's dark, pretty face and answered, "Alice, you must know what an Indian is, for Heaven's sake. You and your folks are Indian. Sam says it ain't true that your Creek mamma is a nigger 'breed."

"What's a nigger, Pearl?"

"A nigger? Everybody knows what a nigger is, you fool girl."

Then, as the blind girl shook her head, Pearl's horizons of understanding widened. She added in a gentler tone,

"Niggers is folks like you and me, only darker skinned and . . . Oh, bother, that won't work with you. Just take my word that they ain't white folk or red folk. They're just different than us."

"How so different, Pearl? I've never been able to get it straight how you whites is different from us Indians. You've let me run my hands over your face to feel how you be featured, but I can't feel you're all that different from me. I sure wish I could see, so's I could find out what the difference might mean. My folks say they can tell a white man from an Indian without even touching him. It must be grand to be able to tell a body afore you even ask them if they be your kind or not," Alice said.

Pearl frowned thoughtfully and said, "I'm not so sure it is, sometimes. When I ride into Fort Smith with Mamma, I sometimes wish the folks looking at us so funny was like you, Alice. But the sun ball's almost down, and we'll have to talk on it another time. I got to get home for supper."

They hugged each other goodnight and Pearl walked home. She arrived at sunset, just as Belle was setting Sam's steak and potatoes in front of him. Belle nodded absently at her daughter, as if she had other things on her mind, and supper was silently consumed. Sam seldom spoke much in any case, but usually Belle liked to jaw at the table. Pearl didn't ask her elders what was troubling them. She knew.

Pearl was doing the dishes, and it had just gotten dark when it happened. The door swung open and Frank James, uninvited, closed it after him, with his Winchester pointed politely at the cabin floor, and breathing like a horse that had been ridden shamefully hard. There was a long stunned silence before Belle Starr, seated near the table darning one of Sam's socks, spoke. "Howdy, Frank. You know Sam, here. Have a seat. Pearl, fetch Uncle Frank some Arbuckle and rustle him up some grub. We just et, Frank, but we'll manage something for you. You should have come earlier. We had steak tonight, but I fear we et it all."

Frank James staggered over to the table and sank down

wearily. "I waited until dark before I closed in. I feared the cabin might be being watched."

"It is," Sam said. "Hear me, Frank James, you can't stay here. We'll grub you and horse you. That's all we can do for you. This is the first place the law would look for you in the Strip."

Belle gasped. "Sam, we can't turn him out into the night like a dog!"

Frank said, "He's right, Belle. I feared the law might suspicion you. I was a fool to come here. I'll stay long enough for coffee, but I'd best not eat. As tired as I am, a warm meal would knock me out for sure. You say you have a mount for me, Sam?"

Sam nodded and Belle cried out, "Oh, take Venus, Frank. She's the fastest horse in these parts. They'll never catch up with you if you're riding Venus."

So Pearl knew, as she served the coffee, that her mamma felt mighty serious about Uncle Frank getting away. Even Sam looked surprised at her offer, and Sam hardly ever showed what he was thinking.

As Pearl placed the tin cup in front of Frank James, he looked up at her and said, "Great balls of fire, is this little Pearl, Belle? She's growed some since last I passed this way. Growed damned pretty, too!"

It flustered Pearl to have a grown man looking at her that way, even though she knew he meant it respectfully. Frank James took the cup in his two hands and drained it in a single gulp. Pearl poured him another as she said shyly, "I know this is growed-up talk, Uncle Frank, but may I have my say?"

"Honey, you can say anything you like to me, for you may be the last pretty gal I'll ever see," replied Frank.

"Sam's right about lawmen skulking about Younger's Bend. Some Cherokee boys I know spotted some in the woods the other day. They're camped all about in a big circle. I was there when Judge Parker told Mamma they expected you to come this way. I think they mean to let you tree yourself here in Younger's Bend."

Sam Starr nodded and said, "She's smart for a child, Frank. You'd not get past them in the woods they know better than you, even riding Venus. But they're sure to close in on us here, if they haven't started already."

"Oh, Jesus, what have I done to you folk? I'd best get going," Frank said.

Pearl said, "You've time to coffee and even grub, Uncle Frank. I've been studying on how I'd do her if I was the law. Even if they suspicion you're here, they won't move in just yet. They'll want to let folks settle down for the night."

Frank James stared up at her in wonder and said, "You're right, Sam, she's smart as anything. I'd forgot how the Pinkertons closed in on my own mamma's farm that time at four in the morning. Lucky for me and Jesse, we wasn't there, but unlucky for Mamma. They come in throwing dynamite bombs and injured Mamma dreadful. You reckon that's what they're planning, Pearl? I'd hate to get you folks dynamited."

Pearl shook her head. "I doubt they'll come shooting unless they know for sure you're here, Uncle Frank. The newpapers took the Pinkertons to task for blowing up an old woman like that, and Judge Parker ain't that wild a man."

Frank James shrugged and said, "I thank you for such small comfort, honey, but I don't mean to be taken gentle, either. Since I likely have half the night to live I'd best move on and let 'em shoot it out with me in other parts. I can see staying here ain't a good notion."

Pearl said, "It's true they'll search our cabin, Uncle Frank, but what if you was holed up somewheres else? Mayhaps in a cabin they wasn't likely to search?"

Belle Starr got up, came over, and threw her arms around Pearl as she cried out, "Lord of Mercy, honey, how did you get so smart?"

Sam Starr grinned and said, "It ought to work, Frank! They'd search the whole Indian Nation if they knowed for certain you'd made her this far, but they won't want to rile everyone agin 'em just on suspicion. I'll run you over to

Bob Ferndancer's place. They'll never think to look for you there. Ferndancer's one of my gang, so we can likely trust him."

Pearl said, "I'd best lead Uncle Frank to shelter, Sam. If the law was to drop by whilst you was out, they'd ask all sorts of questions, but if you and Mamma was to be found setting here alone they'd hardly think of where a young gal like me might be. If they asked, you could tell 'em I was out walking in the moonlight with some boy."

Sam stared up at her, slack-jawed. Then he asked, "Belle?"

Belle nodded. "I don't like it much, but she's right. It's the safest way, when you study on it. You will be careful, won't you, Pearl? I'd just die if anything was to happen to you!"

Frank James said, "You have my word, Belle. If so much as a twig snaps whilst I'm with your child I'll be a country mile from her before anything else can happen!"

So Sam doused the lantern, and Pearl took the desperate man by the hand to lead him out into the darkness. They said nothing until they were well clear of the cabin. Then Frank James asked, "How far is this Ferndancer place, honey?"

"We ain't going there, Uncle Frank. I don't think it's safe for you there," said Pearl.

Frank stiffened and stopped in his tracks, asking, "Oh? Are you saying Sam's friends might Judas me, girl?"

Pearl tugged him on as she replied, "No, but Judge Parker's mighty foxy, and everyone knows Bob Ferndancer works for us. Besides that, old Bob's not much in a fight and his child is a blind girl. I'd be awful vexed if the law found you there and scared poor Alice."

"Where are you taking me, then?"

"Granny Redbird's. She's a spry woman—a conjure witch-woman—as lives well clear of the other cabins in Younger's Bend. She's a friend of me and mine, and has herbs to help you feel better besides. She'd never tell the law on you, and the law would hardly expect a white man and a stranger in these parts to run to earth at Granny

Redbird's. You can rest up there and wait for the trail to grow colder afore you move on. Where are you going, once you're outten here, Uncle Frank?"

"Damn my eyes, I wish I knew, child. I've been running and hiding longer than I've been shaving, and it sure gets tedious. You have no idea what it's like to be chased into your middle years by the law, Pearl. Even when I think it's safe to sleep, I can't. I spook at every shadow of late, and everything I eats tastes the same, like ashes in my mouth. I'm all that's left of the old bunch, and everywhere I run to, every hand is raised agin me."

"We're still your friends, Uncle Frank," said Pearl.

He stopped, swung her around in the moonlight, and said soberly, "That's the pure truth, and I'll never forget it, Pearl Younger. I'm likely just bragging, considering the odds of my seeing daybreak, but I swear to you that as long as I live I'll owe you. You has the spoken word of Frank James that if you ever need anything from me, it's your'n, if I have to bust out of hell to make good on my vow!"

He kissed her solemnly on the brow and they trudged on, hand in hand. After a time Pearl said, "Well, I'm only a child and a gal besides, but I've been studying on the fix you're in, Uncle Frank."

He chuckled and said, "I sure wish you'd started sooner. You're so smart it's spooky. Even Sam didn't think of this Cherokee witch of your'n, and he's a Cherokee. What do you figure I ought to do if we don't get caught between here and there?"

"Well, I've been reading the papers. They seem to think Uncle Jesse was treated shameful by the law, like Robert E. Hood was that time. I read about the law dynamiting your poor old mother, too, and the papers said that was mighty uncalled for."

"Mamma didn't like it much, neither. It crippled her for life, but such talk in the newpapers won't help me much, now," Frank James said.

"I think you're wrong, Uncle Frank. You ain't wanted for murder like Uncle Jesse was. The papers say he done most of the gunning, and that even he was treated mighty shabby. If you was to go back to Missouri and turn yourself in, whilst everyone's feeling upset about the Ford boys playing Judas, the law would have a fine time getting a jury to convict you."

Frank James laughed bitterly, and said, "You're right, you are a child. Hell's fire, honey, it was in Missouri we robbed the Glendale Train!"

"I know, Uncle Frank. I heard the song. In a year or more, folks back in Missouri will likely remember some of the other things you and my daddy and Uncle Jesse did, too, but right now they're feeling sorry for you. There will never come a time when you'll have such a sporting chance in any Missouri court of law. I'd study on it, if I was you."

They got to Granny Redbird's, and the old spey woman greeted Frank James like a long-lost son, to his considerable surprise. She dosed him with sleeping herbs and put him to bed. So, seeing there was nothing further she could do for Uncle Frank, Pearl headed home.

The lamp was lit again and the cabin door stood wide, illuminating the strange ponies tethered out front. Pearl took a deep breath and walked on in. She found her folk entertaining the deputy called Rafe and four other lawmen, including a moody-looking Seminole. Belle looked up brightly and asked in a desperately casual voice if that fool boy had dast to kiss her in the moonlight. Pearl found a stool in the corner and sat down quietly.

Rafe, sitting at the table drinking coffee from the same cup Frank James had used, smiled at her and said, "I'm glad you're here, girl. Judge Parker thinks highly of you and says you never lie. Before we leaves this law-abiding spread I got me a couple of questions to ask you."

Pearl didn't answer.

Rafe said, "Pearl, I want you to look me in the eye and tell me flat out. Has Frank James been here? Before you answer, I'd best tell you this Seminole, here, trailed him to within a country mile of Younger's Bend, and it's a sin to lie to the law."

"Before I answers, I got a question for you, sir. If I tell

you true, do I have your word it won't make trouble for my Mamma and Sam, here?" Pearl asked.

Belle gasped, "Pearl, you just *hesh*, hear?"

Rafe silenced her with a steel-eyed look and said, "You have my spoken word on that, Miss Pearl. Since he ain't here, sheltered with your folk, I see no call to arrest anyone living in this cabin, provided I get some straight answers. I can disremember what your mother and Sam told me just now. Everyone knows they ain't got much sense, but I'm waiting for *your* answer, honey. So what's it going to be?"

Pearl chose her words carefully before she said, "Uncle Frank did come by, earlier. He asked Mamma and Sam to shelter him as you suspicioned he might. Sam told him he couldn't stay here, so he left."

Rafe laughed and said, "What did I tell you, boys? The judge was right about this child. The chief, here, says he's on foot, too, so he won't get far."

Rafe turned back to Pearl, "You have my word that we won't trouble Sam and your mother, here, about the fibs they were just telling us. But I'd take it even kinder if you was to tell us which way he went when he left here, honey."

"Mention was made of the Ferndancer's cabin, sir. I hope you'll approach them peaceable, for Bob Ferndancer's not a fighting man, and there's a blind girl in that cabin."

Rafe nodded and said, "Come on, boys. I know Bob Ferndancer."

Nobody said anything until the lawmen had left. Then Belle said softly, "Don't you do it, Sam. It's a mother's duty to fix her, and I will, as soon as I can figure a punishment as fits such a crime!"

"Mamma, before you kill me, I sure wish you'd let me have my say," Pearl said.

Belle rose ominously and spat, "What can you say, girl, now that you've Judased a man who rode with your own father?"

"Mamma, I never Judased Uncle Frank. The law won't find him over to the Ferndancers. I told him it wasn't safe there. I never lied to that Rafe, but I 'spect I sent him on a wild goose chase."

"What do you mean you sent him on a wild goose chase, girl? If Frank James ain't at the Ferndancer's, where the hell is he?" demanded Belle.

"I carried him to Granny Redbird's, Mamma. He come willing. The spey woman took him in and put him to bed, and he was out like a light in two shakes of a rattlesnake's tail. I carried him there because the law knows the Ferndancer's is thick with us. I doubt they'll ever look for anyone at Granny Redbird's, though."

Sam Starr laughed, a startling sound from a man who laughed so seldom. Belle blinked a couple of times; then she laughed, too, a wild hysterical laugh of pure relief. She snatched Pearl up and hugged her tight, sobbing, "Oh, Sweet Jesus in the manger! You foxed us all, you sly little thing! You throwed the law off and put them in our debt without batting an eye nor telling one lie! I have never met anyone as sly as you, and you're my own true daughter!"

Later that year, they found out just how smart the daughter of Belle Starr was when a tall, lean man strode wearily, if boldly, into the governor's office in the state house at Jefferson City, Missouri. He placed a worn six-shooter on the bemused governor's desk and announced, "Governor Crittenden, not another living hand has touched that gun since 1861, but it's yours now. I have no more use for it."

The governor nodded soberly and said, "I thank you, sir. May I presume you are who you certainly appear to be?"

"Yes, sir. I've got a mite older since them reward posters was first put out, but I am Frank James and I'm here to get it over with," said the tall man.

The governor rose to shake his hand, saying, "Well, since you've surrendered like a gent I see no need for leg irons, but if it's all right with you, we'd best get some of the boys to carry you over to the jail. You have my spoken word on a fair trial, Frank James. I'm awfully sorry about what happened to your mother and younger brother, hear?"

Frank James stood trial for crimes too numerous to list in detail, and, as Pearl had foreseen, they couldn't find a jury of Missouri men who saw fit to convict the brother of their Robert E. Hood. Frank James walked free in the autumn sunlight at the age of thirty-nine.

Pearl's father, Cole Younger, stayed in prison.

6

BY THE TIME Pearl was sixteen she'd become the head-turning young beauty Belle had foreseen. Belle looked much the same, which meant that she was getting better-looking as she aged. Rural womankind faded all too soon. Unremitting toil, repeated pregnancies, together with poor dental and medical care made frontier women middle-aged by thirty. Yet, by the time Belle was thirty-five or so, the ugly duckling teen-ager of Scyene had become the swan among women her age.

Thanks to constant healthy exercise aboard a spirited mount, and far less time than usual bending over stove and scrub-board for a cabin full of demanding kin, her figure was still that of a young girl's. The capricious Mother Nature who'd given her plain features had blessed Belle with good teeth and a smooth complexion that weathered well, so the older she got, the better she looked to folk her own age.

Sam Starr wasn't improving with age. It was generally agreed that he held his drink well for an Indian, but he drank it in awesome quantity. Sam had never heard of Omar Khayyam, but he would have joined the Persian poet in wondering what the vintner bought that was better than he sold. Contraband alcohol passed through Sam's hands in unlimited quantities, and it seemed only natural to sample more than some. His once slim figure thickened and his once darkly handsome face began to take on the puffy look of a middle-aged heavy drinker, but it wasn't Sam's looks Belle worried about; it was the way he was in bed that vexed Belle so.

Sam was a sweet-natured gent and a generous husband, but he tended to just fall asleep and snore beside Belle. When they did make love, it wasn't like it once had been. Sam wasn't up to bedroom acrobatics and, fat as he was getting, one time, if that, was all he seemed up to.

So Sam Starr began to lose his only control over Belle's wilder nature, and if there was one thing Belle Starr needed, it was a common sense man to control her.

Their bootlegging operation was going well and they were prospering. However, Belle found it mighty tedious to break the law the same way day after infernal day. She thought of herself as a natural Amazon, having come from fighting stock, save for her weak-spined father. She didn't like to talk about her elder brother who'd died fighting with Captain Lane's Redlegs in the Border Wars when she was little, but she was proud of him. She was proud of other kin who had fought the Blue Bellies, too, and proud of the fighting son of a bitch who'd sired her daughter Pearl.

Sam was tolerable, she reckoned, but she wasn't sure she was all that proud of him. He had no imagination. He couldn't see a man with hair on his chest could make more money holding up one bank than a bootlegger made in a month of Sundays. But it wasn't just the money to be made on the Owlhoot Trail—Belle wanted action. A heap more loving wouldn't hurt her either, she was sure.

Time had also brought other changes to the settlement on Younger's Bend. President Arthur hadn't been as strict about Indian Affairs as folk expected. Except for a handful of Apaches in another part of the country, the Indians had been acting sensible since Little Big Horn, and Little Big Horn had been years back. President Arthur was more concerned with the new Alaska Territory, and the rebuilding of an obsolete navy. The only thing he did that had any effect on the Indian Nation was his demoralization of the B.I.A., which was due to his newfangled civil service notions. President Arthur expected folk to take written examinations to get a job with the government. Therefore, many men with considerable experience but little education lost their positions as Indian agents. They tended to be replaced by well-meaning gents who crossed every 'T' and dotted every 'I', but wouldn't know a Cherokee if they went to bed with one. This led to demographic changes in the Cherokee Strip.

Any Indian, or any white who's spent much time around Indians, can tell at a glance if a stranger has Indian blood in him or not. Blue eyes or yellow hair don't make no difference. If there's an Indian in the family tree this side of great-grandparents, folk who know Indians can tell. It's not a skill one can read from a book, for there's no way to put it in a book. The American Indian is a distant kinsman of the Siberian Mongol tribes with certain features which doubtless evolved when wandering over his own new continent. He doesn't look like an Oriental and he doesn't look like a European or African. He doesn't even look like other Indians of other tribal groupings. He can be tall and hawk-nosed like the Lakota, or squat and short of limb like a Comanche. His face can be shaped like a hatchet, or it can be round as a pumpkin, but once you know him, he always looks "Indian".

The new agents didn't know their wards. They'd read about them, and they knew as much or more about strange exotic tribal customs as many an assimilated Indian, but they couldn't spot an Indian or a 'breed at a glance. They had no idea that anyone could. The textbooks said that the Cherokee had been sort of fine-featured to begin with, and had interbred a lot with whites, so the professors said it wasn't unusual to meet a Cherokee 'breed who looked more Scotish-Irish than Indian. The professors were right, but a little knowledge is a dangerous toy. Many 'breeds dwelling in the Strip did look distinctly Celtic, Anglo-Saxon, or even

Negroid, whether they owned up to it or not, but more experienced Indian agents wouldn't have been fooled by some of the people moving back into the Strip as things got lax again.

The regulations said you had to be Indian or part Indian to settle on Indian lands. However, free land was getting harder to find as white homesteaders filled in the blank spaces on the survey maps, and many a man was hesitant about filing a regular homestead claim after having changed his given identity more than once. Indians didn't have to fill out infernal forms and pass muster with the flint-eyed lawmen haunting the land office in new territories. Indians just sort of squatted anywhere they had a mind to in the Indian Nation, and who was to say for certain who was Indian or not? Anybody could have an Indian grandmother. It was generally agreed that 'breeds were too dumb to keep records such as birth certificates. Therefore, people with names like Smith and Jones threw up cabins along the Arkansas, and if ever questioned, stared with innocent blue eyes at the inquisitive lawman and said, "Hell, 'course I'm a Cherokee! You reckon a man would brag on being an infernal redskin if he wasn't?"

Naturally, those white squatters tolerated in the neighborhood of Younger's Bend had to be approved by the local tribal council. Which is to say, they had to be able to get along with Sam and Belle Starr, who had their own arrangements with the thirstier members of the same. To get the Starrs' approval, one's complexion and bone structure was less important than one's views on life. Sam and Belle turned thumbs down on trash whites simply moving into the Indian Nation to grow turnips. Sam said he felt more comfortable around his own kind and, his own kind was any man, red or white, who found federal law a needless complication in an already complex world.

Across the line in Arkansas, the folk of Fort Smith grumbled about the "Robber's Roost" they felt Younger's Bend had become. Judge Parker said he had his eye on Younger's Bend but he didn't have the powers to arrest a body just for passing as a blue-eyed Cherokee, and it was up to the Indian Police to do something about Sam Starr getting all those real Indians drunk.

Some likkered-up Cherokee boys went on a wild rampage, robbing and raping and, even worse, running off some white folk's horses in broad daylight. Judge Parker's deputies rounded them up with the help of the Indian police, and when they appeared before him in his court in Fort Smith, he told them he didn't see being Indians cut much ice, and that since they'd been so ornery, they could hang like anyone else. He hung all five of them together on the same scaffold, on the same day. It was a scaffold Judge Parker was proud of. He'd had it built wide, so gangs could hang together as they'd ridden together, side by side.

Folks in Fort Smith said they'd never enjoyed such a grand public hanging before. The B.I.A., however, complained. They said Judge Parker was overstepping his authority in hanging their Indians. Judge Parker wrote back that, as the District Federal Judge, he'd hang anybody, red, white, or blue, that needed hanging. He reminded them that he wasn't Arkansas law, and that his federal jurisdiction extended into the federal lands of the Indian Nation So, if they didn't want their Indians hanged, they'd best make them behave.

Hanging Judge Parker didn't hold with the notion of "wild" Indians. He said Indians had just as much common sense as anyone else, and that everyone knew it was a crime to rob and rape and run off other folks' stock. He held it would be unfair discrimination not to hang a Cherokee or anyone else who had a hanging coming. Did they want folk to say he was a bigot?

Sam Starr warned Belle and his mixed bag of associates to walk the line, and not mix other pleasures with the family business lest they gain Judge Parker's attention and displeasure. A few years back Belle would have listened, but, though she still liked old Sam, she wasn't sure he was worthy of her respect any more.

One night Sam Starr went out to sell white lightning by the light of the moon. Belle was alone with Pearl when a soft-spoken, good-looking stranger knocked on their door. As they coffeed him, the stranger introduced himself as Reed Waddell from Illinois, but hastened to add he'd been too young to ride in the war on either side, and that his kin had been Copperheaded in any case.

Belle was taken with the smooth-talking stranger, but Pearl wasn't sure about him. He looked refined, and could likely talk the horns off a billygoat, but there was something sneaky about his eyes, even though he met one's gaze directly.

After they'd coffeed and caked polite a spell, Belle nodded at the two big carpet bags their guest had placed on the floor just inside the door. She said, "I hope you didn't tote them bags all this way afoot, Mister Waddell. I disremember hearing you ride up on any brute."

Waddell laughed easily and answered, "My, ah, borrowed pony foundered and had to be left behind, Miss Belle. It didn't worry me as much as it might, had I paid money for him and the saddle."

"You just borrowed a mount wherever you found one handy, eh? Well, it's your neck. What can we do for you, Reed Waddell?" asked Belle.

"Well, I met a young gent named Dalton a while back who said you was a smart businesswoman, Miss Belle. You know Grat Dalton, over to Cass County, Missouri?"

"I've heard mention of the Dalton boys. Can't say I think much of 'em. They're just a mess of trashy kids, but I reckon they'll grow. What did young Grat Dalton say about my business, Reed Waddell?"

"Oh, just that you're too smart to turn down a good deal on technical grounds. I'll lay my cards on the table, Miss Belle. I'm on the dodge and I feel a hankering for travel. I need money and a fresh mount."

"I figured you might. Pearl, dear, why don't you run over to the Ferndancer cabin and see if Blind Alice would like to play with you?"

"Mamma, I'm growed past the years of playing, and you know what Sam says about fencing."

"Do as I say, girl. You mind your fences and I'll mind

mine. This is growed-up talk we're having and, no offense, you ain't that growed, even if you are sixteen."

Pearl left reluctantly, and Belle smiled at her visitor.

"Everybody needs money, and you told me why you need a horse. Can I take it you have something to show me in them carpet bags, Reed Waddell?"

Reed got up, grinning, and brought the bags to the table. He took out what looked like a gold brick and said, "This is what I usually sell. It's a family keepsake from my uncle who died of the ague in the mother lode country out west. See the official assay office mark, here? If you want, you can dig into it with my penknife and you'll find it's pure gold, deep as you can dig her."

Belle dimpled girlishly, delighted to meet up with such a rascal after talking so long to laconic illiterates.

"I'd admire buying your gold brick if it wasn't gold-plated lead, Reed Waddell. I know all about the plug of digging out bullion you've got stuck in that pot metal. I'm sore vexed with that silly Dalton kid if he told you I was stupid as well as mortal plain!"

Waddell laughed again. "He told me you were slick, and now that we've met, I'm telling you that you're a handsome woman. Don't go fishing for compliments, honey."

"Don't you call me sweet names, you fool Yankee! It'd take more than sweet nothings whispered in my shelly ears to get me to buy an infernal fake gold brick!" Belle said.

"Good God, you didn't think I wanted to sell you this treasure, did you, Belle? I was just showing you how I generally make my way in this hard world. I wanted you to know it's safe to deal with me. A man caught with a forged federal assay mark on him could go to jail in a clap of thunder. You want to see the die I had made up to mark my pot metal bricks?"

"No. I'll take your word for it that you're a crook. Get to the real deal, Reed Waddell."

He opened the other carpet bag, cascading silverware onto the table in the lamplight.

"This stuff's too heavy for me to carry far, but I swear as a gentleman of the road it's the real McCoy. I sometimes burgle houses as a sideline, when the confidence game is slow. I took this total silver service from a quality house in the county of Conway as I was wending my weary way west. This silver's worth real money, Belle."

"It's hot as hell's hinges, too! The county Conway is just down the infernal river, you fool!" Belle said with a frown. Reed Waddell replied, "Oh, come now, it's over a hundred miles, counting bends in the trail. At the risk of jewing myself down, it's standard pattern Community Plate with no family monograms or anything. The folks who used to own it couldn't swear for sure it was theirs if you served 'em supper with it. I'll let you have it cheap, and it's pure sterling, Belle."

"It sure is pretty, but I have to study on this. I know if *I* lost a set like this I'd let out a right loud howl, Reed Waddell."

He nodded and said, "They did. They even put it in the papers about their house being burgled whilst they was to Church, but there's nothing connecting you or any of your pals to such far-off country, Belle. Hell, you could serve Sunday dinner on it, and did anyone ask, you could say you sent for it from Community Plate like any other law-abiding gal. I'll throw in a bill of sale as says so. I carry all sorts of writing materials against such emergencies."

"Put it back in the bag and follow me out back so's we can hide it and see about a horse and Morgan saddle for you. The horse is lawful, but don't brag on the saddle 'til you're at least as far as the Choctaw Strip. I'll throw in ten silver dollars whilst I'm at it," Belle said.

"You drive a hard bargain, Belle," Reed grumbled.

She said, "Watch your step. It's dark out here. Don't step in horse shit and don't try to horse shit me, old son. I'm making you a generous offer and you know it."

"Belle, you'll get over a hundred for that silver, damn it."

"If I can sell it at all. It'll have to set a spell and cool some afore I dast try. The horse you're getting is worth at least twenty and the saddle would cost more, if you bought it off its original owner, so you're getting way more than the ten percent a burglar generally gets. Why are you fussing so? You never paid one dime for that silver, and once you're out of here, your worries about it are over and mine has just begun."

They got to the stable. It was even darker inside. Belle groped for a burlap feed sack and told him, "Here, put the silver in here whilst I saddle Old Blaze for you, unless you'd rather forget the whole deal. It's no never mind to me."

Reed dropped the bags, took her in his arms, and said, "We got a deal, honey. Let's seal the bargain with a kiss."

Belle gasped and began to struggle without thinking. Then she wondered why on earth she wanted to do a fool thing like that, so they kissed hard and passionately. Reed Waddell seemed to have forgotten what they'd come out there to do as he lowered her to the hay in the corner and ran his free hand down her trembling flanks.

"My, that velvet sure feels nice. I admires what you got under it, too," he said.

"Watch them hands, damn it. I ain't wearing nothing under this riding habit!"

"That's what I meant. Are you in the habit of riding much, honey?"

"I ain't your honey. I'm old enough to be your mother, and a married woman besides, and what do you mean by hauling up my skirts like that and . . . Oh, Jesus, stop teasing me so and just get on with it!"

He moved her skirts up around her slender waist, unbuttoned himself, and mounted her. Belle hissed in surprised pleasure as he entered her hungry flesh. The handsome white stranger was hung better than Sam.

As he started moving within her, Reed Waddell was pleasantly surprised as well. He'd been with no kind of woman at all for some time. Reed Waddell was a man who took from the world as he found it, and expected it to pay him back someday with a bullet. He wasn't given to speculation about his suckers, but if this one was a sucker, she sure was enjoying it. As she wrapped her slender limbs about him and dug her nails into his bare buttocks it wasn't clear who was being victimized more. Like most two-faced men, Waddell was a skilled lover. Belle couldn't get enough of him, and, for a time, she didn't. They climaxed repeatedly in the dew-damp hay; thrice for him and four times for Belle as he began to slow down.

Finally, he said, "Have mercy on me, honey. I fear I'm not the man I was when we came in here a million years ago."

Belle sighed, "That was lovely. Why does everything nice have to end so soon, Reed?"

"Don't know, but it always seems to. I tried to keep eating oysters at Delmonico's one night. Just wound up sick, long before I'd swallowed all the oysters in the sea. But look at her this way. Wouldn't it be awful if we ever did eat our way all the way to the bottom of life's pleasures?"

He started to withdraw and rise from her, but Belle held him tightly and pleaded, "Don't. Not yet. I'll let you go directly, but stay like this and let the old earth turn under us a spell. Where are you headed from here, Reed?"

"Ain't sure," he answered. "The world's a mighty big place, and I mean to see as much of her as I can before they pat my face flat with the shovel. I may go on out to Frisco. I may go to Paris. I won't go to Naples, 'cause I don't mean to see Naples and die just yet."

Then, because he had a gallant streak and was a good judge of human nature, he kissed her gently and added, "I sure wish you could come with me, Belle."

She sighed and said, "Oh, if only I could, but my daughter needs a loving mother's care, so I reckon I'd best not run off with you."

"Well, I'll just have to think of the child, too," he said, and a merciful darkness hid his mocking eyes from the woman in his arms. He moved experimentally as thoughts Pearl's mother wouldn't have approved of inspired him.

Damn, that kid was good-looking, and built even nicer than her mother! He wondered if they were both built the same down there between the legs. He knew the apple didn't fall far from the tree, and if that little dark blonde was any tighter it would be downright dangerous to do this to her. So he started doing it to her mother some more, and Belle was delighted.

She asked, "Do you really want more of me, Reed? Do you really . . . fancy me?"

He said, "You know I did from the beginning, honey."

"Oh, go on, you're joshing me. I know what you needs. I needed it, too, more than I thought I did, but you don't really *like* me all that much."

He moved faster, gasping, "Does that feel like I'm feeling pure hate for you, lover kitten? You gals can fake it, but you know us poor brutes has to feel something for a gal to do it to her like this!"

They went crazy in each others arms again for a time, and when it ended, Belle let him go.

She saddled Old Blaze for him and he kissed her one last time before he rode out into the moonlight and out of Belle's life forever. She knew she'd never forget him. He'd called her his lover kitten. Not even Cole had ever sweet-talked her so.

Belle was smiling to herself as she went back to the house after hiding the silver.

She still felt wistful about the man she'd sped on his way just now, but he'd taught her a grand new notion.

It was true nobody could ever eat all the oysters in the sea, and it seemed impossible that even Cleopatra could make love to all the men in pants, but there seemed to be a tolerable supply of both, and it hadn't scared her at all to tear off a quick casual piece whilst her lazy old Sam was off somewhere on business. Boys who got to love a woman up now and again did what she wanted them to, too. She'd just see who gave the orders around these parts, now! She'd noticed more than one of the gang admiring her discreetly. She'd have to be discreet, too. Not only would Sam have to be kept in the dark, but everyone else enjoying her favors would have to be led to think he was the only one, save Sam, who had such privileges. But hell, she was a white gal and she'd had eight years schooling at the Carthage Female Academy. She knew she could slicker a mess of ignorant men-folk. Even the Daltons over to Missouri allowed she was foxy.

Pearl had come back from the Ferndancers while Belle was outside. Pearl said, "Alice was already fixing to bed down for the night, Mamma. How did things go with that city slicker?"

"Tolerable, daughter, tolerable. I gave him what he needed and sent him on his way."

Pearl smiled wanly and said, "I can see you feel you got the best part of him, for you look downright radiant, Mamma."

Belle started laughing hysterically as Pearl stared soberly at her. Pearl didn't see what her mamma was laughing about. She hadn't said anything all that funny, had she? ∾

7

IN TIME TO come, Pearl would read with some surprise how the notorious inventor of the Gold Brick Game would meet his end in Paris, France, while playing cards with a gent who disputed his sincerity. The man who gunned Reed Waddell must have been surprised, too, when they guillotined him. His name was Tom O'Brian, and even if they did settle things "à la Dodge City" in Paris, Pearl would feel sorry for O'Brien. No matter who he'd been, anyone who shot Reed Waddell couldn't be all bad. She'd never forgiven Reed Waddell for what he'd done to Mamma.

It was the silver he'd left with Belle that made her so angry. For, of course, Belle got caught when she tried to sell it. The quality folk who'd owned it had posted a No-Questions-Asked reward on the family plate.

Reed Waddell had slickered Belle in a way they didn't teach one at the Carthage Female Academy. The silver was real, all too real. It was not the inexpensive Community Plate brand Reed had described in his desperation to be rid of it. So, since the reward totaled more than the value of the silver as bullion to its sentimental owners, the pawnbroker Belle sold it to turned her in after she'd left, of course.

A posse rode out from Fort Smith loaded for bear and spoiling for a fight. They didn't get their fight, so as long as they were out there, they decided they would arrest Sam as well. They wanted to arrest Pearl, but Rafe told them to leave her be.

The kindly deputy warned Pearl not to follow, but she saddled up old Venus and trailed after them anyway. By the time they had Sam and Belle Starr booked and locked up for the night, Pearl had located a lawyer. However, the lawyer wouldn't touch the case with a ten-foot pole.

"Being as they carried the stolen property across a state line, Miss Pearl, that makes it a federal case, and I don't take federal cases. It's tedious losing, and I've never gotten anyone off in Judge Parker's court yet, unless they were innocent. You're not going to look me in the eye and say your mamma didn't carry that silver into that hock shop, are you?"

Pearl tried other lawyers. A couple asked outrageous prices, and one tried to kiss her, and they all agreed that Belle and Sam were in one hell of a mess. Finally, Pearl went to see Judge Parker.

She found him at home, and he invited her into his front parlor and offered her some tea. However, when she told him he had to let her mamma and Sam go, he simply sighed.

"Miss Pearl, you're older than you were the last time we talked, but I'm talking to you just the same, as a minor. What you're trying to do is to compromise the law. You're not supposed to come to a judge social like this with legal matters. I haven't had time to study the case, but it looks like we have 'em red-handed, so anything you have to say for or agin 'em should be said on the stand, with you sworn by the court."

Then, taking pity on her confused misery, he added, "Well, as long as you're here, I'll hear you out, unofficial."

Pearl said, "Your honor, Sam don't even know about that silver, and Mamma never stole it. The man who burgled them quality folk was named Reed Waddell. I can tell on him because he bamboozled poor Mamma. He told her it was just cheap stuff. We didn't know the folks who'd owned it would set such store on it."

"They set store on it indeed. You've no notion how glad they were to get it back. I pointed out this afternoon that the pawnbroker wasn't in such a grand position to pester them for any reward, considering some of the things he's handled in the past, if we could prove it. So, if it's any comfort, they likely won't see fit to come all the way over here from Conway County for the trial. That gives me a little leeway."

Pearl brightened. "Oh, does that mean you can let them go?"

"Not hardly, child. The owners of the stolen property haven't dropped the charge entire. There's their written deposition to satisfy. There's the newspapers to satisfy, too. I can't just turn them loose. There's got to be *some* infernal law and order in these parts, and we all know your folk are guilty of everything but the whooping cough!"

Pearl pleaded, "But Your Honor, sir, they never stole that silver! Sam didn't even know Mamma swapped that skunk an old plug horse for what she thought was a trifle."

Judge Parker frowned soberly at her and said, "Miss Pearl, we're not going to be friends much longer if you try to wool my eyes like that. I'm taking it as a favor that you told me who the burglar was. I'm taking your word that your folks didn't steal the stuff, but don't you go trying to tell me Belle Starr thought that stuff was tin. And don't you try to tell me she didn't know it was stolen property, neither. It's agin the law to receive stolen property, Miss Pearl. You do see how I'm duty bound to slap them on their wrists a mite, don't you?"

"I reckon, Judge Parker. What . . . What are you aiming to do to them?" Pearl said with a sigh.

"Well, if they waive trial by jury, which would be mighty sensible of them in these parts, I can hear the case in my chambers. If they pleads no contest, I can give them the least the law allows. I can't tell you what that is ahead of the trial, but, take it from me, I could make it worse."

Pearl put her teacup down and stammered, "You won't

. . . put them away, will you, sir? I don't know what I'd do if you locked my mamma up!"

"I want you to appear early in my court on the morrow, Pearl. I want you there whilst I finish some business, before your folks appear before me. Things might go a lot smoother if you talk to them before we get down to formalities. Will you do that for us all, Miss Pearl?"

She nodded and he said, "Good. You'll be staying here tonight. I'll direct you to the guest room. In the morning we'll go over to the courthouse after breakfast. You're not afraid to stay here, are you?"

"No, sir. I know you're not as mean a man as folks let on," Pearl said.

Judge Parker rose and rang for the maid. "I know what you think of me, child, and I find it flattering as well as a mite inaccurate. That's why I want you in my court ahead of time on the morrow, Miss Pearl. It's time we got to know each other better."

Judge Isaac Parker's voice was flat and unemotional as he stared at the young man standing before his bench between two armed bailiffs.

"It is the judgement of this court, James Taylor Crawford, that you be taken from this court to your appointed place of execution, and there you are to be hanged by the neck until you are pronounced dead. May God have mercy on your soul. Next case."

Pearl's eyes were as wide of those of the young cowhand who'd gone wrong. As the bailiffs started to lead him away, he twisted free and fell to his knees on the floor, calling out, "Please, Your Honor, I'm too young to die!"

Judge Parker answered softly, "That boy you gunned in the back wasn't much older, son. None of us feel old enough to die when the time comes, and your time has come, so go with these gents and take it like a man."

"Do I have to die today, Judge? Can't it wait a spell?"

Isaac Parker shook his head and said, "It'll hurt just as much in a month. The court sees no call to feed you another day at the taxpaying public's expense. You go along, now, son. You've had your say and been found guilty by a jury of your peers. You're just wasting your time and mine, for you killed a man in cold blood and the time has come to pay for it."

He nodded to the bailiffs. They dragged the weeping young murderer to his feet and out a side door, still screaming for mercy, as Judge Parker studied the papers on his bench and mused aloud, "Let's see, now. That cow thief can wait until this afternoon, and what's this molestation case doing on the calendar? I dismissed that case. All right, bailiffs, clear the court, save for that young lady there. We're holding the next hearing no contest, and private."

The jury box was already empty, but there was the usual modest courtroom crowd of folk who seemed to have nothing better to do but to listen to the trials. As the bailiffs began to herd them out, a distraught looking, middle-aged woman pushed her way forward around a bailiff and cried, "You can't dismiss my complaint, Judge Parker! That nigger trifled with me and you can't throw it out of court!"

One of the bailiffs moved toward the woman, but Parker shook his head and said soberly, "I can and I just did, Miss Hanks. You had no case against that colored man who crossed the Sandy Branch bridge whilst you was swimming nekked in the creek. As I told you at the last hearing, a colored man has the same rights as any other to use a public bridge."

"He didn't just use the bridge, Your Honor. He used my fair white body shameful. I feel he raped me with his eyes!" the woman cried.

Judge Parker repressed whatever he felt about her grotesque charge as he said, "That just isn't possible for any man to do, Miss Hanks. The rail of that bridge is a good twenty yards or more from where you say you was splashing about like a sea lion. He might have stared some, if he crossed a bridge on his way to work and saw a nekked woman in the creek like you say, but most men would have, black or any other color. Staring at ladies who appear in public wearing nothing but their nekked hide ain't a crime.

Indecent exposure is, but even that ain't a federal offense. So let's all just say no more about it."

The woman wailed, "I've more than plenty to say about it, you carpetbagging rascal! It may mean nothing to you if a nigger buck rapes a white woman with his eyes! My husband fell for the South at Pittsburgh Landing and I demand justice!"

"All right. I wanted to drop this tedious nonsense to save the expense and bother of a trial, so here's how we'll do her. My bailiffs will carry you over to the jail, pending your sanity hearing. A couple of medical men won't cost us as much as a jury, and that colored man you charged has already lost a day's work. Putting you away as a lunatic will save us all a lot of bother," the judge said.

Sue Ellen Hanks looked like she'd been whipped across the face with a wet catfish. "Lunatic? I ain't no lunatic!"

"I know what you are, but lunaticing you saves time and trouble. You said you demanded justice, so justice you shall get. You'll get out of the lunatic asylum in a few months if you behave yourself, Mrs. Hanks. If I wanted to go to all the trouble of a perjury trial I'd have to give you a year and a day. That's what the law allows for perjury."

Mrs. Hanks stared wall-eyed and dumbfounded at him.

The judge explained, "Perjury is when you lie to the court under oath, Mrs. Hanks."

"I never lied to anybody, Judge. That nigger wronged me like I said!"

"There you go doing it again, Mrs. Hanks. You see, when you-all appeared before me the other day I knew somebody had to be lying, so I had the marshal and his deputies check out both your tales. At the time you say that colored man was ogling you so, which ain't a federal offense in the first place, he was three country miles away working for Captain Ferris, which means you told this court a whopper."

Sue Ellen Hanks looked uneasy and offered, "Well, mayhaps I mixed that Silas up with some other nigger, then. You-all know they looks alike to us white folk."

"Nice try," Judge Parker said, "but my deputies already

considered that. I asked you in court if you were dead certain the man you accused was the right colored man, and you seemed mighty certain at the time. My boys tell me there's no other coloreds living on the far side of that bridge near your property line. The local law tells me they know of no stray colored men just wandering about Fort Smith, since they discourage such. Whilst my boys was investigating, they found out some other things, Mrs. Hanks. I sort of wondered what a woman of your age and looks might be doing swimming nekked near a public highway in broad day, no offense. So they asked around about your neck of the woods. You have never in living memory gone swimming in said creek before, nekked or no. Furthermore, it's a matter of public record that you asked the accused colored hand to hay your north forty with that mower he drives for Captain Ferris, and that he refused you. So, when you dig to the bottom of the dung pile, Mrs. Hanks, what we have here is a spiteful-hearted woman trying to make trouble for what she considered an uppity colored man. I know some folks hereabouts haven't grasped it yet, but colored folk don't have to work for you agin their will any more, Mrs. Hanks. They tell me Captain Ferris rode for the South, too. Yet he told us the colored man you accused was a decent cuss, and that you paid shameful if at all, and that said colored hand was mowing the Ferris hay at the time besides. So that's why I'm sending you to the lunatic asylum until you can manage to control your nerves better."

He nodded and a bailiff dragged Sue Ellen Hanks out, kicking and screaming like they were going to hang her, too. Judge Parker nodded again and said, "I'm ready for the Starrs, now."

As they waited, he told Pearl what he wanted her to do. When Sam and Belle were led in, Pearl went to her mother and murmured, "You come and sit by my side, Mamma. Judge Parker says it'll go easier on us all if he and Sam do all the talking."

Belle was surprised to find her daughter in court, but she was in a defiant mood.

"Sam don't talk as good as me. I know the law and I got the right to speak out, damn it!" she said.

Pearl grabbed her petite mother by both shoulders. Belle had noticed Pearl had grown to her height, but she was surprised at her strength as she whirled her around, sat her down in a chair near the front of the courtroom and blazed, "Mamma, for God's sake just sit still and hesh! That man has powers, and he ain't as soft as I thought he might be! I've already spoke to the judge for you. Just set quiet and don't go digging yourself deeper with your crazy talk, hear?"

Belle stared up at Pearl in wonder and asked, "What's come over you, child?"

"I'm not a child, God damn it! I'm a woman growed and the only one in this family who acts like one! I swear to you, Mamma, I'll have to lick you if you get sassy with me and the judge!"

Belle laughed. "You sure sound serious, girl. I doubt like hell you could lick me, but I'll set out the first cards."

Judge Parker had been listening. As Pearl sat down by her mother and held her hand, Parker called Sam over to the bench. The burly Indian's face was "cigar store," for Sam was still mighty confused as to what in thunder was going on here.

"Sam Starr, there's a debt to society to be paid here. I'll go easy as the law allows if you agree to waive trial by jury and throw yourself on the mercy of this court. Do you follow my drift?" the judge asked.

"I reckon I do part way, Judge, but would somebody tell me the infernal charge?" replied Sam.

"Receiving of stolen property. To wit, a silver service, a Morgan saddle, and some other odds and ends we may as well get off the books."

Belle called out, "Your men never found that Morgan saddle at our spread, God damn it, Your Honor!"

Judge Parker said, "It was stolen, though. I said I wanted to make a clean sweep of this case. Do as your daughter says, Belle. Keep quiet whilst Sam and I settle up."

He turned back to Sam Starr and said, "Sam, I'm sending you and Belle away for six months. That's the best offer I can make you. If you don't want to accept the sentence, you can demand a regular trial, but we both know what a jury picked from Fort Smith would do to a Cherokee living with a white gal, don't we?"

Sam frowned, "Belle ain't living with me, damn it. We're married up proper. How come we can't be tried in the Strip by my own people?"

"More than one reason, Sam. The stuff was stole by a white man, and given to a white woman to fence. On top of that, we all know your tribal court would find you not guilty, and I'd hate to see you lynched when word of that got about."

Sam shook his head stubbornly and said. "Damn it, Judge, we ain't guilty! I don't know a damn thing about the stuff you say we had!"

Belle said, "He's telling you true, Judge Parker. Sam knew nothing about my, ah, egg money notions."

Judge Parker said, "I told you to stay out of this, Belle." Parker then explained to Sam, "I don't know if you were in on it or not, Sam. It don't matter. That's the advantage of these discretionary hearings. You see, Sam, you folk owes the government a year in jail for acting as receivers of stolen goods. By giving you both six months, it adds up to a year in jail and you're both out six months sooner than either could be if you was to do the year alone."

Sam frowned down at his feet and growled, "It still don't sound fair to me. I never *done* nothing, damn it."

Judge Parker nodded sympatheticaly, and said, "I know, Sam. It's my fond hope you'll settle that up private with your woman in times to come. I reckon some could hold my notions of justice ain't always fair, but they sure seem to work. Since you ain't got a lawyer, I'm duty-bound to tell you that you could stand trial and likely get off scot-free if you was to witness against your woman, but . . ."

"Hold on one cotton picking minute!" Belle protested. "I knows my law. The law says you can't make no husband witness agin his own wife!"

Judge Parker nodded and agreed. "That's true, Belle. The jails are filled with folk who know the law. We ain't talking law. We're talking common sense. If Sam here means to defend himself agin the charge in open court, the only way he can do so is to say he didn't do it. That leaves you holding the bag lonesome. That means you wind up with a year in jail. Are you listening to me, Sam Starr?"

Sam nodded silently. Pearl piped up, "What if you was to let me go shares with my folk. Your Honor? If you split the year we owe three ways, we'd all be out in four months, right?"

Judge Parker laughed. "That's a right generous offer, Miss Pearl, but let's not get downright silly!"

"Why not, Your Honor? I'm just as guilty as poor Sam, since neither of us knew about the stolen goods."

"That well may be, Miss Pearl, but this is the Federal District Court of Fort Smith, not a minstrel show! Besides, I'm sure your mother doesn't want a girl of your tender years to go to jail, if I was crazy enough to send you there. Ain't that right, Belle?"

Belle said, "You know it is. I don't want her in jail and I don't want Sam in jail. I'll take your infernal year and we'll say no more about it."

Judge Parker looked at the silent Indian and asked, "That all right with you, Sam?"

Sam Starr shook his head and said, "No. Hear me, if I can work off half my woman's debt, I just remembered Belle did make some mention to me of that stuff. You'd better give me this six months after all. I have spoken."

Belle rose, went over to Sam and sobbed, "Oh, honey, don't do it. *I* was the one who done wrong."

Sam said, quietly, "I know, and we'll talk about it when we get out. I said I'd spoken, woman. We're ready, Judge."

Judge Parker nodded and decreed, "All right, then. It is the judgement of this court that you, Sam Starr, and you, Belle Starr, shall serve six months at hard labor for the criminal offense of receiving stolen goods, and this case is closed. You can have five minutes in my chambers together afore you go your separate ways. You can join your folks if you like, Miss Pearl. I'm holding you responsible for my furniture, hear?"

It was dire lonesome, yet oddly peaceful out at the spread that night as Pearl supped alone. Judge Parker had offered to board her until Mamma and Sam got out, but she'd said it hardly seemed right to accept charity from the man who'd put her kin in jail. Besides, Sam had told her to tell the boys to lay low and not move any jars of alcohol until he got out again. Pearl knew that even if she couldn't run the bootlegging, she'd still be needed out here to tend the stock and see that nothing was missing when the folks came home. Judge Parker had said it wasn't right for a young she-male to dwell alone out here, but she'd told him that was a mighty odd thing for him to worry on, considering it was all his doing.

She'd nearly finished eating when there came a knock on the door. It was Creek Alice. The blind girl said she felt just awful about all as had happened, and wanted to know if there was anything she could do to help.

Pearl sat her down for coffee and dessert and said, "You can stay and keep me company if you like. I don't mind saying that dwelling alone takes some getting used to. This is the first time I've ever been alone, and the cabin seems bigger and sort of hollow-like tonight."

"I can spend the night with you, if you'd like. My Dad says it's all right. I asked afore I come over. I figured you might be spooked," Alice said.

Pearl reached across the table and took her friend's hand as she smiled and said, "That would be mighty neighborly of you, Alice. I know there's naught to be afeared of, but having you here will be a comfort when the night noises start up. Ain't it odd how the night noises spook one just as you're halfways asleep?"

Alice shrugged and said, "I wouldn't know. I hear the same noises day or night. How come you sighted folk are so scared of the night, Pearl? If seems a mite cooler and quieter the times you folk call night, but I don't notice much difference."

"I can see how you wouldn't, Alice. That's why I'm glad you come so thoughtful. Your ears are even better than mine when it comes to hearing things one can't see. Betwixt us, we should be more than a match for the night noises."

As she poured more coffee, Pearl frowned, cocked her head, and said, "Thunderation! Speaking of night noises, listen to that!"

Alice said, "It's a courting flute. Sounds like that fool Sequanna. He only knows that one tune."

"It *is* Sequanna, damn it! He must have heard about Sam going to jail already. Sam has told him more than once not to pester me, but Sam won't be around for the next six months! You reckon I could get your father to talk to Sequanna, Alice?"

"I don't know, Pearl. We can ask him, but Sequanna's sort of big, and I fear my dad's not a fighting man. Why don't you get one of your father's tougher hands to run Sequanna off for you, Pearl?"

"Oh, sure," Pearl said, "and then what would I do after I owed him and *he* come courting me with a turkey bone flute? I got to study on this, Alice. There's more to this being a woman alone than I considered when I talked so sassy to Judge Parker. He said my blonde hair could make life complex here in the Cherokee Strip."

"Your hair don't feel much different from mine, Pearl. It's a mite finer is all. What's your hair got to do with you dwelling alone out here?"

"It shows from a quarter-mile away I'm a white gal. As Judge Parker explained it, being white's no mortal sin, but folks tend to think poorly of a white gal living amongst Indians. He says many a man feels a white trash gal is fair game, pretty or not, and I'm better-looking than most trash gals, so it's even worse."

Alice smiled and said, "Shoot, Pearl, your folks are tied up with a tolerable sized gang. Any man who raped you would likely get hisself gunned."

"A lot of good that'd do me if Sam's friends gunned him *afterwards*! I don't mind telling you, I wish right now I had black hair like you, Alice. My own hair's getting darker as I age, but it's still too noticeable that I ain't no Cherokee. Now that I study on some of the whites dwelling amongst them out here, I see better what Judge Parker meant. I ain't so worried about the folks hereabouts who know me, but someone just passing through can get the wrong notions, and we're right off the trail, so lots of strange riders pass."

Alice said, "I sure hope you don't get raped. Do you figure Sequanna is studying on raping you whilst your step-dad ain't here to stop him, Pearl?"

Pearl said, "I ain't sure what Sequanna's planning. I doubt he knows either. Sam has always said Sequanna ain't got sense to pour sand outten his boots. I've never given that fool boy any encouragement, and he's been pestering me since I was flat-chested! What do you reckon's wrong with him, anyway?"

Alice answered, "Mayhaps he's in love with you, Pearl. He told Charlie Bluefeather he was. I heard my folks talking about it. It seems that one day as you was passing, Charlie Bluefeather passed a remark about the way you was starting to fill the back of your skirts. He just meant it joshing, but Sequanna was there, and he took it mighty Cherokee. He pulled a knife on Charlie and said if he didn't take it back he'd skin his liver out, so Charlie did. Sequanna said he'd kill any man present who ever trifled with you. He said it like you was spoken for to him."

Pearl grimaced and said, "Oh, Lord, I didn't know he was that crazy. What am I to do if that fool Indian comes knocking on yon door, Alice?"

Alice answered, "He won't. That's not the Cherokee way. You has to invite him to come closer. That's why he's standing out there in the night air tooting like an old owl bird on his courting flute. He's hoping to be noticed."

Pearl said, "Oh, botheration, how am I to deal with him? If I go out in the dark and tell him to hesh up, he'll likely reckon I'm noticing him. If I don't, he's likely to keep us awake half the night with that damned noise. I surely wish he'd at least play another tune once in a while. How would you make him stop, Alice? You're Cherokee; at least half, that is."

Alice shrugged and said, "There's naught we womenfolk can do about boys acting like that. I suspicion that's why they do it. I got a boy pestering me of late. Lucky for me, he don't know how to play one of them old-fashioned turkey bone flutes. He just follows me about like a coyote. Leastways, they say he does. I can't see the fool."

Pearl smiled, surprised but pleased that her blind friend's affliction hadn't gotten in the way of her being so pretty after all. She said, "You never told me you had a beau, Alice. Who is he? Do I know him?"

Alice said, "You might. He's Freddy Brown, and he's a Creek, like my mamma. My dad told him to stay away from me, but Freddy follows me about anyway, when my dad's not around."

Pearl didn't answer. She knew who the Browns were.

"Why do you suppose my dad's so agin Freddy Brown, Pearl? Dad says it's 'cause he's a Creek, but that don't make much sense to me. I know Cherokee and Creek was enemies back east, but that was long ago. Besides, my dad married up with the Creek gal who bore me. How can a man admire one Creek enough to marry up with her, yet tell another Creek to leave his half-Creek daughter be?" Alice asked.

Pearl hesitated, wondering if it was her place to have a say in the matter. But Alice was her friend, and she'd asked. Pearl said, "Well, honey, there are Creeks and then there's Creeks. Let's say the Browns took in more runaways than your mamma's band. I'll take the Brown's word that they're Creek Indians, but, to the eye, they look mighty colored."

"Oh, you mean Freddy Brown's a nigger?"

"Don't know what he is, Alice. But that's what he looks like."

"Oh. Well, is he nice looking? What does he look like, Pearl? It feels so odd to have a boy courting you when you can't see him worth mention."

Pearl said, "I can see how that might fluster one. Let's

see, now. I know it's a waste of time for me to tell you he has blacker skin than most Indians. His hair ain't woolly. It's sort of curly-like. He's tall and built sort of slim. I reckon you could say he was nice-looking in his own way. He's always been polite to me in passing, and he has a nice open smile. He dresses neat and cowboy. He has a beaded hatband and don't pack a gun about the settlement. Carries a bowie in his belt, of course. They say he's a decent cuss. His older brother sometimes drives for Sam. We don't know Freddy all that well."

Alice boasted, "My mamma says he is a cowboy. He herds for the Bar Seven and draws a dollar a day as a top hand."

"Yep. That's what I heard, too. He's got an honest job, for a Brown."

They sat in silence for a time as, out in the darkness, Sequanna serenaded them with sounds more suitable for haunting houses. Pearl asked Alice if she wanted more coffee.

The blind girl said, "No, thanks. If what you tell me of that fool Creek's true, Pearl, I sure wonder what's gotten into my dad. Freddy sounds tolerable enough to me. A gal like me could do worse than a tall, good-looking, honest cowhand, you know."

"I can see how your choice might be limited, Alice, but the boy is colored. Don't that bother you?"

"No. I know you think I'm stupid, Pearl, but I still don't know what in thunder being colored or even being Indian means! I know you're white, and I'm red, and Freddy's black, but what do them words mean to a *blind* gal? I've tried all my life to figure out what these color words mean, and I've never done her yet. Mamma says apples is red and grass is green. I vow I know the difference betwixt an apple and a blade of grass. They feel different and smell different and they taste different. But *folk* ain't like apples and grass. So if this mysterious color business makes folk all different, I'm surely missing something. You take you and me, now. You say you're white and I'm Indian. All right, I know you wouldn't lie to me, Pearl, but I'm sore vexed to fathom what makes us different. I mean, sure, you're named Pearl and I'm named Alice and we have different folk and all, but that's where I lose the trail. We're about the same size and shape, far as I can tell without getting personal with my hands. Our hair and clothes feel about the same and besides, you told me once that if we swapped dresses you'd still be white and I'd still be Indian. But what is so different about us, then? You surely feel and smell more like me than my own father, but you say he's what you call an Indian, too! Now you say a boy who favors me can't, 'cause he's some other infernal color thing! Oh, it makes me so vexed I could spit!" the blind girl cried.

Pearl got up and put her arms around her bewildered chum as she soothed, "Don't cry, Alice. Your folk are trying to do what they feel is best for you, hear?"

"Don't *I* have any say in the matter, durn it? I've never had no beau before, and you say he's pretty!"

"There, there, now. We'll study on this, Alice. Your Freddy ain't out there this evening, so he won't get away afore I've had a chance to sleep on it. I can see how this looks to your kin. I can see how it must seem to you, too. Damn men, why do they make us womenkind do all the common sense chores?"

Alice sobbed, "It ain't fair! I got me a right to have a beau, even if I was birthed like this. I know I'm not much good to a man with my useless eyes, but if Freddy Brown's willing, why can't I at least hear his courting talk, Pearl? I've never had no man but my daddy talking sweet at me, and I reckon I'd like to know what it feels like to be courted."

"I know, honey. You ain't missing as much as you might think. Some of the boys hanging about me of late say mighty foolish things, but it do give a woman confidence in herself to have a man tell her how grand she looks to him," replied Pearl.

"My dad says that nigger Creek's just after me 'cause he can't get no other gals. Daddy says he's out to take advantage of me."

"Well, your dad might have a point, Alice, but you are

mighty pretty, so old Freddy's intent could be honorable. We're not about to find out tonight, though. So why don't we turn in and sleep on the matter? You want to sleep in the lean-to, or shall we go up to the loft? There's beds both places."

Alice said, "Oh, I've never slept in a loft. Can I try her with you?"

"Sure. Lord knows we have lots of room, now."

So the two young girls went up to the loft, and Alice explored it with her hands as Pearl made up the bed she hadn't used for some time. Alice liked to run her hands over things in new surroundings, and Pearl knew she had an uncanny way of finding her sightless way about once she had her bearings. Alice found the edge of the loft for herself without falling to the floor below.

They got in bed together in their undershifts and snuggled innocently. Pearl was still raw-nerved from all the family troubles, and that dumb flute outside was driving her mad, but Alice was soon asleep and Pearl wondered what on earth were they to do about her and that lovesick, colored cowhand?

Pearl was almost asleep herself when she heard a soft tapping on the door below. She stiffened, afraid it was Sequanna, but then she heard the sad distant sound of his twittering infernal flute, so she knew it had to be someone more sensible. She got out of bed gently so as not to wake her sleeping chum. She went down the ladder, hoping it was news of her folk.

She struck a match and lit a candlestick by the door as she called through the planking, "Who's there?"

A male voice replied softly, "It's Reb Collins. Let me in."

She opened the door with a sigh of relief. Reb was one of the white men from Fort Smith who sold white lightning to them. He was big and tough-looking, the kind of man Mamma admired. Maybe he could do something about that pesky Sequanna, after she found out what he wanted.

As she picked up the candle and led him to table, Pearl asked if there was further news on Sam and her mamma.

"Nothing we don't already know, honey. I come out here as soon as I seen you figured to be alone for the next six months," Reb said.

"That was neighborly of you, Reb, but I don't need nothing. I've credit at the trading post when the vittles thin out."

"Mebbe, but you needs a man about the house. You're too pretty a gal to leave here unprotected amongst all these bucks. So I'm moving in with you a spell, see?"

Pearl turned to face him, and she felt uneasy about the way he was looking down at her in her shift. She licked her lips and said, "I thank you for your kind offer, Reb, but I don't think you'd better. It wouldn't look seemly, and I don't think Sam would like it."

"Hell, Sam's in jail, and I don't care what the damned Injuns think. You'll thank me for being so good to you, once you know me better. So, what say we get to that, right off? Put down that candle and give us a little kiss, honey."

Pearl gasped, "Reb Collins, have you been drinking your own stuff? You have no call to talk to me like that!"

The burly man laughed and said, "Don't pull that coy shit on me, girl. You think I don't know what goes on out here in the strip betwixt you white gals and the bucks you lives with? I'm doing you a mortal favor, letting you have some white dicking for a change. I don't generally mess with trash, but what the hell, you're pretty. So here goes!"

He lunged for her as Pearl leaped backwards, dropping the candle and plunging the cabin into pitch black darkness as she cried out, "Get out of here, you maniac! I'll have the law on you if you don't leave this instant!"

She realized she'd made a mistake in crying out in the dark, for he found her with his hands and tried to pull her to him as he joshed, "Go on and call the law. A lot it will do you. You think the word of a bank robber's bastard will mean a thing to the law agin mine? You ain't about to take me to law, Pearl Younger, but if you did, I'd just tell 'em you offered to fuck me for a dollar and upped the price on me once I'd rid all this way!"

There was only one way to tear free, so Pearl did so,

sacrificing her shift to his clenched hands as she danced away from him, stark naked in the dark. She backed into the range with her bare buttocks. Mercifully, the fire had died down and it didn't burn her. She moved around into the angle formed by the wall and the mass of warm cast iron. She stepped on a mouse trap. It didn't hurt her bare foot all that much, but Reb homed in on the loud snap, saying, "Well, well, we wants to play hide-and-go-seek in our bare ass, does we? All right, missy, I enjoy kid games too, once in a time. But you sure are playing hard to get, for a trash gal."

She knew she was cornered in any case, so she spoke out, saying, "Listen to me, Reb. I ain't the kind of gal you take me for. I ain't never gone all the way with any man, I swear."

"Do tell? I think you're full of bullshit, but whatever you may or may not have done with Sam and them other bucks, it's time you learned real loving offen a white man."

He found her with his hands again, mauling her naked young body as he laughed and said, "Hot fucking on the moon! I knowed you was bare ass! Give it up, honey. It's better in a bed by far. You don't really want me to do you on the floor, do you?"

Pearl struggled wildly, punching at him blindly and with apparently little effect as he pinned her hard against the log wall with his weight and ran his hands over her cringing flesh, saying, "I can see you likes it rough and ready. That's jake with me. Just hold still and let me get her in."

He shook her like a rat, slamming her head against the wall as he warned her brutally, "I said hold still and I meant it, gal. You want me to have to hurt you? I'm an easygoing cuss, but I mean to have my way with you iffen I has to kick the shit outten you!"

Reb cuffed her to make his intentions clear, and Pearl went limp against the wall. So this was going to be the way it happened for the first time? She felt more sick than frightened as she felt his knuckles against her nude belly, fumbling with his belt buckle.

"Please, don't," she begged.

He'd dropped his pants and was hauling her down after him to the floor. She tried to break away. He grabbed a fist full of her hair and banged her skull against the floor as he ran the other hand down her, over breast, belly, and between her crossed thighs.

"Open up, God damn it. I'll knock you cold if I has to. You'll hardly enjoy it as much as me that way."

Pearl sobbed and didn't resist as he spread her thighs with his knee and rolled atop her, half undressed and reeking of sweat and white lightning.

Then he suddenly went completely limp, and collapsed atop her like a big dirty bearskin rug.

"Are you all right, Pearl?" Blind Alice asked.

Pearl gasped, rolled out from under the unconscious would-be rapist, and whispered, "Glory be to God! What did you do just now? I can't see a thing!"

Alice said, "Neither can I. I never could. I hit him with the lid handle off your mamma's range. I heard you struggling with somebody down here, so I came to help. I could tell you two was fighting in the dark, so that gave me some edge. I fights better than you sighted folk when you can't see me."

Pearl groped blindly, touched Alice, and grabbed her to give her a big hug, sobbing, "Oh, Lord, you come just in time. I'd clean forgotten you and I thought I was a gone goose!"

"You're nekked as a jay, too. Wait a minute. I touched some cloth with my bare toe, creeping upon you two just now." Alice disengaged herself and moved off in the blackness. "Here it be. It's tore total out one seam, but you can pin it or just hold it. It sure is funny how you sighted folk can't tell what's under cloth with them magic eyes of your'n."

Pearl groped into her torn shift just as the door burst open, spilling moonlight in around Sequanna's outline as the Indian youth called out, "What's happened? I heard Miss Pearl cry out!"

Alice spoke to Sequanna in Cherokee, knowing it wouldn't sound so ugly in a language that didn't have cuss words connected with the facts of life. Pearl struck a light and, not knowing where the candlestick had rolled, lit the coal-oil lamp on the table.

Reb Collin's booted legs stuck out from behind the range, with his pants down around his shins. Sequanna growled deep in his throat, like a yard dog, and moved over to him, reaching in one pocket.

As the tall Indian knelt by the man Pearl asked, "Is he . . . dead?"

Sequanna answered, "He is now. Why don't you ladies go over to the Ferndancer cabin for a spell? I'll neaten up around here."

Pearl sobbed, "Oh, Lord, this is terrible! What's the law going to say about this?"

Sequanna got to his feet by the range, putting away his barlow knife as he answered, "What the law don't know, they won't be saying about. I told you to go off and let me handle things here. I'll come over and tell you when it's safe for you to come back here, Miss Pearl."

Pearl hesitated and the Indian looked hurt.

"Hear me, I will not steal anything in this cabin while you are gone. Did you think I was a thief? Is that why you never notice me, Miss Pearl?"

Pearl smiled at him radiantly and answered, "I've noticed you. Misjudged you some, too, I fear. We'll talk on it later, Sequanna. You'll find I have a lot to learn about men. That one laying behind yon range is the kind I've always been told to admire more than most."

The girls knew it was their duty to tell Alice's parents what had happened, but old Bob Ferndancer said he didn't really want to know all that much, as long as they were both all right. Mrs. Ferndancer fetched Pearl one of her blind daughter's robes, since the two young friends were of a size. Then they all sat on the front steps in the dark, sort of quiet, until Sequanna came to them. Pearl was certain it had taken a million years, but the moon said it wasn't past midnight when the youth who'd offered to help materialized in the door yard and said something to old Bob in Cherokee.

Bob Ferndancer replied in English, saying, "Don't tell me about it, boy. Don't tell Miss Pearl all that much. Just tell her if it's fitting for her to go home again."

Sequanna said, "It's fitting. I'd be proud to walk you home, Pearl, if it's all the same to you."

Pearl said, "I'd be obliged if you would, Sequanna. I'd invite you in for coffee and such, too, but I dasn't until I talk to my kin."

Sequanna said, "I understand. I'll carry you home whenever you've a mind to go."

Pearl rose. Alice started to rise, too. Her mother spoke sharply, albeit softly, in her own tongue. Alice answered in English, saying, "I have to be with Pearl, Mamma. She's feared of night noises."

Pearl smiled at Alice and said, "You'd best stay here for now, Alice. I follow your mamma's drift. If things work out, you can come and stay with me another night, hear? We'll have half a year for visiting, if nobody comes calling sooner."

Pearl turned to Bob Ferndancer and added soberly, "Alice done something for me tonight I'll never forget, but make sure you all forget it if anyone else asks where Alice was this night. I mean to say, Alice didn't see me this evening, which is the pure truth, when you study on it. As for what may or may not have happened to that awful Reb Collins, I can swear with a clear conscience I never did a thing to harm him. That's all they'll get out of me. You have my spoken word."

Bob Ferndancer nodded and said, "You'd best go on home then, child. You have already told me more than I wanted to know. I ain't good at lying to the law. I ain't slick, like your Ma and you."

Pearl sighed and turned away to go with Sequanna. As they walked side by side in the moonlight, not touching, she said, "It's funny how nobody can see I don't tell fibs like my mamma. I hardly ever lie right out, but folk seem to think I'm slick as her."

Sequanna said, "I have heard you're slicker. You're the most dangerous kind of white person. We're not as good as any of you at lying, but we can generally catch white or black folk in a downright lie. You're like those lawyer men who took our lands away in the Shining Times. You know how to twist the truth all out of shape without breaking it to shards you could cut yourself with."

Pearl shrugged. "Well, it's a sin to tell a lie, but a body has a right to stay outten jail as best she can, and that sure can get complex around here. What did you do with that no-good white man, Sequanna?"

"I don't think I want to tell you. I don't think you really want to know. I am not a good liar, so when I don't want somebody to know something, I just don't tell them."

"That sounds fair enough, Sequanna, but don't you think you went a mite far when you come to help us gals? Alice already had the fool knocked out," said Pearl.

He walked on silently for a time before he said, "I was excited. I talked too much. I should have sent you away thinking he still lived."

"I reckon you just lost your head with that barlow knife, huh?"

"Of course not. I did what I had to. What do you think he'd have done once he woke up again? The man rode out here alone, but he belonged to a gang, a bad gang. I hope he didn't tell his friends what he intended."

Pearl gasped as the full meaning of the Indian boy's words sunk in. "Oh, Lord. What am I to do if night riders come a-calling whilst my folk are in jail? What if other like-minded white or red men find me all alone some night?"

"Hear me, Pearl, they will never find you alone. I will be there."

Pearl walked on, choosing her words before she said, "Sequanna, I don't want you to think I don't know I owe you. I'm ever so grateful to you, but you can't stay at my cabin with me."

"I know. People would say bad things about us. I don't care what they say about me, but I don't want them gossiping about you. I know I can't come inside. I'll stay outside, where I can watch while you sleep," he said.

"You mean like an old yard dog? I can't ask you to do that, Sequanna."

"You didn't ask. I offered. You lock up when I get you there. I'll go fetch the saddle gun from my pony. It's hobbled for the night in Bluefeather's pasture. I'll hunker down on your veranda with my Henry .44-40 and we'll say no more about it. I don't mind being your yard dog. I mind I got more bite in me than any other you might find."

Pearl hesitated, then she said, "Well, it will be a comfort to know you and your Henry are watching over me. But will you do me one more favor, Sequanna? Please promise me you won't play that infernal flute no more."

Nobody came that night. Pearl sent Sequanna home at daybreak. She did her morning chores and was fixing to have dinner alone when Rafe and two deputies she didn't know rode in. It was fitting to invite them in, since her folk knew them, so she did so.

As she served them coffee and a peach pie she'd baked for herself and her Indian friends for later, Rafe said casually, "We're looking for Reb Collins, Miss Pearl. His horse come home without him along about four in the morning. You knows Reb, don't you?"

Pearl's legs went watery under her, but she managed a casual smile as she answered, "Sure I do. He's one of the men as works at the likker wholesale in Fort Smith. How come you're looking over here in the Strip for him? I don't remember him having friends in these parts."

Rafe made a wry face and said, "I don't think he had many friends in other parts, but it's my duty. Being the missing man was last seed headed onto Indian lands, that makes it federal."

Pearl refilled one of the other deputies cups as she asked, "What do you reckon happened to him, Rafe?"

"If we knowed, we wouldn't need to look for the cuss," Rafe said.

Pearl said truthfully, "Well, if I knew where he was

right now, I'd tell you, but I don't have the first notion. As you see, he ain't here."

Rafe shot her a curious look and asked, "Now, why would we have any call to expect him here, Miss Pearl?"

Her tongue felt like a wool sock in her mouth as she forced herself to meet his eye and say, "You're looking for him here, ain't you?"

Rafe laughed and said, "We'll pry up your floorboards after we finish this grand Arbuckle, Miss Pearl. Matter of fact, Judge Parker said as long as we was headed out this way it wouldn't hurt to make sure you wasn't missing too. I know you're a bandit princess and all, but it's sort of sobering to think someone big enough to vanish Reb Collins is riding about in these parts."

One of the others growled, "We ain't looking for one rascal, Rafe. Takes a gang to handle a man like old Reb Collins. I've seen that old boy in a bellaroara, and he's strong as a bull and meaner-natured."

Pearl's flesh crawled under her fresh print dress as she recalled the feeling of her attacker's strong hands on her the night before, but her voice was light as she asked, "How come you called me a bandit princess, Rafe?"

He laughed again. "Didn't you read the papers? The headline said Belle Starr, the Bandit Queen, had been sent away to durance vile at last. I ain't sure what durance vile is, but if your mamma is a queen, don't that make you a princess?"

Pearl laughed weakly, and said, "Oh, sure, I got my own Indian followers and everything. Naturally, I don't lead as big a gang as Mamma, but I'm still growing. Anyone else for more coffee?"

Rafe shook his head and said, "We have to get it on down the road, Miss Pearl. Got a lot of looking to do. The way we put things together, for openers, is that Reb must have switched from wholesale to retail with your folk put away for a time. He likely carried some jars out here on his own, looking to make a quick profit off some mighty thirsty Injuns. After that, it can go more'n one way. Somebody might have disputed his prices, or he might have sold his jars and some old boy wanted to share his profits. Or, hell, he might have just got into something personal. Reb wasn't the easiest man to get along with. He's been knowed to start a fight just 'cause it was Saturday night and he had nothing more exciting to do. Let's thank the little lady proper and saddle up, boys. We got a mess of brush to search out yonder."

As they scraped away from the table, one of the other deputies said to Rafe, "What say we pay Granny Redbird a visit, Rafe?" and to Pearl's utter horror Rafe nodded amiably and replied, "I follow your drift, and it's a good notion, Spike. None of these folks are going to come right out and say what they know, but anyone tangling with the missing moose might have had need for a spey woman's doctoring, after."

Pearl blurted, "Don't you pester Granny Redbird! She don't know nothing about it!" She realized she'd blurted too much as they all turned to stare at her.

"How do you know what Granny Redbird may or may not know, Miss Pearl? Was you at her place with the spey woman, recent?" Rafe asked.

"Well, no. But you're crazy if you think Granny Redbird had anything to do with, uh, whatever happened," Pearl answered.

Rafe said, "Spike, here, never said Granny Redbird vanished Reb Collins, but whoever done it might have needed salve for a swollen eye or such. We won't hurt your old spey woman, girl. You have no call to look so upset."

He nodded at the others and they clumped out, muttering their individual thanks for the repast.

After they'd ridden on, Pearl ran to the outhouse to relieve her nervous bladder. Then she forced herself to clean house for hours. She swept and dusted fiercely, and it didn't steady her worth mention. She kept looking at the clock over the fireplace, and the infernal hands moved so slowly she was sure the old Seth Thomas had stopped. An hour by the clock and another million years by her heartbeat, Pearl figured it was safe to ride, so she did.

She rode bareback and astride to Granny Redbird's. The

white lawmen had ridden on, so Pearl could forget the excuses she'd made up as she found herself alone with the old spey woman, pouring out her tale.

The Cherokee woman nodded and said, "Set down, Pearl. You've got yourself overwrought, and I mean to put some calming tea in you afore I send you home."

Pearl sank to a stool as the old woman put some herbs in the pot she had already boiling on her range.

"Oh, Granny, I was so scared when they said they was coming here!" she said.

"Why should you be scared on my account, child? I hadn't done anything the law could trouble me about. That's the pure advantage of not breaking the law. It can sure save a body a heap of bother. I've tried to tell you folks that more than once, but nobody seems to listen."

"Granny, that's not fair. I never started up with that old man. He come looking for me!"

"I know. And he wouldn't have, had your mamma been a schoolteacher out of town on a visit. Like attracts like, if you take my meaning."

Pearl smiled bitterly, and replied, "I do. Wasn't that silly for them to call Mamma a bandit queen, Granny?"

"It was, but your mother's sure worked hard at getting such a rep. Now you're following in her footsteps down the primrose path. Belle would likely be jealous if she knew you'd killed your first man. I don't think she's ever managed that, yet. I don't think you'd better tell her, Pearl. Knowing Belle, she'd never rest until she topped you."

Pearl's eyes widened as she gasped, "Granny, don't you go calling me no killer! I never even bruised that big strong rascal. Sequanna was the one who knifed him. I am innocent of any crime!"

The old woman sat down across from Pearl and said soberly, "Hear me, you are not innocent, as the law sees it. A man is dead. You were in on it. If you had killed that man defending your honor and gone to the law with it, you would be innocent. Now you are party to a murder in the eyes of the law. You must never brag on it again."

"Brag? I never come to brag on it, Granny! I come to tell you what went on over to my spread last night!"

The wise old woman shook her head and said, "There was no need for me to know. Those white lawmen had nothing on me. They were polite-spoken, and I sent them on their way without having to lie to them. Now, the next time I meet them, I will have to, and I don't like to. It is true you came partly out of worry and concern for me, Pearl, but search your heart. Isn't it true you wanted to tell me how you slickered them white lawmen?"

Pearl looked down sheepishly and said, "Well, you have to admit I woolled 'em good."

Granny Redbird looked disgusted and said, "Hear me, child. I know those men. They are good hunters. You weren't smarter than them. When a man hunts coyote he pays little attention to rabbit in passing, but you were dumb, even for a rabbit. You thought you were being clever, but had they suspected you for the flicker of an eyelash, they'd have tricked the story out of you. The trouble with you and your mother is that you've been around so many stupid people that you've both started to think you're smart. That's a very foolish feeling to have, Pearl. Do you understand me?"

"No, Granny. I thought it was good to be smart."

"Only when you know how dumb the smartest person can be, to think brains are all that counts. Hear me, Pearl, a man or even a dog is smarter than a bear. Do you agree?"

"Sure, everybody knows that, Granny."

"Then hear me. What happens to a man or a dog if they go into a bear's den, feeling so much smarter?"

Pearl nodded. "I follow your drift. Bear don't have to be all that smart if you fight him on his own ground."

"Exactly. Your Colonel Custer was smart. He'd been four years to West Point, and he'd even written books on Indian fighting. The man as scalped him didn't know how to read or write, so Colonel Custer must have considered him mighty dumb. Dumb folks can surprise you when they got the numbers on you, and Pearl, there's a heap of folks

out there in that big dumb world. I'd try to avoid fights
with the world, if I was you. That would be *really* slick."

"I ain't out to trifle with the world, if the world will let
me be, Granny Redbird. You gotta admit we handled that
Reb Collins tolerably slick," Pearl said.

"Hear me, you silly child, you did no such thing. You
were very very lucky. Had not your blind friend been
there, unknown to him and unplanned by you, that man
would have had his way with you. Had not Sequanna come
to help, you silly girls never would have gotten away with
it. Had those deputies even suspected a bitty thing like you
could vanish a big tough white man, you'd be on your way
to trial right now. Slick had nothing to do with it. Or, if it
did, it was Reb Collins thinking *he* was so slick that done
him in. He'd studied on how big an edge he had on you
before he came calling last night. He figured a man who
broke the law for a living could likely handle a teen-aged
gal with no growed folk in her cabin to help her. You see
what all his proud thinking done for him? The first thing
you has to study on, afore you set out to slicker anyone, is
that they might not be as easy to slicker as you think."

She rose and moved over to her range, adding, "Your
herbs is about ready. They'll calm you down, and maybe
you won't run about so flighty to tell the whole world it'd
better keep an eye on you."

"Granny, I don't want no sleeping potion. It's broad
day."

"Drink it anyway. It won't put you to sleep. This tea is
meant to steady a woman's nerves. How close are you to
your moon troubles?"

Pearl thought as she took the tin cup. She said, "Mid-
way, I reckon. I ain't upset 'cause I'm getting my period.
It's sort of upsetting to have folks trying to rape one at *any*
time of the month."

"It's good he didn't manage to. Drink. You'll find it a
mite bitter, but it's strong medicine. I gathered them herbs
myself. There's cures for most everything, if you know
where to search for it."

Pearl sipped experimental. "You're right, it's mighty bitter, but I'll drink it. Is there any herb for what's wrong with Alice Ferndancer, Granny?"

The spey woman sat down again with a sigh and said, "If there was, I'd have long since given it to her, Pearl. I midwifed Alice into this world as I midwifed you. I knew as soon as I held that poor tyke up to the light that her eyes were cursed by Spider Woman. I don't know why Spider Woman spins her webs in some folks' eyes like that, but the spirits can be ornery at times. Some say it was 'cause her father took a Creek woman to wife, but I don't know. I've seen pure Cherokee with the same webs in their eyes. I reckon Spider Woman must have had a better reason."

"Ain't there no way to get them spider webs outten her eyes, Granny?"

"No. You've had a dust mote in your own eyes, haven't you? Think what it would feel like to go scraping around in there with a knife."

Pearl grimaced. "I'd rather not. But I don't dust spider webs from corners with a knife, Granny. What if someone was to take a bitty little broom or dustmop to her webby eyes?"

Granny Redbird snorted in disgust and said, "You see what I mean about feeling so smart? Now it's got you crawling into a girl's eyeball with a broom, like a tiny witch! How do you figure to shrink yourself and that broom down to the size of a ladybug, Pearl? And after you do it, how do you figure to get inside that poor girl's eyes? I've treated lots of sore eyes in my time. I've never noticed any doorways into them. There's nought one can do for that blind child's eyes, so forget 'em."

Pearl finished her herb tea and said she'd head home, but she didn't forget her blind friend's eyes. Granny Redbird was mighty smart, but she'd just said nobody knew everything. No white doctor had ever looked old Alice over. Mayhaps there was something white doctors could do about the cobwebs in those eyes. Pearl knew white doctors charged an arm and a leg just to look at you, so there was no use thinking about it 'til she had some money. Lots of money. Mayhaps more money than she'd ever seen in her life.

As she rode back to her cabin. Pearl studied on how a body got lots of money in this world. There had to be more ways than one, for the world was filled with rich folk. It sure would be nice to be rich. The world was filled with even more poor folk, and being poor was mighty tedious when you'd been that way a spell.

Sequanna came just after sundown. Pearl had expected him, and was waiting on the veranda with a tray of fresh-baked biscuits and a pot of coffee.

"You can stay and jaw by my side for a spell, Sequanna, but then I want you to go home. Granny Redbird gave me a thinking potion and I've been thinking good. Folks are going to notice you yard-dogging for me, and that will make them wonder why I needs one. Judge Parker's told his men to keep an eye on me, and the bootleggers who work for us are sort of watching out for me, too. If I have anyone watching really serious, folks are going to wonder out loud what I'm hiding, see?" Pearl said.

Sequanna frowned as he chewed and swallowed before he replied, "What if someone else comes to trifle with you, Pearl?"

"I got a lock on my door and guns in the house. It was my own foolish trust that let that nasty cuss in my cabin last night. That ain't likely to happen again. I've learned a gal can't trust a man just 'cause she's said howdy to him a couple of times. From now on I'll have to know 'em mighty well afore I unbar my door to any man. You may be right about other men having country notions about a gal living alone for the next six months, but having you yard-dogging would be taking even a bigger chance. So you'd best spend the night to home, hear?"

"Do I have to go now?" Sequanna asked.

"No, Sequanna. You can finish your coffee and keep me company a seemly spell. It don't look suspicious for a gent to sit on the veranda with a gal while the fireflies are winking, but when it gets late enough for them fireflies to pack it in for the evening, you'd best leave. My, don't they look pretty, out there over the riverside with the moonlight on the water ahint them?"

"Fireflies are all right, I reckon. They don't bite, like skeeters. Can I ask you something, Pearl? Can I ask you if I'm courting you, sitting here with you like this?"

Pearl thought and replied, "Well, courting may be a mite strong a word for what we're doing, but I won't ask Sam to run you off no more when he comes home, if that's what you mean."

"That's what I meant. Would you marry up with me, Pearl Younger?"

She blinked in dismay and said, "Not hardly, Sequanna. I ain't but sixteen yet."

"What of it? My ma wedded my pa when she was fourteen, and it never hurt her all that much. I want to marry up with you, Pearl. I know you ain't a Cherokee, but you're so pretty it makes a man hurt just to look at you."

Granny Redbird's brew must have steadied her nerves indeed, for she was sure she ought to feel more flustered. Her voice was calm and steady as she said, "I thanks you for saying I'm pretty, Sequanna, but that ain't reason enough for folk marrying up. They got to know one another a spell. We've never spoke, afore last night. I hardly know you worth mention."

He started to reach for her hand, decided he'd better not, and said soberly, "Hear me. I am old enough to get married. I am almost twenty-five. I have thirteen ponies and a herd of twenty-one cows. I have cleared forty acres of bottomland and I'm building my own cabin. I am building it strong, with good elm sills and pin oak walls. No cottonwood for me. If you marry me I will send to Chicago for a real cast iron range. I will buy you a sewing machine. A Singer. I am not a cheap person."

"My heavens, you're downright rich, for an Indian," exclaimed Pearl.

"Is that why you don't want to marry me, because I am a full-blood? I won't expect you to live Indian, Pearl. I'll eat canned food for you if you'll marry me!"

She took his delicately boned brown hand in hers, sensing it would be safe, as she said gently, "I'd be lying if I said I'd been planning all my life to wed a Cherokee, Sequanna. I'd have to study some on that part, but even if you was white as the driven snow I'd still have to do a heap of thinking afore I'd marry anyone. What's your infernal hurry? I told you I was only sixteen. I won't be an old maid for a couple of years yet. So I'll just pass on your kind offer for now."

Sequanna answered, "I am being pestered by my mother to get married up. She says it ain't natural for a man my age not to even have his own gal. If you won't marry me, Pearl, can I say you're my gal?"

"No, dear, that wouldn't be true. You can say I'm your friend if you like, for I mean to be, whatever happens. But I'm not ready to be any man's gal just yet. I got too many other things on my mind."

He sighed, stared off at a passing firefly until it winked out, and said, "They're having a Sunday-go-to-meeting picnic up the river this weekend, Pearl. Could I carry you there if I promised not to tell nobody we was courting?"

"I don't know, Sequanna. Folks would gossip no matter what we said, if we rode in together," Pearl said.

"Damnation, Pearl, it's going to be a grand old picnic, with a dancing fiddle and ever'thing. Please say I can carry you there. I don't want to go alone. It'll do you good to get outten the house, too."

She smiled and said, "My, it do sound tempting. I'll tell you what. I'll ride in your buckboard to the church social if we can take Alice along. That way it won't look like we're sparking personal. How does that suit you?"

"Sure, I'll be proud to take Alice along. But what's a blind gal to do at a dancing picnic, Pearl?"

"Oh, Alice can dance. She dances good, if someone holds onto her. She ain't good at reels and circle dancing, but she two-steps just as good as me. Can I tell her she's coming along, Sequanna?"

He nodded, if grudgingly, and she clapped her hands and said, "Oh, wait 'til I tell her the fun we aim to have!"

* * *

The Sunday-go-to-meeting picnic was a lot of fun, or it started out to be. The mostly Cherokee crowd had assembled from miles around in the meadow near the old frame church. Someone had hung Japanese lanterns from the branches of the surrounding trees, and there were to be fireworks after dark. The different families sat on their own blankets here and there in the grass, leaving a space cleared for the dancing to come. A line of tables groaned under the vittles housewives had brought from far and near.

Women of the Five Civilized Tribes cooked much the same as their white countrywomen, and they prided themselves on their cooking. There were big tubs of corn steamed in the husk with all the butter anyone might see fit to eat it with. There were hush puppies and black-eyed peas, mustard greens deep fried in purest lard, together with basket after basket of fried chicken that just melted in one's mouth. Naturally, there was stuff to wash it down with. There were canisters of coffee and pitchers of lemonade big enough to drown a cat in and although the white Indian agents had promised to drop by, there was stronger stuff for the really thirsty.

Red-eye was trade whiskey in brown jugs. The stronger white-lightning was in fruit jars, looking innocent as water, for it was pure corn alcohol fresh from the still and didn't need aging or the burnt sugar of the red-eye to do its job. White lightning wasn't drunk for its taste. It tasted like its name and was drunk for its no-nonsense effects. By the time the fiddle started up, toward sundown, more than a little of the illegal refreshments had been downed, and some folk were getting mighty noisy. But it was a good-natured, if rowdy, crowd of simple folk, and what was a Sunday-go-to-meeting picnic if nobody there got drunk and silly?

The two girls were seated on their blanket in the grass as Sequanna went to get more lemonade. The sun was low to westward, and the old Chickasaw 'breed who wandered about the Nation with his semi-professional fiddle was making cricket chirps as he rosined and tuned. A girl on another spread out blanket called out to ask when the music would be starting serious, and the old Chickasaw said he aimed to have another drink first, if he ever got this infernal fiddle sounding right.

Pearl's ears picked up another sound, or rather, a silence where there shouldn't be any silence at a Sunday-go-to-meeting on the grass. She turned to see Freddy Brown and some other cowhands making their way across the meadow surrounded by a zone of thoughtful silence. Freddy was the only one in the bunch who looked positively Negroid. A couple of the others looked more white than anything else, but none of them were Cherokee, and none of them had been invited.

They walked with more cowboy swagger than their high heels really called for, the way menfolk did in a strange trail town. Freddy seemed to be the natural leader, so he swaggered the most. He and his sidekicks moved up to the line of trestle tables, and Freddy asked the Elder Swan how much the drinks cost.

"Everything here is free this evening, boys, so wet your whistles on the house, and then, if I was you-all, I'd move on up the road, if you follow my meaning."

Freddy Brown frowned and asked, "Are you trying to run us off, old man?"

The Elder Swan shook his head and said, "Just telling you where you stand, Freddy Brown. This is a Cherokee gathering."

"I see plenty of folk here who ain't Cherokee, old man."

"Sure you do, son. They was invited. You wasn't, no offense."

One of the other cowboys nudged Brown and said, "I told you we was asking for trouble, Freddy."

Freddy said, "I ain't looking for trouble. There won't be none, if nobody steps on my toes. Do you aim to step on my toes, old man?"

The Elder Swan began to fill their cups from a jug as he shook his head and said, "Not me, son. I've outgrowed stepping on toes a long time gone. But there's younger men about, and they outnumber you. I know you're not a bad person, Freddy Brown, but if you ain't got sense to move on, for God's sake take that chip off your shoulder. This is neither the time nor the place for a Creek to sass folks."

Brown picked up his free drink as he scowled and asked, "Didn't you mean to say nigger, old man?"

The Cherokee elder shook his head wearily. "If I'd meant to insult you I'd have done so, Freddy Brown. You don't make it easy for people to treat you polite. I'd best close down the bar for now, boys. I can see you all had a jar or two betwixt you on the way over from the Bar Seven."

The music started suddenly, and the folk around started getting up from their blankets with happy whoops, drowning out the tense conversation as they grabbed their partners. Meanwhile, Sequanna, who'd missed the exchange at the more serious drinking end of the tables, had returned to the girls with their tin cups of lemonade. He hunkered down and asked Pearl if she fancied dancing with him. Pearl sipped her lemonade thoughtfully. Then she shook her head and said, "This first do is a two-step to warm things up, Sequanna. Why don't you and Alice, here, have the first dance?"

The blind girl smiled hopefully. Sequanna hesitated. He knew, as Pearl likely did, that folks tended to think the gal a man asked first was the one he was interested in. But Sequanna was a gentleman, so he agreed.

"All right," he said. "How about it, Alice? You want to dance?"

"Oh, I'd love to!" Alice answered.

"Well, get up, then. I can't dance you on your knees, durn it."

Alice rose, and Sequanna led her out on the grass a ways to hold her awkwardly and dance the blind girl around the meadow as Pearl watched them, smiling. Alice had a new ribbon bow in her shiny black hair, and didn't look blind at all as she and Sequanna and the others danced out there. Alice was about the prettiest young gal dancing in the crowd. Pearl saw some of the other Cherokee men thought so, too, from the admiring glances they cast at Alice in passing.

Over on the sidelines, Freddy Brown was also watching, and he didn't like what he was seeing at all.

As the Elder Swan had surmised, Freddy had arrived well fortified and in an ugly mood. Watching that infernal Cherokee dancing with a gal he admired didn't soothe the unhappy youth's feelings. Like many people trapped in the limbo between two worlds, the fundamentally decent Freddy Brown's uncertain temper was that of a child lashing out at those he justly felt wanted to punish him for something that wasn't his fault. He'd had no say about being birthed with colored looks. It was bad enough to be an Indian in a white man's world, but to be despised by one's fellow tribesmen was a heavier load than Freddy's common sense had been designed to carry.

In truth, many, if not most of the insults the sullen mulatto felt himself subjected to were the products of his own unhappy mind. The people of the Civilized Tribes were inclined to be more easy-going on racial matters than most whites. A lot of the fights he got into were self-fulfilling prophesies, for almost anyone will scowl when a man packs a good sized chip on his shoulder and swaggers about daring folk to knock it off.

Freddy didn't know what an inferiority complex was, but more than one member of the Five Civilized Tribes was carrying his own surly feelings even before Freddy started up with him, so when he dared some 'breed or full-blood to call him a nigger, they generally obliged. Freddy Brown had lots of scar tissue on his knuckles, and more than most young men his age generally wore on their face. But, having had a lot of practice growing up, Freddy Brown was an awesome brawler, who prided himself on the fact that he could likely lick anyone, white, red, black, or in between, who messed with him.

That Cherokee out yonder had no call dancing like that with his Alice. Her father had told Freddy she was too young and to stay away from her. If she was all that young, what was she doing dancing with that infernal

Cherokee? Freddy knew all too well why he'd been told to stay away from Alice, and he didn't like it. He drained his cup, threw the cup over his shoulder and hitched up his pants. Then he headed out across the grass to cut in.

Cutting in was not the custom at a Sunday-go-to-meeting shindig, so when Freddy tapped Sequanna on the shoulder and told him to stand aside and let a real man dance, Sequanna shook his head and said, "Not hardly, friend," and tried to move on with Alice.

Freddy grabbed Sequanna's shoulder and spun him around as Alice, off balance, fell to the grass, bewildered.

Sequanna glared and shouted, "Now look what you've done, you fool cowhand!"

Freddy snapped back, "I never knocked her down, you dumb Cherokee, and didn't you mean to call me a nigger?"

"All right, you fool nigger, if that's the way you want it. I stand ready, so what's it to be, fists, blades, or guns?"

Naturally, it couldn't go any farther, surrounded as they were by cooler heads and many strong hands. As the menfolk dragged the two angry young men apart, Pearl ran over to Alice.

"What's going on? What's happening? I was having such a grand time afore I wound up in the durned old grass!" Alice wailed.

Pearl saw the men were carrying the two boys off in opposite directions as they both called out dreadful things about each other's mammas. She led Alice off the green to the blanket, saying, "Lord of mercy, I never should have put that ribbon bow in your hair this afternoon. You've got men fighting over you."

"I have?" asked Alice, brightly. "My heavens, I've never been fought over afore! Who was that as started up with Sequanna, Pearl?"

"Oh, that fool Freddy Brown tried to cut in on you two. Sequanna took it unfriendly and I mean to have a word with him about that later. Right now there's too many older men sitting on both those dumb boys for anyone to talk to. You want me to carry you home, Alice? This party's getting a mite rough even for folk as can see to duck."

Alice sat down on the blanket and said, "I don't want to go home yet. It's just getting interesting. Tell me how they looked when they was fighting over me, Pearl."

"They looked like a pair of idjets. You look mighty dumb to me right now, too. It's nothing to be proud about, Alice. Only trash gals encourages men to fight over them."

Alice protested, "Hold on, I never asked them to fight over me, Pearl." Then she giggled and asked, "Which one does you think is better looking?"

"Neither one, damn it. Men look ugly when they go at one another like that." Then she laughed, took her blind friend's hand, and added, "Well, at least you'll have to admit I was right the time I told you it didn't matter all that much if a body was blind, as long as she was pretty."

"I ain't sure what pretty is, Pearl, but I'm sure glad I am. You reckon they're both in love with me? I surely hope so. My mamma told me once not to get my hopes up along them lines, but it don't seem as hard as she thought to get men to fall in love."

"Hush, there's some men coming," Pearl warned as a clump of sober-faced Cherokee led Freddy Brown over to their blanket.

One of the young cowhand's eyes was swollen, even though Sequanna had been swarmed before he could raise a hand to the mulatto. One of the older men nudged Freddy and he stammered, "I have come to say I'm sorry afore I ride out, ladies. I never meant to lay you on the sod, Miss Alice. I was just funning."

Alice smiled up at him and said, "No offense taken, then. I wasn't hurt and I accepts your handsome apology."

Freddy Brown might have wanted to say more, but they dragged him away as someone called out, "Let's hear that fiddle, dang it. Folks come here to dance, not to watch a dog fight!"

The fiddle was playing a reel when Sequanna rejoined them, with the sleeve of his shirt torn. He hunkered down between them and said, "Where's that infernal nigger at? I mean to have a word with him in private."

Pearl said, "They drug him off and forked him aboard

his bronc, Sequanna. His friends are likely taking him back to the Bar Seven about now."

"Well, I know where the Bar Seven is, so we'll settle up later. You want to reel with me, Miss Pearl?"

"Not just yet, Sequanna. We got something to settle here and now. What just took place out there on the grass was uncalled for."

"Damn it, Pearl, I never started it."

"I know, and I ain't finished. It was a misunderstanding on both your parts, Sequanna. Freddy Brown's been paying court to Alice, here, so he must have took your dancing with her wrong."

Sequanna frowned and asked, "That nigger boy's been sparking Alice?"

"There *you* go with that nigger business. Oh, if only my eyes worked, so I could understand what in thunder you're all talking about!" Alice complained.

Pearl squeezed her hand to hush her as she said to Sequanna, "I want you to leave it be, Sequanna. Will you promise me you won't go looking for that Freddy at the Bar Seven?"

The Cherokee shrugged and said, "Well, if you don't want me to I won't. He's mighty annoying, even for a Creek, but if he leaves me alone I won't go looking for him. What if he comes after me? Can I fight him then?"

"He won't come looking for you. I mean to have a talk with him first. Oh, look, they're lighting the Japanese lanterns. Ain't they pretty? This shindig might not turn out so bad after all, and if you promise to behave, I'll be proud to join you in the next reel if Alice don't mind," said Pearl.

Blind Alice sighed and said, "I don't mind. I'll just set here and listen to the music whilst I study on this pretty business. I can see being pretty is a mite more complicated than I thought."

❧

8

At the Woman's House of Detention, Belle was enjoying herself some, too. She'd settled who was boss in her cell block by snatching that sassy lizzy woman nearly bald. Though she'd have much preferred the admiration of men, it was nice to be looked up to by the other she-male prisoners.

Belle's cellmate was an older confidence woman named Gypsy and they had quickly become, "thick as thieves". Some of the other prisoners whispered that they were lizzy lovers, but that was the last thing on their minds. Gypsy admired Belle for being such a fair scrapper. The older, weaker, and more refined Gypsy was afraid of lizzy women. Belle was drawn to her cellmate by her manners and awesome knowledge of criminal lore. Gypsy seemed to have been all over and done everything. She enthralled Belle with tales of badger games in Louisville, and tipping a mark in glamorous-sounding places like Virginia City and Leadville. Gypsy said you had to go where the silver was mined if you aimed to line your pockets with it.

Belle didn't get sore when Gypsy told her she'd been mighty foolish fencing her own silver. Belle had already figured that out for herself. Gypsy explained how one fenced slick. She knew all sorts of tricks that seemed simple, once they were pointed out. Belle enjoyed her stories and listened well.

"It's not for me to say whether you should stay with that Indian buck or not, honey, but it ain't natural to let a man do your thinking for you. Anyone can see you're smarter than most gals and, no offense, your Sam sounds sort of backward," said Gypsy.

"I've told Sam time and time again, I'm the slick one in the family. But he says it's the man's job to plot agin the law. I'll have to admit my recent notions didn't work out too well. I doubt he'll be in a mood to listen, once we gets out. You reckon he'll take a whip to me for getting him throwed in jail like this?" Belle asked.

Gypsy laughed. "Honey, after he's spent six months with his fist for company at night, taking a whip to you will be the farthest thing from his mind. He don't like boys, does he?"

"Lord, no. As a matter of fact, he ain't all that anxious to screw women, lately."

"Don't worry, six months at hard labor will have him horny as a billy goat. Even experienced gents of the road who've spent enough time behind bars to resort to using punks for pleasure, generally come forth from prison with rekindled desires for the real thing. He'll likely keep you in bed a week afore he even mentions that dumb move you made with the burgled silver. The Lord sure gave us gals amazing powers over men. Ain't it funny how easy it is to overpower the strongest man, just by raising your knees a mite?"

Belle laughed, and told Gypsy about her plans to enlist more support by discreetly doing just that with other members of Sam's gang.

"Well, you'd have to be mighty careful, and pick gents who don't kiss and tell. Just what did you have in mind if you had more of a say in your gang's comings and goings, aside from their comings in you, that is?"

"I'm still working on that. I showed you what they put in the papers about me being a bandit queen. In truth, I've only slept with bandits. I've never bandited my own self," replied Belle.

Gypsy sat up on one elbow on her cot and said, "Listen to me, Belle. Road agenting and sticking up banks is for suckers. As I've told you more than once, the really slick crook gets her money without making so much noise. You take me, now. I got a year and day for taking that old rancher for ever'thing but the gold fillings in his teeth, and I had the money his foolishness cost him well hid afore they arrested me, so it's still out there waiting, and my year will soon be up. I took that joker for twelve thousand and change. He fooled me a mite by going to the law with it, for most men don't like to admit they've been slickered. But the point is, even though the take cost me a year and a day, that's all it cost me. You think I'd have got off with a year had I took it off him at gunpoint? I would not have. Robbery at gunpoint is good for five years at the least, and damn few suckers wander down the hughway packing twelve thousand and change on them. Robbing banks is even dumber. They start bank robbers off with twenty at hard, and if they think you've made a habit of it, they give you life, like that Cole Younger of your'n."

"Yeah, but they have more'n twelve thousand in most banks, Gypsy," said Belle.

"Damn it, Belle, pay attention! You might get fifty off a bank if you're lucky. Let's say you're mighty lucky and get a hundred. It takes at least half a dozen folk to pull off a bank job right. More, if you use unskilled labor like them trashy boys you're figuring to seduce into wilder ways. So figure what you wind up with, once you share the loot out. Then consider that the maximum for embezzlement is three, and add it up. You can make a million conning folks with less risk to your hide than robbing anyone for one silver dollar with a gun."

"Easy for you to say, Gypsy. You're a handsome gal with fancy manners for robbing folks with your jawbone. I doubt like hell I'd ever talk a rich man into paying off a mortgage on my gold mine, whether I raised my knees for him or not!" Belle replied.

"Hell, Belle, a man would pay off his intended's debts for her before he'd stick folk up for her. Besides, a she-male riding in ahead of armed robbers would attract more attention than the law allows. The papers already have you writ up as a bandit queen, so you'd get caught in no time if you really started banditing. You'd be the first gal they'd come to. Everyone knows how you've bedded down with the James-Younger gang in your time."

Belle sighed and said, "Not all of 'em. But your point's well taken. All right, if you're so smart, Gypsy, what would you do if you had your own gang of gun hands?"

"I'd have them steal for me. I wouldn't ride with the bunch. I'd stay put and let 'em bring the stuff they stole to me. Then I'd sell it for a profit."

"Hell's bells, Gypsy! That's what I done, and the first time I tried I got caught at it!"

"Then pay attention, and I'll teach you how to do it right, next time."

Sequanna worked stripped to the waist, for it was a hot afternoon and elm is a heavy wood and mortally hard to hew with an adze. He now had his cabin walls and rafters up, and he was hewing planking for the roof. Some said it was foolish to use such hard working timber for planking, but elm didn't rot when it got wet, and it rained on roof-tops, didn't it?

Sequanna wanted to finish the cabin before Pearl's parents returned. They'd been away over a month now, and things had settled down in Younger's Bend. Pearl had told Sequanna not to speak of her marrying up with anyone 'til she had her folks to home again.

He'd said he wouldn't. But meanwhile, it would be another string to his bow if he could point out that he had a fine new cabin waiting, as well as a couple more acres cleared. It seemed to put strength in his arms when he thought about how Pearl would look at night by the fire-place under his roof.

Pearl had asked him if he didn't think Blind Alice wouldn't look as nice, but that was woman talk. Everyone knew Alice was a Creek. Sequanna had been terribly embarrassed by the silly talk about him and that blind Creek gal after the dance last month. He'd told everyone he'd only been trying to be polite, but some people still teased him about his Creek gal. Sequanna hadn't told them about his plans regarding Pearl, of course, Pearl had asked him not to.

He finished the timber he was working on and stood straight to ease his tired spine. They were right about the elm being a devilish wood. He had many more planks to hew, but he'd just get his breath back before starting the next.

As he stood alone in the sunlit clearing, a rifle cracked from the tree line. Sequanna flinched at the noise just as the bullet hit him with a loud wet smack. He blinked his eyes at the fading light and muttered, "Heya, I think I've just been shot!"

He was right. The bullet had entered his back just under the floating ribs and severed his aorta. He took a couple of bewildered steps in the sudden darkness, then the rest of his nervous system followed his eyesight into the oblivion of eternity. His body was found a few hours later when a kinsman came to fetch him home for supper.

Naturally, everyone knew who'd done it, or thought they did, so the law rode to the Bar Seven and arrested Freddy Brown as he was washing up to eat with the other hands. He said he hadn't been anywhere near Sequanna or Younger's Bend that afternoon. They took him in anyway. He would stand trial for his life before Judge Parker, and Pearl was among the witnesses called.

The courtroom was packed with Indians as well as whites, but to Pearl's surprise, the notorious hanging judge didn't even empanel a jury after hearing the first presentation.

Judge Parker heard what Pearl had to tell him about the dispute at the dance. He listened, staring sober, as everyone else told him of the fighting words. Some didn't put it as charitably as Pearl had. Then, when everyone had had their say, Judge Parker called Freddy Brown and his court-appointed lawyer to the bench and stared a long hard time at the sullen cowboy.

"Freddy Brown," the judge said. "I'll tell you true, I think you're guilty as hell. But thinking isn't enough. The law requires evidence, and you either done it mighty slick or there's an outside chance you never done it."

"I never, Judge." said Freddy Brown. "I was out hunting strays that afternoon, like I said."

"Hesh, I know what you said, boy. It's mighty odd how none of the hands you ride with can alibi you. But, on the other hand, since you were off alone that day none of 'em can say they saw you shoot that Indian boy. Sequanna couldn't say, even if he was still able. The coroner tells me he was hit in the back, and likely died before he could have turned to say howdy. What we have here is a Mexican standoff in the eyes of the law. Just the smell of a skunk around the henhouse won't cut the mustard to the law unless someone seen the skunk and can point out the right one, so I've no choice but to free you for lack of evidence, and that's what I mean to do. Before you go, though, I'd like to give you some fatherly advice. If I was you, Freddy Brown, I'd go out that door, fork my bronc, and ride for other parts right sudden. What the court has to say on your dubious innocence is one thing. The Cherokee Nation might see it another way. Are you paying mind to me, son?"

"I reckon, Judge," answered Freddy, "but I ain't scared. I never shot that old Sequanna and I don't mean to run."

Judge Parker sighed. "We'll likely be having another case here afore long, then. I doubt you'll be called on to testify. You just do as you've a mind to, Freddy Brown. Case dismissed."

Then, as the lawyer led the accused away from the bench, Judge Parker called out, "I want the rest of you folk to stay in your seats and give this boy a running start, hear? Lawyer Barnes, get that kid out of here and see if you can't explain on the way how pretty California is this time of the year."

Later that night, Pearl was loading Sam's Winchester

when there came a knock on her door. It was her Uncle Frank James.

"I come as quick as I heard, Pearl," he said.

"My, you must have traveled like the wind, then, Uncle Frank. It was only yesterday Freddy Brown shot Sequanna in the back, just like that other rascal done Uncle Jesse. Come and set whilst I coffee you. You are welcome to stay the night, of course, but I mean to be out a time this evening," said Pearl.

Frank James took a seat at the table as he smiled and asked, "Who on earth are you talking of, honey? I came because I heard about Belle and old Sam going to jail. I've been living in Lee's Summit, near Kansas City, since the law let me go. It sure feels good, living quiet at last. That old ulcer has just died a natural death, thanks to your good advice. You were right as rain, Pearl. The jury never left the box when I stood trial. The judge even shook my hand when he said I could go and just behave myself. When I heard you was alone, though, I did some riding to get here. What's that gun and ammunition doing on the table, honey? You fixing to go hunting at this hour?"

"Yes, I'm out to shoot me a skunk, but it can wait 'til I've coffeed you. I'd offer to let you come along, Uncle Frank, but now that you've turned law-abiding, you'd best not."

Frank James frowned and said, "You'd best tell me about this skunk you mean to shoot. I'll see how I feel about being law-abiding after you tell me how he's wronged you."

Pearl told him as she fed him. When she got to the part about the infernal judge letting Freddy Brown go, Frank James nodded and said, "I can see he had no choice, Pearl. If I was you, I'd let it lie, too."

"Let it lie? Why, Uncle Frank, that ornery cuss gunned Sequanna, and Sequanna was my friend."

"I know," said Frank. "But leave it lie, anyway. It hardly seems right for a young gal like you to be out gunning for grown men. If as many as you say think he done the deed on that Cherokee boy, you won't be the only one out hunting him. Be slick, child. Let the Injuns kill the rascal for you."

"I can't. I owed Sequanna personal. Before I ride, tell me what you're doing here, Uncle Frank."

He put down his cup and said, "I told you. I heard you were in trouble, so I came."

"I ain't in trouble, Uncle Frank," replied Pearl.

"You ain't huh? Then how come I found you loading up a Winchester as I come in the door? You may need more supervising than I thought, Pearl Younger. I figured I was riding over to protect you. I can see I got here just in time to protect that poor doomed colored boy as well. I'll tell you what my original plannings were, honey. I mean to carry you back with me to Lee's Summit. Don't look wall-eyed at me. I meant that fatherly, for as pretty as you are, I got me my own woman as well as a tolerable quarter section. I told her before I left to make up the spare room for you. We got us a fair house, and there's horse for you to ride and all. We'll carry you into Kansas City and introduce you to fine folk. It's a funny thing but since I've retired as an owlhoot I seem to be a sort of celebrated man. Folks keep coming up to me on the street to shake my hand and ask for my autograph. Ain't that something?"

"I'm glad the law ain't after you no more, Uncle Frank."

"Not half as glad as *I* am, girl! Lord, it feels so good that some mornings I wakes up singing, and I want to clack my heels like a fool!"

Then he sobered and added, "That's why I want you to come with me, Pearl. I owe both you and your father, Cole Younger. I writ to him about you and he says he's glad you turned out pretty, even though he was a mite surprised to hear he had a daughter down here in the Strip. This ain't no place for a gal like you, Pearl. Come with me to Missouri and we'll rear you right, hear?"

"I've already been reared to womanhood, and I have to go shoot a skunk this night," she said stubbornly.

"That's what I mean. When a man has a son he worries. When a man has a daughter he prays. You ain't as grown-up as you think, honey. The next few years are a delicate time for anyone, male or she-male. My own life would have been spent more sensible had I had someone to guide me a mite better. I can see the road purely forks ahead of you, Pearl. If you has a lick of sense, you'll come with me back to Lee's Summit," he said with a sigh.

"I can't. My place is here. I have to watch the property for Mamma and Sam. I have important business ahead of me tonight, too, so I'd best get to it."

Frank James shook his head and said, "Pearl. You ain't going nowhere with that Winchester. I ain't asking. I'm telling, so put the fool gun back on the wall and we'll just say no more about it."

Pearl smiled uncertainly and asked, "How do you figure to stop me, Uncle Frank? You ain't my real kin, no offense, and even if you was, I'm a mite old for you to put over one's knees for a licking."

Frank stared at her judiciously. "I ain't sure it would be seemly to spank a gal built so womanly, Pearl, but I reckon I'm still tough enough to stop you one way or another. I told your father I'd look after you. I mean to do it. Since I've reformed, it's my bound duty not to let you kill folk. Put away your gun, honey. You ain't about to gun anyone whilst I draw breath. Could I have some more of that nice peach cobbler? You surely cooks nice for such a murderous little gal."

She fetched his second helping, but asked, "How long are you planning to stay, Uncle Frank?"

"Long enough. I follow your drift, honey. If you won't ride back with me to Missouri, I'll just camp here long enough to keep you from doing anything dumb."

Pearl put the gun aside. Her score with Freddy Brown could keep until her Uncle Frank got tired of being a pest about the matter.

Later that evening, as Frank James smoked by the fireplace while Pearl mended some clothes, there came another knock on the door. It was Rafe, Judge Parker's deputy. Pearl invited him in and introduced him to Frank James.

"I'm proud to meet up with you at last, Frank. Last time I tried to meet up with you, you gave me the slip," said Rafe.

Frank James laughed. "Yeah, I don't do things like that no more. Mayhaps lucky for both of us, since I hear you're pretty good with that S&W. It's double action, ain't it? Always favored single action myself, but everyone to his own taste."

Pearl asked Rafe if he'd like refreshments. The tall saturnine deputy shook his head and said, "Like some. Can't stay that long, Miss Pearl. I was wondering if you folks heard anyone riding through these parts this evening. Likely riding hard."

They both shook their heads with puzzled smiles. Rafe shrugged and said, "He must have headed another way, then."

"Who are we talking about, Rafe?" Pearl asked.

Rafe said, "The man who gunned Freddy Brown, of course. Didn't happen long ago. Indian cuss just strode into the bunkhouse out to the Bar Seven and emptied his gun into Freddy afore he could rise from his blankets. The others was too thundergasted to move afore he backed out, looking mighty pleased with himself, considering what Judge Parker has in store for him. He rode out and the Bar Seven sent a man in to tell us about it. The trail's still warm, if only we could cut it. Since he didn't ride through here, we just have to look somewhere else. I'm sorry I troubled you all, but it's my duty to ask about."

As she followed him to the door, Pearl asked, "What do you have to take the poor Cherokee in for, Rafe? Everyone knows Freddy Brown had it coming!"

"That ain't exactly true, Miss Pearl." said Rafe. "You know Freddy likely murdered that Cherokee boy. I know Freddy likely did it, too, and so does the judge, but in the eyes of the law, Freddy was innocent. That makes gunning him a hanging offense. When we catch the man who done it, he'll have to hang. This time there was a bunkhouse full of witnesses."

Rafe left, and Pearl came back to the fire, saying,

"Don't look at me like such a smug old cat, Frank James.
I'd have done it slicker."

Frank James shook his head and said, "Honey, there
ain't no way you could have done it slicker. Letting justice
flow to its own level like water is about as slick a move as
anyone can make. Ain't you glad you wasn't met up with
on the trail tonight, packing a loaded Winchester? I said I'd
come to look after you, and Pearl, you surely need some
looking after!"

Ben Franklin had been right when he'd said guest folk
and fish began to smell stale after three or four days.
There was no way Frank James was going to stay in
Younger's Bend until Sam and Belle Starr got out of
prison, but he insisted he'd stay until things quieted, if
Pearl wouldn't ride back to Lee's Summit with him. The
trouble with that notion was that things hardly ever quieted
in the Cherokee Strip.

Sam had warned the gang to stay low, and Belle had
vowed to cut the nuts off any man who trifled with her
daughter while she was working off her time, so the boys
seldom visited, and when they did they didn't even come in
for coffee.

Gossip had it that the Brown family had moved out of
the Strip since Freddy Brown's disgrace and murder.
Being colored was enough of a chore, even without the
Cherokee nation gunning for you in a blood feud.

So Pearl was stuck with Uncle Frank's company alone.
Even Alice seemed to be occupied. Her notoriety as the
blind "Helen of Troy" who'd got two men gunned, had attracted more than one curious young gent. Then, once
they'd seen how pretty she was, they didn't want to leave.
The blind girl's folk were a little worried and mighty proud
to have so many young suitors hanging about their front
steps of an evening.

Pearl had never met a reformed drinker or smoker, but
her Uncle Frank did tend to go on about being a reformed
outlaw. One sunset as they were jawing on the veranda and
he'd just finished telling the story of robbing the Glendale

Train for the seventh or eighth time, Pearl smiled and interrupted.

"No offense, Uncle Frank, but you've gotten past confession into bragging again."

He laughed good naturedly, and said, "Yeah, it was sort of fun, when me and Jesse and the world was younger. My old woman says I'm getting to be as boring as an old soldier. It's a funny thing, folks back home pay me to come and lecture them on the terrible things a life of crime can lead to. You might say I've gotten to be Missouri's answer to Niagara Falls. Sometimes I suspicion they attend my lectures just to enjoy a thumping good yarn. I haven't noticed any decrease in the way boys steal apples around Lee's Summit since I've been doing my reforming work."

"You say they pay you to brag on what you and my father and Uncle Jesse done?" Pearl asked.

"Yep. They can't hardly open a new bridge or railroad station back home without parading me by like an elephant. They don't pay me all that much, but it's a funny thing, Pearl, betwixt the farm, my horse trading, and the public appearing, I generally have more to jingle in my jeans that I ever had in the bad old days. Why do you ask? You need some money?"

Pearl shook her head and said, "Not for me. I got credit at the trading post and a few dollars saved besides. I was wondering what a doctor would ask to look at Alice Ferndancer's eyes for us."

"That's a generous notion, child, but I'd leave well enough alone if I was you. Granny Redbird says Alice is always going to be blind, and the little Indian gal seems used to the notion. It's dangerous to play God, Pearl. It hurts to have one's hopes dashed, and that blind gal's likely to have high hopes, if you go pestering her with doctor talk."

"Well, Granny Redbird says herself that she don't know everything. I'd like to see what a real doctor would say about them cobwebs in poor Alice's eyes."

"Honey, Alice don't know she's all that poor. She has a mamma and a pappa and a lot of young jaspers telling her how pretty she is. You've got to learn to leave sleeping dogs lay. I know your feelings. I used to try and change things more to my liking, too, but fighting on after Lee surrendered just got us in a dreadful mess. You're almost pretty enough to pass for an angel, but don't try to play God, girl. You'll just cause hurt."

Pearl set her jaw in a way Frank James remembered with a sinking heart. He reached in his pocket, took out a roll of bills, and peeled some off as he said, "I'm likely making a big mistake, but afore you go robbing any infernal train, I'd best give you the doc's time of day. Tell me what he says and if there's any way to cure that poor kid, I'll manage somehow."

The next day Pearl took Alice into Fort Smith to have her eyes examined. They went to Doctor Long, who was said to specialize in bad eyes. Doctor Long was a grave old man who received the two girls in friendly style and said they'd talk about money after he had a look-see. He put Alice in a big barber's chair, and the blind girl's eyes were filled with hopeful anxiety. Pearl stood by, holding her hand to steady her as Doc Long peered at her eyes with funny looking little spyglass things. Pearl asked if it was true white docs could put a body to sleep whilst they cut 'em open.

The kindly old man nodded, but said, "I don't see as we have a called-for operation, here, miss."

"Oh, you mean it ain't that serious, Doc? What did I tell you, Alice? I told you a fine doc could likely give you drops or something. Ain't that right, Doc Long?"

The doctor straightened up with a sigh. He was a good and kindly man, and dealing with blindness had put extra lines in his face as he'd grown older. He searched for the right words, but he'd had conversations like this before. He shook his head and said, "I'm afraid it's congenital, ladies."

"What does that mean, Doc? Mamma says Spider Woman spun webs in my eyes in her womb," Alice said.

"Close enough I guess. You see, Miss Ferndancer, your mother must have had a fever when she was carrying you. We call that frosting a cataract. I know you can't see to follow my meaning, but try to think of it as the way sand-blasted glass feels," the doctor said.

Alice nodded. "I know what glass feels like. Mamma says sighted folk can see through glass even though they can't see through cloth. I've never understood that, since glass feels thicker."

Pearl said, "Hold on, now, I remember reading about some doc cutting them catar things out of folk's eyes, Doc."

"It's been known to work, mayhaps ten percent of the time. But the ruined lenses isn't the problem. Look here."

He shone a beam from a little mirror into Alice's wide eye

"Folk with nothing ailing them but cataract can still tell light from dark. Their pupils contract like anyone else's when you shine light into their eyes. Miss Ferndancer's pupils are dilated permanently." He moved his free hand through the little beam and added, "Do you notice anything at all, Miss Alice?"

Alice said, "No. What are you doing, Doc?"

"Testing, dear heart. Just testing."

"I see what you're doing, but I don't follow your big fancy words, Doc," Pearl snapped.

"Let me put it this way, then," the doctor said. "The optic nerves are dead. Your friend is totally, one hundred percent unable to see. There's not a thing anyone can do about it."

Pearl's heart sank, but still she asked, "Even in Kansas City, in one of them big fancy hospitals, Doc?"

The small town ophthamologist gave her a wounded look. "You could take her to the moon and you wouldn't find anyone who could restore those optic nerves that just never got around to being born, Miss Younger. I can see your young friend here has learned to cope well with her affliction. There's nothing else we can do for her."

Pearl felt sick. She licked her lips and said, "Well, we'd best go home then. How much do I owe you, Doc?"

"Nothing, dear heart. It wouldn't be Christian to charge when there's nothing for me to do."

Pearl placed a dollar bill on a nearby metal tray and helped Alice out of the chair. She tried not to cry. Understanding, Doctor Long escorted them out in discreet silence. When they reached the street, Alice asked, "Is the sun ball high, Pearl? It sure seems hot out here."

Pearl sobbed, "Oh, just hesh and let's go find the wagon, you fool Indian."

"What did I do wrong, Pearl? You sound mad as anything at me," Alice asked in confusion.

"I ain't mad at you. I'm mad at me," Pearl said. "My Uncle Frank was right about playing God. It's vexing as hell when your God powers fails you."

When they were almost to the parker buckboard, they met the tall deputy, Rafe, coming down the walk. Rafe tipped his hat, "Howdy, gals. You come to take in the hanging this morning?"

Pearl frowned up at him and replied, "No, we just got to town. What hanging are you talking about, Rafe? Who got hung?"

"Oh, didn't you know we caught the rascal as shot that boy Sequanna? Half the Cherokee Nation came to see him do the rope dance this morning just at break of day. From the way they carried on, it's a shame you can only hang a rascal once," Rafe answered.

Pearl shook her head, confused, and said, "Hold on, now. How on earth could you hang Freddy Brown for killing Sequanna, Rafe? He's buried out by the Bar Seven."

"Well, sure he is, but it seems we was wrong about Freddy Brown all the time. That Creek-nigger told us true when he said he wasn't the man as bushwacked Sequanna from the trees. It was a white boy named Dawson as done the deed."

"Hank Dawson, that rider for the Bar Seven?"

"Yep, that was him. Only he'd been fired off the Bar Seven a few days afore he gunned Sequanna. That's why his name never come up on the list of witnesses at Freddy Brown's trial. Dawson was fired for drinking on the job, so Brown never called him to say one way or the other about where he might have rid that day. I'll allow we was all a mite asleep by the switch at the time, but when Hank Dawson tried to sell some cows, it made us wonder. A fired cowboy hardly ever has cows to sell that he came by honest, you know."

Pearl gasped and said, "Thunderation! I'd forgot all about the herd Sequanna told me he had! I never saw his cows, but he bragged on having some."

Rafe continued, "He did, and his brand was registered with the B.I.A., too. Old Hank Dawson likely figured there wouldn't be a record of Indian brands in Sebastian County and he was right. But it did seem odd about a worthless kid like him having stock to sell, so we asked about it and he busted down and confessed as soon as we arrested him. He said he figured everyone would figure Freddy Brown would get the blame, since the two boys had been fighting over a gal, Miss Alice, here. He had to shoot Sequanna in order to drive off his herd, since he knowed Sequanna and his Cherokee pals would trail said herd, and likely act sort of testy about him stealing it. Dawson told Judge Parker he'd heard gunning an Indian didn't count as murder. Judge Parker told him he was wrong, so his body's been shipped home to his kin in Tennessee. That's likely why them Cherokee enjoyed his hanging so much, They still hold hard feelings toward the whites who got their old lands in Tennessee. Can't say as I blame them. Hank Dawson sure took killing and robbing Indians casual."

Pearl leaned against a hitching post and started to cry hysterically after Rafe had excused himself. "What's got into you, girl? You wasn't fond of Hank Dawson, was you?" Alice asked.

Pearl sobbed, "I hardly knew the awful thing. That ain't what's got me so upset. Can you hold a secret, Alice?"

"Sure I can. What is it? I can see it's upset you mortal."

"I was loading my stepfather's Winchester to go gunning for Freddy Brown when my Uncle Frank came by unexpected to make me stop."

"I see. Well, I don't blame you. I'd have gunned Freddy Brown for killing our Sequanna if blind folks could do things like that."

"Damn it, you fool Indian, Freddy Brown wasn't the one who murdered Sequanna!"

"I know. I just heard, but you thought it was him, right?"

"I did, God forgive me. I was murder-bent on mere suspicion and, well, I reckon because poor Freddy was colored, too. All of us were wrong to judge that boy the way we did on the color of his hide, Alice."

"I didn't. I still don't know what a nigger might be."

"You might be lucky at that, Alice. I see what Uncle Frank means about playing God. None of us mortals have the powers of the Lord, and sometimes I suspicion He makes mistakes, too!"   ❧

9

FRANK JAMES WENT home to Lee's Summit, having likely
found Younger's Bend tedious. Pearl hadn't expected to
miss his jawing in the evenings, but she did, and Alice
seemed too busy with her new-found popularity to come
over often. It was odd how the boys stayed clear of Pearl.

She chored and ate and slept alone, night after endless
night, until, after a long spell of peace and quiet, six months
had passed and Belle came home with Sam Starr. The re-
union was joyous and noisy, but then Belle sent Pearl over
to visit with Alice. She and Sam hadn't been within hug-
ging and kissing range for six months, and Belle didn't
want an innocent maid about the premises when they made
up for lost time.

The moon was high and it was fair late when Pearl
found Alice saying goodnight to some shy boys on her own
steps. The boys seemed even shyer when Pearl said her
howdy-dos and they rode off quickly. Pearl made a wry
face as she sat down by Alice.

"My, ain't we ever popular these days?" she said.

Alice's blind eyes were radiant in the moonlight as she
answered, "I like being popular. Which one of them two
boys just now was better looking, Pearl?"

"I don't know. They were both tolerable, for 'breeds. Which one do you like best?"

"Both of 'em. I sure wish I was Shoshone, Pearl."

"How come? Ain't it enough of a chore being Creek-Cherokee, Alice?"

"Shoshone gals is allowed to have more than one husband. Mamma says Shoshones don't have Christian ways, but I vow it sure would be grand to be a Shoshone gal when one can't choose betwixt two or more boys. How do you reckon the Shoshone work it out in bed, Pearl?"

"Disgusting, most likely. It ain't natural to have more than one man and one woman living together, Alice."

Alice sighed. "That's what Mamma says. She says Shoshone are mighty wild Indians, even for Indians. My Dad says Cheyenne allow a man to have more'n one wife, but nobody but the Shoshone hold with a wife having more than one husband. Save the Crow, of course. Dad says Crow don't have no rules at all, and even sleep with their sisters. He might be making that up. Most Indians hate Crows. You reckon it's 'cause the Crows spend so much time scouting for the army?"

"It sounds likely, but why worry? You don't have no Crow boys courting you, do you, Alice?"

"Nope. I got me a couple of 'breeds, a Creek and an Osage paying court to me, but mostly I got Cherokee hanging about. Mamma says I'll likely have less in-law troubles if I marry up with a 'breed. Both full-blood Creek and Cherokee kin can be proddy about impure blood like mine, so I reckon I got it narrowed down, some. But you said both them 'breed boys was good-looking."

"I said they was tolerable, durn it. The Rogers boy has a better job. A blacksmith's likely to be home more than a cowboy like that Jim Mahoney."

"I think I like Billy Rogers best, too. He let me feel his biceps the other night and he's ever so strong. I admire a strong, soft-spoken man."

"Most women do. I'll have to study on it, Alice. There's more to being a man than being strong."

"Your mamma, Belle, has always fancied strong men, hasn't she?"

"She has. That's what I meant."

Meanwhile, over at the Starr spread, the conversation was less concerned with probable futures then it was with the recent past. Now that Sam had made rugged love to Belle, he was speaking broodingly about his six months in prison. He still lay in bed beside her, sipping a jar of white lightning.

Belle lay nude, at his command, in the moonlight. She had hardly warmed up for the night she'd planned for months. She fondled his limp shaft as she smiled up at him and pleaded, "Put down that infernal jar and do me right some more, darling. This is a hell of a time for a man to think of getting drunk. Did you miss me all them months in prison?"

Sam finished draining the jar, threw it across the room to smash on the stones of the hearth, and said, "Some. I missed a heap of drinking, too. Damn it, Belle. You had no call to get us locked up like that."

"Hell, Sam, it wasn't my intention to get caught. What say we try her dog style, now?"

"I ain't in a fucking mood, woman. I'm talking to you. I just spent six months of my life making little rocks outten big ones and I'm sore as hell about it."

"Well, don't take it out on me, Sam. I never sent you away. It was Judge Parker. Mayhaps you'd feel better if we got the boys to gun the rascal for treating us so ornery."

Sam stared aghast at her and said, "You're crazy, Belle. You know that, don't you? I don't know what in thunder I'm to do with a wife as crazy as you."

"Well," she suggested coyly, "you could pleasure me some more for openers, you big growly bear."

"Let go my pecker, damn it. I already done that to you. I'm studying on what else I ought to do about the way you carry on."

"Well, why don't we go French, then? Come on, Sam, I'm still horny as all get out!"

He shoved her roughly back down as she tried to sit up.

"Don't try to change the subject, damn it. You got me throwed in jail and I'm so sore I've a mind to whup you good."

"Aw, Sam, you don't want to do that."

"The hell I don't. I've a mind to get out my drover's whip and beat you 'til you promise never to act crazy on me again."

He started to rise, but Belle rolled out of bed with cat-like grace ahead of him, and by the time his feet were on the floor she was standing by the fireplace, stark naked with the fireplace poker in one hand.

"You go ahead, Sam. You just go and fetch your drover's whip, and we'll just see what happens!"

Sam sat on the rumpled sheets, staring silently at her for a long time. Then he laughed uncertainly, and said, "Come on, Belle. I was just funning. You know I'd never whup you. Come on back here and give old Sam some sweet loving, hear?"

Belle moved closer, still holding the poker, and her eyes gleamed wildly in the moonlight shining through the window panes behind Sam as she said, "I'll give you something, you drunk old Cherokee! I'll give you this poker wrapped about your skull if you ever mention whupping me or mine again! I mean it, Sam. I may be married up with you, but I'll have you remember I'm a high-born white woman. You ever raise a red hand to me and I swear you'll draw back a stump!"

Sam shook his head and said, "I won't raise one hand, Belle, but you sure look pretty, standing nekked like that with the moonbeams on your tits and all, and I got something else with red skin that I've raised like hell for you. Come on, old gal, let's screw some more!"

Belle laughed, dropped the poker, and climbed back in bed. He'd meant what he said and they went hot and heavy for a time, but it seemed all too brief to Belle. He soon rolled off, turned his back to her, and fell asleep like an innocent babe.

She lay beside him, frustrated, and wondered, as she fondled her own turgid flesh why she'd defended herself against the lizzy women in prison. The Good Lord knew Sam didn't know how to treat a woman right down there, and she'd heard them in the other cells at night, giggling dirty at each other by the hour. She wasn't sure just what lizzy women did to one another, but she knew it lasted more than a quarter-hour, damn it!

Gypsy had said it was best to hang tough whilst doing time. Fooling with the lizzy women crowd could lead to prison-yard knifings. Anyway, there was a mess of nicely hung men out there in the world. Gypsy was likely right, but Belle doubted she'd gone out to spend her first night of freedom with a fat drunken Indian.

Belle wondered what Gypsy was doing, and if her man was good-looking. Gypsy said she even enjoyed making love to her marks, though she never forgot while doing so that the real goal was to relieve the rascal of his gold. Women were more pragmatic about such matters. They could enjoy it as well or better than a man, but, since they didn't lose their breath so much while doing it, they could relax and let their mind sort of wander.

Belle was glad she'd teamed up with the older con woman in prison. Gypsy had told her all sorts of things she'd never known about making money. Belle's only problem, now, was this infernal redskin snoring at her side. She knew she'd cowed Sam out of outright whupping her, but getting him to go along with some of her new plans was going to be a chore.

Belle was still awake when there came a soft tapping on the door. Belle rose with a puzzled frown. Pearl had her own key to the lean-to, and it hadn't been her rap in any case. She slipped on a robe, moved cautiously to the door and whispered, "Who's there?"

A male voice answered, "Pete Ironhand, Miss Belle. We just heard tell you and Sam was out, so I come over to see if there was anything you needed."

Belle started to say no, then she remembered what the young buck who ran jars for them looked like. She opened the door and stepped out on the veranda, barefoot and smiling in the moonlight as she said, "Sam's sleeping off a celebrating jar, Pete. Let's you and me walk around out back so's not to disturb him."

Ironhand was surprised to have her take his hand that way, but he kept his dry-mouthed thoughts to himself.

"Set yourself down in the hay and we'll have us a get-to-know-you talk, Pete. You'd best not try to smoke 'mongst all this hay, but there's other pleasures to be had in the moonlight."

The young, good-looking Cherokee had noticed her robe was open as she sat down beside him. He looked away nervously and said, "Well, like I said, I come over to see if I could be of any service, now that you folk are out. Will Sam be going back in the likker trade, Miss Belle?"

"Of course he will. I'm thinking of starting my own business, too. That's what I wanted to talk about, after."

"After what, Ma'am?"

"Well, I'll tell you, Pete. We're going to have to be mighty careful, but I've had my eye on you for some time as a likely lad. I'm right fond of old Sam, you understand, but a woman as young as me has needs as well as ambitions. Why don't we get out of this ridiculous setting up position and I'll tell you all about it later."

Thus, unbeknown to Sam Starr, the Starr Gang, as the papers called it, divided like a growing germ. Most of the boys still helped Sam sell bootleg to deprived Indians, and Sam prospered like the rose. However, on the rare occasions he was sober, Sam was too busy selling jars instead of opening them to bother much with what his womenfolk might be up to.

His step-daughter, Pearl, was mostly working at the house and resigning herself to being an old maid. She was sorely vexed, a year or so after her folk got out of prison, when Alice Ferndancer posted her banns with David Tallchief. Alice hadn't asked Pearl's opinion on the infernal Osage-Choctaw cowboy. But Pearl still went to the wedding, since she'd been asked to be the maid of honor, and she had to admit that David Tallchief looked handsome enough in his rented finery.

He wasn't as tall as his name said he ought to be, but he was tall enough. He drew the wages of a top hand off the Double Diamond, and said he was saving up for his own herd some day. He kept looking down at blind Alice like she was some kind of fairy princess, and they said he didn't drink, neither. It made Pearl so mad she could have spit.

The only boys who ever came to call on her seemed to be the kind who led more interesting lives than David Tallchief and, though her mamma approved, Pearl gave outlaws short notice to vacate the premises whether they brought flowers or not. Mamma said real he-men were the only kind to trifle with, but Pearl had other notions on what made a man in her eyes.

Belle didn't press her only child to spark with outlaws. She was having too much fun with them herself. It was curious how easy it was to climax with a man in a stand-up stolen moment in some dark corner when one considered how long it took nekked in bed with a man you'd gotten used to. She even liked Sam better now, since he offered a novelty to her other paramours.

The best-loving boy in the bunch was a Creek gone wrong called Jim July, who'd been run off by his tribesmen for having unusually sticky fingers to their way of thinking. "Old Sam," as Belle now called a husband younger than herself, had taken Jim July on as a moonshiner, but Belle had other more exciting things for Jim and her other lovers to do.

The commerce of the time literally ran on horsepower, in town and country alike. Therefore, horses were valuable, and Frank James was hardly the only Missouri-bred person who could judge good horseflesh. Keeping her Indian lovers in the dark about one another, Belle sent them out to steal horses off the spreads within easy reach of the Cherokee Strip. The result was an awesome decline in local horsepower.

Belle warned her gang never to steal a horse easy to identify. They therefore, passed on calicos, whites, dapple greys and such. Most work and saddle horses were, of course, various shades of brown, and few wore brands like

cows. Once a nondescript but likely horse was in Belle's
hands, it was easy enough to sell in other parts. More than
one local white or Indian grumbled to the law about their
missing livestock, but it was one thing to suspect a horse
thief and another thing to prove it. After a couple of mysterious midnight barn burnings, people no longer saw fit to
voice their suspicions quite so openly. However, that didn't
mean they thought anyone but Belle and her bucks were
behind the decline in the equine population in those parts.

The matter of night riding was discussed at the grange
hall with some heat, but wiser feelings prevailed. It was
one thing to track down a horse thief or two and settle the
matter with a rope and a convenient tree branch but riding
against the Cherokee Nation called for more desperation
than a few horses called for, and the infernal woman was
said to be well connected with the Cherokee.

Belle was only half aware of the terrible things folk said
behind her back as she rode grandly by on her horse, Venus. She was pleased with the little she did pick up, as it
was mostly about her being a bandit queen.

Old Venus was finally getting too long in the tooth for
any kind of queen to ride. Belle had had the chestnut mare
longer than most horses lived. While Venus still looked like
a high-stepping race horse, she was losing her get-up-and-
go. Much as it pained Belle, for she was fond of old Venus,
it was time she switched mounts.

She explained to Jim July one lazy afternoon as they
made love in a haystack, that one chestnut thoroughbred
looked a lot like any other, once you studied on it. Jim said
he knew of a man in Sebastian County who raced a mare
that was the spitting image of old Venus.

Belle sent Jim to see how closely guarded the thoroughbred was. Then, after supper, she asked a husky young Osage called Murphy if he'd ride with her to Saunders
Slough, since Sam Starr was away on business and Saunders Slough was a mighty spooky place after dark.

It was spooky. The slough was a stretch of bottom land
that flooded every high water and bred all sorts of bugs
and crawly things in the meantime. Nobody lived there or

even went near it if they didn't have to. Murphy wondered why Miss Belle had brought a spade along. She explained once they got to their destination.

"You want me to dig you a hole, Miss Belle?" asked the Osage warily. He'd said a few country things to her in the past, just trying to find out if she was as wild as some allowed she might be.

Belle laughed as she tethered Venus to a willow and sat on a log to supervise.

"Don't worry, son, I only bury my help in hallowed ground, but you'd best get cracking, for we're meeting up with Jim July here around midnight and I want the hole dug by then," she said.

Murphy tested spongy soil with his borrowed spade. "Well, the sand's pure soft, but it surely is heavy with all this water in it. How big a hole do you want, Miss Belle?"

Belle looked thoughtfully at her tethered mare and answered, "Oh, eight-by-five ought to do."

"That's a mighty big hole, Ma'am."

"I know, Murphy. That's why I chose you to dig her. I surely admire your shoulders, old son."

The young Osage glowed with the compliment and dug the spade deep as he observed, "Yeah, some do say I'm strong as a bull. I've been told I'm built like a bull in other ways, if you take my meaning."

Belle did, but she didn't comment. The Osage was young and good-looking, but he'd never shared Belle's favors up to now. It was up to Belle whether he ever did or not. The erstwhile ugly duckling had discovered a new game; a cruel little game better-favored girls tended to discover at a more tender age. A gal didn't have to give herself all the way to a gent to find out if he admired her or not. Sometimes it was more fun to leave them sort of halfway there, squirming like worm-bait on the hook. Belle's instincts told her that no matter how good a gal might be betwixt the legs, a man hungering for her always thought she was better than any woman could be. It gave her a nice warm feeling of power to tease Murphy.

As he dug in the moonlight, Belle took a dip of snuff

and said, "My, you sure are strong as they said you was. Mayhaps even stronger. Look at that dirt fly."

"Aw," said Murphy, "you ain't seen half how strong I be, yet." He proceeded to dig like a lovesick prairie dog trying to reach China before the dawn.

Even the husky Osage had to rest, so Belle rewarded him by letting him sit by her side on the log from time to time. The second time he did so, Murphy tried to kiss her. She eluded him gracefully and joshed him friendly, saying, "Behave yourself, you horny rascal. You'll never finish with that hole if you weaken yourself with country matters."

He laughed. "That ain't the only hole I'm interested in and you know it, ah, honey."

"I know the kinds of holes you menfolk are all interested in, but we'll talk about mine after."

"Hot damn! Will you let me, honey, after I dig that big whatever for you?"

"Mayhaps. I have to study on it, Murphy. Your sudden admiration has me totally flustered up. I didn't know you was so interested in me as a woman."

"Go on, Belle, you knew I was a natural man, didn't you?"

"Well, if I'd known you were that natural I might not have rid out here alone with you in the moonbeams. As long as you're all full of beans, what say you use some of that infernal energy on my hole? The one in the ground over yonder, I mean."

And so, between spells of digging and restful tussles on the log with Belle, Murphy got the monstrous grave dug about an hour before midnight. Even Belle had to agree that there was no sense digging below the water table. When Murphy had the hole dug to where the water was up around the ankles of his boots, she told him he could stop. He stood the spade on its blade in the spoil heap and came at her again. As he dropped on his knees by the log and put his arms around her to kiss her, she let him. She let him kiss her hard and hungry, but when he stuck his tongue in her mouth she bit it and pushed him back, saying, "That's enough, now. You're getting me all hot and flustered, Murphy."

"That's what I was aiming to do, honey. What do you have under this here skirt?"

She slapped his wrist and said, "Stay outten my skirts, you fool boy. Jim July should be here any minute, and what would he think if he saw a married woman giving her all to a young rascal like you? Lord of mercy, I'm nigh old enough to be your mother. Jim wouldn't know it I was laying you or giving birth to you! Behave yourself and have some snuff with me as we wait."

"Don't want snuff. Want you. Don't tease me, Belle. I wants you so bad I can taste it!"

"Do you like to taste gals, Murphy? My, you do sound tempting, but there's a time and place for everything, and this ain't it. You must simmer down and be good, hear? I'll let you know when it's the time and place to be bad."

"Hot damn! Does that mean you'll let me, later?"

"Well, we'll see, Murphy. I got to study this new relationship you're proposing. A woman in my position can't be too careful, you know. Old Sam would kill us both if he even suspected we was more than friends."

Murphy's voice became conspiratorial as he said, "Hell, honey, I'd never give the show away. I've pleasured more than one married gal in my time and I've never been found out yet."

Belle spat out her snuff and kissed him again, putting her back into it this time, but pushing him away when his hand was halfway up her thigh. "Not now, durn it. I'll let you know when I'm ready."

Then she kissed his cheek as she regained control. "You wouldn't want to waste our first lovings on a hurried wrassle in an old swamp now, would you?"

"Oh, Lord, are you saying it's all right with you. honey?"

"I'm saying I'm praying to the Lord to give me strength, Murphy. You're a mighty hard man to say no to."

"I'm hard as hell, all right. You want to feel what I've been saving up for you, Belle?"

"Not hardly. I'd likely swoon and give in and then what would we say when Jim July rode up?"

In the end, of course, they wound up rutting in the sand behind the log. Belle had started to just satisfy him for now with her hand, to calm his nerves and satisfy her own considerable curiousity, but Belle was a warm-natured woman, and once she'd grasped that big Osage creation and felt how nice it was, it seemed a shame to waste it in mid-air, so she let him put it where it seemed more natural to both of them. After they'd both climaxed a time or two, she told Murphy to leave. She said she'd never manage to meet Jim July's eye innocently with her new lover standing about, grinning like a shit-eating dog.

She was sitting on the log alone, throbbing warmly from her unexpected moonlit thrills, when Jim July rode in, leading the stolen thoroughbred.

Belle sprang up and went over to pet her new Venus.

"It went slick as silk, honey," Jim said. "They had her in a paddock with a lock they should have been ashamed of. I vow this thoroughbred's worth at least a thousand dollars, for she won the race at Ozark Downs last month. What's this big hole doing here, Belle? Godamighty, it's big enough to bury us all."

Bell sighed as she said, "I know. Help me change my saddle and bridle from my old mount to my new, Jim. I'll show you in a minute why I had the hole dug."

Jim dismounted, saying, "I get it. Everyone for miles knows Belle Starr rides a chestnut thoroughbred, but having *two* such critters might call for some tall explaining, right?"

"That's about the size of it, Jim. I sure wish I didn't have to do old Venus so dirty. She's been a mighty fine friend to me all these years, but like you say, I can only prove I bought one such mare. I bought Venus proper, down Texas way. I have the papers to prove it. Are you sure this new Venus don't have no blaze or markings to give the show away? Standing here in the moonbeams they sure favor one another, but . . ."

"Belle, honey, when it comes to judging horseflesh, you

can't beat old Jim July. I told you this here thoroughbred was as good a match as one can ask for. Just let me cinch this sidesaddle and . . . there you go, Belle. She's the spitting image, save for being mebbe a hand taller and being a few years younger, of course. You, ah, want me to take care of your old mare?"

Belle shook her head sadly. "I'd best do it, Jim. Venus trusts me, and besides, it seems more fitting to be finished by a friend's hand."

Belle grasped her stripped-down mare's forelock and led her away from the other two tethered horses. "Come on, old girl. Mamma wants a word with you in private."

Venus balked near the edge of the gaping hole as the sand gave under her hooves.

"Simmer down, honey. You know Mamma wouldn't hurt you, don't you?" Belle said.

She patted the skittish mare's neck with her free hand to steady her before she reached for one of her ivory-handled six guns, musing aloud, "It's a shame us human folk don't get to end like this when we gets old and doddering. There's worse ways to die, Venus. You'll never know what it is to get old and ugly and feeble-minded."

Belle placed the muzzle of he revolver in the indentation over the mare's eyes, and whispered, "So long, old pal." Then she pulled the trigger.

The other horses whinnied nervously, but Venus just fell away like a tumbleweed rolling in a gentle breeze and landed in her soggy grave with a mighty splash. Belle gazed down at what she'd done and said, "Never even twitched. I'm glad I done it right by her. Would you fill in the hole, Jim? I'm feeling sort of weak at the knees for some reason. I'd best sit down and steady myself."

It didn't take Jim July half as long to shovel the spoil back as it had taken Murphy to dig it out. Even though the night was cool and the dirt was loose, Jim was sweating by the time he'd finished.

Jim put an arm around Belle's waist and said, "The grave's mounded some, but it'll settle once she rots a mite. She ought to turn back to clay soon, as wet as the soil is in this slough. How's about a little kiss, Belle? Don't I rate a kiss for fetching you such a fine new mare?"

"It ain't a new mare. Make sure you remember that. That chestnut over yonder is my old Venus, sort of rejuvenated," Belle said.

"Hell, everyone knows that, Belle. Let's kiss on it."

Belle started to say no, but she did feel oddly excited for some reason. She kissed Jim July, and when he started to feel her up she said, "Wait, I don't want to mess my dress. Let's do it right."

He let Belle go and she got to her feet, taking off her hat and guns before she peeled her black velveteen riding habit off over her head. Jim July gasped as he saw how the moonlight played on her petite, well-formed body. He popped a button fumbling with his hickory shirt as he called out, "Wait for me. I want to get nekked too!"

Belle walked nude to the soft mound of the big grave. Jim joined her, stark naked, and took her in his arms again.

"You sure have odd notions of a fitting love bed, Belle. I can feel that dead horse under my damn feet."

Belle sank to the clean sand, pulling Jim down with her. "I know. It feels exciting and what the hell, we surely can't put a marker or flowers over her. I feel like leaving her in a loving place. Jim, let's make lots of love above her afore we leaves her here forever."

They did. Even Belle was surprised how passionate she suddenly felt. It was odd how death and sex had such exciting effects on a body. Mayhaps, she thought, that was why she'd always enjoyed the company of killing men. Nobody felt as alive in a woman's arms as a man who found it easy to kill. She felt young and alive, even though she hadn't killed anybody more important than old Venus.

By break of day, the new Venus didn't really look as much like the old Venus as Belle had expected, but a chestnut thoroughbred was a chestnut thoroughbred, so what the hell. Sam never commented, if he noticed at all. Pearl said Venus looked sort of odd for some reason, but didn't press it when her mother said it was likely the new grooming brushes and the way she'd trimmed the old mare's mane. Folk less accustomed to tending the old Venus were less sharp-eyed as Belle rode by, sitting proud on her spirited steed.

Colonel Lewis, however, the original owner of the fastest mare in the county of Sebastian, took it mighty hard when his stablehands reported her missing from the paddock. He posted a five hundred dollar reward for information about her, and that tended to sharpen eyes a mite all over the neighborhood.

One morning, as the Starrs were just finishing breakfast, Rafe, Spike, and a couple of other deputies rode in to say Judge Parker wanted a word with Belle and Sam, and to bring the horse along.

Spike wanted to arrest Pearl too, but Rafe told him not to talk so surly. Pearl saddled her own painted pony and rode along with them, arrested or no.

Judge Parker held court out in the yard that forenoon, since horses were not allowed in his courtroom, even as witnesses. Colonel Lewis and some of his hands were there, and the colonel looked mad as a wet hen.

As the newcomers dismounted in the courthouse yard, Colonel Lewis pointed with his riding crop and shouted,

"God damn it, I knew it! That's my thoroughbred, Judge Parker!"

Judge Parker pursed his lips. "It sure looks like the critter I saw racing over to Ozark Downs, Colonel. How do you want to plead this charge, Belle Starr?"

Belle remained in her sidesaddle as she reached disdainfully into the saddlebag behind her hip.

"Not guilty, of course. I don't know this man and I don't know what he's thundering about. I brought Venus, here, lawful in Texas, back in '72 or '74."

She took out her wilted bill of sale, unfolded it, and thrust it out. "Here it is, Judge. It's dated '74. I've rid old Venus so long I'd sort of forgot when I got her."

She handed the paper down to Judge Parker, who read it over and said, "I'll keep this for now as Exhibit A, Belle."

He put it in the side pocket of his frock coat and turned to Lewis, "The lady has papers granting her full rights to one chestnut thoroughbred mare, Colonel. It's your turn."

Lewis gasped and said, "I don't care if she has papers from here to the moon and back, God damn it! That's my horse she's sitting and I'll thank her to get off and go direct to jail!"

Parker shot him a frown and warned, "I'll do the deciding on such matters, no offense."

The Judge moved around to the disputed mare's head and took the bridle in hand to examine her teeth.

"You say you got this horse back in '74, Belle?"

"I did. I'll allow she 'pears younger than she might. I takes good care of her, Your Honor."

Parker smiled crookedly and said, "That's for damned sure. Most horse traders would judge her as a three-year-old, but it's true no two horses age at the same exact rate, so I fear these here teeth ain't concrete evidence. You have some identifying marks on record on your missing horse, Colonel?"

"She isn't missing anymore, damn it! She's standing right in front of us with that infernal she-male hoss thief setting on her, bold as brass!" Colonel Lewis spat.

"That isn't the question I asked, Colonel," said the judge, "I'll take your word this appears to be your stolen thoroughbred, but the lady says it's hers and she has the papers to prove it."

"God damn it, Judge! Don't you see what she done? She's using papers on another mount to pass off as the papers on mine!"

Judge Parker nodded soberly, and asked, "How about that, Belle?"

"He's lying, Judge. Ask anyone and they'll tell you I've had this mare long afore his was stole. If this ain't the Venus I've always rid, where the hell might she be, save under my rump as always?"

Judge Parker turned to the arresting officers as Pearl, sitting on her pony nearby, held her breath. Now that she studied on it in broad day, Pearl could see the mare Mamma was riding was a total stranger.

Judge Parker asked for Rafe's opinion. Rafe shrugged and said, "Well, I've seen her more than once aboard a chestnut thoroughbred, Your Honor. I can't rightly say if this is the critter or not. It sure looks like Colonel Lewis' race horse. But, on the other hand, it sure looks like old Venus, too."

The judge asked, "Did you boys think to scout about for other chestnuts whilst you was out to the Starr spread this morning?"

"Sure we did, Your Honor. We never expected Belle, here, to say any mount but Venus might be Venus. They ain't got any other chestnut thoroughbreds out yonder. None we saw, leastways."

Judge Parker looked over at Sam Starr, sitting silent and bemused on his own dun gelding. Parker asked, "What have you to say about this, Sam?"

Sam shrugged and answered, "Nothing. My woman never told me about it if she stole a horse the other night. She's rid that critter or its twin since afore I ever knew her."

The Judge looked over at Pearl, but didn't ask her anything. He turned back to the colonel and said, "Well, what we have before this court is a missing mare, chestnut, thoroughbred."

"I can see that, Your Honor, and that infernal woman's sitting on it!" the colonel insisted.

Judge Parker said, "Hold on. We've still got one horse unaccounted for. Belle, here, has papers allowing her to ride about on a chestnut thoroughbred. I'll allow it's suspicious, but suspicious won't do. If that isn't the mare she's supposed to be riding, where is the infernal critter?"

"Hell, Judge, how should I know? She must have sold her old mount to someone else!"

"You got someone in particular in mind, Colonel? It's one thing to accuse and another entire to prove. Since you posted that reward, folks have been keepin' an eye out for any chestnut mares at all. Nobody in this neck of the woods seems to have acquired such a critter in recent memory. So, as I said, we're still missing a horse here."

"God damn it, Judge, don't you want to arrest her?"

"Want to. Can't. There's no solid evidence that the mare she's setting isn't the one she bought lawfully in Texas, and she has papers to back her story."

"Oh, hell, I got my own papers on that same horse, Judge!"

"No you don't, Colonel. You have papers on a horse that was stolen. Belle, here, has papers on a horse she says is her'n. I can say for the benefit of all here present that I think you're right, Colonel. I suspicion Belle of slickering us with ring-papers, and she ought to be ashamed of herself. But you can see she ain't, and unless you can do a better proving job, this court has no further say in the matter. Case dismissed for lack of evidence and I'm going home for lunch. It's hot as hell out here."

Pearl couldn't believe it, but she was glad. She saw Colonel Lewis and one of his hands talking to the deputy, Spike, and shooting mean looks their way. She moved over to Belle and Sam and suggested that they do some riding.

Belle allowed that that was a good notion. Sam said he had business in town as long as he was here, so the two women rode for home.

As soon as they were alone on the trail, Pearl asked, "No fooling, Mamma. Did you steal that mare off Colonel Lewis?"

Belle laughed and replied, "As God is my witness, child, I never went within a country mile of the Lewis spread."

"Well, I know you wouldn't lie to me, Mamma, but that sure don't look like Venus, no offense."

"No offense taken, honey. I have noticed this critter's changed some of late. She might be getting old. Horses are like people that way. We all look a mite different as we age."

"Mamma, that mare don't look older. She looks younger. A heap younger."

"Well, mayhaps she's getting her second wind. I know

I've been feeling more spry of late. Let's not talk about the fool mare no more, daughter. How come you wasn't nice to that Winslow gent the other evening? You know he likes you, and he's nigh pure white."

"I know he's wanted for a gunning in Waco, too. My daddy might have been an owlhoot, Mamma, but I ain't interested in the breed."

"You ought to get interested in *some* young gent, then. You're pushing near the brink of twenty, and you don't mean to be an old maid, do you?"

Pearl set her jaw stubbornly and answered, "I ain't twenty yet, and if it's a choice betwixt being an old maid and an outlaw's woman, I'll take old maid."

Meanwhile, back in Fort Smith, Sam Starr had spoken to the boys at the liquor warehouse and gone over to the nearby saloon to celebrate. He wasn't sure what he was celebrating, but a man didn't get turned loose by Hanging Judge Parker every day, so it called for some serious drinking.

Sam was bellied up to the bar, enjoying the calming effects of Maryland Rye in a shady place, when the part-time deputy, Spike, came in.

Spike walked over and stopped, two paces away, staring hard enough at Sam for the men around to sort of edge back. Sam nodded at Spike and said, "Howdy. Can I buy you a drink to show there's no hard feeling, Spike?"

"I don't drink with Indians. It's agin the law for Indians to drink at all, and I'm going to have to arrest you some more," Spike said.

Sam laughed and said, "Not hardly, Spike. That law only applies on the reservation, which, as you see, we ain't on. Indians working in white parts is allowed to drink like anyone else."

"You ain't working in Fort Smith, you thieving son of a bitch. You're over here on the decent side of the line looking for trouble, and trouble is my middle name."

Sam Starr's eyes went sleepy and a man in the corner muttered, "Oh, oh,"

Most of the others in the bar knew what was happening.

Folk used to Indians know that you don't have to worry about an Indian when he's yelling bright-eyed and bushy-tailed.

Sam's voice was curiously soft as he said, "I'll overlook your bad manners, Spike. I see you're a poor loser. But don't call me a son-of-a-bitch no more. I don't like it."

Spike sneered and said, "You don't, huh? Well, I'm trying to be neighborly, so I won't call you a son-of-a-bitch no more. How does thieving mother-fucker please you?"

Sam sighed, put his glass on the bar, and went for his gun.

Spike had hoped he might. He'd come in on the prod and was expecting it. He slapped leather, too, and the other men in the saloon dove every which way as the two men opened on each other at point blank range.

It got mighty silent. Nobody breathed as they crouched in corners or behind overturned tables, waiting for the smoke to clear.

When it did, Sam Starr was still on his feet, leaning against the bar. Spike lay sprawled on the sawdust covered floor, staring blankly at the pressed tin ceiling with a row of wet red buttons added to the ones already on his shirt front.

"Damn it, Sam, you've killed that boy," the bartender yelled.

"Yeah, ain't that a bitch?" Sam said as he let go of the bar to fall wearily to the same dirty floor. He was dead when they rolled him over on his back.

And that's how Belle Starr got a new horse and lost a husband, all in the same week.

Jim July moved into the cabin in Sam's place. Pearl didn't like it much, but what was she to do about it? At least her mamma seemed to be bearing up well in her widowhood. ❧

10

BELLE KEPT THE name Belle Starr after she'd buried poor
Sam and taken up with Jim July. Jim offered to marry up
with her, but Belle said she was in mourning and didn't
fancy being called Belle July. Some of the neighbors in
Younger's Bend were scandalized, not so much by her living with another man so soon, but because Jim was a
Creek.

Jim didn't look colored, but one never knew with Creeks.
Many a neighboring white said Jim July was a thieving
nigger, as if mean-mouthing Belle would make her a lower
outcast than she already was. Belle didn't feel like an outcast. She felt more like a bandit queen than ever, for Jim
July, while younger and nicer looking than Sam, was a
weaker willed man. Now Belle really had the bit in her
teeth and was prepared to do some spirited fence jumping.

She had enough cunning to act quiet for a spell, and let
folk get used to the idea that the new Venus wasn't really
the property of Colonel Lewis after all, so she stayed
mostly around the cabin with her new lover, drinking and
carrying on in broad day in a way her daughter Pearl could
hardly abide.

Pearl had discovered a vice of her own, over in Fort

Smith. It was called the public library. Thánks to her mother's casual tutoring, Pearl could read. What was more important, she liked to. Some of the words had mighty long
handles, but she could wade through most books if she
moved her lips a mite.

She'd found a tabled nook in the reading room where
nobody bothered her as she pored over the endless books in
the stacks. She had the curiosity and attention span of the
self-educated, so she liked the encyclopedias best. It was a
thundering wonder how many things there were to learn
about the outside world.

She learned that folk had lived before the coming of the
Lord, for that was what B.C. meant, and that Robert E.
Hood didn't hail from New Mexico after all. The books
said his real name was Robin and that the feud he'd had
with the sheriff of Lincoln County had happened almost
B.C. and in the old country. But otherwise, he sounded a
lot like the folk she been reared amongst.

She found a book one afternoon on the writing of proper
letters, so she composed a proper letter to her father in the
Minnesota State Prison. She explained that she'd hired a
post office box in Fort Smith, so's he wouldn't have to
write back to her at an address he might feel awkward
about, considering what Uncle Frank had said about time
off for good behavings. This time she sealed and sent it
herself, and a few weeks later she found an answer in her
post office box.

She sat on a bench out in front of the library and opened
the letter written on prison stationery. It read . . .

"Dear Miss Pearl Younger:
I was mighty pleezed to heer from you and it's not
true I didn't want to. I did not know I had yew by
Belle Shirley until Frank James paid me a visit a spell
back. If I had got yewr other letters I wood have writ
to you yew, you? sooner. Frank gets to travel about
the cuntry telling boys not to go wrong and he's bin by
tew see me more than once, as has your Aunt Retta,
who is my sister. She says if Frank says you are all

right, that's good enough for her. Your Uncle James joyns me in wishing you well and so does your Uncle Bob Younger, who's feeling poorly. Bob has consumption and we sure hope they set him free to die at home amongst his kin. Your Uncles and me has asked for parole, but it don't seem likely. So if I never get out to see you in the flesh, pay mind tew Frank James and don't go getting yourself put in jail like me. You wouldn't like it. Frank tells me you has growed up mighty nice and so I am mighty proud on you. I hope sum day to meet up with you. But I don't know what we can dew after. You are tew old to buy a circus baloon and tew young to drink with, but we'll work something or other out.

Your loving father, Cole Younger.

P.S.Don't you go wrong. I mean it. They got enough Youngers in jail for now."

Pearl read the letter over twice and sat there in the sunlight crying softly. A shadow fell across the letter in her lap and a male voice asked softly, "Is there something the matter, Ma'am?"

Pearl looked up. It was a boy she'd seen about the library before. He was tall and blond and gentle looking in a manly way. He wore a Stetson hat and riding boots, but most of him was dressed "townie," in a tweed suit.

"There's nothing wrong. I just got a letter from my kin as choked me up a mite. An uncle I didn't know I had is sick," she said.

"That could put one off her feed. My name is Steve Logan."

"I'm Pearl Younger. Are you kin to the Logans they named Logan County after?"

"That was the richer side of the family, Miss Pearl." He laughed. "I have to work for my keep. I clerk for my uncle, over at Logan's Dry Goods Store."

"My heavens, that's about the biggest store in all Fort Smith. You must be mighty sharp, clerking in a big store like that."

"I went to the twelfth grade. It isn't all that hard. You live around here, Miss Pearl?"

"No, why?"

"Uh, I thought I'd see you home, if that's where you'd be headed."

Pearl shook her head and answered, "I'm fixing to go in and read. If you must know, I live over in the Cherokee Strip at a place calt Younger's Bend."

"Do tell? You don't look Cherokee. Your dad must be an Indian agent, right?"

"Some called him an agent in his time. He ain't with us right now. He's, ah, working for the state up Minnesota way. My mamma and me are waiting for him to get out, I mean, done."

Steve Logan nodded and said, "Well, I'd need to go home and get my pony if I was to see you that far. If you mean to be in town when I get off work at the store . . ."

"I reckon I know the way myself, Mister Logan, but I thank you just the same."

"I'll be on my way, then." He sighed, adding, "Uh, there's a social at the grange this week-end, Miss Pearl. Has anyone asked you yet?"

Pearl dimpled shyly and replied, "No, I don't know many boys from Fort Smith. But I'd have to study on it before I took you up on your kind offer, if it was an offer."

He grinned and said, "You know it was an offer, Miss Pearl. Will you be about the library some more this week?"

She said mayhaps she would and mayhaps she wouldn't, so he went off to do whatever clerks did in stores, looking like a prospector who'd just noticed color in a creek he'd never panned before.

That night at supper, Pearl told her mother about her meeting up with Steve Logan. Jim July wasn't home. The Creek was mighty busy after sundown since he'd taken over Sam Starr's bootlegging in addition to the chores Belle set up for him and the boys.

Belle heard Pearl out, looking at her sort of wistfully until the girl said she was studying on going to the grange social with Steve. "You're just riding for a fall, girl. You'd best forget your sissy townie boy. What's the matter with that nice Frank Dalton, if you cotton to boys from Fort Smith all that much?"

Pearl frowned and said, "Mamma, Frank Dalton's a *Dalton!*"

"Hell, girl, everybody knows that. The Daltons are kin to the Youngers, too. But Frank's a decent cousinhood removed from you. He's right nice-looking, too. As for being a Dalton, Frank ain't as wild as his brothers. I hear tell he's asked for a job as a lawman. Since Sam left a vacancy in Judge Parker's staff like he done, Frank may get it."

"Mamma, I wish Frank Dalton well with his job hunting, but he ain't my cup of tea at all. Haven't you heard what his brothers, Bob, Bill, and Grat did over to the Osage Strip a while back? They'd signed on as lawmen, too, but that never stopped them from running off with a herd of Indian beef!"

Belle laughed. "I heard. Ain't they little rascals, though? The Dalton boys are just spirited, Pearl. They've never been posted for anything serious, and Frank Dalton's said to be almost a disappointment to his wilder kin. He's the honest living Dalton boy. If you're so set on sparking sissies, Frank's about the one for you."

Pearl shook her head stubbornly but Belle insisted, "Study on it, honey. You'd get the best of both worlds if you encouraged Frank Dalton some. He'll never wind up in jail, riding for the law, and a lawman for an in-law would be mighty comforting to me in my declining years, if you follow my drift."

Pearl did. She stared aghast at her mother as she asked, "Is that why you want me to give myself to Frank Dalton? So's you and Jim July could get away with even more of your stealing?"

"Now, daughter, nobody said a thing about you giving yourself to anybody. Frank Dalton would have to marry up with you afore you gave him more than a kiss on the veranda! Land's sake, Pearl, didn't I rear you more proper than that?"

"I ain't sure just who reared me, Mamma. Sometimes I fear I mostly reared my own self. But whoever it was, I ain't about to spark lawmen as my part of the family business!"

Belle frowned and said, "Don't mean-mouth your mamma, girl! It's no never mind to me whether you fancy Frank Dalton or a dozen others. I'm only trying to keep you from getting hurt, honey. What's that Steve Logan going to say when he finds out who you are?"

Pearl frowned back as she asked soberly, "I don't know. Who *am* I, Mamma?"

"Who are you? Thunderation, girl, don't you have a looking-glass in your own room? You know blamed well who you are. You're my loving daughter, Pearl Younger."

"I had that part figured out, Mamma, but who am I to folk like Steve Logan and his kin?"

"I'll tell you who you are to them, Pearl. You're pure trash. Don't frown at me so. I never said it. Folk like the Logan boy's kin talk like that 'bout us folk in Younger's Bend. I know you ain't trash. Hell, you're so prissy it makes me broody at times. But face it, Pearl. To folk like the Logans, you're the bastard child of a convicted bank robber and . . . well, me."

"Do you have to go on being you, Mamma? My daddy's never likely to come back, and poor old Sam's in his grave, too. Why couldn't you go straight like Uncle Frank James? He says it don't hurt."

Belle grimaced. "Frank James is him and I'm Belle Starr. I can't change my nature, Pearl, even if I wanted to, which I don't."

She saw Pearl didn't understand. She put a hand on her daughter's and added, "Honey lamb, it wouldn't do you no good if I could turn myself inside out for you. We could take in washing like infernal Chinese, and all it would mean in the end was that we'd eat poorer. To them fancy folk in Fort Lee, we'd still be fallen women, living over here in the Strip with an Indian buck."

"Durn it, Mamma, why can't you tell Jim July to go live somewhere else? I don't like Jim July."

"That's likely why you ain't sleeping with him, then. Has he been acting forward with you, daughter?"

"No, he ain't like Blue Duck was, but I still don't like him. Why can't you get a decent white man, Mamma?"

Belle snorted in disgust. "With what, my dowry from my secret Vanderbilt kin? Getting a white man ain't all that impossible, I reckon, but then we'd have to move off Indian land, and where in thunder would we go? Besides, any white man willing to take up with me at my age would likely be worthless, next to old Jim. I'm staring close at forty, Pearl. Where's an old gal like me to find a man better than Jim July? A woman has to study on her future, and Jim's a hard-working cuss."

Pearl wrinkled her nose and said, "Hard at stealing, you mean!"

Belle nodded amiably. "Don't think stealing ain't hard work, girl. I can see I might have made a mistake in not insisting you follow the family calling as close as me. You wouldn't think stealing was so easy if you'd done some."

Pearl got to her feet and flounced out, angry with the whole world. She knew her mother was mostly wrong but partly right. She'd heard what folk in Fort Smith had to say about Younger's Bend.

She headed for the Ferndancer's cabin out of habit. Alice had moved out to the Osage Strip with her new husband. Pearl missed Alice. Ma Ferndancer did, too, so they sometimes sat and jawed on Alice of an evening. They had nothing in common to talk about but a girlhood past, but there was nothing else to do in Younger's Bend if one didn't drink or raise hell.

As she started to cross the wagon trace, a couple of 'breed boys came down it whooping and yelling and firing their guns at the moon. They saw Pearl and a gal alone was fair game. Then they saw who she was and let her be, riding past with a friendly whoop. They didn't have anything better to do, either.

When Pearl reached the Ferndancer's she found the Elder Swan there, seated on the steps talking to Alice's folk in Cherokee. They switched to English as she walked up.

Pearl said, "I could just as lief come another time if y'all are having a private conversing."

"Set down, girl. You're family," Bob Ferndancer insisted.

"I am glad you are here, Pearl," the Elder Swan said in the stiff way he had when he'd first switched tongues or when he was feeling official. "Hear me, we are very worried about your mother, Pearl."

"I'm worried about her too, sir. What's she done lately?" Pearl asked.

"Nothing locally, Pearl. She and Jim July know better than to raid stock off Indian neighbors, but they are becoming a holy terror to the white settlers across the Arkansas line."

Pearl sighed. "I'd noticed they seem to be starting up again, but they don't run stock back here in Younger's Bend. They don't listen to me, either, so I don't see what I can do about it."

"Hear me, Pearl, someone must do something. The whites are talking ugly. I recall when we lived in Tennessee, so I remember the Pony Boys. I don't want Pony Boys bothering my people here."

"Pony Boys, sir?"

The old Indian nodded and said, "White men, riding ponies, with sacks over their heads and firebrands in their hands. There were good persons in Washington who said to leave the Five Civilized Tribes alone, because we were not wild Indians. The Pony Boys did things to make us wild. They raided. They burned. They did bad things to our women. Sometimes they got shot. Even a civilized Indian has feelings. In the end we were forced to move away. It was said white people and Indians just couldn't live as neighbors. It was said there would always be trouble."

"I know about the Trail of Tears, Elder Swan."

"Then hear me. I don't want to move again. It has taken me a lifetime to get used to these dry red hills out here. There is no more land left that anyone can live on. If they move us again, it will be to the great desert of Apacharia, where even the Apache can't live as honest men. We Cherokee are a forest people, Pearl. What would we do in country even more dried-out than this?"

"Starve, I reckon," answered Pearl. "But I don't figure they're planning another Trail of Tears sir. I've been reading a lot at the library in town, and there's been no talk in the papers about it."

"I can read, too. That is why I'm on the tribal council. Have you read what the papers say about the Cherokee Strip, Pearl?"

"Well, yes, they make it sound sort of rough-hewn in those Wild West magazines."

"They call it a no-man's-land, a country where there is no law; an empty land where only outlaws roam."

"I said I'd read the fool things, sir. That dude, Ned Buntline, writes all sorts of silly notions about the country out here. He's got an awful lot of it down wrong. My Uncle Frank James says they had him and Uncle Jesse doing things they never done, and that Wild Bill was really named Jim and wasn't all that great a bullfrog anyhow."

"It doesn't matter if they tell the truth or not. People act on what they *think* is true. They think the Strip is a den of thieves. They are partly right. Hear me, Pearl, the people doing bad things in the Strip are mostly whites," the Elder Swan said.

"I heard about the Dalton boys running off that Osage herd, sir."

"You have thieves closer to home than that, Pearl. I have just told Bob Ferndancer, here, that he must stop working for your mother. I mean to tell other Cherokee the same. Do you think you could get your mother to move out of the Strip willingly?"

Pearl sighed and said, "Not willingly, sir. I've asked her more than one time. As to asking Indians not to work for her, you can try. Jim July and some of the others ain't Cherokee. I doubt some of the Cherokee working for us will listen."

"Us, Pearl? Have you become party to the moonshining and stock raiding?"

"No, sir. I don't mean to, neither. But if it gets down to

that, I reckon it'll be us agin you. Mamma and me is kin, and I love her."

The old man nodded grimly, and said, "I see. I understand. Don't worry about barn burnings or bushwackings, Pearl. It is not our way, but when you do warn your mother, tell her I think it is time she moved on. She has worn out her welcome here in the Strip. We don't want her and her kind here any more. I have spoken."

Pearl nodded, got to her feet, and trudged home in the suddenly unfriendly dark. When she'd retraced her steps to the cabin, she found Belle with Jim July and a couple of other men. One was Choctaw and the other was mostly white.

Belle smiled as she came in and said, "I'm sorry I fussed at you about that grange dance, honey. You can go if you like, and I'll buy you a fetching new dress to boot."

"I ain't made up my mind on the dance, Mamma. Can I talk to you private just one minute?" Pearl asked.

Belle nodded and led her out on the veranda, asking, "What's wrong? Are you having she-male troubles, girl?"

"No, Mamma. You're the one with a problem."

Pearl repeated her conversation with the Elder Swan as Belle listened. When she'd finished, Pearl added hopefully, "We could go live with Uncle Frank in Missouri, Mamma. He says it's grand in Kansas City."

"Hmmph, what would I do for a living in Kansas City? Besides, Frank's offer was to you, not me. You just go along to Lee's Summit if you don't love your old mamma no more, hear? I'll get by as I always have with the friends as like me."

"Mamma, I like you. Hell, I love you. You're my mamma!"

"Then why are you studying on leaving me?" Belle said.

"Mamma, I never said I aimed to leave you. I said I wanted to leave this infernal Cherokee Strip!"

Belle sniffed and said, "It's the same thing, daughter. I'll never leave the only home I've ever owned. I growed to womanhood here. I gave birth to my only living child here. I got bones buried in this red clay, Pearl. I'll never leave the Strip willing. They'd have to kill me and carry me off before I'd leave."

"Mamma, the Indians don't want us here no more!"

"Shoot, what Indians, girl? What do you reckon them boys inside is, Zulus? Ain't no Indians talking on running us off. It's just one old Cherokee who's too big for his britches. I'll deal with Elder Swan. We'll just see who's got the final say in these parts!"

Pearl blanched and gasped, "Mamma, you're not to hurt the Elder Swan! You dasn't!"

Belle smiled thinly and asked, "Now, did I say word one about hurting that old cuss?"

"No, Mamma, but you got a look in your eye as scares me."

"Well, go look somewhere else, then. Go inside and look at your pretty self in the looking glass, for I mean to gussy you up to be the prettiest gal at that Grange Dance this weekend, hear?"

"I'd sure like that, Mamma. But, about the Elder Swan . . ."

"Honey, I said I wouldn't hurt him. Don't you take your mamma's word no more? I swears on my honor as a southern woman of gentle birth that I'll not lift a finger agin that dumb old Cherokee. Is that good enough for you?" said Belle.

"I reckon. Does I have your word nobody else will do so, Mamma?"

"Well, now, that's asking me a little much, girl. I can only speak for my own self. I won't order him gunned, if that's what you mean, but I can't do better than that. Hell, I'm only a poor widow woman. You know how much control I have on men."

"Yes, Mamma, I knows exactly how much control you have on men, and I'll be sore vexed if anything ugly happens to that old Indian!"

Pearl sat in the Fort Smith library reading intently as she waited for Steve Logan to show up. He generally spent his lunch hour there, she knew, but he hadn't come yesterday or the day before, and the dance was to be this very night.

It was long past lunch time. The clock on the wall said it was going on three, but she'd heard the Logan Dry Goods Store closed early of a Saturday, so Steve had likely gone home to change into his party duds before coming by. That had to be it, Pearl thought.

She was sitting in her new dress, with ribbon bows in her dark blonde hair. She'd left her paint pony at the livery down the way, since Steve would likely drive them to the dance proper. She wondered what could be keeping him.

She was reading about Constantinople when the librarian came over to her table and whispered, "I'm sorry, miss, but we're fixing to close."

"Close?" Pearl gasped, "I thought you stayed open to six."

"That's on weekdays, miss. We close early of a Saturday."

The librarian, not much older than Pearl, added with a secretive little smile, "To tell the truth, I have to go home and get ready for the dance at the grange hall."

"Oh, are you going, too? I'm waiting here for my beau to pick me up," Pearl said.

"I noticed the way you had yourself fixed up, but I really have to close. Can't you meet him somewhere else?"

Pearl sighed and got to her feet. "It surely looks like I'll have to, but I don't see where."

She went outside and sat on the park bench, where she and Steve had met. A little while later the librarian came out to lock the doors and wave goodbye to her. Pearl waved back, angry enough to spit. She felt a fool sitting there in her fancy duds, and if that infernal Steve didn't come by sudden she'd just . . . what?

She couldn't go to the dance alone. She hadn't been invited and didn't know anyone there. She could mayhaps go to the dry goods store and see if he was working late or something, but that wouldn't be seemly. They'd just tease him if a gal acted so bold towards him, and it might give

him notions she was anxious. She'd drink turpentine before she'd let any boy think she was anxious.

She sat there twisting the white cotton gloves her
mamma had bought for her to look proper at the dance.
She wondered if Steve would try to kiss her coming home,
and if she ought to let him. Then she wondered where in
the hell the fool boy was. Didn't he know she'd be waiting
here at the library?

"Oh, Lord," she murmured, "He's a townie, so he knows
the library closes early on Saturday! He won't expect me to
be here, sitting in the hot sun like a big ass bird!"

But if he didn't mean to meet her there, where in thunder was she supposed to wait for him? She waited as the
sun moved lower in the western sky. She kept looking up
hopefully as each surrey or carriage came down the street,
but none of the men driving past were Steve Logan. She
waited and waited and after she'd waited several hours she
saw a couple driving by all dressed up to go dancing.

"That tears it," she said aloud, and got up.

He wasn't coming. She knew he wasn't coming, but she
didn't know why. She headed for the livery, thinking up all
sorts of reasons why he hadn't shown up and hoping some
of them hadn't really happened to him. He'd tell her in his
own good time why he couldn't take her to the dance, and
she vowed the excuse would have to be a good one.

Then, as she was almost to the livery, she saw Steve Logan talking to another boy on the corner. They were both
dressed up mighty nice, so she knew he hadn't forgotten
the dance. She walked toward them with a puzzled smile.
Steve spied her, looked embarrassed, and grabbed his chum
to duck into a saloon, where of course she couldn't follow.

Pearl froze in her tracks, staring slack-jawed at the
swinging doors of the saloon for a long heartsick moment.
Then she nodded and said to herself, "I see. Somebody told
him." She raised her chin and walked past the saloon.

"Take a good look, damn you! Have a gander at the
bastard daughter of Belle Starr! See if I give two hoots and
a holler!" she muttered.

She didn't start crying until she was mounted up and

riding back to the Strip, and by the time she'd sidesaddled most of the way home she'd recovered, or at least gotten too mad to cry. It was starting to drizzle, and the sunset was blood red. She hoped it would rain fire and salt that night and soak all those snooty townie gals 'til the colors ran on their party dresses. She'd be indoors and dry whilst they got soaked, for she was almost home and figured to make it before the sky really opened up.

She cut across the back lot and put her pony in his stall. By the time she was making for the cabin it was raining hard, so she ran across the damp ground to the side door of her lean-to and yanked open the door.

She froze in the doorway and gasped, "Oh!"

Belle was in her daughter's bed with a man. They were both stark naked with the coverlet thrown down. They quickly stopped what they'd been doing and Belle looked mighty sheepish. Pearl stepped back and closed the door. She moved around to the veranda and sat on a box, staring red-faced into the falling rain.

A few moments later Belle joined her, fastening up her robe. "Sorry about that, honey. I thought you'd be at the dance 'til midnight."

"I know what you thought, Mamma. That was my bed you was doing it in, and that wasn't Jim July, neither!"

Belle laughed. "I noticed. You see, Jim never goes in your room."

"I had that figured out already, Mamma. Do we have to study on it? Just get that damned buck outten my bed and we'll say no more about it."

"Honey, we has to talk about it. I wouldn't want you to think your mamma was a wicked woman."

Pearl stared at her aghast, and asked, "Thunderation, Mamma, what else have you ever been? I just caught you rutting with a total stranger in my very own bed!"

"Oh, shoot, I meant to change the sheets afore you come home from the dance. What happened at the dance, anyways? How come you left so early?"

"I never went. Somebody must have told Steve Logan about. . . . you."

"Well, good riddance, then. What do you want with a boy who cares what the neighbors think? About that Seminole boy and me just now, I'm trying to get him to join my gang."

"Is that what you calls it, Mamma? No offense, but it sure looked like you were screwing."

Belle laughed again. "That's for sure. I like to bring young men home to raise, but I was doing it for us all, Pearl. That Seminole's with the Indian Police, and I've been trying to win him over to our side. I doubt Jim would cotton to my methods, but a woman in my position has to sacrifice some for her family."

"Mamma, you wasn't sacrificing. You was screwing, and in my bed!"

"I promise I won't do that no more, and I said I'd change the bedding."

"Mamma, I just don't want to talk about it."

"We has to. I wants you to understand how it is with me. I never set out to be a fallen woman, Pearl. Had not the South lost the war I might have turned out different, but . . ."

Pearl rose to her feet, blazing, "Mamma, forgive me, but you are purely full of it! I've heard all my life how the war turned you and others bad, but that's a mighty poor excuse. I know my uncle got kilt riding with the red-legs. I know Frank and Jesse James was mixed up with Quantrill. But what of it? Robert E. Lee rode some in the war, too, and the last I heard he was running the University of Virginia for a living! Lots of folk lost their slaves and whole plantations in the war and no doubt it left them mighty upset, but do you see men like Jeff Davis and Robert E. Lee holding up banks and robbing trains? Of course you don't. And what in hell did you or the Youngers or the James boys lose that was so all-fired important? Nobody burnt granddaddy's house in Texas. Nobody on my father's side had anything worth losing."

"Now, honey, you know how the Missouri Pacific tried to steal land off the poor folk in Clay County," Belle said.

"Mamma, that just ain't true. In the first place, nobody

never took an acre of them hard-scrabble farms. In the second, there's an Atlas in the library as shows the railroad right-of-ways, and let me tell you something. The Missouri Pacific don't run anywhere near the county of Clay. To rob that Glendale Train they had to ride clean across the state, near Saint Lou! The Missouri Pacific never come looking for trouble with the James-Younger gang. The James-Younger gang went looking for them!"

"Lord have mercy, you're starting to talk like a Pinkerton! What's got into you this night, Pearl dear? I told you I wouldn't use your bed no more!"

Pearl sank wearily back on the box and sighed, "Mamma, it's no use talking about it. You just can't tell right from wrong."

"Now don't you go getting high and mighty with me, girl. I reckon I know right from wrong as well as you or better. I know the law says some of the things I does is wrong, but what's the law? Who writes it, folks like us? You ain't that dumb, Pearl. Laws are writ by men who owns factories back East where little kids of six or nine is working hot and sweaty this very moment. Laws is writ by men who throws men in jail for trying to form a union in the mines and mills they owns. Laws is writ by men who use the same to run our Indian friends off their land. Laws is writ to keep folk like us in our place.

"But I don't fancy the place they chose for me, Pearl. I have my own notions on right and wrong. I mean to live by my own laws; the laws of real folk. Real folk do what's fitting, not what some jasper in a stuffed shirt has written for him by his tame politicos. Real folk see that their kin don't go hungry, and if anyone hurts their kin, they pays them back. That law code is older than any others; older than the hills. All that other stuff is just meant to keep us little folk down."

"You've told me all this afore, Mamma, but is your way the only way? Do we really have to be at war with the whole world?"

Belle shrugged and answered, "Hell, honey, we didn't declare war on them. They declared war on us, a long long time ago. They calls it law, but it's war to the death betwixt those who want to run this world like their very own plantation and us freedom-loving folk who don't want to chop cotton for them. That's what they really want of us, you know. They want us to be their niggers. Do you want to be their nigger, Pearl?"

"No, I got treated like one this afternoon and I didn't like it all that much. That boy I told you about stood me up. Somebody must have told him who I was. But, Mamma, he didn't do so 'cause he thought I was colored. He done it 'cause I'm your child. You know how they talk about us in town."

"Let 'em talk, the sissy things. I told you not to trifle with townie boys. They're all alike. They think they're special. Hell, have you ever seen that Steve Logan fight? I'll bet he'd run like hell if even a woman like me challenged him to slap leather!"

Pearl laughed a trifle wildly and said, "I think you could be right about that, Mamma. It's a mighty wild notion, but when you're right you're right."

"You want me to settle his hash for him, daughter?"

"No, Mamma. Leave Steve Logan be. I just don't ever want to see him again."

11

IT WAS MORE than a week before Pearl rode into Fort Smith again. She'd told herself she didn't want to go to the public library any more, but there was nothing else to do. It was a free country, and she had as much right to spend her time there as any infernal boy named Steve Logan.

He wasn't there. He never came again. She didn't care. She'd come to read the books, and they were just as interesting as any sissy boy.

One afternoon as she approached the entrance, Rafe and another deputy riding by reined in when they saw her. Rafe got down, tipped his hat, and said, "Howdy, Miss Pearl. Where might you be headed?"

Pearl pointed with her chin at the library entrance and answered, "Yonder. I came to steal some books, if you must know."

Rafe chuckled. "We may have to stake the library out, then. I wonder if you've seen that old Cherokee, Swan, lately."

"The Elder Swan? Let's see, I spoke with him about a week ago, over to Bob Ferndancer's."

"Ferndancer ain't seen him since then, neither. The Indian Police have been searching high and low, but they ain't seen hide nor hair of the old gent. I don't suppose you'd see fit to tell me if he's been around your place, huh?" Rafe asked.

"I would so see fit, had he been to our cabin, but I am telling you true he never was. Why do you ask?"

"Well, Miss Pearl, there's been talk about him and your mother, Belle Starr."

"Good heavens, is she supposed to be having an affair with that poor old Indian?"

"Not hardly. Seems the old gent was making war talk about your white mother dwelling on Indian lands."

Pearl nodded and said, "He did say something along those lines to me, but I don't think he spoke to my mother about it. Wouldn't the whole tribal council have to vote on it?"

Rafe nodded soberly, and said, "Yeah, they would and they did. Seems the others don't care if you folk stay on there at Younger's Bend. It likely could get a mite thirsty if they run you off. Sure is odd how the one old man who didn't drink much never turned up at the last couple of meetings, though."

Pearl took a deep breath, let half of it out so her voice wouldn't crack, and said, "All right, let's stop this infernal cat and mouse game, Rafe. If you've got an accusation to make, let's hear it!"

"I don't hold much with accusings, Miss Pearl. I'll take your word you don't know what happened to old Swan. I never figured you did, as a matter of fact, but it's my duty to ask fool questions."

He turned to remount. Then he pointed to the other younger deputy and asked, "Do you know Frank Dalton, here, Miss Pearl?"

Pearl nodded. "We don't know one another all that well, but we're distant kin."

"Pleased to meet you, Pearl Younger. I've heard some about you, too," Dalton said.

Now that she'd had a close look at him, Frank Dalton didn't look like an owlhoot. There was something missing. He didn't have the haunted look in his eyes that she'd learned to associate with the breed. He was a nice-looking boy and wore his deputy badge like he meant it. They said he'd shot it out with a gang of bootleggers one time, working for the B.I.A., so he likely didn't hold the same views on the law as his wilder brothers. She was glad he hadn't met up with any of Mamma's boys that way. She could see why Mamma wanted her to cultivate him some. But he was kin, damn it, and Pearl wasn't the kind of gal who'd trifle with a man that way.

Sometimes she wished she was. It was pure hell being an old maid, and she knew no decent man would ever fancy her. She went inside and pulled a romance from the stacks to read. She wondered what it felt like to make love like her Mamma did, but how was she to find out, unless she tried it with some old boy from the Cherokee Strip?

"I'd give myself to a law-abiding colored boy first!" She grimaced, trying to concentrate on the book. Folk sure talked fancy about love in books. That Heathcliff dude sure was a sulky devil, but he talked decent to gals and never came right out and asked for a lay. Pearl wondered where a gal met up with a gent like that.

She found out a few minutes later when a boy sat down at her table and said, "Excuse me, is this seat taken?"

"It is now. Ain't you the boy I saw talking to Steve Logan the night of the dance?" Pearl asked.

He nodded and said, "I am. I told him he was a fool, too, Miss Pearl."

She closed her book and looked him over. He had curly brown hair and nice wide-set grey eyes. He was gussied up in a checked jacket and bow-tie.

"My name's Larry, Larry Woods," he said. "I live up the road from Steve, but let's not talk about him. It's generally agreed he's mighty dumb."

"He likely had his reasons. What did he tell you about me?" Pearl asked.

"Oh, you know how folk gossip. I like to judge for myself, Miss Pearl."

"Well, go ahead and judge me, then. I was birthed out of wedlock and my pappa is doing time in prison for robbing banks and trains too numerous to mention. As for my mother, the less said the better."

Larry chuckled and said, "Everyone knows who Belle Starr is, Miss Pearl. Can I call you Pearl?"

"You may as well. Ain't you scared I'll hold you up at gunpoint? We're alone in this corner nook, you know," said Pearl.

"I know. Steve told me how he'd met you here at the library. I was hoping you'd be here. I don't figure to get robbed by you, Pearl. You see, I asked myself, and they say you aren't like your mother at all."

"Now, don't you go mean-mouthing my kin, Larry Woods!"

"I won't, I promise. I meant some say you're a lady, and that's how I mean to treat you."

"Do tell? How do you figure ladies ought to be treated, Larry Woods?"

"Well, for starters, there's to be a concert on the green tonight. How do you feel about going to her with me?"

She hesitated and he quickly added, "You don't have to ride back home for supper. I'll take you to a restaurant. Have you ever et at the Franklin Arms?"

"Lord, no, that's a mighty fancy place! I've passed it, but I've never even seen the insides. Are you sure they'd serve a gal like me in such a high-toned restaurant, Larry?"

"There's only one way to find out. Say you'll go, and after, we'll go over to the green and listen to the German Band. How's about it?" Larry asked.

Pearl looked at the clock on the wall. "There's time to study on both moves. I'd have to know you a mite better," she answered.

He suggested that they take a walk, and the next thing Pearl knew, they were in a creamery having ice cream sodas. It smelled elegant. Larry talked almost as nicely to her as that Heathcliff feller, and wasn't nearly so sulky. He said he worked in a feed store and that he hadn't gotten the job through kin. He said he was the assistant manager and that he lived in his own hired digs, even though his folks had a farm on the far side of Fort Smith. Pearl was too polite to ask how much he made, but she could see he drew top wages and didn't have to steal. He was almost as good-looking as that durned old Steve Logan, too.

They walked about some more and, when they met some other young folk he knew, Larry introduced her to them. The boy shook friendly, but the gal with him looked sort of scornfully at Pearl.

When she commented on it after they'd parted, Larry laughed and said, "She was just a mite jealous, 'cause she's fatter than you. She's not as pretty, either. You'll be about the prettiest gal at the concert tonight, Pearl."

"I thank you," Pearl said, "but I've been worried about something, Larry. What are your friends likely to say when you show up with the daughter of Belle Starr?"

"Heck, I don't care what folks say. It's what they can *do* as counts, when you get down to brass tacks. It's a free country, isn't it? I can take anyone I like to a public concert, and I like you a heap, Pearl," replied Larry.

They went to the Franklin Arms, and by the time they were half finished, Pearl decided she was either in love or getting there. Larry wasn't at all awkward with the fancy linens of the grand restaurant. He told the colored waiter how he wanted his steak done, and here, too, Pearl was afraid to say one word to the snooty waiter. She'd never in her life seen such fancy service. There was even a rose in a cut-glass vase on the table betwixt them. He said she could have it if she wanted, but she said to leave it be, so's the next folk dining there could enjoy it. The waiter brought little silver bowls of what looked like plain water with slices of lemon floating in them. Pearl was about to put her spoon in hers, until she saw Larry rinsing his fingers in his. So that was what a finger bowl looked like! She'd read of the fool things, but had never seen one before. It felt sort of silly washing one's hands at the table like that, but it made her feel sort of grand, too.

They had apple pie with cheese afterward, and by the time they'd finished, Pearl was full. She'd ridden to town in a corset, for she was a woman of near twenty, but she was sure glad she hadn't laced it as tight as she had the night of the dance.

By the time they got to the green, the music had started. Larry took her by the hand and led her closer to the stand, not caring at all how many of the folk there saw him with her. They sat on the grass and Pearl felt like she was in heaven. The sky above was clear, and winking stars and the paper lanterns all about were glowing romantically in the soft night air. The German Band played beautifully without missing a note, and between the sets, Larry bought her some orange soda pop and introduced her to others sitting nearby. Some of the gals looked sort of like they wanted Pearl to go away and drown herself or something, but the boys all grinned at her and Larry as if they admired his gumption.

The concert ended all too soon. As Larry helped Pearl to her feet, she brushed off her skirts and said, "Well, that sure was nice. I'd best go get my pony from the livery now, though."

"Aw, do you have to go home so early, Pearl?" Larry asked.

"I don't have to. I haven't anyplace else to go. It's pushing eleven o'clock," Pearl said.

"Heck, Pearl, we're just getting to know one another. Can't you stay in town for a while?"

"I reckon I could, but where could we go next? There's nothing open at this hour, is there?"

"Yeah, this surely is a one-horse town. If we were in a real city the night would just be starting. But, heck, we can make out we're in some grand place like Little Rock and make our own night life, right?"

"Mayhaps, but where?" asked Pearl.

"We could go over to my place. It's not far, and I've got glasses and stuff."

"Oh, all right," Pearl said.

Larry took her arm, laughing, to carry her home to his furnished digs. He had a private entrance off the alley, and his place was sure fixed up nice. He had lace curtains and a leather chair near his bed, but Pearl wasn't sure she approved of the picture of the naked lady on the wall.

Larry sat her on the bed and said, "Don't talk prudish, honey. That's a very artistic print, painted by a Frenchman over to Paris, France."

"She still ought to have more duds on. A fig leaf, at least."

Larry laughed as he finished mixing their drinks, sat down beside her on the bed, and handed her a thick glass tumbler, saying, "Bottoms up. This'll take care of your fig leaves, I'll bet."

Pearl took an innocent sip, gasped, and asked, "Lord of Mercy! What on earth is in this stuff?"

"It's whiskey, honey. Don't tell me *you* don't know what whiskey is?"

"Not to drink. I reckon I'll just pass on this refreshment, Larry. You sure has a nice place here. Are the roses on yon lamp hand painted?"

Larry answered coyly, "I'm sorry if the light hurts your eyes," and reached to trim the wick.

Pearl frowned and asked, "What did you do that for? It's nigh pitch black in here, now."

He put his own glass aside, took her in his arms, and lay her on her back across the bed as he kissed her. Pearl admired the way he kissed, for she'd been wondering what it felt like to kiss like that. Then he put his free hand on her breast and she said, "Hold on, now. I don't want to go that far."

He moved his hand away from her breast, but ran it down her bodice as he said, "Don't play hard to get honey. You know you wants it as bad as me."

She flinched as his hand cupped her mons through the skirting of her lap, and she grabbed his wrist, gasping, "Stop that, you fool thing! I never come here to be bad. You said you wanted to get to know me better."

"I do, honey. Oh, do I ever! But all these infernal clothes are in our way! What say we shuck 'em and do this right?" he suggested.

"You just stop, hear? I don't want to do it right or

wrong, Larry Woods! What do you take me for, a fallen woman?"

He snorted in disbelief and said, "Hell, we both know what you are, Pearl Younger. What are you acting so silly for? Once the loaf's been cut, what does another little slice hurt?"

She shoved him away and sat up, trying not to cry as she said, "Well, the loaf you seem so sure of ain't never been cut yet, and the man who does it won't be *you*! You ought to be ashamed of yourself, Larry Woods! I took you for a nice young gent. Now I see what you took *me* for, and I'll just be going, now, if it's all the same to you!"

He grabbed her and tried to force her back down, but the daughter of Belle Starr did take after her mother in some ways. She was just as strong and her nails were just as sharp.

Larry Woods flinched away in the dark, holding his cheek as he gasped, "You little bitch, you clawed me! I'm bleeding like hell! What in the hell's wrong with you? Is it money you want?"

Pearl sobbed, rose from the bed, and ran out of the dark room. She didn't stop running until she'd gotten all the way to the livery and surprised the night man there as she dashed in, shouting, "I want my pony!"

She got it. The night man didn't want to argue with a lady as wild-eyed as Belle Starr's daughter was just then!

Pearl was so mortified she didn't visit Fort Smith for weeks. She therefore didn't hear what they were saying about a whole herd of prime beef missing from a spread in the Boston Mountains north of town. She never heard of a certain rustic gallantry that transpired in her behalf, either.

Larry Woods enjoyed his reputation as the lady-killer of Fort Smith, and his friends had seen him sparking the notorious daughter of Belle Starr, so it was only natural that some sniggering boys should ask, and only natural that Larry entertain them with tales of his prowess.

Unfortunately for Larry, he was overheard in the saloon

when he told Steve Logan, "You should have brazened it out with her, old son. You don't know what fine screwing you passed up."

Steve Logan, who wasn't the kind of youth Larry was, snorted dubiously and said, "Go on, you never! I told you she seemed a nice young gal. I wanted to take her, but my daddy said he'd whup me black and blue when he found out I'd asked her to the grange dance. I still don't think she's what they say she is, but you know how folk are once they're old and set in their notions."

Larry laughed and said, "Your daddy was right, praise the Lord, but your loss was my gain, old son. You see these scratches on my cheek, here? That's how she likes to screw, like a real wildcat. She damn near screwed me into the ground. She even wound up on top, hollering at me for more."

Steve said, "I think you're full of it," and got up to leave.

Larry called after him, "You go along and see if she won't do the same for you, boy. Take it from a man who knows his women. It's them quiet ones who'll bust your back ever' time!"

At the next table, two boys dressed cow stared soberly at one another, unnoticed by the braggart. One said softly, "He sure talks a lot. Reckon there's anything to it?"

His friend shrugged and answered, "Don't matter if it's true. It still ain't seemly to talk like that about any gal."

"I found it a mite ugly, too. What do you reckon we ought to do about it?"

"Ain't sure. The wronged gal ain't kith or kin to neither of ussen, but ain't Frank Dalton a Younger on his mamma's side?"

"By jimmies, I think he is. You want to tell him, or shall I?"

"I'll tell him. I know him better than you. Finish your beer first. It's early, and this sounds like night riding business."

Frank Dalton didn't hold with night riding, so when the

boys got word to him about what Larry Woods was bragging on, Frank took off his badge, put it in his pocket and
walked over to the feed store.

He had timed it so he would get there just before closing.
The boss had gone home and Larry was fixing to lock up.

As Frank Dalton came in, Larry said, "We was about to
close, but what can I do for you, friend?"

Frank Dalton took out his barlow knife, unfolded it, and
calmly ripped open one of the feed sacks piled near the
stove. As he watched the milled oats cascading to the floor
he said quietly, "I'm not your friend. I'm Pearl Younger's
kin. Her daddy and my mammy was cousins back in Missouri."

"Do tell? Well, it sure is a small world. How come you
ripped open that feed sack, mister? That's an awful mess
you just made for me to have to clean up," said Larry.

Dalton nodded soberly and said, "Yeah. Be even more
of a mess if there's blood on the floor when I leave. But
don't worry, *you* won't have to clean it up."

Larry Woods was pale as a ghost as he stammered,
"Look, the boss emptied the cash box afore he left for the
day, but if it's money you want . . ."

"Now, boy, do I look like I come in here to hold you up?
When in hell did you ever hear of a grown man holding up
a feed store?"

He ripped open another sack as he added, "Jesus, some
idjets just don't have a lick of sense."

Larry pleaded, "What do you want then? Why are you
ripping things up so?"

"Just testing, boy. Testing my blade, here. Ain't cut anything important with it recent, and I seem to be here on a
cutting matter."

"For God's sake, what do you want to cut *me* for? I ain't
never done nothing to you, mister!"

"You're wrong, boy. That's what I mean to discuss with
you after I see what's in this here bag and . . . well,
what do you know, corn meal. Ain't it pretty, streaming
down all goldly like that?"

Then he turned his cold gunmetal eyes directly on Larry

Woods. He didn't have to brag on the men he'd killed so far. Larry knew. His bladder betrayed him and he wet his pants.

Frank Dalton smiled thinly and said, "Now look what you've done to the floor, boy. I understand you've been saying about town that you know my kinswoman, Pearl Younger, in the Biblical sense."

"Oh, hold on, I only took Miss Pearl to the band concert!"

"Do tell? That's funny, I heard you said something happened after."

"No, never, so help me God! I never trifled with that girl!"

"Well, I believe you, boy. What are we going to do about the dumb story going about, that Miss Pearl's no better than she should be?"

"Nobody will ever hear a word agin her from me, I vow!"

Frank Dalton stared long and hard at the frightened young man. Then he said, "I sure hope you mean that, boy. If I hear any more gossip about you and my young kinswoman, I'll come back and fix you so's you won't ever be able to brag on any woman."

"You has my bound word I'll never mention Miss Pearl or even her mamma again, so help me God!"

Dalton stood undecided for what seemed a million years. Then he said, "All right, why don't you go over there and set yourself down to watch?"

"Watch? Watch what, mister?" Larry asked, trembling.

"Oh, I'm going to wreck your store afore I leave. You didn't think I'd just walk off without wrecking the place, did you?"

"I surely wish you wouldn't, mister. I'll only have to clean up after you, and what am I to tell the boss about all this mess you already made?"

"Why, boy, you just go ahead and tell him anything you've a mind to, as long as you leave me and my kin out of it. I'm letting you off mighty easy, considering. I want you to ponder, as you clean up after me, what some of the other gents in the family might have done here. It's mighty lucky for you I'm on the law-abiding side of the family."

Nobody ever found out what had happened to Elder Swan. Nobody knew what had happened to a dozen head of Lazy Eight cattle, a matched pair of high-stepping show horses, a prized cutting horse, and the whole infernal team of the Fort Smith Volunteer Fire Department who'd been left out in the meadow one moonless night.

It's probably not true Belle and her gang were behind the mysterious disappearance of those expensive piebald Poland-China hogs, and the lady who accused them of rustling her Shanghai rooster was just talking silly. Like the James-Younger gang before them, Belle's bunch tended to get more discredit than was due them. It was said to be dangerous to speak openly about Belle and her kith and kin, so people spoke in whispers, and whispered gossip is the wildest, since the voice of common sense isn't there to debate it.

Belle never had more than a dozen or so working with her at a time. They came and went. Some of the men she entertained on the sly never even kept their promises to fetch her this or deliver that. Some were willing to tote a jar across the line but not willing to steal stock. Others stole stock on their own and took it to Belle to dispose of.

The James boys would have considered her petty criminal operation small pickings in their day, but the folk about Fort Smith had her riding by moonlight across the countryside at the head of a hundred desperado Cherokees. Some said they'd seen her riding naked, siddesaddle, with her long black hair trailing behind her like a witch-woman's as she jumped her ever-young Venus over three strand barbed wire, laughing like a lunatic in the night.

This was not true, but anyone could see old Belle was getting mighty strange. One evening Pearl went up to see Granny Redbird about the wild feverish look in her mother's eyes.

The old spey woman met Pearl on her front steps, and didn't invite her in. She listened impassively as Pearl said,

"Granny, there's something wrong with Mamma. I don't mean the way she carries on, or even the way she's been drinking more of late. There's something else the matter with her. She coughs a lot in the night, and there's these twin blooms of pink on her cheekbones agin how pale the rest of her face is getting. I fear she's sick."

Granny Redbird shrugged and said, "Your mother has always been sick. Sometimes I think all you white people are sick. There's an evil spirit haunting you white people. You're all like bears clawing at a honey tree. You take and take and you never seem to have enough to fill your hunger."

"Granny, we both know Mamma has ever been a taking woman, but it's getting worse."

"What do you expect? She's a white woman. Go away, Pearl Younger. I used to have high hopes for you, but Elder Swan was a good person. I will never forgive you white people for whatever you did to him."

Pearl blanched and gasped, "Granny Redbird! You don't know what you're saying! Surely you don't blame *me* for the way that old man vanished?"

Granny Redbird's dark eyes were cold as she asked, "Who am I to blame, then, the jay bird cawing in yon willow? Hear me, there are many ways to do evil, Pearl Younger, and sometimes I think your way is the worst! Evil is not wise and clever. He needs help to get by in this world. The most help Evil gets is from the people who say they are good, but do nothing to stop Evil from happening."

Pearl looked hurt and said, "As the Lord is my witness, Granny, I don't know what they done to Elder Swan. I confronted Mamma about it when the old man turned up missing. She looked me in the eye and swore she hadn't laid hand one on him, and that she didn't know where he was, alive or otherwise."

"Your words buzz like flies about a dead dog, Pearl Younger. You are not a stupid person. Of course your mother didn't murder that old man and bury him somewhere in the red clay of the Nation. No white person could

bury a litch where the Indian Police could never find it. It
may even be true she never ordered the men she ruts with
to do it. She only had to say, batting her eyelashes at them,
that if something wasn't done, she'd have to move out of
the Strip, and then where would those trash bucks get their
jars and other comforts? Go away, Pearl. I don't like you
anymore."

Pearl sobbed, "Granny, you can't mean that! Since the
Ferndancers followed Alice out to the Osage Strip, you're
about the only friend I has left near Younger's Bend!"

"Friend? You want friends, as well as all the honey in
the tree? My father was right. You white people are all
crazy. You're not content to rob people. You want them to
like you as well! Hear me, when an Indian steals your pony
or lifts your hair, does he expect you to like him? Of course
not. He expects you to be his enemy. He wouldn't have
attacked you if he wanted you to like him! What is wrong
with you white people? You take and take and take, and
then you get angry and pout like children when an Indian
or a colored person gives you a dirty look!"

"Granny, you ain't being fair to me! You know I've
never stolen a thing in my born days!" Pearl said stubbornly.

Granny Redbird said, "You haven't? Where did that
nice dress come from? Did your paint pony arrive from
your Santa Claus on a Christmas Eve? Many, maybe most,
of the white people farming our old lands by the Tennessee
this day can say they never raised a hand against the Cherokee Nation, but they are there and we are here. Shall we
tell them what good people they are? You can't share in the
misfortunes of others and have them for friends, Pearl.
There's not a thing you own that you came by honestly.
You say you have never stolen. Heya, have you ever done
an honest day's work in your life?"

"Granny, I've chored about our spread hard as anything.
I ain't lazy."

"Mayhaps your bones are not lazy. Your mind certainly
must be. Go away. You are not my friend anymore. You
will never have anyone but trash for friends, since trash is

of your own choosing. Go home and cook supper for your mother and her trash. The moon will rise late tonight. No doubt they will need their strength for night riding!"

Pearl sobbed, "Granny, wait. Mamma really is feeling poorly."

"Take her to a white doctor, then. I have taken an oath never to give the medicine I'd like to give her for what ails her!"

Granny Redbird went inside and slammed her door in dismissal. Pearl stood agape for a few moments. Then she remounted her pony and rode home, crying.

Belle was sitting on the veranda alone when Pearl rode in. She frowned and asked, "What's fretting you so this evening, honey? You look like you just buried your best friend."

Pearl dismounted and joined her wearily as she said, "I reckon you did that for me, Mamma. Will you promise to do something for me, come sunrise?"

"Well, mayhaps, if it don't hurt. What's your pleasure, girl?" said Belle.

"Mamma, I want you to see a doctor man with me."

"Lord of Mercy, are you ailing, child?"

"No, Mamma, but I suspicion you are. I don't like your color, and the other night I heard you coughing through the wall. You was coughing fit to bust."

Belle laughed. "Hell, I ain't sick, honey. I got me a summer cold I can't seem to shake, is all. Once I'm up and about it passes. I feels just fine, most of the time. Ain't nothing I can't clear up with a little booze to clear my pipes."

"Mamma, you ain't been dosing yourself with a little booze. You been drinking like a fish of late. Promise me you'll come to the doctor man with me, hear?"

"Oh, hell, I may as well, since this is the tenth time you've brung it up, and I can see you're as willful as your pappa. But you'll see it's just a waste of time and money, Pearl. I'm sound as a dollar; maybe sounder. How many gals my age still have their teeth and shape, eh?"

Belle was wrong. The next morning they rode together

into Fort Smith, and while the doctor examined Belle, Pearl went down to the post office to see if her father had written to her again.

Cole Younger hadn't, but his sister, Retta, had. Pearl was surprised by the strange handwriting. It was cribbed and carefully done in a woman's hand. The envelope was expensive and scented. She opened it in the post office and read . . .

"My Dear Pearl:

Since your father allows you are his and he's my brother, that makes me your aunt, and that's jake with me, because Frank James says you're all right. The reason I am writing to you is because we've been hearing worrisome things up here in Missouri about the way your mother has been carrying on. I never met your mother and I know she's your kin. But we are your kin, too, and since your father, who's my brother, don't figure to ever get out and have more childer, he's worried sick about you. I am worried, too. It don't seem likely I will ever have another niece. So you had best come here and stay with us. We are simple folk and our house ain't fancy. But it's frame and clean. We got lilacs in front and apples out back. The room I'm fixing up for you is small, but it looks out over the valley and in the summer it catches the breeze. It is yours until you get married or find some place better. I hope you won't take me for a forward woman. But I want you to come and live with us right now.

You have to get out of there, Pearl. You are a Younger, not a Cherokee. Nobody in our family has ever been mixed up with folk like you are living with. Save for some of the Daltons, everyone else in the family has been living lawful of late and you'll doubtless find it more settled here. So please write and say you will come and live with me. If you don't have the money to come, I will send you some.

Your Aunt Retta."

Pearl carefully folded the letter and put it away. Then she went back to the doctor's office. She found her mother fully dressed again, and looking broody as a wet hen.

"I told you it was just a summer cough. Let's go. As long as we're in town, I has some business over to the warehouse," Belle said.

Pearl saw the look in the doctor's eye and answered, "You go along and I'll meet you later at the livery, Mamma. I ain't interested in the kind of talk you'll doubtless have at the warehouse, and I has some errands of my own to do."

"All right, but don't take all day," Belle said as she stomped out, muttering, "Doctors. A lot *they* know!"

As soon as she found herself alone with the grey-haired physician, Pearl asked, "All right, Doctor, what ails her?"

"Slip off your bodice and sit over on that table, Miss Younger, I have to examine you, too," the doctor said.

"Me?" Pearl smiled uncertainly, adding, "There's nothing the matter with me, sir. My mother is the one who's been acting queer of late."

"Small wonder. Here, take this thermometer under your tongue while you undress the top part of you. Don't be shy, miss. You don't have to undress completely, and I assure you I've seen everything you might fear to show me."

Pearl frowned and took the thermometer as she unbuttoned her bodice. She felt mighty shy undressing that much in front of a strange man, but he looked kind and decent, and after she'd exposed her small firm breasts it didn't seem as strange as she'd thought it would be. He thumped her back, then he took the glass stem from between her lips, held it up to the light, and said, "Ninety-eight on the nose. Your lungs are sound, too. Thank heavens for small favors, Miss Younger. You don't have it."

"Have what, Doctor? What's this all about?"

"Tuberculosis. Your mother has it. You don't."

Pearl gasped in dismay and asked, "Is that the same as consumption, sir?"

He nodded and said, "They used to call it that. Of late

we understand it better, so we've given it a name. We don't know how to cure it, but at least it has a name."

Pearl nodded, numb-lipped, and said, "I read about it in the library books. I has an uncle dying from it, too. Ain't there a German doctor working on a cure?"

He nodded and said, "Doctor Koch. He's identified the germ that causes tuberculosis, but we're a long way from any cure, Miss Younger. Your mother has a dose I'd say she's carried some time. That's why she has the chronic low-grade fever you were sharp enough to notice. She seems a mite manic. That's another classic symptom."

"How . . . long does she have, Doctor?"

The physician shrugged and said, "Hard to say. I've seen people with worse cases last ten years or more. It's a slow-killing illness. It depends on how well she takes care of herself. That drinker's nose of hers doesn't signal a long life for anyone, with or without her lung condition. But with rational diet, plenty of rest, clean air . . ."

"What if I was to take her out to that sanitarium I read about in Colorado?"

"It might help, if she'd go. T.B. is a funny bug, Miss Younger. We can't do a thing for it, but sometimes the body heals itself. I've heard of total remissions in folk who moved out to the high, dry country, but even that's only a fighting chance. They die a mite slower out in Colorado or Arizona, but most of 'em die, sooner or later."

Pearl had been listening with half her mind as she thought back on some of the things she'd read in the library and what Uncle Frank had told her about a gun slick called Holliday.

"Let me ask you something, Doctor. Seeing as I'm sitting here half nekked and we're talking personal, is it true that folks with what Mamma has get, uh, sort of horny?"

He looked away as he answered, "That seems to be one of the side effects of tuberculosis. They think more than one notorious courtesan may have had it. Mention was made of the high coloring of Madam DuBarry and some others. The constant low fever and nervousness associated with tuberculosis makes its victims overactive and, well, prone to passion."

Pearl buttoned herself up, feeling very detached and adult. "Then some of the things she'd done were never really her fault at all. It was them little boogers as made her so wild. I'm glad we came to you, Doctor. I understands thing better now. What can be done to help her? She's my mamma and it's my duty to try," she said.

The doctor hesitated. He was a resident of Fort Smith, too, and so he knew who Belle Starr was and the kind of life she was said to lead.

He said, "Any calming influence would be an improvement. If you could get her to sleep more and drink less, it might buy her another ten years or so."

"And if she goes on the way she has been, sir?"

"A year. Maybe two, if she's lucky. Look, Miss Younger, this may not be my duty as a physician, but you're a patient, too, in a way. So may I give you some personal advice?"

"Of course, That's what I'm paying you for."

"All right then. Give it up. I know she's your mother and I can see you love her, but she's a lost cause. I tried to tell her what I just told you about her unwholesome habits, and she cussed me for my trouble. She's not going to change her ways. She's set in them. You have your own life to consider. Go out and live it, Miss Younger. Loyalty is a fine thing, but loyalty stops short of suicide, and she has no right to ask you to follow down after her!"

Pearl smiled wanly. "She hasn't asked me to do anything, sir. I know my own self what I must do. Somebody has to look after her, and she has nobody but me who really cares."

So Pearl went down to the livery to wait for her mamma. She read the letter from her Aunt Retta again. Then she crumpled it and threw it away. It was a nice letter, but Pearl didn't mean to answer it. She couldn't answer it. What was there to say?

* * *

In the months that followed, Pearl nagged, pleaded, and threatened Belle not to consume quite as much white lightning. She chased men off with a broom when they'd come calling while Jim July was off raiding stock or selling moonshine. Belle, however, met them on the sly, and of course Pearl could hardly run the lusty Jim July off. The boys said Belle was sure a hot old bawd, drunk or sober, and Belle didn't seem to be getting any worse.

The same could not, however, be said for the Cherokee Strip. The old wild days were dying with the eighteen-nineties, but they were going out with a bang. The terrible winter of '87-'88 froze cattle dead on their feet from the Canadian border to south of the Red River into Texas, which finished the free and easy era of the open range. The price of beef was down and the country was heading into the terrible depression of the Gay Nineties, which would only be gay for those few holding steady jobs. As the was between the states had done a generation before, the economic troubles starting in the late eighties would leave a lot of semiliterate and active young men with nothing much to do but raise pure hell.

So, as the star of the cowboy began to set, many a hitherto honest young puncher turned mean. There were still parts of the country unfenced and wild, and they started getting wilder.

The Indian Nation was one such place. Big enough to form the future state of Oklahoma, it was a vast expanse of rolling, partly wooded country, inhabited by a simple folk who didn't gossip much with white men. It was policed casually, even by western standards, and there were endless nooks and crannies where a man and his mount could bed down next to timber and water without being pestered. So, just as a magnet draws steel filings, the Indian Nation drew the remaining outlaws.

The Burrow gang were Alabama-born and white besides, but they found a home in the Indian Nation and held up trains in other parts. Ned Christie was white, or said he was, but he raided out of the Cherokee Strip too, and, like Belle Starr, ran illegal firewater to the Indians who covered

for him. Mysterious Dave Mather was said to be somewhere in the Strip, but nobody knew for sure. Nobody
knew where he'd come from or where he'd gone after gunning Tom Nixon in Dodge.

John Wesley Hardin was a Texas lunatic who made the
Strip his home from time to time between senseless killings
in small trail towns all over the West. Cherokee Bill
Goldsby was an Indian, or said he was. He could be said to
belong in the Strip, since he'd been born there, and it
wasn't a good idea to comment that he looked sort of colored. He'd already shot a colored man for calling him
"brother" and he was said to gun Creek and Seminole on
general principles.

Over to the north, where they couldn't vex their badge-
toting brother, Frank, the other Dalton boys were making
themselves a reputation as general hell-raisers and cattle
rustlers. An older drifter named Bill Doolin was about to
lead them further astray. He and his sidekick, Red Buck
Weightman, sure admired the bank in Coffeeville, Kansas,
just outside the Indian Nation.

There were others. There was Dynamite Dick Clifton,
Bitter Creek Newcomb from Wyoming Territory, Tulsa
Jack Blake, and old Charley Pierce who didn't need a nick-
name to frighten everyone he met. There was Arkansas
Tom, and the fighting Daugherty clan, Little Bill Raidler,
who stood six feet tall, and the really short and surly Little
Dick West.

Honest folk said the Cherokee Strip was a caution, and
Judge Parker said he was doing his best, dang it! Young
Deputy Frank Dalton surprised a trio of bootleggers one
moonlit night and killed all three in the resulting discussion
of their wicked ways. The bodies were photographed
propped up on cellar doors, and when Rafe showed copies
to Belle Starr she said she had no notion who they might
have been. Rafe decided that since all three were white and
decent-looking, she was likely telling the truth.

Pearl pleaded with her mother to give up the life she led,
for it looked like she was riding for an awesome fall, but
Belle had started drinking heavily again and she was feel-

ing cocky and full of beans. She knew she was slicker than anyone around and, in a way, she was right.

The law knew what Belle was up to, but the law was mighty busy. Belle would have felt highly insulted had she heard Hanging Judge Parker instruct his deputies to, "Go after the really dangerous killers and let the trash thieves be for now."

Belle had started to believe she was the bandit queen folk said she was. She bought a little pearl-handled revolver, and tucked it in the belt she already had two Colt .44s hanging on. She put a white plume in her hat and liked to ride into town without opening gates, but instead just jumping the fences that got in the way of her bee-line. She enjoyed the way the more "sissy" housewives looked at her, and she laughed like hell when she heard that mothers were warning naughty childer that Belle Starr would get 'em if they didn't behave.

Her daughter Pearl began to look more sick than her tubercular mamma.

Pearl's young face was drawn from sleepless nights, spent worrying when her mother took it in her head to ride with the boys. She lost weight and there were dark circles under her eyes. Yet she still held her head high when she went into town, and while small boys jeered and hissed at her, they knew better than to throw things. The pale gal on the painted pony that their mothers called "The Younger whore," with sardonic double meaning, was not only likely a witch-woman like her mother, but kin to Deputy Dalton, and he'd passed word that he'd take it mighty personal if anyone knocked off his cousin's hat with a hoss turd.

By unspoken mutual agreement, Pearl and Frank Dalton seldom saw each other on the streets of Fort Smith, and when they did, they only nodded. Pearl knew that, like his brothers, she was a considerable embarrassment to the young lawman. She was his kin, so he had to do right by her, but he didn't want to brag on it.

One day Frank Dalton got a worried letter from another distant kinswoman. Pearl's Aunt Retta couldn't understand

why the girl had never answered her letters. She begged
Frank to advise her.

Frank didn't want to write back, but a man did what he
had to when called on by his own blood. So he wrote:

> "Dear Miss Retta:
>   I think Pearl should go and abide with you-all too. I
> would tell her to, if I thought she would listen. But I
> know she won't. She is a good girl, like you heard from
> Frank James. She is quiet and sober and talks like a
> fine lady with lots of book learning. She's never been
> caught stealing and my side-kick, Rafe, says he's
> known her all her life and she never has been bad. But
> she is sure willful about her no-good trashy mother.
> Since you asked me about Belle Starr in your letter, I
> hope you won't take it as unkind when I say your
> brother, Cole, must have been blind drunk when he
> took up with that woman. She is no-good total. Your
> niece, Pearl, seems to be the only one who can see any
> good in Belle Starr. What that might be is a total mys-
> tery to yours truly. But Pearl loves the crazy old horse
> thief and there's no use talking. I am as sorry for her
> as you-all are. But I am just as helpless to do anything
> about it.
>
>   Cousin Frank."

Pearl's concerned distant kinsman was correct in saying
she was well-spoken. Like many another young spinster,
Pearl lived much of her life in books. She no longer spent
much time in the reading room. She'd made friends with
the librarian and was allowed to check books out, even
though they'd had to fake an Arkansas address for her library card, since the Cherokee Strip was off limits to bor-
rowers.

Pearl had discovered poetry as her vocabulary expanded,
and she'd even written some poems to lighten the hours at
the spread. They tended to be fairly banal, if judged by the
standards of the literary world, but since it never occurred
to Pearl to submit any of her poetry for possible publica-

tion, she was unaware she was no threat to more established poets, and Belle was quite impressed.

One night on the veranda as Pearl let her read what she's written about the moonlight on the Arkansas, Belle sighed and said, "Lord, you surely has a way with words, honey. I have never noticed how the old river looks like crumpled tinfoil when the moon ball's rays is slanting like you say here, but now that I study on it, you are right on the money. I sure admire that part about the tree branches being black lace agin the blue silk of the night sky, too. Who'd have thought you could make old willow and alder seem so pretty? You sure sees the world prettier than I do, Pearl. How come you sees beauty where others only see ugly sticks and muddy water?"

Pearl shrugged and said, "I guess we look at the world a mite different, Mamma."

"That's for damn sure, but I sure like the way you writes these things, Pearl. Will you promise me a favor?"

"What is it, Mamma?"

"This stuff you write. Would you write a poem about me?"

Pearl hesitated and Belle reassured her. "You don't have to do it right now. You can do her after I'm dead, all right?"

"Mamma, you have no call to talk about being dead. The doctor says you could live another twenty years if you'd behave yourself."

"Oh, hell, who wants to live another twenty years? I'd be over sixty if I lived that long and I'm old enough already."

"Not to me, Mamma, so let's not talk on dying just yet, hear?"

Belle shook her head. "I ain't figuring on doing her tonight. I feel spry as anything. But about this poem. You know the kind of poem they puts on grave markers?"

"You mean epitaphs, Mamma?"

"Yeah, that's what I mean. You sure talk pretty. So, listen, when I ain't on this earth no more, I want you to write a nice poem about me for my grave marker. Something as will make me sound as pretty as I always wanted to be. Will you do her, Pearl?"

Pearl smiled and murmured, "When I'm gone, and in my grave, no fancy tombstone will I crave. Just lay me down in my native peat, with a jug of rum at my head and feet."

"I ain't sure I cotton to that one, honey. It sounds more suited to a man's grave marker, if you want my true opinion," Belle said, frowning.

"I was only funning you, Mamma. I couldn't use that. Another poet already wrote it."

"Oh, then you mean to do better by me, right?"

"If I have to, Mamma, but please don't talk about dying any more. It makes me feel all blubbery inside. I don't want you to die, Mamma."

Belle put her hand on her daughter's shoulder and whispered, "I know you don't. You never have had much sense, but it warms me to know you care, honey. I sometimes feel nobody else in the world would care if the ground just opened wide and swallowed me."

"Oh, come on, old Jim July acts mighty fond of you, Mamma."

"Shoot, Jim's fond enough of what I got betwixt my legs, and the likker we drink together helps him admire my looks. But you're all I really has, daughter. You're the only thing on this earth that really loves me. And you know what, I loves you, too. I mean, I loves you with my heart alone. The way I've always loved men, even your father, can't hold a candle to the way I feels about you, honey. Can I ask another favor?"

"Sure, Mamma. What do you want from me?"

"Well, would you put your arms about me and give me a great big old hug? I don't want you to think I'm turning lizzy woman with my own kin or nothing, but we ain't hugged good since you was little and, I don't know, tonight I feel like I want you to hug me."

Pearl's eyes glistened in the moonlight as she took her mother in her arms.

Belle warned, "Don't kiss me. I wouldn't want you catching what that fool sawbones says I might have."

She leaned her head against Pearl's bosom and said, "My, that feels so nice. You know, your grandmother used to hold me like this when I was a little girl, and now my own daughter is holding me the same way. It seems mighty strange, but it sure feels comforting. Can I tell you something, Pearl? You won't think I'm getting queer in the head?"

"What is it, Mamma?"

"I've tried to feel this in the arms of many a man, but I never. I mean, I likes to be helt by men. More than I should, I reckon, but being helt by a man ain't as comforting, when a gal feels scared."

"Are you frightened, Mamma? Whatever for? The doctor says you don't have a bad dose of consumption and . . ."

"Pearl, I ain't scared of consumption. I ain't even scared of dying. I've seen the valley and I've seen the hill and I ain't scared of old man skull-and-bones all that much," Belle said.

"What are you scared of then, Mamma?" asked Pearl.

"I don't know. That's why it scares me so. Just hold me a spell and it'll pass. It always does, even when I ain't got my strong brave daughter to comfort me."

"You've had these spells before then, Mamma?"

"Sure I has. Hasn't everybody? Sometimes, when the wind is still and you're all alone in the night, don't you get to wondering how high is up and how long is forever and what the hell you're doing here?"

Pearl sighed and said, "Yes, Mamma," as she held the confused woman close. She didn't comment on the many times she'd cried herself to sleep, alone and frightened and wishing someone was there to hold her. ❧

12

THE LAST LEAVES fell and everyone settled down to get through the winter of '88-89 as best they could. It got colder than it had any need to, even when the sun was shining on the ice-edged Arkansas. The cabin was as cold as a well digger's socks, even with the stove heated cherry red halfway up the pipe. Pearl had to spend more time than she really would have liked to with Belle and Jim July.

Jim July sensed that pretty Pearl didn't like him all that much, although he was a good-humored rogue who genuinely liked most folk who didn't wear a badge.

Therefore, as Christmas approached, the lusty, innocently stupid Creek broke into the Logan Dry Goods Store and brought back a buckboard load of presents for both the gals. Pearl was too polite to ask where he'd gotten all the play pretties, and warm-heartedly praised her presents. She tried to be nice to Jim July. He treated her mother decent and never got forward with her, even when they were alone together, but she never managed to get past common courtesy with anyone as obviously moronic as old Jim. However, since he was stupid, that was good enough for him.

The winter passed, taking a million years but not doing anything worthy of record, and then a robin bird was chirping on the veranda rail one morn as it paused on its way north. As January moved toward February, skunk cabbages poked cautious shoots out of the snow melting along the river bank. They knew the worst of the northers were likely over, and the dreadful muddy earth of that never-never time betwixt winter and the green-up, was on its way.

One day Pearl bundled up and rode into Fort Smith to the library. She knew Jim and the boys wouldn't go raiding while the ground was soft enough to lead a posse right up to the dooryard, and her mother seemed to be breathing easier in the crisp, cold air.

As Pearl left her pony at the livery and headed up the street to the library, Steve Logan fell in at her side, smiling sheepishly.

Pearl said, "Get away from me, Steve Logan. I've no words for you a lady dast say in mixed company."

"I got a lot of ugly words coming, Pearl, but afore you hit me with a snowball, hear me out. I've been looking for you all winter. I reckon I owe you an apology," he said.

"That's for durned sure. So, all right, you've said you're sorry and I'll thank you to go stick your head in a horse trough."

"Look, Pearl, I said I was sorry. I acted like a fool. I was younger in them days. I've had half a year to study on the way I done, and I'd sure like to make it up to you."

"Do tell? How do you aim to make me feel good? Have you got your own furnished room in town, now?"

"Aw, Pearl, you know I never believed that dumb old Larry. I called him on it, too. I said I'd punch his nose if he said he'd had his way with you, and he said he'd only been joshing and that you was a decent gal."

"Well, it's good to know I meet with your approval. I suppose I'm supposed to roll over and butter myself 'cause a fancy Dan from the Logan clan don't aim to call me a whore in public," Pearl said sarcastically.

"Pearl, you sure aren't making it easy to be nice to you."

"I don't need you to be nice to me. I got me a whole tribe of Indians out to get in my britches. Didn't anyone tell you that?"

"Pearl, I'm asking you to be friends. I told my father he had no call to tell me who I may or may not be friends with. I'm over twenty-one and self-supporting. He still thinks I'm crazy, but my mother says she'd like to meet you. Can you come to dinner with us this Sunday?"

Pearl stopped, sincerely shocked. She frowned up at him and said, "Are you telling me true, Steve Logan? Are you saying Miz Logan of *the* Logans is ready to recieve the daughter of Belle Starr?"

He nodded. "I told you she was, didn't I? My Ma's a free-thinking woman, and when she heard about you and me she asked around town. There's some in Fort Smith as thinks highly of you, Pearl. Ma says if Judge Parker and Tillie the librarian think you're all right, it's good enough for her. Say you'll come, Pearl, please?"

Pearl shook her head and said in a kinder tone, "It wouldn't work, Steve. You might not think I'm bad; even your folk might be willing to meet me open-minded; but this is a small town, and I'd only be making trouble for you and your'n. I thanks your mother for her lady-like offer, but I must refuse it. It wouldn't be fair to take her up on it."

"Aw, can't we just sort of be friends on the quiet, then?"

"Where, Steve? Where do you suggest we tryst in the dark? Here in this bitty one-horse town, or mayhaps over in the Cherokee Strip, in the bushes?"

"Pearl, I wasn't studying on meeting you like that, durn it!" exclaimed Steve.

"All right, let's say we was to meet on the sly and just hold hands for now? What would be the point, Steve? You're from a quality family here in the county, and me, I'm an outlaw's child and an outcast."

"Damn it, Pearl, you don't have to be! You could move away from Younger's Bend, you know. You're above the age of consent. Your mother couldn't stop you."

Pearl laughed bitterly and said, "I'm not a fairy princess

being held prisoner by ogres, Steve. My mother wouldn't stop me if I said I wanted to leave, so you've no call to put on that armor and come riding to my rescue. They'd likely hoorah you about that tie, anyways."

"I'm not afraid of being hoorahed, Pearl, but I can't understand why you want to live along the river with those trashy folk."

"Don't want to, Steve. Have to. One of them trashy folk you speak of is my mother, and she needs me. So, like I said, pay your mother my respects and let's say no more about it."

"Can I walk you to where you're heading, at least?"

"No, Steve. I like you. I like you a heap, if that's any comfort. That's why I don't want you seen on the streets of Fort Smith with me, now or ever."

She turned away and walked on, not looking back. She went to the library and checked in the books she'd borrowed, wondering why she felt so awful, like something had been cut out of her. It wasn't the time of the month when a gal was supposed to feel awful. It was likely her corset was too tight. She felt all faint and fluttery in her chest and her legs dragged like empty rubber boots.

She picked out some new books and went back outside. The sky was grey like it was fixing to snow some more. She wished it wouldn't. The ride home was tedious enough without having to ride through snow.

As she approached the livery, a man called her name. Pearl walked on without looking back. She was used to the things men called after her this close to the saloon where Sam was killed. If she pretended not to hear, they never bothered her further.

So she was surprised when a hand gripped her coated elbow and the same voice repeated, "What's got into you, Pearl? You have no call to snub me, have you?"

It was Frank James. He was older and more respectable looking, but it was still her Uncle Frank. Pearl hugged him, sobbing, "Oh, I thought you was somebody jeering me, Uncle Frank!"

He patted her and said, "Yeah, Frank Dalton's told me.

Let's get out of this bitter wind, girl. The tea shop yonder looks decent."

She went with him into the tea shop, and as they sat facing one another over a checkered tablecloth, she said, "My, you sure look mighty fine, Uncle Frank. What's that hanging on the chain across your vest?"

"Oh, that's my lodge token from Kansas City." Said Frank. "I'm member of a lot of lodges and such, these days. Seems everywhere I go, men want to shake my hand and join me up to their lodge. I'm on my way to Texas now, to give a talk at a boys reform school. I had to change trains here in Fort Smith. I was hoping I'd meet up with you. Your kin back home are worried about you, Pearl."

"The only kin I've ever known is over to Younger's Bend. What do you mean you were *hoping*, Uncle Frank? Weren't you fixing to ride out to the cabin and see Mamma and me? asked Pearl.

Frank James stared awkwardly down at his teacup and said, "I studied on it, honey, but you see, since I've gone straight . . ."

"I understand. Frank Dalton don't pay many sociable calls in the Strip, neither."

He sighed and said, "Honey, I paid a visit to your father, up north in that prison. He'd sure worry less on you if you was to take your Aunt Retta up on her offer to board you."

Pearl shrugged and said, "I know you all would, Uncle Frank. But I can't leave Mamma."

"Sure you can, honey. I'll tell you what, I got the money right here in my pocket to put you on the train for Missouri and wire your Aunt Retta to expect you. You can leave a message for old Belle and be long gone afore she knows it."

"Do Jesus! All you fool men seem to think I'm a maiden to be saved!" Pearl said with a sigh.

"Well, ain't you, Pearl?"

"Of course not. I just got done this very day with another such dumb conversation with a man out to save me from whatever. I don't need no saving. I'm staying with my mamma 'cause she needs me, durn it!"

"Do tell? What does she need you for, running brands or loading guns?"

"Be serious, Uncle Frank. Mamma is sick. She has consumption, like my Uncle Bob Younger."

Frank James stared soberly across at her and said, "That *is* serious, ain't it? How long do you reckon Belle has to live?"

"We don't know. She could go in a year. She might last twenty."

He nodded thoughtfully and said, "Making you a middle-aged woman when you was finally free of her." He reached across the table, took her hand, and said, "Pay heed to my words, Pearl Younger. I know all too well what it means to waste a youth on a lost cause, for I've done it, and it hurts like hell to even think about it! Look at me, Pearl. You see before you a middle-aged man, and I ain't much older than you'll be in another twenty years. Is that all you want out of life? Do you mean to throw your golden years away on someone who can't even appreciate it?"

"What else can I do, Uncle Frank? She's my mamma, and she needs me. I could never run off and leave her to look after her own self. She'd likely be dead in a year or less if I was to be so selfich hearted!"

"Honey, your mother has her good points, I reckon, but when it comes to a selfish heart, she's got us all whipped by a mile. She chose the life she leads, and when she meets her certain end, she'll have chose that, too. Don't sink with the ship, Pearl honey. The leaky old tub just ain't worth it!"

Pearl shook her head and insisted, stubbornly, "She's my mamma."

Frank James nodded and said, "Yeah, God help you, that she is."

The federal deputy rode into Younger's Bend bundled against the cold in sheepskins. He held a cocked Winchester across his saddle swells.

As he turned into Belle Starr's dooryard, Belle opened

the cabin door and called out, "Rafe, git in here and warm yourself, hear? You look like you're half friz!"

Rafe dismounted, relieved by the friendly reception, and said, "I sure could use me a gallon of Arbuckle to set in, Belle. You're dead right about it being cold on the trail today. Damned wind has shifted to the north again."

He stamped his boots politely on the veranda and followed her inside, where he found Pearl. It wouldn't have been polite to say what he was doing there while they were serving him coffee and pecan pie, so he didn't. He waited until he'd finished his second cup and shook his head when Pearl offered to pour him more. Then he asked if it was all right to smoke, and when Belle nodded, he took out his makings and started to roll thoughtfully as he said, "I don't see old Jim July about, Belle."

Belle answered cautiously. "Jim rode up the trail a ways to visit some friends. I disremember who he said they was."

Belle waited while the deputy finished rolling his smoke. Then she moved her head impatiently and asked, "Are you looking for Jim, Rafe?"

The deputy thumbed a wooden match alight, lit his smoke, and said, "Yep. Matter of fact I am. I'm sorry, Belle, but I got a warrant on old Jim."

"Do tell? What's the warrant for, Rafe?"

"Oh, a little of this and a little of that. Mostly robbery. You, ah, wouldn't mind if I had a look about your spread, would you, Belle?"

"Is my name on your warrant, Rafe?"

"Nope, can't say as it is."

"Then I mind."

"I figured you might, Belle. That's why I asked the judge to write you up, too. But you know what a nit picker Judge Parker is. He says the eyewitnesses to the robbery never mentioned anyone in skirts being along. Just a couple of gents who might have been Indians or 'breeds."

"Have some more coffee, dang it," said Belle. "This is sort of interesting and it's still friendly. How come them witnesses couldn't say for certain whether the robbers was 'breeds or pure-bloods, Rafe?"

"Oh, didn't Jim tell you? They wore kerchiefs over their faces at the time. You could tell they wasn't Swede gents, since they had dark skin and Injun hair where they wasn't covered. Mention was made of a red plaid shirt, too. Don't Jim have a red plaid shirt, Belle?"

She shook her head and said, "Not no more. I think a goat must have et it. No offense, Rafe, but you sure has a mighty poor case agin my man, if you ask me."

"Didn't ask you, Belle. Asked Judge Parker if I should pick up an old boy who tallied with the descriptions. He thought it was a fine notion. So here I be. When do you expect Jim back?"

"Can't say, Rafe. His friend was mighty sick, so Jim could well spend a day or so nursing him. You want me to ride out and see if I can fetch him for you?"

Rafe laughed and said, "Not hardly, Belle."

He took a thoughtful drag on his smoke and then he shrugged and said, "Well, I could go looking for him and freeze my fool self to the very bone, or I could stay here and wait for a man who likely won't ever come back here lessen you signal to the tree line that's it's safe. So I'll tell you what let's do. I'll leave the warrant here with you and let you serve it on him, Belle."

Belle snorted in disbelief and asked, "Me? Do I look like an officer of the court, Rafe?"

Rafe said, "You don't have to be. Any law-abiding citizen can serve a man with notice to appear in court, and you are a law-abiding citizen, ain't you, Belle?"

"I'd sure be a fool to deny it. What if I do as you say, Rafe? What if I hand the warrant over to Jim when and if, and he tells me to just shove it you know where?" she said with a laugh.

"I don't think he'd want to do that, Belle. I'm riding back to tell the court I served the warrant as close as I could get to Jim. You knows your law, so I don't have to tell you what'll happen if old Jim ain't in court when the judge's bailiff calls his name," Rafe said.

He took out the arrest warrant and placed it soberly on the table.

"It's addressed to Jim July, but you can read it if you like. I got to get on home. If you don't want to attend Jim July's funeral, make sure he's in court come morning, hear?"

Belle followed him to the door as Pearl remained at the table, frozen faced. Rafe wondered what was wrong with the girl. He'd been as decent as he could to her mamma, considering.

Belle waited until the deputy was out of sight before she barred the door and called out, "You hear all that, Jim?"

Her Creek lover appeared at the edge of the loft, where he'd been hiding since spotting Rafe through the window. He came down the ladder before he said, "I sure did, honey. I reckon I'd better start riding far and sudden, don't you?"

"Sit down and behave yourself, you fool Creek! Why in the hell would you have call to ride off anywheres?" Belle said with a frown.

"Belle, has you got wax in your ears? I was up there trying not to wet my britches all the time that lawman was talking about the robbery we pulled off!"

Belle gave him a disgusted look. "I heard him. Jesus H. Christ, who ever heard of wearing a red plaid shirt to a holdup! You're pure dumb, Jim July! Every time I think I know how dumb you are, you prove me wrong by pulling something even dumber! Pearl, get this fool some coffee to wake him up so I can talk sense to him!"

As Pearl moved to the stove, Belle said, "All right, fortunately for you, you don't own a red plaid shirt no more."

"Belle, has you gone blind? I'm setting right here *wearing* the infernal shirt!"

"No you ain't. It's going in the stove as soon as we undress for bed. Let's see, you boys took money, and money all looks the same. So they got no shirt and they can't prove one silver certificate from another. You had enough sense not to let nobody see your face. You didn't introduce yourself by name or carve your initials on the counter as you was waiting for them to open that safe, I hope?"

"Course not," he said with a grin. "I ain't that dumb. I

never said word one. Osage Mike done all the talking. I just stood there covering the old rascals."

"There you go, honey. They got no case agin you," Belle said.

"What do you mean they got no case, Belle? I done it, didn't I?"

"Hell, no you didn't, Jim honey. Some other thieving rascals done it. Don't ask me who, for how are *we* to know, right?"

Jim grinned moronically, and Pearl felt sick as she served him. Belle nodded, pleased with her own astute grasp of the rules of evidence, and assured him, "It's our word agin theirs, Jim. Me and Pearl here . . . never mind, you and me, Jim, will just stand before Judge Parker and tell him how you was here in my loving arms when some no good 'breed pulled that robbery and likely wore a shirt like your'n to throw the blame on you."

She struck a dramatic pose and orated, "I ask you, Your Honor, does the accused look like a man dumb enough to wear his own loud shirt to a robbing?"

Jim July laughed. "Hot damn! You reckon we can slicker him?"

"We always has, hasn't we? You see, Jim, the trouble with boys like you and the others is that you run afore you study on things. If you was to run, they'd put that together with your fancy shirt and add it up to a heap of trouble for you. My way, it's just a tedious morning session in court and we can forget all about it."

"Gee, Belle, you sure are slick. I don't know what I'd do without you."

Belle jabbed him playfully in the ribs and answered, "You'd likely wear your poor hand out." Then she caught her daughter's eye and asked, "Didn't you say you wanted to go early to your room and write some poems, Pearl?"

Pearl nodded and rose to her feet, red-faced. They were going at each other before she'd closed the door behind her.

As she sat alone in her tiny lean-to, wondering if it was worth the lamp oil to try and read herself to sleep, she heard a coarse vulgar yell through the log wall. She grimaced and undressed for bed in the dark, as she tried to ignore the orgy going on within earshot. She knew she wasn't going to get much sleep tonight. Mamma was never hornier than when she thought she was putting one over on someone.

Pearl lit the lamp and tried to read, but damn, the book was dirty, too! Tillie at the library had said it was by a new and saucy author, and Tillie had been right. The words were more polite than the ones she kept hearing through the log wall, but Pearl knew what the characters were up to.

"Write a poem?" Pearl snorted, sitting up and reaching for her note pad and pencil. "I'll right you a poem, Mamma!"

She scribbled, angrily, "Pricks and cunts make the world go 'round. It's just cunts and pricks 'til we're all in the ground. And when I get to heaven's gate, Saint Peter will likely masturbate!"

She balled the paper and threw it away, breathing hard as she muttered, "Now why on earth did I ever do that?"

She found another book and started to read, but the new book was about some fool girl-child and a black horse she spoiled like a hound dog. Pearl suspected the writer had no notion which end of a horse the turds come out of, for she'd met folk who weren't half as smart as that Black Beauty!

She decided she might as well try the first book again, but as she reached for it, the ball of paper on the floor caught her eye.

Pearl tried to ignore it. Then she got up, picked up the dirty poem, and carefully put it in the lamp chimney to burn away to nothing. Lord of mercy, what if Mamma was to ever find a thing like that she'd written? What would Mamma think?

Leaving Pearl to mind the cabin, Belle and Jim July rode to Fort Smith in a jovial mood. They were well fortified by white lightning, and carrying along a couple of jars in case they met up with any snakes on the frozen trail.

When they got to Judge Parker's court, they were told the judge was out of town and wouldn't be back for a couple of days. Belle swore roundly.

"Jesus H. Christ, after we rode all this way to settle this little misunderstanding, too! Come on, Jim, let's go home."

That's when Rafe, who'd been sitting quiet in a corner, stood up. "You can go, Belle. Jim's staying here!"

Belle regarded Rafe owlishly and said, "Say again? The man here says the judge is out of town. How in thunder can poor Jim stand trial if the infernal Judge aint here?"

"Oh, we'll keep him comfortable in the jail 'til the judge gets back, Belle. I told you it was an arrest warrant, didn't I?" Rafe said.

"Thunderation, this ain't fair! Jim and me come in volunteer!"

"I know that, Belle, and I'm sure the judge will feel obliged, but I was told to arrest Jim when I caught up with him, and here he is, so he's under arrest. I'll take them guns from you now, Jim. You do mean to hand 'em over sensible, don't you?"

The Creek looked like he was fixing to burst into tears as he undid his gunbelt and blurted, "Belle? What went wrong here?"

"Nothing, Jim," Belle soothed him. "They're just being mean. I told you they have no case and I meant it. You just play along with the rascals for now. I'll get you off. You'll see."

Rafe said, "Let's go, Jim. You wouldn't want to come along with him, would you, Belle? I could likely fix it up for you if you wanted to tell me a tale about some Rocking Six yearlings."

Belle smiled bitterly and answered. "Not hardly. Them yearlings is likely cut and sold for someone's supper by now and you know it. You ain't got the evidence to hold poor Jim, neither, you sneaky scoundrel."

"Well, I'll tell you, Belle, I'm holding him, at least until the judge sees fit to weigh the evidence. That ain't my job. I just arrests the gents and the judge decides."

"Shoot, you know he'll let Jim go. What if I was to post bail for him?"

"You can't hardly do that, Belle. The judge has to decide on bail or not, and, like I said, he ain't here."

"I sure misjudged you, Rafe. I never thought you'd do us like this. I suspicion you're just holding my Jim out of pure ornery spite. You just mean to hold him as long as you can, 'til the judge has to turn him loose, right?"

Rafe nodded. "When you're right you're right. If we can only keep old Jim here, under lock and key one night, that's one night folks can breathe easier about their personal property. Move it on out, Jim. You knows the way to the detention cells by now."

Some of the other men were snickering and Belle didn't like it much.

"We'll see who has the last laugh, here," she said. "I mean to sue for false arrest, soon as I have it out with old Judge Parker."

She marched grandly out, but she stood undecided on the walk, looking like a small shabby figure bundled against the wolf-wind, as she tried to decide if there was any point in hiring a lawyer this soon. Then she shrugged, went to her tethered mount, and climbed up in her sidesaddle to head on home. It was broad day, but the sky was overcast and the world looked twilight as well as frozen stiff.

Her thoroughbred's steel-shod hooves rang on the icy clay of the wagon trace. Both the mount and its rider left a trail of visible breath in their wake as they moved along at a brisk, mile-killing trot. Belle fumbled in her saddlebag for a whiskey jar. She felt better after she'd had some medicine, but she was angry and frustrated and she knew she faced a lonesome bitter night. She didn't mind being alone in daylight, but when owl birds hooted a woman needed a man's arms around her. Any man's arms were better than sleeping alone in the dark.

She and the jar were halfway home when Belle and New Venus rode into Basket Thicket, where the still bare willows crowded close to the trail as if they wanted to claw passers with their branches. Belle reined in when she saw a tall, dark figure seated silently among the willows on a large dark horse. Her guns were under her heavy coat. She shivered, and then she let out a sigh of pure relief.

"Oh, Lord, it's you, Frank James. For a moment you gave me a whopping start. You looked like old Mister Skull-and-Bones setting there in the half light! What are you doing in these parts, Frank? I didn't know you were anywheres near Fort Smith."

"Nobody else knows neither, Belle. I was to speak in Texas today. They'll likely believe me when I explain how I missed connections in the bad weather we've been having," Frank said.

"Well, it's not for me to ask why you needs an alibi, Frank, but I heard you'd gone straight."

"I have, Belle. At least, I mostly has, but there's some things a man must do, when his blood cries out for help."

Belle rode closer, frowning at his odd words and sad-looking face. She asked, "Who are we talking about, Frank? Who's calt on you for a kinsman's help?"

"Your daughter, Pearl. She never *called* on us for help. I want you to know that, Belle. It's important that you know none of what must be is the sweet girl's doing. You see, Belle, Cole Younger is her father, and Cole Younger is my kinsman as well as my friend. That makes me kin to Pearl, too, and a man stands by his kin."

"Well, sure, Frank, everybody knows that. She's always calt you her uncle, ain't she?"

"She has, and I mean to live up to the name. Her father saved my life one time, so you see, there's a blood as well as a kinship debt connecting me to that girl. I'm sure sorry about this, Belle. I've studied on it a long time, but, like I said, a man does what he has to for his kith and kin."

Belle shook her head impatiently and demanded, "Get to the infernal point, Frank James! If my child is in trouble I got a right to know it, too. What's going on here? Who's been causing trouble for my Pearl?"

"You have, Belle. I know you doubtless meant well, but you are at the root and heart of all that troubles Pearl. You got to let her go, Belle. She's a good and decent young gal, who deserves the chance you and me never had."

Belle blinked in surprise and gasped, "Let her go, Frank? Let her go where, for heaven's sake?"

"Anywhere would be an improvement, Belle. And it's for heaven's sake I'm asking you. Will you let her live her own life, Belle?"

"Hell's fire, I ain't never stopped her from doing anything she wanted to. Some even say I spoiled that child by not paying more attention to her rearing. But hell, she turned out all right, didn't she?"

"She did, Belle, and I can see you've no notion of what I'm talking about. You can't let her go, 'cause you don't see how tight you're holding on to her. I was afeared it would be like this. So we'll just say no more about it."

Belle nodded and said, "Well, if you're done talking queer as hell, let's go on out to the spread and I'll feed you some supper. You wouldn't, ah, like to spend the night, would you, Frank?"

He shook his head and said, "I has a train to catch. Goodbye, Belle."

She shrugged, told him to suit himself, and swung her mount around to ride on. She'd only ridden a few paces when the world around her exploded in a thunderous roar and something tore her from her saddle like a big steel claw, and she landed face down on the frozen trail, muttering in dull wonder, "Thunderation, I do believe I've been shot!"

Some instinct warned her not to move, and as she lay there playing possom, she heard hoofbeats moving away at a steady lope. She groaned and tried to roll over and get her guns, but the air before her eyes was filled with little pin-wheeling stars, and it was far easier just to let go and fall down into the suddenly warm soft darkness.

Belle Starr was unconscious but still alive when some people came along in a buckboard and found her. They knew who she was. Everyone knew who she was, so they carried her home to Younger's Bend and to her daughter Pearl.

The sobbing, dutiful daughter had her mother laid out, and then sent for Granny Redbird. She knelt beside the bed, clutching Belle's cold hands and begging her not to die. Granny Redbird never came, but as Pearl and the others hovered over her, Belle opened her eyes, smiled, and asked, "Is that my Honey Pearl? Where am I?"

"You're home, Mamma. Home where you belong. We've sent for help. Try to hold on like a good girl, hear?"

Belle smiled roguishly and said, "I've never held with being all that good, but does you love me, Pearl? Does you really love me?"

Pearl couldn't answer as she put her arms around the dying woman and sobbed against her breast.

One of the men in the room asked, "Who did it, Miss Belle? Who bushwacked you like that?"

Belle frowned and murmured, in a barely audible voice, "I never would have thought it of him."

"Who was it, Belle? I'll get some of the boys and we'll string him up for you, but we has to know who to string."

Belle reached up a hand to run it over Pearl's hair, sighing, "Pretty. So pretty. And I've been ever so proud on her. Pearl? Are you listening to me, Pearl?"

"Yes, Mamma. I'm here. I'll ever be here."

Belle coughed and croaked, "No you won't. I sees now what Mister Skull-and-Bones meant. You didn't say, before, when I asked you if you loved me."

"Of course I love you, Mamma. I'll always love you!"

"Who shot you, Belle?" a male voice insisted.

Belle closed her eyes and murmured, "It don't matter. She said she loves me."

Pearl held her head closer to her mother's breast. She bit her lip and listened hard. Then she let out a low lost sound and fainted across her mother's still form.

One of the men put his hand to Belle's throat. Another asked, "Is she?" and he said, "She is. Now we'll never know who done it!"

A man was having a shave and a haircut in a Fort Smith barber's chair the next day. He was a stranger in town. He was a freelance journalist looking for a story on some new outfit called the Dalton Boys, but people in Fort Smith didn't talk to strangers about a deputy marshal's kin, so he was ready to move on.

Another man came it, sat down to wait his turn, and asked the barber, "Hey, Pop, you hear about Belle Starr?"

The barber snipped on as he answered, "I'm always hearing about Belle Starr. What's the fool woman done now?"

"You mean you didn't know? She's been shot! Bushwacked on the trail she was. She's dead as a kitten down the well!"

"I always figured someone would shoot her sooner or later. Who was the rascal?" the barber said with a shrug.

"Nobody knows, Pop. Belle died afore they could get it out of her. The lawmen think it could have been a jealous lover, a short-changed Cherokee, or any of a dozen who'd have more than enough reason. To tell the truth, I suspicion they ain't looking all that hard."

"Can't say as I blame 'em. Whoever it was did the world a favor."

The journalist interrupted, "You boys are way ahead of me. Who on earth was Belle Starr?"

The barber said, "Oh, just a crazy old white trash woman, screwing Injuns over in the Cherokee Strip. When she got drunk, she liked to call herself a bandit queen. Bandit queen, ain't that a bitch? You want water or bay rum on your hair, mister?"

"Bay rum, please. What do you mean she was a bandit queen? What bandits was she queen of?"

"Hell, stranger, *I* never said she was no bandit queen. *She* did. She had some Injun bucks and white trash stealing for her. Some said she and her gang was responsible for stealing last year's harvest, but most of us never took her and her trash all that serious."

The journalist got out of the chair and paid, but stayed to chat with the other customer, who was more willing to green an eastern dude with impossible yarns.

A short time later, the newspaperman was over in the Western Union office to send his night letter. It read:

WILL TAKE SPACE RATE OR CENT A WORD FOR EXCLU-
SIVE NEW WILD WEST CHARACTER BANDIT QUEEN OF
CHEROKEE STRIP STOP FORGET DALTONS THIS IS HOT
STUFF STOP.

Then he went back to his hotel, locked himself in with pencil, paper, and a bottle. He knew they'd buy it. The readers were getting tired of rehashes about Buffalo Bill, and even Billy the Kid had been written into the ground after laying there seven years. He set to work with a few sketchy facts, a vivid imagination, and a lot of whole cloth, to write one gully-washing feature story.

As the Legend of Belle Starr grew, she became a raven-haired beauty on a spirited black stallion, riding hell for leather at the side of her brave husband, a Confederate officer fighting on for the lost cause against the wicked carpetbaggers who'd framed him on a false charge to seize the old plantation from him and his young bride, who was southern spitfire, and an all-around swell kid. In the legend, Belle would kill more damn-yankees, crooked Indian agents, and generally ornery rascals than the Kid and Hickok between them.

Pearl was not mentioned. A hard-riding female bandit carrying a baby in her lap sounded a little silly.

Pearl wasn't going to mind that omission.

It was raining the day they put Belle Starr in the ground; a raw, grey rain that turned the red clay to gumbo, oozing blood. Few of the crowd who came to the burial ground were friends, at least of Pearl's.

Granny Redbird was there, wrapped in a blanket under an umbrella, but she didn't come near Pearl and Pearl didn't go to her.

She'd wired to her Uncle Frank, inviting him to the funeral, since she knew he'd always admired Mamma, but

Uncle Frank had sent a wire saying he was busy and that he was afraid he couldn't make it.

Most of the people standing around were curious strangers who'd come as they and others came to public hangings and other entertaining events in an otherwise mighty dull little town. Pearl spied Frank Dalton, and when he nodded soberly, she knew he'd come out of respect. Federal men weren't called upon to keep order at a simple country funeral.

When she saw Steve Logan moving toward her through the crowd, she didn't know just why he'd come, but when he stood beside her and said, "I sure am sorry, Pearl," she nodded and said, "So am I. It was decent of you, Steve. Mamma would have been proud of all the quality folk here today, even if they come just to say they've been."

"You should be under an umbrella, Pearl." Steve said. "I got one in my shay."

"Don't bother. I'm already as wet as I can get, but it's funny, I don't feel it. I feels sort of numb all over, you know?" Pearl said.

He nodded and said, "I felt the same when my aunt died last winter. She wasn't my mother, of course, but I was mighty fond of her and I hated this part. We living folk feel so useless at a time like this. You keep wishing there was something you could do, instead of just, you know, standing here."

"I know," Pearl replied. "I've done all I could. My kin up to Missouri sent me some money as soon as they heard the news, and we already had some set aside for a rainy day."

She grimaced and added, "My, it really *is* a rainy day, isn't it? Anyhow, as you see, I bought her a right handsome casket. She's holding violets in her hand inside. They're silk violets, on account of the time of the year, but it was the best I could do. She always liked violets best."

"I'd say that was a handsome thing to do, Pearl. Listen, after this is over . . ."

"I wrote what they carved on that grave marker," continued Pearl, not listening to him. "I had to pay the monument man extra to get it ready in time, but it was a promise I made to Mamma. She always admired my poetry and she asked me one night to write one for her grave if ever the time came. The time came sooner than we expected. I stayed up all night, and after I'd tore up a hundred sheets of paper, that was the best I could come up with. How do you like it?"

The boy craned his neck to see around the preacher man who droned on about life everlasting to a lot of folk who doubted that more than they let on.

Steve read the epitaph and said, "That's mighty nice, Pearl."

"You reckon it's fitting? I wanted her remembered right."

"Well, if you remember her that way, that's all that counts. Listen, Pearl, I said I got my shay parked nearby, and I can see they are almost finished here. What say I drive you anywhere you want to go? You need some coffee or hot chocolate, too. I'll take you home to my mother, or I'll drive you home to . . . where will you be staying now, Pearl?"

She frowned and said, "You know, I hadn't studied on that. When you study on it, I can go 'most anyplace now, can't I? I reckon I'll stay out at the cabin 'til I get things settled. After that . . . who knows?"

The preacher man finally finished and nodded to Pearl. She moved to his side, accepted the little scoop of mysteriously dry soil, and tossed it into her mother's open grave. She asked the preacher man if he thought her mother's soul was at rest.

He had his private opinion about that, but he was a kindly man, if a mite long-winded, so he nodded and said, "Go home and dry off, dear. You've done all that a daughter could, and the sextons will finish up here. It's not comforting to look on."

Steve was still waiting for her answer as she turned away from the preacher man.

Pearl smiled wanly and asked, "Won't it be crowded in a shay?"

He said, "Some. I won't try to take advantage of the one seat, Pearl. You just tell me where you want to go, and I'll see you get there, hear?"

"We'll talk on it as you drive, Steve. It's just starting to hit me how many directions I can go from here," she said with a frown.

She took his arm and they walked away. She felt oddly light on her feet of a sudden, as if some great weight had been lifted from her shoulders. Her Victorian mind would never openly face the reasons, but as she walked away from her mother's gravesite, Pearl Younger looked prettier as some worry lines began to slowly fade from her brow.

They just made it to the covered shay when the sky opened up and it began to rain fire and salt, scattering the remaining curiousity seekers as if the heavens, too, wished to leave Belle Starr at peace in the little lonely burial ground.

The workmen cursed as they hastily filled the grave in the driving February rain. Then they, too, left, and the monument Pearl had placed there stood over her mother's grave in the falling rain under a dark and sullen sky.

The letters emblazoned on the stone glittered like diamonds, or maybe teardrops, as the rain ran down over the carved cold slab, and the tormented soul of Belle Starr would have laughed, or maybe wept, to read:

R.I.P.

BELLE SHIRLEY STARR 1848–1889
"Shed not for her the bitter tear
Nor give the heart to vain regret
'Tis but the casket that lies here
The gem that fills it sparkles yet."

THE END